PRAISE FC

"If you have read any of Leslie Wolfe's books, then you know you're in for an excellent read!"

"Leslie Wolfe has assumed the role of the feminine counterpart to the Tom Clancy, Lee Child, Ian Fleming set, proving that indeed women can equal if not surpass the established norm."

"Loved Las Vegas Girl, excited for this next book in the series."

"This was well thought out and really a good mystery. The story unfolds little by little, making you want more."

"This book has it all: murder, mystery and intrigue! Not only is there a great plot, there are several good subplots masterfully woven in."

"Bestselling author Leslie Wolfe weaves another great mystery, thriller and suspense, with intriguing twists and turns that will easily captivate the reader's attention from the beginning."

PRAISE FOR LESLIE WOLFE

"Leslie Wolfe has the talent that is comparable to the likes of a Tom Clancy or a Michael Crichton, or even James Patterson."

"Leslie Wolfe writes suspense thrillers that keep you interested from start to finish."

"Leslie Wolfe is a new favorite author."

CASINO GIRL

BOOKS BY LESLIE WOLFE

TESS WINNETT SERIES

Dawn Girl
The Watson Girl
Glimpse of Death
Taker of Lives
Not Really Dead
Girl with A Rose
Mile High Death
The Girl They Took

DETECTIVE KAY SHARP SERIES

The Girl From Silent Lake
Beneath Blackwater River
The Angel Creek Girls

BAXTER & HOLT SERIES

Las Vegas Girl
Casino Girl
Las Vegas Crime

STANDALONE TITLES

Stories Untold
Love, Lies and Murder

ALEX HOFFMANN SERIES

Executive
Devil's Move
The Backup Asset
The Ghost Pattern
Operation Sunset

For the complete list of Leslie Wolfe's novels, visit:
LeslieWolfe.com/books

CASINO GIRL

LESLIE WOLFE

Italics Publishing

$\coprod$ ITALICS

Italics Publishing Inc.

Edited by Joni Wilson, Susan Barnes.
Cover and interior design by Sam Roman.
ISBN: 978-1-945302-67-1

ACKNOWLEDGMENTS

A special thank you to Mark Freyberg, my New York City authority for all matters legal. Mark's command of the law and passion for deciphering its intricacies translates into zero unanswered questions for this author. He's a true legal oracle and a wonderful friend.

A warm thank you to Jessica Berc, whose sense of style and knowledge of fashion brings vivid colors to my favorite characters. Jess uses fashion to complement personalities and bring dimension, and glamour, to everyday attire.

If anyone knows Vegas, that's Bill Zimmer, whose entire career was spent on casino floors, learning the games, running the games, mastering the games. My warmest thanks for his willingness to teach me the specifics I needed to know to make my story come to life with full, authentic Vegas shine.

1

ODDS

They're called quasi-strippers.

They don't really bare it all, like real strippers do behind the darkened glass doors of specialty adult clubs, but they aren't exactly fully dressed either while they perform.

Crystal preferred the term exotic dancer. Five nights a week she took the small stage at the center of the high-limit blackjack tables, in the glamorous Scala Casino. Five nights a week she danced and smiled and undulated her perfect body to the rhythm of sultry songs, carefully chosen to lure the gamblers' attention away from the cards and the ever-diminishing stacks of their chips. In the background, nothing is more Vegas than the Scala Casino floor, filled with a million noises, dazzling lights, and excess adrenaline. Nothing is more alive.

That's where she belonged, among the glitter and the gold, the glitzy and the rich.

She wore strappy lingerie with black and gold lace accents on beige silk, designed to trick the mind's eye into believing she was naked. Black, knee-high stiletto boots completed her attire; her black, garter-belt straps attached to them, sexy and kinky and fun. The appreciative looks she basked in that night told her she'd chosen her ensemble well. It was going to be a profitable evening.

The familiar music seemed a bit too loud, making her wince, a little dizzy. She grabbed the pole tighter, aware she was dancing out of rhythm, but knowing the customers were too far gone to notice. It was almost four in the morning, and by that time, most of them were pleasantly inebriated, high on their own excitement and maybe more, living the Vegas dream.

The only danger was that asshole, Farley, a fat, lewd pig who liked to scream at the girls, giving them a hard time for everything they did, right or wrong regardless. Two minutes of being late or changing clothes mid-shift and she'd get pulled inside the pit manager's office for another scolding session.

But she held her head up during those moments, aware they were going to pass and even more aware they were meant to intimidate her into offering sexual favors in return for a privileged work atmosphere.

Oh, hell, no.

Not ever. Not even if the prick turned blue in the face from too much screaming, or his waiting-to-happen stroke knocked him dead right before her eyes.

But even Stan Farley was looking away that moment, focused on a newly arrived high roller who'd taken a seat at one of the blackjack tables with a view of the stage. She didn't know that one, but judging by the way Farley fawned over him, he must've been someone important.

Someone rich.

Someone who didn't care that the odds at his blackjack table were stacked higher against him, just because the table came with a view of full, inviting cleavage and tight little buns.

Hers.

She felt beads of sweat bursting at the roots of her hair and forced some stale air into her lungs. Maybe the air conditioning was off, or something. The cigar smoke made it nearly unbreathable, but it was an acceptable tradeoff for being allowed to work the high roller pit, not some fifty-cents-minimum roulette floor, where the tips were always Washingtons, never a Franklin and rarely a Lincoln, and not a whole lot of them to count at the end of a shift anyway.

No, she'd been lucky, and her luck had started to play in her favor about a month after she'd been hired. For that she had Devine to thank.

Her sweaty palms made it difficult for her to get a good grip on the shiny, chrome pole, but she managed a back-hook spin and landed facing Devine. Her best friend danced some thirty feet away, on a small, elevated stage set among four high-limit roulette tables.

She waited until she could make eye contact with Devine and waved discreetly at her best friend. Just seeing her smile back made her feel less lonely, less vulnerable. Maybe she was going to be okay. Maybe things would work out after all.

Without realizing, she put her palm on her belly in a soft, caressing gesture, aimed to comfort the tiny sparkle of life growing inside her. She wasn't showing a baby bump yet, but soon that would change, and with it, her entire life as she knew it.

She skipped out of rhythm again, but soon snapped out of her trance, motivated by Farley's mean glare. She focused on her customers for a while and, within a few minutes of smiling provocatively and wiggling her rear, a crisp fifty-dollar bill landed under the thin strap of her thong, delivered by long, hairy fingers that reached lower and lingered longer than was necessary.

Sometimes she was happy the payout was 6:5 instead of 3:2 on a blackjack at the tables facing her; those jerks deserved to bleed.

But she smiled at the man who'd delivered the tip and mocked a reverence without letting go of the pole. Then she let herself fall into a back bend and frowned when she saw Farley was approaching.

"What the hell is wrong with you, huh?" he snapped, after grabbing her arm and pulling her close. The music was loud, and no one could hear his words; not that anyone would care if they did. "Could you be bothered to do your job tonight? A deaf penguin has more rhythm than you."

"I'm working it, Stan, what the hell? I haven't taken a break in two hours."

"The hell you are, bitch. You see those bozos? If they're looking at their cards instead of your ass, you ain't earning your keep."

He let go of her arm and disappeared before she could say anything. He was a two-faced creep; with her and the other girls he showed his real charm. For all the patrons and the rest of the Scala staff, he was a perfect gentleman, always dressed in an impeccable suit and starched, white shirts, pleasantly smiling and accommodating.

She knew better than to let him get under her skin.

But her head was spinning, and she held on tight to the pole, not as part of her routine, but for much-needed balance. The music changed, and she welcomed the new beat, one of her favorites. She knew the playlist by heart; the casino had a limited supply of premixed tracks, but the customers didn't seem to care.

Cheers erupted at the table in front of her, and one of the players lifted his arms in the air, beaming. The croupier pushed an impressive pile of chips in front of the man, and she quickly flashed her megawatt smile and made lingering eye contact. He didn't disappoint; he picked one of the chips and sent it flying her way. She caught it gracefully, then placed it on the floor, next to the pole. Her barely there panties weren't made to hold casino chips.

When she looked up, she startled.

It was him. It was Paul, and he was furious, by the angle of his eyebrows, by the deep ridges flanking his mouth.

He stood right there, next to her stage, glaring at her with a loaded gaze filled with such hatred that her breath caught. He beckoned her to come closer without making a single gesture. She approached him hesitantly and crouched to bring their eyes on the same level, aware not even Farley would dare say a word. She shot a quick glance toward Devine's stage, but she was gone, nowhere in sight.

His eyes drilled into hers, close enough she could see his dilated pupils. Without a word, he shoved a purple and white chip deep inside her bra, then grabbed the thin strap, pulling her closer to him. He said something, keeping his voice low and menacing. She couldn't make out his words but didn't dare to ask. She wanted to explain herself, wanted him to understand her motives, but she couldn't find her words.

She didn't want his money, and she didn't deserve his anger.

When he finally let go of her strap and pushed her away, she almost fell. Her knees were shaking, and she felt the urge to sit for a moment, to catch her breath. She grabbed the pole tightly and did a clumsy back slide against the shiny surface, landing hard on her butt, then folded her legs to the side. She let her head hang low, and her long, wavy hair covered her face, hiding the fear in her eyes until it subsided a little.

Then she wrapped her hands around the pole again, planning to stand and do a pirouette, but her arms and legs felt numb, listless. She tried to breathe, but air refused to enter her lungs. Frantic, she looked around, searching for someone, anyone, who could help. Only one man was looking at her, but her desperate and silent plea was misunderstood.

The man licked his lips, arranged his crotch with a quick gesture, then looked away at another dancer.

She gasped for air a couple of times, then the bright lights of the casino seemed to dim, inviting darkness to engulf her view of the lively floor. Silence came, heavy, palpable. Against it, not even her own heart beats could be heard.

Defeated, she let go. Her body landed on the stage floor with a loud thump that no one heard. Unnoticed, the white and purple casino chip fell out of her top and rolled onto the floor, stopping under a table.

For a long moment, Farley thought the immobile pose was part of Crystal's routine, some new dance move that she was trying. Customers really enjoyed seeing girls crawling on the stage; it made the viewers feel powerful, superior, in control. By the time Farley realized he'd been wrong, she was already gone. His chubby fingers felt for a pulse and found nothing.

Now he'd have to call the cops and close the pit. His worst nightmare.

2

ASSIGNMENT

I pulled into the familiar parking lot at the Henderson Police Department, then walked quickly toward the entrance, while memories flooded my mind. That modern building had been my precinct for years, before being transferred to the Las Vegas Metropolitan Police Department, Sector M. It felt familiar, yet strange somehow, already eroded, faded from memory, although it had only been a week since I'd moved.

What a week that had been.

I hadn't even met my new boss, who happened to be vacationing in the Caribbean at the precise moment I reported for duty. I was going to meet him today; Captain Morales, the head of the Homicide and Sex Crimes Bureau of the Las Vegas Metro PD. Famous for his crime-clearing rate, the captain had a reputation for being a stickler for procedure.

Fantastic. Just what I needed.

He'd probably be *thrilled* to meet me, the disciplinary transferee who's lucky she still had a badge. I cringed, and not even a deep breath of fresh, cold, desert air could scatter the gloomy thoughts that invaded my mind.

As for my new partner, I didn't even want to start. He's a good cop but... How did I manage to get the relationship between us so bloody complicated in only one week? I had no excuse... I had years of experience as a homicide detective in Las Vegas, well, in the neighboring City of Henderson, but still. And that's on top of the years I'd beaten the streets of my native London as a detective sergeant, then as the youngest inspector in the city's modern history.

Then, why did I feel like a rookie, like one who screwed up?

Well, that's because maybe I did.

I let him get too close, and for that, there's no logical explanation, no rhyme nor reason.

Ah... Bloody hell.

I shook off the feeling of uneasiness, straightened my back, and walked through the main door situated at the center of a façade made entirely of glass panels in a modern arrangement that reminded me of a barcode, of all things. I expected to see smiling faces greeting me as I crossed the lobby, but there were none. Most cops were out in the field already, and the receptionist was someone new. I actually had to show my badge and sign the registry, and she didn't crack a smile the entire time. She sized me up with a quick look, head to toe, and only the faintest glimmer of envy lit her eyes before her self-imposed, cold indifference returned in full flux.

"Detective Baxter, yes, I have you picking up Darrin Casarez," she stated with the professional tone that receptionists always take with people they don't know.

She directed me, but I already knew where I was going. The perp, handcuffed and secured to the bench he was sitting on, shifted in place and rattled the chain that attached his cuffs to the bench when I approached.

"*Hola, bonita,*" he called in a guttural voice, "set me free and I'll be yours forever."

I stared blankly at him, while making an effort not to laugh. He was a skinny fellow with oily hair and numerous piercings, including a nose stud that sparkled, most likely a real diamond. Whenever I saw nose jewels, all I could think of was how were people managing such accessories when they caught a cold? Did it hurt when they sneezed?

Seeing I had stopped in front of him, he continued his plea with increasing enthusiasm and dramatic inflections worthy of a five-season, prime-time, soap opera. "I'll do whatever you want me to do, okay? I swear... anything. Just break me out of these chains, *te lo ruego!*"

He was the only detainee lined up for transfer to Central Booking, so I assumed he was Darrin Casarez, the cargo I'd been asked to haul over to my new precinct, just because I lived in

Henderson and it was on my commute. I ignored his plea and walked over to booking, accompanied by his calls for help and mercy. Someone yelled, "Shut the hell up," from the bullpen, but that only bought us a minute or two of silence. I signed him out and said goodbye to the booking clerk, one of the few who remembered who I was.

Then I took out my handcuff key and approached Mr. Casarez.

"Yes, yes," he shouted, his pitch high with delight. "Yes, I'll be your sex slave, do anything you want." He grinned widely, showing two lines of small, crooked teeth.

If he thought his banter was going to earn him anything but annoyed indifference, he was sorely wasting his breath. But then again, he didn't strike me as the rational, thinking type, just the smart-assed, big-mouthed variety. He wasn't much of a challenge, this bloke. He weighed maybe a buck-fifty or less, and was three inches shorter than me, even in my work flats. I had every reason to believe the transfer was going to be uneventful, albeit irritating, but Darrin Casarez had other plans.

He watched me unlock his cuffs, getting ready to restrain him again with my own zip tie handcuffs, at which moment his grin died and his jaw slacked under the weight of disappointment, while a flicker of despair glinted in his eyes.

"You a cop, *bonita*?" he asked quietly, disgust seeping through his voice. "What a waste of a fine piece of ass."

Then, lightning fast, he wriggled free from my grip and made for the exit. He stopped abruptly, practically tripping over himself, when he noticed a cop's service weapon in an open drawer of a desk in the bullpen. He grabbed it with shaking, unsure hands, then he sprinted forward, quick as a rabbit.

"Gun!" I yelled from the top of my lungs, giving the few people in the bullpen a heads-up. I cursed under my breath and ran after him, while an unwanted thought slowed me down, making me a little hesitant.

Only last week I'd been transferred for beating a detainee while he was in my custody. The fact that I had a reason for it had made little difference; barely enough to keep me employed, on notice, and with a twelve-month reduction in pay. Hence, I thought I'd better not do any damage to Mr. Casarez, not put a single fingernail scratch on his face. Definitely not put a bullet anywhere in his body.

Ah, the hell with it. That didn't mean he got to play prison break on me before I had my first cup of tea for the day.

"Freeze," I shouted as I pulled out my gun, but he kept on going fast, halfway to the front door. I holstered my weapon, sprinted forward, and caught up with him just as he threw himself against the glass panels, bouncing off into a heap on the floor. He'd slammed against the wrong door, the one that is always locked. The gun he'd stolen clattered as it fell onto the tiles. I picked it up, secured it, collected my unruly cargo with a firm grip around his thin arm and slammed him against the wall. As I zip-tied his wrists behind his back, I uttered a few words only he could hear.

"Do this again, wanker, and I'll release you in your own neighborhood, and let everyone know how grateful we are for your help."

Fear dilated his pupils and I felt his muscles relax under my grip. He wasn't going to pose any more issues; he'd given up.

"Clear," I shouted, and the three cops who were approaching with their weapons drawn holstered their pieces and drew near, inspecting Casarez with angry glares to see who'd disturbed their early morning routine.

One of them was lingering, seemingly uncomfortable; he wasn't someone I knew well, just some rookie fresh out of the academy, his uniform still new and well pressed.

I looked at his sidearm holster and saw it was empty. The weapon he'd drawn earlier was his backup, now secured on his left ankle. I smiled and pulled out the gun that Casarez had swiped from his drawer and offered it to him.

"Lost something?"

He blushed before managing to reply. "Um, y—yes, thank you."

Moments later, I loaded Casarez into the back of the borrowed cruiser and slammed the door behind him. When I climbed behind the wheel, he only had one thing to ask in a subdued, hesitant voice.

"What's a wanker?"

I didn't bother to educate him.

Instead, I drove by Starbucks on Eastern and picked up two ventis for Holt and me; black coffee for him, green tea for me. I don't believe the procedure manual allows cops transferring detainees to make coffee stops, but I really couldn't remember, nor did I believe anyone would mind.

Fifteen minutes later, Mr. Casarez was in the hospitable hands of LVMPD's Central Booking, while I handed Holt his order of coffee, right as Captain Morales showed up.

"Thanks," Holt said, taking the paper cup from my hand. Our fingers brushed in passing, and that brief, loaded contact brought a grin to his lips and a frown to my forehead.

Never again, I thought. *Not in a thousand years.*

One mistake was enough. Well, okay, there were two to be precise, but I'd learned my lesson.

"Come on in," Morales invited us.

He had an unexpected smile on his face and the gaze of an intelligent, open-minded man.

We remained standing in front of his desk, watching him go over some paperwork in a cream-colored personnel file. I couldn't read the name affixed on the cover, but it was probably mine.

"Welcome to LVMPD, Detective Baxter," he said, and all I could do was gawk in disbelief. What, no threats? No huffing and puffing over taking someone else's disciplinary transferee? No putting me on notice that I was going to be kicked out of the force for the tiniest mistake? I was prepared for *that*, not for this. Not for what appeared to be a clean slate with my new boss.

Holt elbowed me discreetly and I swallowed, then muttered a strangled, "Thank you."

"Technically, you were a part of LVMPD before, while at Henderson," he added, sounding apologetic. "You knew that, of course."

I nodded.

"We're lucky to have you," he continued, reading from the file. "Degree in psychology, trained at Scotland Yard, deception detection and advanced interrogation techniques."

Holt whistled quietly, shooting me a side glance. He probably wondered why I'd kept my background a secret, despite his many questions. The answer was simple; as soon as people learned of my abilities, they started shunning me, as if I were a mind reader and a dangerous one at that. Couldn't've been further from the truth.

"You two had a terrific first week as a team," Morales continued, thankfully changing the subject. "I read the report. Great job. Keep it up, both of you."

I shifted my weight from one foot to the other, ready to get out of there in a hurry, willing to sprint faster than Casarez running for his life.

"You bet," Holt replied.

"Detective Baxter, you weren't assigned a desk, a computer, or a car yet. We'll get that sorted out today."

"Thank you, sir," I managed to articulate, still stunned, unsure how to behave.

"Until then, there's been an incident at the Scala early this morning. The coroner's already on site." He pushed a brown, thin file across the desk and Holt grabbed it.

"You got it," Holt replied for both of us, then turned and allowed me to leave the room first.

We walked in silence all the way to the parking lot, where he stopped short of unlocking his unmarked Ford Explorer.

"What the hell happened in there? Never seen you pretending to be a functional mute before."

"Nothing like that," I said, stopping to take a sip of tea. "I was expecting something different, that's all."

"Different, how?"

"Colder, more hostile, considering what's in my file. Morales didn't seem to know, or, if he knew, to give a damn."

"He likes to think for himself and draw his own conclusions. But don't let his friendly demeanor fool you. He's tough. He doesn't care about the national crime solve rate being as low as it is these days. He wants us closing *all* the cases, *all* the time."

I shrugged. So did I, and from what I could tell, so did Holt. I didn't see an issue.

He unlocked the car and we climbed inside without another word. The heavy silence continued for a long moment, while Holt's hand hovered above the ignition. He seemed preoccupied by something he wasn't yet sharing. I waited.

"Okay, I'll give it to you, that was too nice, even for Morales," he eventually said. "You are a disciplinary transferee and I've never seen him compliment anyone before you. Typically, he hands them a polite, yet firm warning not to screw up again."

Tension firmed his jaw line, and I felt his uneasiness seed anxiety in my gut. What were we missing?

"Should I be jealous?" Holt suddenly quipped, replacing his grim expression with a seductive grin. "I saw the way he was looking at you."

"Shut up already," I replied, working hard at hiding a smile. "Do we know anything about the Scala case?"

Holt opened the file and frowned, seemingly intrigued. "Oh, that's a new one. One of their exotic dancers died during a performance."

3

CRIME SCENE

The most stunning thing about the Scala Hotel and Casino wasn't the steel-and-glass, semicircular towers, forty-five stories high, housing thousands of rooms. To me, the fountain in front of the entrance was the one piece of lavish, exotic décor that spelled *Scala* more than anything else. When LED technology met computer-assisted fountain flow control, combined with what I'd learned since I'd seen it for the first time was called laminar flow, the result was a stunning, unpredictable, and mesmerizing game of light, color, and water. Water that didn't splash, didn't cascade, didn't whirl, water that was turned into a fluid conduit for light; disciplined, intricate webs of perfectly contained jets, reminiscent of fiber optics.

But I wasn't there to look at the fountain; the drop-off driveway that went around it was already filled with crime scene vehicles with their flashers on, and all access was blocked. Beyond the yellow do-not-cross tape, hundreds of gawkers took countless photos and endless videos on their cell phones, so we walked quickly toward the entrance, avoiding the cameras as much as we could.

The coroner's van was already there, backed into the hotel's entrance, on standby with its rear doors open. Two crime scene unit vans were also present, and the technicians, much to the disappointment of the camera-happy tourists, wore full-body coveralls complete with hoods and facial masks. Famous since the TV show *CSI* had achieved its notorious success, tourists always greeted the Vegas crime scene units with enthusiastic interest, and today was no exception, despite the fact that they couldn't even get a glimpse of their faces.

But that wasn't the reason why the technicians wore the white coveralls known as moon suits. Their focus was preserving the integrity of the evidence collected and avoiding the risk of contaminating the crime scene with even the tiniest of fibers or specks of dust. Put in perspective, when the primary crime scene was the busy floor of one of the largest casinos in Las Vegas, such care to preserve the evidence might've seemed pointless, but it never was.

I followed a technician through the main doors, with Holt walking briskly by my side. Not a single word was exchanged between us on the ride over, and maybe that was for the best. The man rarely had anything to say that wasn't a question, more often than not driven by the innate curiosity that made him the excellent cop that he was. But I wished he'd stop looking at me with the same level of suspicion that cops looked at the rest of the world, given the things they saw on a daily basis. Fact was, the man didn't trust me worth a damn.

But had I done anything to gain his trust? Yeah, sure, I had his back on a couple of occasions, helped him out of a jam or two, but had I been open and truthful to him about anything of any importance? Not really. I opted to keep him in the dark, avoiding sharing any information about myself, about my past. That wasn't because I'd just met him, or because I wanted to play coy. It was because nothing of my past could be shared without talking about Andrew and thinking about him still ripped through my heart like a serrated blade.

I was thankful when a crime scene tech directed us to the escalator, dissipating my gloomy thoughts. I gazed briefly at Holt and caught a frown wrinkling his forehead before he could wipe it off and paste his signature bad-boy grin on his face.

"What's on your mind?" I asked, my voice casual, yet friendly.

"Just wondering what else is there to find out about my new partner, that's all. Scotland Yard, really? And you didn't think of mentioning that?"

I shrugged, feeling a little defensive. "Is that it?"

"That, and the thought of the awkwardness we're all going to experience as soon as we start talking to the coroner."

"Why?" I frowned, pretending I didn't understand.

"Because you and Dr. Anne St. Clair obviously have a long history, a good one, but you won't talk about it. I have my own history with her, not so good, but at least I told you about it."

The escalator ride came to an end and I stepped on the second floor without replying to his comment. There was nothing I could say without making it worse. The fact remained, despite my best efforts, that my partner knew I was keeping a few secrets from him.

I thought of lying, of serving him a well-crafted tale told impeccably by someone trained in the art of deception, but my conscience held me back. He was a good man and a good cop. He deserved better; he deserved the truth, but I wasn't ready to share.

Silence was golden, given the circumstances.

We walked the rest of the way in silence, a loaded stillness that tugged at the corner of his mouth and put a glint of sarcasm in his eyes. I focused on my surroundings, taking in everything.

After the stroll through the immense, familiar lobby, decorated in white marble that matched the modern chandeliers, each of them at least two stories tall, I entered uncharted territory. The second floor was new to me, because I rarely gamble; there's no room for such extravagances while living on a cop's salary. I was unfamiliar with the vastness of the Scala's casino floor and completely unacquainted with the high-roller gambling rooms.

I'd read somewhere that the Scala had recently piloted opening up the high-limit gaming rooms to a larger number of players, by lowering the minimums, in an attempt to make more of their customers feel like VIPs. The pilot included bringing in a bit of pleasure-pit experience to the rooms, complete with music and dancers, instead of the elegant, yet cold and stark atmosphere one would expect when the chips on the table easily exceeded what I made in a year.

The first thing I noticed was the smell. It had discreetly changed as I entered the restricted area. The cigarette smoke was now blended with bitter, suffocating cigar fog, and the fancy scent of the vapes I'd picked up downstairs was completely absent.

As soon as I entered the high-limit area through dark-tinted glass doors flanked by uniformed staff, the noise subsided, muted by the thick carpet that felt soft under my shoes.

The service lights were on, and the room was flooded with a white, bright glow coming from ceiling-mounted fixtures. These lamps were never on during the times the room was open to customers; from what I could tell, the room had its own club lights in bright colors, now turned off.

I stopped a few steps inside the entrance and observed the layout. Clusters of four gaming tables surrounded several small, elevated stages, each grouping about thirty feet apart from the others. In the center of each stage, there was a stainless steel pole that went all the way up to the vaulted ceiling. Blackjack, roulette, poker, even craps in the far corner, the setting was the same regardless of the game. The tables were close to the stages where dancers performed, enough to allow customers to offer a tip without leaving their seats, or to watch the dancers from across the table, not more than ten feet away.

I put on shoe covers and approached the elevated stage where technicians swarmed. Then I saw her.

She was stunningly beautiful, even in death.

She couldn't've been more than eighteen, maybe nineteen years old. She lay on her side, her arm extended over the edge, and her head leaning on it as if she were sleeping. Long, wavy strands of blonde hair partially covered her face and draped around her shoulders. She seemed peaceful, as if in her last moments her young body hadn't agonized, desperately trying to live, to survive; none of that anguish had left a mark on her elegant, relaxed features. Her lips were parted slightly, as if she were breathing gently while dreaming of something only she knew. Whatever her secret, she'd taken it with her.

"Finally," I heard Anne St. Clair say. "Sure took you a while."

I watched her crouch next to the body, gently removing the long strands of hair off her face and her neck. She leaned closer to the girl's head and examined her eyes, then muttered, "Uh-huh," only to herself.

"Do we have an ID?" I heard Holt ask a uniformed officer.

"Yeah, her name was Crystal Tillman," he replied, holding a driver's license with his gloved hand. "That man over there, the one in the suit and red tie, is the pit manager," he added, pointing at an overweight man whose jowls extended beyond the collar of his perfectly starched, white shirt.

"Any background?" Holt asked the coroner's assistant who was taking a reading on a mobile fingerprint scanner.

Erika didn't look up from the device's screen. "She's not in the system."

"Thanks," Holt replied.

I climbed up on the stage next to Anne and crouched by her side.

"Hey," I whispered, and she looked briefly in my direction and nodded quickly in lieu of a reply.

She never smiled when she worked, and there was a story behind that. I knew better than to be offended by her coldness; it wasn't about me or about anyone present. Like most of us, Anne still fought the ghosts of her past.

"What can you tell me?"

She sighed before replying. "There are signs of asphyxia, see these petechiae here, and here?" She pointed with her pen at the small, ruptured blood vessels around the girl's eyes. "But they're not marked enough."

"What do you mean?"

"We see more petechial hemorrhaging associated with a COD of asphyxia. In this case, we only have superficial petechiae, as if she had started to suffocate, but then her heart stopped."

"By itself, in a girl this young?"

Anne sighed again. "Yeah, my point exactly. I'll know more once I have her on my table, but I don't believe a heart this young just stops without a reason."

"Any signs of trauma?" Holt asked.

"None that I can see," Anne replied.

"Could you venture a guess as to what killed her?" I asked, and she promptly frowned at me. She didn't like it when I voiced that particular question, but I had no choice. The first forty-eight hours in a murder investigation are critical; we had no time to waste.

"If I had to speculate, which you know I can't do, I'd have to say some kind of poison," she said, lowering her voice as if she were doing something illegal by formulating an educated guess. "I'm not smelling anything, nor seeing the usual signs of poisoning, like foam at the mouth, vomiting, and so on. It's either that, or something else stopped her heart."

"Could it be natural causes, like a birth defect?" Holt asked.

"Theoretically it could, but I seriously doubt it," she replied, and the temperature in the room dropped by at least ten degrees, possibly from the tone of her voice. She really didn't like Holt one bit. "I'll let you know soon enough."

"How about time of death?" I asked, eager to dissipate the tension between the two.

"We have a time-coded video, from that camera over there," Anne replied, pointing toward the ceiling, "and my findings confirm it: 4:12 AM."

"But it's almost eight-thirty now," I said, the pitch of my voice expressing surprise and disappointment. Usually, we're called within minutes of someone's death, not hours.

"That's your mystery to solve, not mine," she replied coldly, while beckoning her assistant. "For some reason, they took their sweet time before calling nine-one-one."

I felt the blood rush to my head. Out of the critical forty-eight hours, the most important four had been wasted.

Moments later, Anne and her assistant, Erika, took away the gurney carrying the lifeless body of a beautiful, young girl who had barely begun living. And the stuffed suit over by the lounge had wasted precious time.

I walked over to the pit manager and propped my hands firmly on my hips. "You have some serious explaining to do."

4

WITNESSES

"Wait a minute," the manager reacted, heaving heavily while his cheeks turned an unhealthy shade of dark red. "You can't pin this on me!"

"Tell us who screwed up, then," Holt intervened, in a lower, sympathetic tone. Only the deep ridge above his eyebrows revealed the frustration he must've felt.

"Um, Joe, he's the security manager," he replied, pointing at a thin man wearing a three-piece suit. He stood a few yards away, talking to a group of people seated in the lounge area. Judging by his body language, he was pacifying them, trying to accommodate whatever it was those customers were demanding.

"Last name?" Holt asked.

"Deason, Joe Deason," the manager replied. "He should've called nine-one-one, it's his job, not mine. I had them to deal with," he added, gesturing loosely with his hand, pointing at the lounge area.

"And your name?" Holt asked, just as calmly as before.

"Stan Farley," he replied quickly, then cleared his throat. "I'm the high-limit gaming room manager," he added.

"Quite the mouthful job title," I reacted. "You're telling me you stood here for hours, without asking yourself how come the cops weren't showing up?"

"Listen, I had to keep the customers calm, keep them from leaving, you know? Do you have any idea who these people are? They buy and sell people like you and me on a daily basis. I was going crazy trying to keep them calm. At least they're all here, so you can talk to them."

"They better be," I added, then made for Joe Deason, the security manager.

He noticed me coming and nodded toward the customers he was speaking with and met me halfway.

"Detectives Baxter and Holt," I introduced us when Holt caught up. "You're the one responsible for sitting on a crime scene for hours without calling us in?"

"No," Holt intervened, "he's the one we're booking for obstruction, right this minute."

Deason flinched a little. The corners of his mouth tensed and dropped lower, and his pupils dilated for a tiny fraction of a second.

"It's nothing like that, Detectives," he replied. "It was an honest misunderstanding. I assumed, because Crystal died on Farley's floor, that the first thing he did was call the cops. Unfortunately, I didn't think to ask; I rushed to secure the video, to close the area, to preserve the scene. To keep things contained, if you wish."

"You're throwing me under the bus?" Farley shouted from where he'd followed us. "You son of a bitch! Whose job is it to deal with the authorities?"

"All right," I intervened, raising my hands in the air in a pacifying gesture, before they could get at each other's throats. "We get it. Who called us, eventually?"

"I did," Deason replied coldly, shooting Farley a deathly glare.

"What about them?" Holt asked, pointing at the lounge area. "Are these all the people present at the time of Crystal's death? Eleven men and one woman?"

"Y—yes," Deason replied, after a split-second hesitation.

"Are you sure?" I asked.

"Positive."

"Walk us through the events," I asked, turning to Farley. "What exactly happened, and when did it start happening?"

"Crystal was dancing the blackjack tables, over there," he said, pointing at the stage where her body was found. "There weren't many players at those tables; it was late. Maybe two or three."

"Was it two, or was it three?"

"Um, three," Farley replied, looking left and right frantically, as if seeking help from someone. "I'll ask the croupier, if you'd like, but I'm fairly sure there were three men playing blackjack before she dropped."

"Then what happened?" Holt asked.

"Nothing," he replied. "She just fell to the ground, slowly."

"Slowly?" I asked. "How does one fall slowly?"

"I thought it was her routine at first. She had the pole, and held on to it, you know."

"Okay, go on."

"But then, she didn't get up, and I got worried. Players, too. I went over there, but she was dead already. I tried CPR, but—"

"How long had she been dancing before she died?"

"About two hours," he replied, shooting Deason a quick glance.

"Precisely two hours and eight minutes since she came back from break," Deason replied. "I checked the video."

I exchanged a quick look with Holt.

"So that's what you were doing, instead of calling us?" I asked, drilling my eyes into his. "Checking what happened, to see if and how you needed to cover up anything?"

Deason shook his head. "No, Detective, I would never do that. No job is worth going to jail for."

"We'll need that video, all of it, raw," Holt said.

"Absolutely."

"Were there any other girls dancing?"

"Yes," Farley replied. "Brandi was dancing the craps, and Devine was there too, at the roulette tables."

"We'll need to speak with them," I said.

"Brandi is over there," he pointed toward a girl carrying a tray with half-filled, stemmed champagne flutes.

I watched her incredible body as she walked on stilettos with undulating grace, making quick stops near each player, replacing their empty glasses, smiling, chatting casually with them in a low voice, thanking them for the tips they placed on her tray.

"How old is she?" Holt asked.

My thoughts exactly.

"Everyone here is over twenty-one, Detective," Farley replied, seeming sure of himself, more so than I'd seen him yet. "I vet the girls myself. They have to be twenty-one or older to be serving alcohol."

"Do all your dancers wait on tables?" I asked, intrigued by Brandi's visible experience with carrying a tray filled with drinks. She'd hauled that across the floor in four-inch heels without spilling a single drop.

"They do, yes," Farley replied. "We can't ask them to dance their entire eight-hour shift, right?"

"How considerate of you," I remarked, not even trying to hide the sarcasm in my voice.

I walked toward Brandi, who smiled widely when she saw Holt and me approach. She wore her hair like Marilyn Monroe, but in a slightly darker, tamer shade of blonde. She had large, expressive eyes and a thin, long neck. She was a nine-point-five, at least.

"Hello," she greeted us with a professional smile. "What can I help you with? Would you care for something to drink, coffee, maybe?"

"No, we're fine," Holt replied, his eyes lingering on her half-naked body long enough to piss me off.

"What can you tell me about Crystal?" I asked. "What kind of person was she?"

Brandi looked around quickly, discreetly, to make sure she was out of everyone's earshot. "She was interesting, to say the least," she said, speaking barely above a whisper. "Lots of hot shots buzzing around her, lots of action. One day she gets hired out of nowhere, three days later she dances the high-roller tables. I used to dance blackjack before; tips were way better than they are now, over at craps."

"How did she pull that off?" I asked. "Getting promoted, or assigned here, in your section, replacing you?"

"No idea," she replied, shaking her head with sadness. "Honestly, if I knew how, I'd do it too, whatever it was. But the thing is, if there's a chopper landing on the rooftop at night, chances are that's not some Saudi prince on his way to lose a fortune. No, that's Crystal's private ride."

"What? She had a chopper?" Holt asked, just as surprised as I was.

"No, not her, but whomever she's seeing sent one for her quite regularly. She flew out of here last night, right before her shift."

"What time was that?"

"Maybe nine-thirty or so? Yeah, I believe it was after nine-thirty."

"Then her shift started...?" Holt asked.

"At midnight," Brandi replied. "She was here on time for that. She worked drinks for the tables for two hours, then took the stage. That's how our shifts are scheduled."

"I guess it's easier this way, huh," I said, thinking out loud.

"That's just a gimmick to make it legal for the bosses to fire the wait staff if they gain weight. Law says you can't weight discriminate anymore for waitresses, but you can for dancers. See? Problem solved. For us, it's the same; same heels, still on our feet all day long, still naked."

I couldn't find my words for a moment, suffocated by the anger bubbling up in the pit of my stomach.

"Did she have any enemies?" Holt asked. "Maybe other dancers, like—"

"Like me?" Brandi laughed quietly. "I didn't hate her for taking my spot. It wasn't her fault, and even if it was, that's life, you know? But no, none that I can think of. She and Devine were besties, you know. She might know more. They share a place together."

"Yo, missy," a player hollered from the lounge. "Cut the chitchat and give us something to drink, will ya?"

I felt tempted to tell that player he could wait his turn in the back of Holt's unmarked Interceptor Utility vehicle, but I thanked Brandi instead and turned to Holt.

"A bloody chopper?" I asked quietly.

"Uh-huh," he replied. "Might be something. Let's talk to those high-priced bozos first."

We approached the lounge area where eleven men and one woman were seated on red, plush armchairs and sofas, drinks in hand, ashtrays nearby on glossy, black end tables. One of the croupiers stood near the wall, ready to beckon a waitress if any of them desired anything.

"It's about damn time," one of the men said angrily, standing and coming aggressively toward us. "We've been sitting here for hours. My lawyer will be in touch; you had no right to detain us without due process."

I refrained from telling him it wasn't us who'd detained them; it was their favorite casino's pit manager.

"Thank you for your patience," I replied instead, as politely as I could force myself to speak. "I'm sure you're eager to assist us in finding what happened to that poor girl, right?"

"Hey, I didn't see anything, my back was turned. I wasn't anywhere close to the blackjack tables. Can I go now?"

I saw no signs of deception on his face, no microexpressions, no flicker in his eyes. Later, when we'd have time to review the surveillance video, if he'd lied, we'd know. And we'd find him.

"Leave your contact information with the officer over there, by the door, and don't skip town," I said.

He practically ran toward the exit; it would be a while before he returned to lose any more of his money in that particular high-limit gaming room.

The next man we spoke with had even less to say. It wasn't until the fifth witness that we got anything interesting. He was an older bloke, maybe seventy or so, wearing his bright white hair styled youthfully. Not many men his age could boast a full head of hair, but he looked as if he hadn't lost a single strand his entire life.

"There was a guy who came to speak with her while she was dancing," the man said. "It was about three in the morning. I'd just returned from the restroom, and I saw the clock on the wall on my way back."

"Your name, sir?" I asked.

"Cline," he replied with a quick smile, sizing me up shamelessly. "Jonathon Cline, with an O."

"Mr. Cline, tell us about that man, their interaction, any detail you can recall," Holt said.

"He was angry with the girl, really angry. He grabbed at her bra, but she didn't scream or anything, she just—"

"That man shoved a chip in her bra," the woman cut in. "I saw it clearly. I was right there, at the blackjack table."

I turned toward her, a little surprised. Farley had said that only three men were seated at the blackjack table. He must've been wrong.

She sat cross-legged in a deep armchair, smoking menthols and drinking Evian. She was stylishly dressed in a black sequin dress with high slits on both sides and a deep cleavage in the front. She had nicely shaped, toned legs, but her face still told her age, despite the elaborate makeup. This particular high roller was pushing fifty.

"Did you hear any words exchanged between them?" I asked her, hoping for a miracle.

"No," she replied. "He seemed intense rather than angry, but he shoved the chip in her bra and let her go. He disappeared, and she carried on with her dancing as if nothing happened."

I looked toward Deason and Farley, who'd stayed near, observing every move we made. I caught them exchanging glances and called them on it.

"Who was the man they're talking about, Deason? You seem to me like the kind of guy who knows who everyone is."

"I'm afraid I don't know what you're talking about, Detective. I didn't see anyone."

"How about on video, the one you had plenty of time to review?"

He shook his head a little too enthusiastically and ran his fingers quickly along his goatee, as if to check if it was still there, all hairs straight and smooth and accounted for. "I'm sorry, Detective, I didn't notice anyone."

Deason was definitely hiding something. I turned to Farley. "You're responsible to keep these girls safe from rude customers, aren't you?"

He fidgeted in place, shifting his weight from one foot to the other. "Yes, but no one gave Crystal a hard time. I didn't see anyone."

I gave them both a long glare, knowing they both lied, letting them know that I knew. Holt finished talking to the rest of the witnesses, released the last of them, and joined me in my staring match with the two casino officials.

"Better not be a single millisecond missing from that video, gentlemen," I said. "We would have a field day making an obstruction charge stick for both of you. Easy-peasy." I let them squirm for a long moment, while they reassured me the recording was intact, then I asked, "Where can we find this Devine? She was Crystal's best friend, wasn't she?"

5

ROXANNE

We followed Farley through a door marked "Authorized Personnel Only," and it was as if we were stepping into a different world. All the glamour and luxury that made the Scala Hotel and Casino a world-renowned attraction stopped abruptly at the doorsill. Beyond that point, we walked through dimly lit corridors with cement floors and scratched, stained, off-white latex paint on the walls.

I grabbed Holt's sleeve and held him back a little.

"Are you buying the bystander effect explanation for not calling us in earlier?" I whispered.

"It's a hell of a stretch," Holt replied. "My money is on trying to contain the fallout. Their high-limit customers spend a lot of money here, and most of them won't be returning anytime soon. But I'm curious to see if they gave anyone a head start."

"The killer?" I asked, doubting it could be that simple. It never was.

"Or someone who shouldn't've been there in the first place. Some fat cat they might be protecting from being associated with something as trivial as a stripper's murder."

"Yeah, I thought of that too. One thing's for sure, they're lying; both of them are. They're professionals, trained for situations like this. They're playing dumb with us, hoping it will stick."

Farley stopped in front of a closed door and knocked against the scratched plywood panel.

"Are you decent in there? Can we come in?"

No one answered, and Farley soon repeated the knock and the call, this time louder, more persistent. He pulled a universal access key card from his pocket and opened the door.

We entered a small dressing room, furnished with little else except three vanities lined up on a common counter and littered with scattered makeup items, hairbrushes, and a variety of cosmetic products. Clothing racks held the dancers' stage attire on plastic hangers, although some were hung from seatbacks, drawer knobs, even the door handle. A walk-in closet, dark and small, opened to the back of the windowless room.

"She's not here," Farley said, while Holt and I exchanged a quick glance.

Poison was a woman's weapon of choice. If Anne was right in her preliminary findings and Crystal had been poisoned, that meant the killer had access to Crystal, close enough to slip her the poison. That someone would doubtless hang around to see what happened next.

In the brief moment of silence that ensued, I thought I heard a sniffle coming from the back of the room.

"Devine?" I called in a gentle voice.

The sniffle repeated, closer as I stepped into the dark closet. I felt the wall looking for a light switch, which turned on the saddest, most underpowered light bulb I'd ever seen hanging from a hotel ceiling.

I saw Devine, curled up underneath a rusty, banged-up clothes rack loaded with garments. She had her back against the corner and hugged her knees tightly to her chest, her face buried against them. She seemed numb, inert, apparently going through what psychologists call bereavement shock.

Not what a killer would experience. Maybe I'd jumped to conclusions.

I crouched next to her and touched her arm gently. "Devine? I'm Detective Baxter, and I have my partner, Detective Holt, with me. We're sorry for your loss."

She raised her swollen eyes and looked at me without saying a word. Tears had left streaks in her makeup and had stained her white, glitzy top. She let out a shattered breath, a contained, quiet sob.

"We need to ask you some questions, please."

She nodded once, then stood slowly, shakily. She wiped her tears with the back of her hands, grabbed her waist-long, silky hair and twisted it into a loose knot she brought forward, letting it hang over her right shoulder.

"Tell me what you need," she said quietly, squinting from the bright vanity lights as she exited the dimly lit closet.

"Tell us about Crystal," I said, then my eyes fell on Farley's excited demeanor. The man was a creep. I turned to him and removed all sympathy from my voice when I spoke. "We'll be fine from here, Mr. Farley. You can wait outside."

His jaw dropped for a moment; he must've felt offended. But he complied, and as soon as he left the room, Devine's body language changed. She relaxed a little, the tension in her neck dissipating, making room for more grief.

"Thank you for that," she said quietly.

"You're welcome, Devine. What can you tell us—"

"My name is Roxanne," she said, halfway through my question. "Devine is my stage name, so the freaks can't find me. Crystal liked it."

"Was Crystal a stage name too?"

She nodded, and a fresh tear rolled down her cheek. "She hated her given name, Carole Sue. Said it was her hillbilly name and wouldn't hear of using it. She was from Arkansas, you know."

"Can you think of anyone who could've hurt her?"

Roxanne shook her head, while her eyelids stayed lowered, moist with tears. "She was kind, caring. Ambitious like I've never seen before, but kind. Too kind..." she added, then quickly stopped her train of thought, as if she'd let something slip out involuntarily. "She was working hard, going to school during the day, and doing *this* every night." She gestured with her hand to emphasize the word, loading her voice with contempt.

"She was going to school?" Holt repeated.

"Yeah, she was in her third year. She took business administration accounting at UNLV. She had a future," she added, her last word choked by a sob.

"Was she seeing anyone?" I asked, thinking of the mysterious helicopter rides in the middle of the night.

"She had a boyfriend, Ellis. He's married, but that didn't seem to matter much to him; he was in love with Crystal. He's famous somehow, I recognized him when I first met him, but can't recall from where. Some kind of artist; plays the cello."

Artists didn't normally fly choppers, but this was Vegas. Many things were different here.

"Does Ellis have a last name?" Holt asked, frowning.

She shrugged, her thin shoulders seeming frail under the thin fabric of her top. "I don't know his last name, I'm sorry."

"How about a helicopter, Roxanne?" I asked. "Was he the one flying Crystal out from the hotel's helipad?"

"Yes, that was him," she replied, after a flicker of surprise lit her eyes. She didn't expect us to know about that. "He spared no expense when it came to Crystal. But not in a bad way, no. She wasn't like that; she wasn't for sale. She rarely accepted his gifts."

"What's he like, this Ellis?" Holt asked, his frown deepening, as if he knew something I did not.

"He's charming, a perfect gentleman, not like those bastards we see at work every day. He loved Crystal, I have no doubt in my mind. A little moody, unstable, but he was always good to her, generous, attentive."

"Violent?" Holt asked.

"No, absolutely not. He's in love with her, I told you."

"Then, moody, how?" I asked.

"He'd turn sad sometimes, tearful. Other times he'd be the life of the party, so to speak. Cracking jokes with Crystal and me, showing us a good time."

"Did you and—"

She shook her head with such determination her hair became loose. "I'd never do that to Crystal, and he only had eyes for her. I was just her friend, passing by on my way out or something. Those were the only times I saw him."

"Roxanne, we'll need to take a look at Crystal's, um, your apartment, if that's okay," I asked.

"Sure," she said, then reached into a Chanel knockoff purse and pulled out a set of keys. "Here you go, let yourselves in."

"And you?" I asked, taking the keys from her frozen hand.

"I'll use Crystal's. Her bag's over there," she replied, pointing at a black, leather purse with a gold, shoulder, chain strap.

"Why don't we take Crystal's purse instead, okay?" I offered, handing back her set of keys. "We'll need to log this in as evidence."

Holt was already going through Crystal's purse and had extracted her wallet. He pulled out a few plastic cards, then stopped his search with a whistle of surprise. Without a word, he handed me a driver's license issued for Carole Sue Tillman, Crystal's real name.

Based on that piece of government-issued ID, Crystal was barely eighteen years old.

6

BACKGROUND

I ran into Fletcher as I entered the building and almost didn't recognize him. At first, I thought he must've been some thug who just got released or something. He wore baggy track pants, and until then I didn't even know such a thing existed. Maybe it didn't, and they were just three sizes too large, like his T-shirt was. The message printed on the light gray shirt in red, block letters read, "Born to party, forced to work," and got a quick laugh out of me. The young man climbed down the stairs two at a time, his entire body moving to the rhythm of whatever music he was listening to on his earbuds. His long, curly hair bobbed in the same rhythm, partially covering his eyes and making me wonder how he managed to see where he was going. Then again, Old English Sheepdogs have hair covering their eyes, but don't trip over themselves either.

"Whoa, not so fast," I said, stopping him before he reached the ground floor. "We need you badly."

He looked at me with inquisitive eyes, then at Holt, who nodded and muttered, "Uh-huh." Then he let out a long sigh and started climbing up the stairs with significantly less enthusiasm than he'd demonstrated on his way down.

"I still can't get over how you manage to stay employed with your blatant disrespect for the LVMPD dress code," I said, smiling. He barely seemed old enough to work, although I knew he was a Caltech computer science graduate, top of his class.

"That's 'cause I'm irreplaceable," he replied jokingly, showing off two rows of perfectly white teeth. "Can you do what I do?"

"No, I—"

"See?" he cut me off before I could finish my statement. "That's why. No one can."

He was probably right about that. I'd only met him last week, but I was already impressed. Holt called Fletcher a techie, but he was a genius. There wasn't a single shred of data out there that he couldn't find. Thankfully, he was on our team, and it seemed to me that he and I had hit it off beautifully.

He walked quickly with both of us in tow until he reached his desk, where he collapsed into his seat and put his hands over his keyboard, ready to type.

"Shoot," he said, then slurped some dubiously colored liquid from a transparent, half-pint mug. "You're standing between me and my burger."

"We need background on the Scala victim," Holt said, handing him Crystal's real driver's license. "She's eighteen based on this ID, but her roommate says she's taking classes at UNLV."

"Got it," he said, typing crazy fast and flipping through countless database screens displayed in stacks on his dual monitors.

"We need anything you can dig up," I added, "tax reports, family background, criminal record, the works."

"Okay, I said I got it," he replied, his voice not conveying the typical frustration that accompanied those words when other people spoke them. "I'll let you know when I got something for you."

"Uh-uh," Holt replied, "we'll wait. We've already been handed a late start on this one."

Fletcher shrugged. "As you wish." A few moments later, he started delivering, speaking a little too loud, because he hadn't removed his earbuds nor stopped the blaring music player. "Yeah, she's eighteen, got her birth certificate right here. No criminal record whatsoever, not even a parking ticket."

I stared at the screen, trying to keep up with Fletcher's maneuvers between the various databases. He searched state and federal criminal records, the Interstate Identification Index, IRS, DMV, Crime Information Center, even the Homeland Security ATS, or Automated Targeting System.

"Tax records show her employed with the Scala, okay, we knew that," he mumbled, to himself. "Last year's reported income was a dime short of seventy-five grand, but she's a stripper, right?"

"Exotic dancer," I clarified, although he wasn't exactly wrong. It just felt disrespectful to call her that. If I closed my eyes, I could still see her body, lying lifeless on that stage, beautiful and serene and young, as if asleep, as if dreaming of a secret lover. Her being so young made it even harder.

"Yeah, yeah," he said dismissively. "Most strip—um, dancers underreport their tips by at least sixty percent on average, and that puts her real income somewhere above six figures. Nice! I'm in the wrong line of work."

I laughed. He and I both, but at least I had the looks for it.

Holt patted Fletcher on his back.

"Sorry, dude, can't think of anyone who'd pay to see you take off your clothes."

"You never know," Fletcher said, still searching. "Okay, family next. Your vic was born in Grady, Arkansas. Father deceased when she was, um, nine. Mother, Elaine Tillman, thirty-seven, works as a shift manager at Outback Steakhouse, the one on West Sahara. There's a sister, Tina Tillman, now twelve. They all moved to Las Vegas after the father died, looking for work. The mother never remarried."

We took notes, while he typed another string into a search screen and waited for a couple of seconds. Then the screen shifted and displayed a man's DMV record.

"I checked to see if anyone else had reported the same current address as the Tillmans with the DMV. Meet Norm Chaney, forty-two. Must be mom's boyfriend or something."

"Mom's brother, maybe?" Holt asked.

Fletcher typed a few words, then replied, "Nope, mother was a single child. Must be the boyfriend or sublet tenant."

"What does he do?" I asked.

"Tax records have him working a construction site as a foreman. But here's something unusual: income was reported on a 1099, not on a W2. These guys are typically unionized."

"How about Crystal? Was she really a third-year college student at eighteen?"

"You mean Carole Sue, your vic?"

I nodded, and his fingers danced on the keyboard some more.

"Believe it or not, she was. She graduated from high school two years early, and UNLV admitted her immediately. Based on her SATs she could've gone anywhere she wanted, but she chose to stay close to home. She claimed tuition on her taxes two years in a row, so, yes, she was a third-year college student."

Unexpectedly, a wave of sadness engulfed me. There was something about this girl that tugged at my heart. She danced to put herself through school; how cliché that sounded, but to her it wasn't. She wanted to get ahead, to have a chance for a better life. She fought hard, worked hard, and chose to study twice as much at the age when all her girlfriends obsessed over boys and makeup and parties. And somewhere along her uphill path she'd made an enemy. A deadly one.

"Can you trace her phone, see where she's been?" I asked. "We need the phone dumped, calls and messages, you know the drill."

"Don't I know it?" he said quietly, thumping his foot against the floor in the rhythm of the music only he could hear.

"There's video surveillance from the hotel coming in," Holt said. "Start poring over it, frame by frame. There was someone who spoke to her while she danced last night; witnesses say he seemed angry. We need him identified, pronto."

Fletcher typed notes on a separate screen, a quick and unpretentious to-do list.

"Crystal flew out in a helo last night," I said, and for some reason Holt shot me a surprised glance. "Let's find out who owns that eggbeater."

"What else?" Fletcher asked.

"We need to map her last twenty-four hours," I said, speaking to both of them. "Sometime in the last few hours of her life, someone got close enough to kill her."

7

INTERNAL

I checked my email while Holt brought us coffee from the local swill machine and I saw only one new message. As I read it, dread spread through my body bringing a chill along with it.

The Internal Affairs Bureau wanted to speak to me immediately, specifically my old nemesis, Lieutenant Steenstra. *Bloody hell...* I'd thought that entire thing was over, finished.

I hesitated for a moment, thinking what took priority: catching a killer or wasting my time with the rat squad. Of course, if I were to play by those rules, I'd never willingly sit down with them, not ever. Still, I had no choice.

I scribbled a quick note on a Post-it, affixed it to Holt's computer monitor, and took the elevator to visit with my least favorite of all cops. On the way up, I repeated to myself the only two words that were going to matter in the following minutes.

Keep calm.

The elevator doors whooshed open and I stepped out, pasting a professional smile on my lips and doing my best to look relaxed, unfazed. The receptionist didn't reciprocate the smile and invited me to take a seat in the adjacent conference room, while she called the lieutenant.

I'd been in that room before. Sternly decorated with two opposing chairs and a table, a one-way mirror and a video camera, with its red dot on, attached to the wall near the ceiling, the room did little to make visitors feel welcome. Quite the opposite. The IAB called it a conference room, while everyone knew exactly what it was: an interrogation room. The only thing missing were the shackles, designed to keep the perps chained to the table while they were being questioned.

Lieutenant Steenstra opened the door abruptly and I almost flinched. I smiled, but she didn't smile back. She was dressed smartly in a blue gray pantsuit and matching, button-up shirt, an attire that was an excellent expression of her uncompromising attitude. Her blonde hair was cut short in an unpretentious style, reminding me of something I've read somewhere: beware of the woman who cuts her hair short; if she doesn't have the patience for herself, she definitely hasn't got any for you. How fitting.

Steenstra nodded once, put a half-inch thick folder on the table and took a seat across from me.

"Detective Baxter," she said in a cold voice, "we are disappointed, to say the least."

"Why is that?" I asked, while in my mind I recited my new mantra. *Stay calm.*

"I was under the impression that you and I had reached an agreement," she announced. "Seems to me I was wrong."

"What are you talking about?"

"I'm talking about your career, something we've allowed to continue despite the things you've done to jeopardize it," she added, tapping rhythmically on the folder's cover with long, French-manicured fingernails. "I'm talking about the cooperation you had promised us, that has yielded zero results so far."

"Oh, I see," I replied before I could contain myself. "You're talking about Detective Holt and the allegedly missing cocaine."

"The cocaine *is* missing," Steenstra corrected me. "Not allegedly, Detective. I'm telling you how it is, and you, because you're on a probation that otherwise would've never happened, believe what I say and respect our agreement. Is that clear?"

"Crystal," I replied, bitterly using the name of the victim I was supposed to find justice for, in a twisted pun that only I understood. "I thought that this was over, because—"

"Because we weren't for real?" she cut me off angrily. "Because we were part of some kind of cockamamie conspiracy looking to frame your partner? Is that it, Detective?"

I smiled hesitantly, apologetically. "Pretty much."

"Well, news flash for you, Detective. That kilo of cocaine is still missing, and we know your partner took it. We need you to bring us the evidence, so we can lock him up. That's all there is to it."

"But what if he didn't take it? You haven't shown me a single piece of evidence leading to him as the perp in this case."

She sighed, visibly irritated, frustration seeping through every pore of her skin. She undid the buttons of her tight suit jacket and leaned into her elbows over the table, then opened the file.

"Maybe we haven't shown you any evidence regarding Holt, because you're a detective, and we're asking you to do your job, nothing less, nothing more, to find us the evidence we need. We can, however, show you plenty of evidence regarding your own guilt in a number of situations where you broke the law."

She turned the file my way, so I could see clearly. Video camera stills taken when I'd punched a suspect in custody, a drug dealer who'd killed my husband, only I couldn't prove it. Pedro *El Maricon* Reyes, a twenty-something-year-old thug who'd put two bullets in my husband's chest, just because Andrew happened to stumble across a major drug deal going on in our neighborhood. Reyes had left no evidence behind, not enough to prosecute. Andrew's dying words described him and his rather unique heterochromia, but the DA had refused to prosecute because, apparently, odd-eyed people aren't that rare after all.

Andrew died before he could pick Reyes out of a lineup. Heartbroken and restless, I kept looking for my husband's killer at night, never giving up.

Until one day, when my former partner collared yet another drug dealer and I recognized him: his eyes, one green and one brown. Reyes recognized me too, he knew exactly who I was and made jokes about my lonely nights.

And I lost it.

As shown beyond any reasonable doubt in the photo stills from Steenstra's file, I'd punched him, again and again and again, wanting him dead, wanting him to pay for the life he'd taken, for the happiness he'd destroyed, for the never-ending loneliness in my heart.

Steenstra touched my forearm with the side of a Kleenex box and only then I realized I'd been crying silent tears of grief over Andrew's absence from my life. My grief turned to rage as I dried my eyes and glared at the woman who'd stirred up old wounds just to get an edge, then at the camera on the wall.

Bloody wankers, all of them. They didn't deserve to see me cry.

"What exactly do you want, Lieutenant?" I asked coldly.

"You're on probation for twelve months, Detective, and that's because we, Internal Affairs, put in a good word for you when your Henderson commanding officer put in a request for your termination with prejudice. We *own* you for these twelve months. Is that clear?"

"And what exactly does that mean?" I asked again. I was unexpectedly calm, calmer than I'd been in a long time.

"I can't believe you're asking me this," she replied angrily, pushing her chair away from the table and starting to pace the room. "You work your caseload like you'd normally do, and on top of that you help us investigate whomever we choose, whenever we choose. You will close all the investigations the IAB assigns to you during these twelve months quickly, correctly, with well-documented evidence that will stand up in court."

"And if I don't?"

"If you don't, you won't be holding on to your badge for much longer, Detective. We can always flip the switch on you. We've got enough to bury you for good, as you well know. Your extracurricular activities are nothing short of appalling."

With those simple words, I felt a chill freeze my blood; it wasn't just Reyes they were throwing against me. My job was everything I had left. I couldn't think of a life where I wasn't a cop. However, what they were asking for was preposterous. If

I'd read them well, they didn't care if I planted a kilo of coke on Holt myself, as long as I made it stick and got him nailed for it. They didn't seem to care about the presumption of innocence where Holt was concerned; the almighty judge and jury of the IAB had decided Holt was guilty and wanted him executed. Soon. Yesterday, if possible.

I was only a pawn in their bloody game.

My breath caught as I fully understood my options. I leaned against the back of my seat and looked at Steenstra unequivocally.

"Okay, I get it," I replied. "What's my timeline? With Holt?"

"You have a week, Detective. Not a single day more."

"A week? I can't possibly be expected to pull this off in a week," I reacted, not having to feign any of the anguish in my voice. "We just caught a murder case; I won't have the time. I need more—"

"Make the time, Detective," Steenstra said, collecting the scattered photos from the table and getting ready to leave. "I expect a full status report on my desk by noon, next Monday. Close the case on Holt, or we close the case on you."

She turned and left the room and the door sealed quietly behind her, pulled shut by a hydraulic mechanism. Stunned, I stared at the door for several minutes before I collected myself enough to head downstairs and face my new partner, the man I was supposed to bury.

Waiting for the elevator to arrive, I realized that never, during the conversation with Steenstra, had I wondered if Holt was indeed guilty; not even once. He was a good cop; I knew that in my gut, although he was also a recovering addict. The fact that he'd become addicted to cocaine while working an undercover drug operation mattered to the higher-ups just as much as it had mattered what Reyes had done to me, to my husband. Until that day, I'd thought people understood what drove me to come down on Reyes, and that's why I still had a job. Sadly, it turned out that wasn't the case; the rat squad needed fresh meat, and that's all there was to it.

No empathy. No compassion.

The IAB needed collars to look good, just like the rest of us did. But for the rest of us, there was enough real crime in Vegas to investigate and meet our arrest quotas. We didn't have to go around framing people; we had good collars to show.

What if the IAB didn't have enough things going on to justify its existence? Maybe someone else had taken the missing cocaine and framed Holt for it. Or maybe the IAB had an axe to grind with Holt and had decided to jam him up permanently.

My mind kept spinning, weaving layers of explanations, no matter how far-fetched, because I couldn't think of a single scenario in which Jack Holt, my new partner, could be the criminal the IAB was saying he was.

8

PRELIMINARY FINDINGS

I took a deep breath just before the elevator doors opened on the ground floor. I had to summon all my strength to smile casually in Holt's direction, as if nothing were out of the ordinary, although on that particular occasion I didn't manage to fool him one bit.

He frowned and came straight to me. "What's wrong?"

I'd learned a trick at Scotland Yard while training on deceptive tactics; it's called half-truths. A lie had better chances of ringing true if it was built on a foundation of truth or, even better, if it's sandwiched between two slices of factual information. Even share a little vulnerability, expose something that you wouldn't otherwise expose about yourself, and the person you're talking to would zero in on that particular aspect and not see the fib blooming right in front of their eyes.

"It's that stupid probation I have on my record," I replied, stating one truthful statement about the entire situation. "This supervision will make the next twelve months of my life interesting, to say the least."

"What do they want now?" Holt asked in a lowered voice.

I led the way to the parking lot and didn't reply until we'd left the building. "These HR people and their never-ending requirements." That was the lie. "Did you know I have to see an anger management shrink now?"

The part about the shrink was also true, albeit not new. I'd been seeing a court-appointed shrink for a few weeks, hating every minute of it.

As expected, Holt relaxed a little when he heard my response, not doubting it, from what I could tell. "Better watch what you're saying in the office," he said. "It could come back and bite you in the rear."

I smiled briefly and nodded a couple of times. "I know it. It's just a waste of time, that's all."

"Want to deliver next of kin?" he asked. "I called the restaurant and Mrs. Tillman is off today."

"Let's stop by Anne's first, to see what she's got so far."

"Deal," he said, then started the car and put the AC setting halfway to the max.

It was a cold, yet sunny day that had managed to make the inside of his Ford as unbearably hot as if it were summer. Winters in Vegas are short-lived and not cold, and the crisp blue of the sky contradicts the notion of winter, which, by definition and association, was supposed to be as miserable as I was remembering it from my native London. Back then, darkness gloomed for days in a row, while an incessant drizzle fell from the sky and a bitter cold pierced through to the bones, regardless of how many layers of clothing attempted to shield it. But in Vegas, the air was crisp and the sky cloudless; you had to remind yourself it was Christmastime. Between the palm trees and the powerful rays of the desert sun, there wasn't any hope for a white Christmas, and the idea of winter holidays seemed surreal, unless you climbed nearby Mount Charleston.

Holt made small talk during the few minutes it took him to drive us to the coroner's office on Pinto Lane, while I let my thoughts grab and twist me into a knot, trying to figure out what to do. How was I going to deliver on the IAB's demands and still be able to live with myself? One alternative required I didn't have a conscience; the other meant I didn't have a job.

The cold air filled with the smell of formaldehyde pulled me into the present the moment we walked through the double doors that separated the autopsy room from the coroner's front office. As always happened when I visited the morgue, I froze in place, willing myself to take a few more steps and move near the autopsy table where Crystal's body lay bare.

I felt a chill in my blood as if it were my skin touching the stainless steel table. Nothing made me think of my own mortality more than seeing death's handiwork, exposed and analyzed under powerful lights, dissected with sharp instruments, interpreted by mass spectrometers, visualized with digital microscopes, and separated into core components by whirring, spinning centrifuges. Death had won that round, and Crystal's body lay still and vulnerable in testimony to some bastard's victory. But death had been but an instrument wielded by a hateful hand, one I was soon going to snap handcuffs around.

I breathed, willing the thumping of my heart against my chest to slow a little, and approached the autopsy table. I looked at Crystal's perfect face, glowing under the powerful exam lamps, beautiful and serene. How could someone so young, so innocent have stirred up such immense enmity in another human being? What could she have done, if anything? Or had she been a random victim of a killer yearning to satisfy urges of a dark, perverted nature?

In my mind, there wasn't a single shred of doubt: that beautiful, young girl had been murdered.

"I'm not done yet," Anne announced, not raising her eyes from Crystal's abdominal cavity.

She wore her lab coat and a see-through, polyethylene protective gown on top of black jeans and a black T-shirt. Her hair was buzzed even shorter than usual, her firm response to the invasive smells of death and decay that accompanied her daily labor. It was difficult to see, behind the rigid, authoritarian appearance, the kindness and warmth of Dr. Anne St. Clair—the person, not the ME. The medical examiner was all business: cold, factual, analytical, a dedicated and perceptive investigator.

I swallowed hard, finding it difficult to voice words or make sounds near Crystal's motionless body. That was a part of my job that never got easier, despite the many years I'd accumulated investigating homicides on both sides of the Atlantic.

"Anything you can tell us?" I asked, shooting Holt a quick look.

He seemed uncomfortable, even more than I was. He was pacing slowly, his hands tucked deeply inside his pockets, and his broad shoulders hunched forward, walking back and forth by the drawers stacked against the back wall in two rows of four refrigerated body storage units. Five of them had labels; it had been a busy few weeks for the Clark County coroner's office.

Anne looked up through her safety goggles with scrutinizing eyes. She seemed to have an unspoken question on her mind but decided to keep that to herself after shooting Holt a cold glance.

"Got your message about the chip in her bra," she said, "but I didn't find anything. All her clothing has been swabbed, bagged, and tagged, and there was no chip. I don't remember seeing one at the crime scene either."

"I went over the crime scene photos and there was no chip anywhere," Erika, her assistant chimed in from the lab's computer desk.

I sighed, feeling a wave of frustration building. That chip could've had that mysterious man's fingerprints and DNA on it. "Okay. Anything more on the cause of death? Something we could use?"

Anne put her scalpel on a tray by her side and took off her gloves, then her goggles.

"I will rule this death as suspicious circumstances, until I can identify the chemical that was used."

"So, she was poisoned?" Holt asked, approaching the table. "This is officially a homicide, then?"

"I will rule her death as suspicious for now," she repeated her earlier statement. "Her heart stopped moments after she started showing acute symptoms of poison-induced asphyxia."

"What was it, Doc?"

"Do you know how many poisons and toxins there are in this world, Detective?" she asked, but Holt knew better than to venture a response. "We will have to test for each one until we find what killed her."

"So, no idea what it was?" I asked.

"I have a long list of what it wasn't," she replied, "but that list isn't nearly long enough to make testing a quick task. I'll start testing for the more common substances used that deliver the symptoms I've seen."

"Anything else relevant?" Holt asked.

"Again, this is preliminary, Detective. My guest is still on the table," she stated, going back to her earlier position next to Crystal's body. "I swiped her chest in case that chip left any trace material. At first sight, the area was clean. Well, that's a relative term, considering I found dust particles, hair and carpet fibers, and other trace elements we're working to identify."

"Do you know how she ingested the poison?" Holt asked.

"That's one of the things I didn't find, evidence that she had actually ingested it. See here?" she pointed her finger at the stomach, opened up for examination in a metallic tray by the organ scale. "Typically, in ingested poison victims we see signs of chemical burns in the stomach lining. Here, there are none. But there are several known toxins and poisons that don't leave any visible marks on the mucosae."

"If you had to guess?" I asked quietly, knowing how much she hated the question.

"There's one big problem with guessing," she said coldly. "It can point you in the wrong direction, giving you clues where there aren't any. No, Detectives, I don't want to guess. The only thing I can say is that based on my experience with poison victims and the literature I reviewed, I'm inclined to start testing for toxins before poisons."

Holt frowned, then rubbed his forehead with one quick gesture. "Meaning?"

"A toxin is a poison that was produced by a living organism, animal or plant," she replied. "I believe what killed her had been engineered by a living organism."

"Could it be possible a snake bit her?" I asked.

"I didn't see signs of a snake bite anywhere on her body. Typically, when people get bitten by snakes they go to the hospital and seek help."

"Then, what are you telling us?"

"I'm telling you I will start testing for toxins before I start testing for poisons, and that I can't tell you yet how the toxin got into her bloodstream. I'll take tissues samples from all her organs, including her skin, and have those analyzed. As soon as I know, you'll know. I've already sent a blood sample for a tox screen, but it will take a while to get the results back."

"How about stomach contents?" Holt asked.

"Still working on that, Detective."

"Okay, then," I said, "we'll get out of your hair. Call us when you get something."

"I always do," she replied simply. "Oh, there is one more thing. She was ten weeks pregnant."

9

FAMILY

That was another part of my job that never got easier; delivering death notifications to victims' families. The worst of them all was telling a parent that her child was never coming home.

Elaine Tillman lived with her younger daughter, Tina, and Norm Chaney, most likely her boyfriend, in a small house in Spring Valley. It was a beige, single-story, two-car garage, traditional house with a small backyard and little distance between neighboring homes, the tell-all sign of a newer development. Nothing stood out about the property, except a bike abandoned on the driveway, Tina's, judging by the pink frame and the handlebar streamers in pink and purple. It was almost dark; Tina was possibly at home, eating dinner, telling stories about her day, in a preteen chipper voice.

I took a deep breath before ringing the bell and glanced at Holt quickly. His eyes were lowered, and a couple of deep ridges marked his forehead. He must have dreaded these house calls just as much as I did.

Elaine Tillman opened the door, and her smile vanished when we showed identification and I said our names. She wiped her hands on her green-and-white striped apron and ran her hand quickly against her hair, as if to make sure everything was in place.

"May we come in, please?" I asked, and she stepped aside, making room for us to enter. She closed the door behind us and gestured an invite to take seats in the living room, while pallor took all the color away from her cheeks.

"Who is it, Mom?" a young girl asked, as she burst into the living room at a sprinter's pace. I recognized Tina from the photos we had in our systems, dating a couple of years back when she got a passport issued for a trip to Cancun. She had the most freckled face I'd ever seen, complemented by long, curly, and seriously entangled hair, so red it didn't seem natural. Her mother must've spent hours combing through that mess every day.

"What can we do for you, Detectives?" Mrs. Tillman asked, while Tina drew near her mom, wrapping her thin arms around her waist.

"Please, take a seat," Holt invited, and they both obeyed silently, fear altering their features, changing the expressions in their eyes, bringing slight tremors to their mouths.

Then Holt and I looked briefly at each other.

"Mrs. Tillman, I'm afraid we have sad news," I said, feeling my throat dry all of a sudden, making it difficult for me to articulate the words. But I pulled myself together; if it was tough for me to say the words, for them it was much worse to hear what I was about to say. "Your daughter, Carole Sue Tillman, died early this morning during her shift."

Mrs. Tillman's mouth gaped open and, at first, not a single sound came out. Her eyes, open wide, moved erratically as she tried to make sense of my words, as if she were looking all over the place for help, for someone to tell her it wasn't true, for a sign that everything she'd heard was a nightmare she was going to wake up from.

"No... Are... you sure?" she eventually asked, her voice choked, raspy, and trembling.

My eyes were riveted on Tina's reaction. Her big, blue eyes had shifted from shock to pain and immediately to anger, while she threw a fiery glare at a door, most likely leading to a bedroom. Behind that door, the muted sound of a TV delivered some baseball news I could only partially hear.

"Yes, I'm afraid we're sure," Holt replied. "She died this morning at 4:12, on the casino floor where she worked. Her heart stopped."

Mrs. Tillman covered her gaping mouth with her hand, but to no avail. Her sobs burst from her heaving chest, while her tears mixed with Tina's, mother and daughter in a tight embrace, their cheeks touching, their wails buried in each other's hair.

"What the hell is going on?" a man said, and with his appearance, the TV sports commentary resounded louder, now that the door to the bedroom was open.

That was Norm Chaney, and my first impression of him was instant, undeniable dislike sprinkled with wariness. It wasn't because of the sleeveless shirt he was wearing with brown, worn-out shorts and flipflops. It wasn't the large number of tattoos that marked his skin in faded blue ink. One of them caught my attention though, some kind of broken, thick line, only partially visible above the neck of his shirt. It seemed familiar, although I couldn't tell what it was; when he saw where I was looking, he placed his hand on top of the tattoo as if to hide it. However, not even that quick, reflex gesture was the reason for my suspicion.

No, it was something in his cold eyes that I saw glimmering for a fraction of a second. Irritation that his televised entertainment had been disrupted. Annoyance with what was going on, with Elaine's sobs, with Tina's fiery glares. Visible displeasure with our presence in his home. But what *I didn't* see in his eyes was equally worrisome. Not a single shred of empathy, of curiosity even, over what could've caused the women in his life such immense grief.

A fraction of a second later, that glimmer of who Norm Chaney really was had vanished, and the worried, apparently empathic companion came out, played to perfection. He rushed toward Elaine as she pulled herself out of her younger daughter's arms, stood, and buried her face in his chest, her wails renewed.

I kept my eyes riveted on Tina, the twelve-year-old freckled kid whose reactions were nothing I'd expected. She wiped her nose with the back of her hand, stood, and rushed into her room, slamming the door. Well, maybe her reactions were starting to become a little more normal; most teenagers would forego the use of a tissue and run and lock themselves in their room in a situation like that.

Only half a minute later, she emerged from the room calmer, a look of fierce determination in her dry eyes, and that was unusual. She wore jeans and a black hoodie over a white, V-collared T-shirt, and kept her hands in the hoodie's pockets. She walked calmly across the room, then threw Chaney another death glare and let herself drop on the sofa, seemingly more struck by anger than by grief.

That kid knew something about her sister's death.

I looked briefly at Holt, but he'd already picked up on the girl's demeanor. He took a step forward toward her, but I stopped him with a touch on his forearm.

"Mrs. Tillman, I know this isn't the best time, but we have some questions about Carole."

"Crystal," Tina said sharply. "She hated that name. Everyone called her Crystal. She was legally changing it, or had already changed it, I don't know."

"Crystal, yes," I replied, wondering if they knew she was an exotic dancer and that was her stage name. Her mother knew her age, so my guess was she probably didn't know what Crystal really did for a living.

Mrs. Tillman made a visible effort to contain her sobs. Her shoulders still heaved while she wiped her tears on her apron, then mumbled an apology and disappeared for a moment inside the kitchen, from where she emerged with a box of tissues.

"Tell me," she said, looking at me directly, "how did she die? Did someone…"

She couldn't bring herself to say the words.

"We're investigating, ma'am," Holt replied. "There are no signs of violence. Her heart stopped, apparently for no reason, while she was working. Are you aware of any heart condition she might've had?"

"N—no," she replied. "She was a healthy, happy girl, full of life. She worked really hard, always pushing herself to be first, to finish school early. She must've been tired, but I don't believe a strong heart like hers could just stop." Fresh tears started rolling down her stained cheeks. "No, my baby wanted to live.

Her heart... didn't just stop." Then she turned to me and took two steps forward, then grabbed my hand with both of hers. "Please, promise me you'll find out who killed my baby. Please."

"We'll do our best, Mrs. Tillman," I replied, while in my mind I said the words we weren't allowed to say out loud. *Yes, I promise I'll catch your daughter's murderer. I swear I will.* "When's the last time you saw her?" I asked, looking at Tina first, then at her mother.

"Last weekend," she replied. "She came home for Sunday dinner."

"Please, sit down, Mrs. Tillman," Holt said, and she let go of my hand after prolonging her pleading look for one more moment. She sat on the couch and Chaney took a seat next to her, holding her hand. Tina kept her distance from Chaney and glared at him every few seconds, in the typical insistence of teenagers who don't immediately get what they want. All that time her hands stayed deeply hidden in her hoodie's pockets, and her jowls showed the tension of firmly clenched teeth.

"And you are...?" Holt asked Chaney, pretending we didn't know already.

"Norm Chaney," he replied, while his eyes flickered, avoiding Holt's. Visibly nervous, he ran his hand across his face, and scratched his nose in passing. Those hand movements were definite signs of deception; Norm Chaney was lying.

"Is Norm short for something?" Holt asked, and by the tone of his voice, I knew he was aware of Norm's dishonesty.

"No," he replied quickly.

"What do you do for a living, Mr. Chaney?" Holt asked unperturbed.

"I'm a construction foreman at Sun Builders," he replied, also a little too quickly, rehearsed.

"What are you building these days, Mr. Chaney?" Holt asked.

"That new hotel, over on East Sahara," he replied, his frown deepening. He fidgeted, ostensibly nervous, then shifted in his seat and crossed his hairy legs. One of his flip-flops fell off his foot, and he struggled with coordination as he put it back on.

"Could we see some identification, Mr. Chaney?" I asked.

He didn't reply. Instead, he grunted as he stood and walked over to a pair of jeans abandoned on an armchair, near the dining room. He returned with his wallet and extracted his driver's license. His fingers shook a little, almost imperceptibly.

I studied it and didn't see anything wrong. It seemed legit. Maybe he was hiding something else other than his identity, or maybe he was just not comfortable talking to cops. It's known to happen.

"Mrs. Tillman," I asked, handing Chaney his license back, "where was Crystal going to school?"

Her red eyes filled with pride and renewed sadness. "She could've gone anywhere she wanted," she replied, stifling a sob. "She had acceptance letters from lots of places, but she wanted to stay here, with us. She went to the University of Nevada."

"Did you help her pay for tuition?" I asked, careful not to kick a hornet's nest and cause damage without any gain. Holt looked at me briefly, intrigued.

"No," Mrs. Tillman replied, lowering her eyes. "I, um, don't really make that much, and she didn't want to be a burden. No, she had financial aid, and I cosigned her application."

It felt as if I walked through a maze, at each step a new, unexpected turn. A web of lies, with no end in sight. That meant we couldn't take any information for granted, no matter where it came from. Everything had to be checked and double-checked, then checked again.

Crystal had been a talented liar; thus far I understood all her reasons. But had we uncovered all her lies?

As if reading my mind, Holt cleared his throat and asked, "Do you know if anyone wanted to hurt Crystal? Did she have any enemies that you know of?"

She shook her head, then said, "No, no one. Everyone loved Crystal."

That wasn't true; at least one person had disliked her enough to want her dead, but I couldn't bring myself to tell her that.

"Tell me about Crystal, Mrs. Tillman. What kind of person was she?" I asked instead.

Her eyes met mine with a softer, warmer light in them. "We moved here from Grady, Arkansas, after my husband died," she said quietly. "Crystal was ten, and this one," she pointed toward Tina, whose fierce demeanor hadn't shifted a single bit, "was only four. We didn't have a choice; there aren't any jobs in a place like Grady. Here I could make a living, keep a roof over our heads. It wasn't easy."

She stopped talking for a while, then patted her eyes and nose with a tissue she kept in her hand, clutching her fingers tightly around it, as if afraid to let go.

I allowed her time to collect her thoughts.

"Crystal noticed how tired I was every day, coming home from work after pulling at least four, five hours of overtime each day," she continued after a while. "One night she asked me, 'Mom, how can I make money to help you?' I told her she had to finish school first. She was a high school freshman when she asked me that. A year and a half later she graduated from high school with honors, in a rush to make money for her family. Two years after that, at only eighteen, she's a third-year college student. Can you believe it? That's who my Crystal was."

There was little left to be said. I thanked her, offered my condolences again, then headed for the door. As I shook her hand and presented my business card, Tina sprung off the sofa and came near us, apparently waiting in line to say goodbye, uneasy, agitated. Holt noticed her too and moved in front of Chaney, blocking his view of Tina, while he asked him more questions about the hotel his employer was building on East Sahara.

Nothing happened for a long moment; I reiterated my commitment to find out what had happened to Crystal while shaking her mother's hand. I turned to leave just as Tina tripped over the edge of a tasseled rug and flailed, trying to grab on to something for support. I reached out and grabbed her right arm but felt her other hand reach inside my pocket.

Our eyes locked and I saw the plea for silence in hers. Discreetly, I pulled out another business card and, pretending to straighten her clothes, slid it into one of her bottomless hoodie pockets.

10

DINNER

I breathed the cold air thirstily as soon as the Tillman's door closed behind us. It was late, almost seven, when residential streets found their nightly peace while the Strip awakened, welcoming hundreds of thousands of tourists as it did every night. December was a slower time of the year for gamblers and vice seekers, but the city still came alive each night, with its myriad lights and incredible colors.

I climbed inside Holt's SUV and rubbed my frozen hands together. It was cold; the temperature had dropped to maybe forty-five or so, and I only wore a light jacket on top of my shirt. I zipped it up and slid my hand into my right pocket, expecting to find something that didn't belong.

I pulled out the piece of notebook paper and unfolded it carefully, squinting in the dim light.

"What's that?" Holt asked, throwing me a quick glance after taking a right turn on Flamingo.

"Tina Tillman slipped me a note. It says, 'I know who did it. I'll call you.'"

"Interesting," Holt replied, cussing under his breath after three tourists ran in front of his car, jaywalking. "After tonight, I think I know too. This guy, Chaney, no way he hasn't done time. Did you see the tattoo on his chest?"

"The one he was trying to hide? Yeah, I noticed it, but can't place it."

"Aryan Brotherhood," he replied. "Our Mr. Chaney has been on the inside."

"We ran his rap sheet," I replied, thinking that Holt's theory sounded plausible. Chaney looked just like the ex-cons we collared each day. We both knew one when we saw one. "His driver's license seemed legit, and if he's living under a false identity, that's two in a row."

"Two? You mean, with Crystal's?"

"Precisely. I wonder who has the ability to deliver such perfectly executed fakes."

"Maybe they're not fakes," Holt replied.

"What do you mean?"

"Maybe someone at the DMV has a little side business," he offered, shifting lanes and signaling a right turn as soon as the Paris Las Vegas Hotel and its scale reproduction of the Eiffel Tower appeared in sight.

"Where are we going?" I asked.

"To dinner. I don't recall us eating lunch today, and I'm not suggesting dinner, I'm buying."

The moment he mentioned it, I realized how famished I really was. Maybe the chill I felt in my entire body had something to do with that, with the lacking calories that deprived my body of much-needed energy to function, to live. I smiled but turned my head away from my partner, hiding my smile.

He pulled his unmarked SUV into a restricted parking spot and flashed a badge for the Paris Hotel valet who was approaching us in a bellicose march. The valet stopped in his tracks and sketched a timid smile, then disappeared before we entered the hotel lobby.

"I don't think Chaney is the killer," I said. "He's too butch for poison."

"Too butch?" Holt repeated, laughing. "Is that a technical term?"

"He's more of a blunt force trauma kind of lad, or maybe even gunshot trauma, but not poison. It just doesn't feel right."

"We'll see. For now, *après vous, mademoiselle*," he said, as he opened a massive door for me.

"Where are we going?" I asked, surprised at how excited I was, although it wasn't the first time I was having dinner on the Strip. Nevertheless, I was smiling widely, and felt proud seeing the appreciative glances my partner got from practically every female, and some men too.

"The HEXX," he replied, leading the way to the restaurant's back entrance. "Outside, in the cold? Or inside, without the view?"

"Outside, definitely outside, and we'll ask them to pull up one of those space heaters I know they have."

The hostess greeted us with a perfect, little smile and then escorted us to a table out on the terrace facing the Bellagio fountains. Holt pulled out my chair and I sat, feeling the coldness of the metal against my thighs but not minding it that much.

"How come you can afford dinner at the HEXX on a cop's salary?" I asked, the sudden tinge of anxiety and suspicion ruining my mood and reminding me of the skinny and wicked Lieutenant Steenstra.

"I *can't* afford it," he replied. "That's why we're only going to have appetizers and dessert," he said jokingly, his crooked smile bringing a warmth that dissipated the cold December air.

"Then I'll cover the entrées," I replied. "No way I'll settle for appetizers and dessert after a twelve-hour day."

"No, that's not necessary, Baxter," he replied laughing. "I'll feed us tonight."

"Yes, it's necessary," I insisted. "It's also fair. This isn't a date, you know."

The moment I said it, I regretted it. Why did I have to bring it up? His widening grin told me he saw right through my words. He knew I still thought of our night together sometimes, mistake as it might've been.

The thought of that night brought a sigh to my lips, one I tried really hard to hide. Yeah, I'd shagged my partner after only knowing him for a few days. Words could not describe how guilty I felt, or how much I wished I could do it again. That conflict of emotions made me angry, nervous, hesitant, in one word, a complete idiot. Well, in three words, to be exact.

When I had the courage to look at him again I didn't like what I saw, not even a bit. He leaned against his backrest, a crooked grin tugging at the corner of his mouth, and his eyes, half closed, were sizing me up.

"Then, what is it, if not a date?" he asked me in a low, sultry voice that sent heatwaves through my veins.

"Just two cops having dinner," I managed to say.

"Uh-huh," he replied, his expression unchanged. "Thanks for clarifying."

Our eyes met across the white tablecloth and the winter chill dispersed as if it were never there. I couldn't think of a single thing I could say that wouldn't make things worse. Or better, depending on perspective.

Ah... Bollocks.

"Good evening," the waitress said, after having approached the table completely undetected. "My name is Michelle and I'll be your server tonight. Can I start you off with something to drink?"

I wanted to scream, tell her to bugger off for a minute or two. They should teach those waiters to read their customers, not barge in like that.

"Pellegrino for me, no ice," I replied, hating to be the first one to break eye contact.

Damn Holt and his innuendo.

"Same here," he added. "We're ready to order, I believe?" he asked, the question being meant for me.

"Sure. What's good here?" I asked, as I couldn't seem to focus on the bloody menu enough to place an order, unwanted thoughts and memories clashing in my mind.

"Our specials tonight are—"

"Go for a steak, partner," Holt cut in over the waitress. "Ribeye or filet for you, and you must try the crispy broccolini. You'll love those."

I nodded, and then clarified, "Ribeye, please, medium-well."

"I'll have the same," Holt added, then handed Michelle the menu and thanked her. She accepted with wanting, lingering eyes and an openly inviting smile, raising in me the sudden urge to scratch her face and see her bleed. I was becoming ridiculous, and the only one to blame was Holt.

Of course, he was... Heaven forbid I had to take any responsibility for my own actions, and ideally a cold shower.

The waitress finally disappeared, leaving us in peace.

"You sure about that?" he eventually asked in the same loaded voice.

"Yeah, ribeye is fine with me," I replied absentmindedly, still mulling over the intrusion of the waitress and the emotions she'd stirred in me. I didn't want to think what it all meant, but I couldn't put a lid on it either.

"Are you sure that's all we are?" he repeated, unfazed. "Two cops having dinner?"

I steeled my eyes before looking at him. "I'm positive," I replied sternly.

"It doesn't have to be that way, you know."

The hell it doesn't, I thought.

"But it does," I replied, as firmly as I could muster without sounding bitchy. "We made a mistake... *I* made a mistake, and I'm sorry." I lowered my eyes, unable to look at him, at the curl in his lip, the glimmer of amusement in his eyes, and the unspoken words on his breath. "We have jobs, we need to be able to count on each other, Holt, as cops. No emotion, no luggage. Let's admit it, we made a mistake."

The waitress returned with our food. I wolfed it down in silence, barely taking the time to savor the exquisite taste. Those broccolinis with their orange-flavored dressing were to die for. Holt didn't say anything either, and his sixteen-ounce steak disappeared at an incredible pace.

I sighed with satisfaction as I dabbed my mouth with a starched napkin, then placed it on the table next to the plate. "Thank you, Holt, this was amazing."

"I can think of a few other amazing things I could offer," he replied with a crooked smile.

Typical male; he'd heard nothing of what I had to say earlier, just because he didn't agree with it. Too bloody bad.

"Well, thanks, but no thanks," I replied seriously, but almost burst into laughter when he licked his lips. I managed to refrain from doing that, keeping it all bottled up inside and holding his gaze without flinching. I could play this game too and win at it. If anyone was going to go home crying tonight, it sure as hell wasn't going to be me.

"Can I offer you the dessert menu?" Michelle inquired.

"Strawberries," I heard him say without looking at her, his eyes still riveted to mine.

"We have strawberry cheesecake, strawberry soufflé," the waitress started chanting, but we both glared at her so intensely she clammed up and disappeared.

Holt's hearty laughter made a few heads turn, although there weren't many bracing the cold on the Strip at that hour.

"What?" I asked, biting angrily into a piece of a leftover roll.

"God forbid anyone interrupts our twisted foreplay, huh?"

I laughed lightly, lowering my eyelids to hide my guilty eyes. He was right, although I'd never admit it to him. Our interaction reminded me more of flirting than of typical detective chatter. I admitted that obvious fact to myself, immediately doubting my own sanity. What the hell was I doing here with him if that were the case? Why wasn't I eating an omelet by myself, at home, where I could avoid making more mistakes?

"Get over it, Holt," I replied, "it will not happen."

Michelle put a bowl of strawberries on the table, then another with whipped cream and a thin layer of chocolate syrup. She placed two spoons in front of us as quickly as she could, eager to disappear.

Still looking straight at me, Holt picked up a strawberry and dipped it in whipped cream, then offered it to me. I accepted, then took a bite. The moment my teeth sunk into the delicious fruit, his eyes closed halfway and his grin widened.

"Damn you, Holt," I said, but my voice betrayed me, the laughter swelling my chest.

Our phones chimed at the same time, but he was the first one to read the message. His smile vanished, replaced by a deep frown and an intensity I'd never seen before.

He pushed himself away from the table and put some cash under the bottle of water. "Come on, we've got to go."

11

Night Caller

Anne liked the silence at the morgue, late after hours. Now that Erika had finally gone home, she was the only one left and wasn't planning on heading out anytime soon. Crystal's body still lay on the exam table, more questions than answers keeping the Clark County coroner from filling out the autopsy report.

How did an eighteen-year-old girl's heart just stop, in the middle of her dance routine?

Very few poisons and toxins could claim such performance in execution, but Anne didn't see a trace of either.

Cyanide, for example, can kill a person within seconds, but the smell of almonds it leaves behind is unmistakable. There was no trace of that smell on Crystal's body, and the mass spec didn't find traces of cyanide on the tissue samples she'd tested.

Arsenic is another favorite poison, but it gives out a heavy, garlic-like smell, not something she'd overlook on a preliminary exam nor during an autopsy.

There were some other poisons she could think of that could stop a heart, but none of them had left any traces in Crystal's body. The most inconspicuous of them all, potassium chloride, rarely left any traces for the medical examiner to find in its terrible wake, except one: the concentration of potassium in heart blood. Anne had tested by comparison with femoral blood and found the two values close enough to eliminate potassium chloride poisoning as a potential cause of death.

One by one, she'd worked through most poisons known to stop hearts and impair respiratory function, although she'd already sent a generous blood sample to the crime lab for a preliminary tox screen. She just didn't have the patience to wait for the results, while the killer could disappear.

It seemed logical the killer had used a toxin, not a poison. Okay, but which one? There were thousands of plant toxins that could kill in that manner, countless venoms, and on top of that, deadly bacteria like Clostridium botulinum, also known as Botox.

Where could she start narrowing these down? After the preliminary tox screen came back, perhaps negative, she would've eliminated the most likely poisons and toxins. Then she'd have to order additional testing, one toxin at a time. The entire process could take years of trial and error.

Unless she could think of something creative to do, like find the point of entry into Crystal's body, before she could identify the toxin itself.

She'd examined the entire body under a 10x magnifier glass, then under a fluoroscope, looking for any signs of trauma, no matter how small, like that given by a needle, for example. She'd found nothing, not a single puncture mark.

She measured the skin color with a method called colorimetry, looking for hidden bruises under the skin, too new to show, and through special imaging techniques like reflectance spectrometry or hyperspectral analysis.

Still nothing.

Suddenly feeling tired after a thirteen-hour day, Anne let herself drop into the massage chair she kept in the adjacent room, hoping some inspiration would come if she distanced herself from all the things she could still try and look at the big picture instead. Who was this killer? How did he or she think? How does one instantaneously poison someone who has been dancing in plain sight, under video surveillance, for at least two hours before collapsing?

She rubbed her forehead with frozen, achy fingers and closed her eyes, trying to visualize the scene at the casino. The four blackjack tables situated around the elevated stage where Crystal performed. Her grabbing the pole, every now and then, for balance, as she twisted her body in the advanced choreography she'd seen her perform on the video recordings.

That pole... Maybe poison had been dripping down that pole, and she'd been absorbing it through her skin? She grabbed it with her palms, or wrapped her thighs around it, her inner thighs, where skin is soft, thin, permeable.

Damn it to hell, how did she not see this sooner?

She almost sprung out of her seat when she remembered she'd swabbed every inch of Crystal's skin, looking for trace evidence, and the lab was still running those. She could only try one more thing, highly unorthodox, but enough to point her in the right direction. She could prepare tissue samples from areas of her skin she suspected of contact with the toxin and run them through the mass spec, looking for significant discrepancies among the various samples.

She sighed and let herself lean back into her chair again. She remembered Erika had swabbed the entire length of that pole and already ran it through the mass spec. Nothing out of the ordinary, no unknown element or elements that would be indicative of a toxin.

Nope, she had nothing but a fierce migraine starting to develop.

She rubbed her forehead, trying to push the migraine cloud away, but then she froze. A clattering noise came from the morgue.

She wasn't alone anymore.

Quietly, she got out of the massage chair and tiptoed toward the door. The pair of swinging doors that separated the autopsy room from the storage room were fitted with see-through glass panels, installed to prevent the staff from running into one another when moving between the two spaces. Walking quietly along the back wall, careful not to make a sound, she approached the doors and peeked inside the autopsy room, still hoping against all reason that it was one of her employees who'd forgotten something.

At first, she smelled gasoline, even before she saw him. Tall and well-built, dressed in a black tactical parka and wearing a ski mask, the man didn't seem like someone she could easily take down on her own. She pulled out her phone and dialed nine-one-one, then placed the phone under some towels, so the operator's voice wouldn't give her away.

Then she realized where the smell of gasoline was coming from. The man had brought a canister with him, had removed the cap, and started pouring the liquid along the walls.

She couldn't sit and wait for him to destroy all the evidence she had yet to examine.

Her weapon was locked in the front office, where she kept it during the day. There was no reason to carry a gun in a morgue, at least not until that moment. Swallowing a detailed curse, she grabbed a scalpel from a spare kit stored on a shelf and made it through the doors, as quietly as she could.

Then she leapt forward, planning to slash his throat from behind, her only chance against someone with twice her body mass.

She slipped on some gasoline and grabbed the side of the exam table to stop her fall but dropped the scalpel. The tiny object clattered loudly against the cement floor, and the intruder turned to face her.

She didn't hesitate; she'd been trained in hand-to-hand combat during her two tours in Afghanistan, and she wasn't going to go down easily. She charged at the man with her bare hands, aiming for the most sensitive areas of the human body. A clawed finger to the eye, a quick fist in the laryngeal prominence, then a strong, angry-as-hell kick in the side of his knee, just as he delivered a bone-crushing blow to her ribs.

At least two of the blows she delivered hit home, because the man fell to the ground groaning in pain, but the sound he made was unnatural.

"A shattered larynx does that," she said, panting heavily, and coming around him to deliver one final blow to his neck.

He pushed himself away from her and reached inside his pocket. She heard a familiar sound and froze. The man had pulled the pin out of a grenade and was holding it in his hand, ready to throw.

She looked around, thinking hard. Where could she take cover? Could she outrun an explosion? Not likely.

He pulled himself up and limped toward the door, while Anne retreated toward the back wall, putting as much distance between them as possible. She took her eyes off him and saw the gasoline puddle spreading toward her. In a second, her feet would be soaked in it. She backtracked a few more steps but ran into the wall. There was nowhere else she could go.

He threw the grenade toward her and took off. The grenade bounced against the wall and rolled under the main exam table, now empty. She had four seconds at best.

"One, one-thousand," Anne counted, gasping for air and desperately looking for a way out. She made for the body storage units, built with solid, insulated stainless steel walls. "Two, one-thousand," she counted again, opening an upper level storage unit and pulling the shelf out halfway. "Three, one-thousand," she said, painfully hopping on the shelf and pulling herself inside the storage unit.

Once inside, she couldn't close the door; instead, she rolled herself over the body stored in there, landed on the last unit and curled up in a ball, shielding her head under her folded arms. "Four, one-thou—"

The explosion shook the room and the entire building burst into flames, fueled by gasoline and the many chemicals she stored in her lab, letting out toxic fumes that would soon get to her. She felt singeing heat coming from the fire and a cloud of black smoke soon engulfed her. She choked, desperately gasping for air.

Then everything faded away into still darkness, the heat of the fire, the smell of the toxic fumes, her own choked gasps for air, the thumping in her chest.

12

FIRE

By the time Holt pulled near the morgue, the fire had been extinguished, but the building was still smoldering. Parts of it had collapsed into a pile of rubble, but half of the autopsy room was still standing, and so was the entire back storage area.

The street was engulfed in red and blue flashing lights, while three fire trucks still pumped water through hoses, suffocating the flames wherever smoke coiled up toward the night sky.

My heart stopped when I saw the body covered with yellow tarp near the entrance. I felt Holt's hand squeezing mine as I climbed out of the vehicle, afraid to move, afraid to discover Anne's body underneath that tarp. Tears streamed from my eyes, making it difficult to see anything clearly.

I forced a deep breath into my lungs and rushed to the body. Holt had run ahead of me and was talking to one of the officers on the scene. I kneeled next to the frail silhouette, afraid to touch it. Holt crouched next to me and grabbed my hand again.

"It's Erika," he said, "Anne's assistant. Her neck was broken."

"Oh, no," I whimpered, covering my gaping mouth. "Where's Anne?" I sprung to my feet, looking around, searching for her with frantic, illogical moves that led nowhere.

"The coroner wasn't here at the time of the explosion, Detective," a first responder replied.

"The hell she wasn't," I snapped, then pointed across the street. "That's her car right there, under that tree, and her phone keeps going to voicemail. She's here, I'm telling you."

I rushed to the entrance, crushing glass shards and debris under my feet, but didn't make it all the way inside.

"Baxter," Holt shouted, catching up with me and grabbing my upper arm in a steeled grip.

"Let me go, Holt. You don't know her like I do. She's strong; she's a fighter. She's in there somewhere, I know it."

"I can't let you go in there, Baxter," he replied calmly.

"You can't go inside, ma'am," one of the firefighters said, standing in my way. "The fire is still active and there could be more explosions."

His attitude, although logical, made me immensely angry all of a sudden. Their job was to save everyone, not play it safe, just because there might be more explosions down the road.

"Yes, I *can* go inside, and I bloody will," I replied, freeing myself from Holt's grip with a violent gesture and I sprinted ahead.

As I moved past the firefighter, he grabbed my arm firmly. A split second later, Holt flanked me on my left side, locking his grip on my other arm.

"Really?" I snapped. "Two macho men against one woman? Let go of me, right this instant," I told them in a low, menacing voice. "My friend's in there, and I'm going in."

The firefighter looked at me for a long moment. "Are you sure?"

"No, I have a bloody death wish and a fetish for chemical fires, you tosser," I replied, and he instantly let go of my arm, visibly insulted. Holt released his grip before I could sling insults at him too.

After a moment's hesitation, he took a mask fitted with an oxygen canister and gave it to me. "At least wear this, ma'am," he said, fitting the mask over my face. "There are noxious fumes inside."

He led the way and I followed closely, watching, observing every detail, visualizing the explosion and the seconds that had preceded it. Right behind me, I heard Holt's footsteps and I felt grateful for him being there for me, for having my back.

"This is where it went off," I said, pointing at a crater in the floor. Holt nodded, while keeping his mouth and nose covered with the flap of his jacket.

My heart sunk when I saw there was no place Anne could've taken cover from a blast that strong. Contorted metal and equipment tables ripped to pieces stood testimony to the force of the explosion.

Anne was nowhere in sight.

Water still dripped from the remnants of the ceiling. The power had been cut off, but the occasional smoke swirl still climbed from beneath smoldering concrete debris. Various glass containers had been shattered in the blaze, fueling the fire with the chemicals normally found in all morgues, most of them highly flammable, like alcohol or formalin. It was a miracle that the single-story building hadn't been completely leveled by the force of the detonation.

I stopped, not knowing where to go. Other than the dripping of water and the humming activity outside the morgue I couldn't hear anything. Against all logic, I called out loud.

"Anne! Where are you?"

A faint thumping coming from the back wall caught my attention. It was so muffled I wasn't sure it was real at first, but it continued, rhythmical, increasingly persistent.

I rushed toward the body storage freezers as my heart swelled with hope. One of the shelf doors was missing, torn from the hinges, as if it were open when the explosion happened. I looked inside, but it was too dark to see anything. The firefighter lit his flashlight and gave it to me.

She was covered in blood and soot and debris, curled up on her side, barely breathing. "She's in here," I shouted, as I opened the last door of the unit and pulled out the shelf as far as it could go.

"We need a gurney in here," the firefighter called into his radio. "On the double."

"Hey, sweetie," I said, letting my tears fall freely as I caressed her hair.

"Hey," she whispered in a raspy voice. "I knew you'd find me." She held her right hand up and I reached for it, but she stopped me. "Don't touch me," she said, and I instantly pulled back, afraid I was hurting her. "Bag this hand in plastic and tape it around the wrist," she said, barely intelligible.

I smiled, because I knew why.

Two firefighters carried a gurney over the rubble, then put it alongside the freezer shelf, getting ready to haul Anne out.

They took positions on both sides of the freezer shelf and one of them said, "We'll move her with the shelf tray, on my count: one, two, three."

She whimpered a little while they slid her over the gurney but kept her hand up in the air the entire time.

"I want you to wrap this hand carefully to preserve evidence," she told the firefighter. "I scratched that bastard before he threw the grenade. I have his DNA under my fingernails."

13

EVIDENCE

I'd been camped out in front of the emergency room at the University Medical Center for a few hours, waiting to hear what was going on with Anne. A doctor had come out after an hour or so and told Holt and me she wasn't critical; she was stable. She'd been lucky, the man said, while I looked at him with suspicion, noticing he seemed too young to drive. But his ID had MD after his name so I listened, fighting hard against the urge to ask him for a more experienced doctor to take over Anne's case.

She had two cracked ribs and some internal bruising, a cut on her forehead that had required a few stiches, and she was being treated for smoke inhalation. She was in good spirits, taking it like a soldier.

Oh, if only you knew, I thought, but it wasn't the time or the place to start sharing my knowledge of her military record with her attending physician. Instead, I nodded and thanked him right after he told me they were still running some tests to eliminate the risk of a concussion, and then they would release her in a couple of hours, because she was adamant about not spending the night.

That was the Anne I knew. A fighter. A survivor.

I smiled widely, lowering my head to hide my tears. When I looked up again, he was gone.

But Holt was still there, and without a word he took me in his arms and held me, while I buried my face in his chest and tears of gratitude stained his shirt. We were both covered with soot anyway.

He caressed my hair gently, and said, "She isn't just the coroner you've worked with for the past few years, is she? You two seem way closer than that."

Holt and his questions, for crying out loud... I pulled myself away from him and wiped my eyes with the back of my hands.

"Don't you have somewhere else you have to be?"

He seemed confused, but I wasn't entirely sure he wasn't playing it dumb, trying to back out of our deal. He was supposed to attend an AA meeting every night for a year, or for as long as I needed him to, until I could be sure his addiction wouldn't relapse. That was the price I'd asked for in exchange for my silence, for the countless rules I was breaking by not telling the IAB about him being hooked.

I held his gaze firmly, with an unspoken, "Cut the crap" message in my eyes.

He lowered his head and said, "All right, I think I might still find a meeting, although it's late."

"Wait," I said, "I need your laptop. Could you please leave it with me?"

He nodded and disappeared for a couple of minutes. When he returned, he had his laptop with him and a grim expression on his face.

"What's on your mind?"

"I'm wondering if Anne's still a target," he replied. "He might come back, and I won't be here."

"But *I* will, Holt," I replied. "I don't believe he was after Anne. My gut tells me he was after the evidence in Crystal's case. We might be getting close to uncovering a thing or two about her killer."

"Okay, I'll give you that, if you tell me what an eighteen-year-old stripper could—"

"Exotic dancer," I said, frowning.

"Okay, exotic dancer," he conceded, "have done to earn herself the attention of an assassin, a pro. Not everyone walks the streets of Vegas with grenades in their pockets, Baxter. I'm taking your bet, you know. Your coroner friend is the target. What other cases is she working on?"

I clammed up for a moment, accepting the hypothesis. What if the timing of attack on the morgue and Crystal's murder had been coincidental? Either way, I was a capable cop who didn't need a man to take care of her and her friend.

"We'll be fine, Holt, I won't let her out of my sight."

"Where are you taking her when you leave here?"

"My place, if she'll have it. Her fridge is always empty," I added with a tiny smile. "Now, go to your meeting."

I took a seat in the waiting area near the ER doors and fired up the laptop. I hesitated a little before starting my search; what should I start with? What did we really know about Crystal Tillman?

Not much, and most of what we thought we knew were only versions of truth, seeding suspicions in my mind that we might soon uncover more lies.

She was eighteen, an early graduate, a college student, an exotic dancer using a fake ID to gain access to a well-paying job. And that about summed it all up, everything we really knew about her.

As my old Scotland Yard trainer had said in a previous life, always start small. "How do you eat an elephant?" he'd asked. "One bite at a time," was the answer, a wise course of action for deciphering Crystal's multifaceted life.

I opened a new document and started typing questions freely as they popped into my mind. Who issued the professional grade, fake, driver's licenses? How did Crystal afford one, *before* starting to make money as a dancer? That level of craftsmanship rarely goes for under a thousand bucks apiece, and that's only if you know the right people. That seemed unlikely for a girl from Grady, Arkansas. Maybe she had help.

Help from a man who had his own helicopter, came the immediate conclusion. Was that man Ellis? Probably. He would've had the financial resources and the pull to get anything to happen for the young lady of his heart. But wait, if he was so in love with her, why would he have helped her become an exotic dancer, so she could take her clothes off onstage, in front of other men? It didn't make sense.

Was there another man in the picture? Maybe someone younger than the helo guy, maybe someone Crystal really loved, but couldn't be with because they were both poor? Okay, now I was speculating, my brain turned to mush from an endless day, a rollercoaster of emotions and interiorized conflict about my own involvement with Holt.

Bloody hell... I could still smell his aftershave in my hair, from when I nestled my head against his chest. I could still feel the warmth of his strong arms wrapped around my body. And I could still recall the irritation I'd felt when he started his overprotective male routine a few minutes earlier, forgetting I was a cop just like him, always carrying two loaded weapons on my person. Why? Because I'd allowed that to happen. It was all on me.

And it wasn't going to happen again. Not ever. Not even once.

Bloody hell.

Focus, Baxter, focus, I told myself, as I started typing more questions.

What if Crystal was a high-end call girl? It's been known to happen, especially here, in Sin City, when good girls can't think of a different way to survive, to make ends meet, or, in Crystal's case, to help her family.

If that part was even true.

If so, did Crystal have a pimp then? Where would she have met the famous, rich, yet married Ellis? Those things don't just happen, like in fairy tales. Maybe she had a pimp, or maybe she had an agent, a new version of pimp for the entrepreneurial, expensive, and exclusive call girls. A different kind of business deal altogether, where the agent recommended vetted clients, set the appointments, and managed any interference, all for a hefty percentage, of course. Such an agent would have a business front set up, so the client could use corporate invoicing or a company-issued credit card without raising any suspicions. The agent's corporation would pay the call girl as a 1099 contractor. Apparently all legit, all tax-deductible, until someone looked closely enough at the actual services being rendered.

It made sense, the call girl theory. It explained the helo rides in the middle of the night, why she'd kept her job as a dancer, why a mysterious man had been seen shoving a casino chip in her bra. Most of these men were power freaks, alpha males who took rejection badly and competition even worse. If that were the case, then Crystal's best friend, Roxanne, knew much more than she'd shared. "Well, of course she did," I whispered. Why would she be the one to tell the truth?

The automatic doors swung open and the young doctor pushed Anne through in a wheelchair. She was pale and tired, and four stitches marred her forehead at an angle above her right eye. She was restless in her seat, holding on to the arms of the wheelchair as if she were planning to make a sudden run for the door.

"Here you go, Detective," the doctor said, "she's all yours."

I almost touched her forehead and whispered, "Oh, sweetie, I'm so sorry."

She shrugged and dismissed my concern with a wave of her hand. "I've had worse."

There was still some soot on the side of her neck, and I used my sleeve to wipe it off.

"All right, Mother Hen," she quipped in a faint voice, "I'll be okay. I'm ready to go home now, if you'll take me."

"Of course, I will," I said, taking the wheelchair handles from the doctor's hand.

"I'll pretend I don't know she's a licensed physician and prescribe a recovery regimen she'll undoubtedly ignore," he said. "Bed rest is mandatory, and I'm sending her home with oxygen and a mask. Please make sure she uses it."

"Thanks," I said, over my shoulder, and crouched in front of her. "Do you have any idea who did this?"

"No," she replied, seemingly ashamed, as if it were her fault. "He was wearing a black ski mask and moved around like a pro. I almost had him, but he had a grenade."

"You're so tough, Dr. St. Clair," I said, smiling widely. "He's probably in worse shape than you are. Now let's get you home."

"You should put out a BOLO for a six-three, Caucasian male with a torn left knee and a deep laceration under his right eye," she said, sounding proud.

"Will do, as soon as I get you to bed."

I started pushing the wheelchair down the long corridor toward the exit and asked one of the parking attendants to get me a cab.

"We lost everything, didn't we?" I asked, thinking of Crystal's body, charred to a crisp and buried under rubble.

"Not really," Anne replied. "All the physical evidence was in the back-room fridge. The blast didn't damage it."

"Why would you—"

"She was poisoned, and we still don't know by what and how. Until we do, I need every bit of evidence preserved. Some poisons are volatile and can dissipate in time. Even room temperature can accelerate the evaporation process."

"You mean, we still have, what, exactly?"

"Everything, more or less. Her clothing and shoes, her purse, and all the swabs we'd already taken from her body that we hadn't had the time to process yet."

"How about blood, fluids, fibers, the body?"

"Her organs were removed and stored in the big fridge; I wanted to be able to take another look once we have the toxin identified," she said, counting on her fingers. "I've sent blood out for a tox panel already, a large sample; they'll have to be careful with how much they use until we finish testing, but I believe they have enough. Vic and fetal DNA are with the Crime Lab already, but the body was burned to a crisp."

"How could you possibly know that?" I asked. She'd been in the ER the entire time since I'd found her.

"It was on my side exam table, and the entire room was engulfed in flames. That much I remember seeing before I—"

She stopped talking, and I didn't push. Instead, I glared at the parking attendant, wondering why that cab was taking so damn long.

"Anything further I find on the body will likely be disputed in court," she continued. "A good defense attorney will claim the evidence was contaminated by all the chemicals that were dispersed by the explosion, the gasoline, the water and suppressors they used to put out the fire, and so on. We'll never hear the end of it."

"Yeah, but the perp won't know that, right?" I replied. She turned to look at me, wincing a little, and I winked. "He won't know what samples had already been sent to the lab."

"Yeah, but in court, I couldn't—"

"No one's asking you. We're cops; we're allowed to lie, as long as it's not under oath."

"That is correct," she replied, smiling.

"You keep on digging and give us something we can use. We need to know how Crystal died. Nothing we've uncovered so far makes any sense."

"On it," she replied with a shattered sigh. "I just need to clean up the morgue as soon as possible, because whatever that goon thought he was achieving by torching the place didn't happen."

"Oh, no, first you take a few days off," I replied, pushing her wheelchair toward the cab pulled in at the curb.

"We'll see," she said, grunting a little when she got up and climbed inside the minivan.

I slid next to her and clutched her hand. It was frozen, and she was shivering, although the heat was on in the vehicle.

"Your place or mine?" she asked faintly.

"Mine," I replied, then gave the driver the address and asked him to crank up the heat. "It's girls' night in."

The moment I said those words, a heavy silence fell between us. Only one other time we'd spent the night at my place; the night after Andrew had been killed. Anne had been there for me every second of that terrible night, the first night I grieved the loss of my husband and she mourned the death of the fellow Marine and helicopter pilot with whom she'd served two tours overseas.

I felt her hand squeeze mine and realized she knew exactly how I felt. I willed away my tears and smiled.

"Got liquor?" Anne asked.

"After a day like today, you get to pick your label, woman," I replied, then hugged her gently, afraid I'd see that wince on her face again. "Do you believe alcohol mixes well with oxygen?" I quipped, pointing at the gas canister in her lap. "I don't want to blow up the house."

She didn't reply; she just let her head rest on my shoulder and closed her eyes.

Later that night, as I pulled the curtains shut on my living room window, I thought I saw Holt's unmarked Ford parked across the street.

Bloody hell, Holt.

14

ANXIETY

Roxanne's hands trembled as she unlocked the front door. The house was unusually dark and quiet, and she reached for the light switch without daring to step inside, terrified as if there was someone lurking in the shadows, waiting to pounce.

With the floor lamp on, she dared to come in and closed the door behind her, turned the deadbolt and slid on the chain. She walked toward the small table where she and Crystal usually dropped their purses when they came home, but her keys fell to the floor. The clatter of rattling metal against the granite tiles startled her, seeming much louder against the still silence of the house.

She wasn't used to that much silence. Crystal always had music on, as if the music she danced to wasn't enough for her and she always needed more. But Roxanne didn't feel like breaking the mournful peace. She wandered aimlessly through the living room, noticing where the two detectives had opened closets and looked through their stuff. Briefly, she stopped in front of Crystal's bedroom, the closed door bearing her name in girlish, glittery letters sprinkled with tiny hearts and gold stars. She didn't dare enter the room, as if she risked bringing upon herself the rage of a restless ghost, still hurting to be yanked so brutally away from the land of the living and deep into nothingness.

She turned away from there, breathing with more ease as she distanced herself from the haunted room. She stopped for a moment in the middle of the living room, heaving, still terrified after the events of that morning. She picked up her purse and clutched it tightly, thinking how lucky she'd been. She could've been in jail that night if the dice would've rolled a different number.

She unzipped the purse slowly and fished out the gun with frozen, trembling fingers, her entire body reacting to the sensation of the cold metal against her skin.

She looked at the weapon as if she'd never seen it before and wondered how she could have possibly thought of shooting Crystal. She must've been insane... The gods must've smiled down her way, no matter how unlikely that seemed, when they didn't let her find the guts to pull the trigger the night before. They'd smiled again when the detectives didn't find her in possession of an illegal weapon.

Her breath shattered, and she let herself slide against the wall, until she hit the floor. The coldness of the granite grounded her but didn't do much for the chill that sent icicles through her blood, coming from inside her heart. It didn't matter that she hadn't pulled that trigger; she'd wanted Crystal dead, and she'd bought the gun to take her friend's life. She was still a murderer.

Tears started rolling down her cheeks in steady rivulets, blurring the image of the weapon she held in her hands. She'd loved Crystal, and she'd always felt they were like sisters, closer than family, thicker than thieves. Until...

She picked herself up from the floor, put the gun back in her purse, and pulled the zipper shut. Tomorrow she'd have to figure out a way to get rid of the gun, before the cops came to visit again.

Once the echoes of the purse zipper subsided, silence engulfed the house once more. Roxanne shivered and opened the fridge door, looking for something to warm up her frozen soul. She poured herself a shot of Grey Goose without bothering to close the fridge door, downed it, then filled the glass again. She hesitated for a moment, held on to the bottle and kicked the fridge door closed with the tip of her foot.

Better.

She looked at the clock on the wall and realized how late it was. He was soon going to be there, and she wasn't ready for him. Regretfully, she abandoned the bottle of vodka on the table and took off her clothes, letting them fall in a heap on the floor. She rushed into the shower, letting the hot water cleanse her body and her burdened conscience.

She spent more time than usual in there, applying lather after lather of her favorite scented shower gel, savoring the smell, anticipating how Paul would savor it too, breathing against her heated skin. She washed her hair thoroughly, knowing only long minutes of shampooing would remove the stink of the casino, the smell of cigars and of metabolized alcohol that reeked in the high-limit gaming room.

She stepped out of the shower stall, letting water drip from her body onto the thick carpet before she patted herself dry with a soft towel. She blow-dried her hair while running a brush through every long, blonde strand, making sure it shined and crackled and settled into perfect waves around her face.

It wasn't the time for stage makeup; just a tiny touch was enough, a little foundation, a bit of blush, and discreet, pink, lip gloss. They weren't going out that night. As they usually did on her nights off, they stayed in, savoring each other, spending precious time away from the prying eyes of everyone out there.

For the final touch, she opened a vanity drawer and extracted a small cosmetics jar. The container didn't have a label, but she knew quite well what was in there, not something you'd find in a store: a custom-made mix of concentrated hashish extract and an edible, slightly fruit-flavored gel. She dipped two fingers into the gel and applied some to her nipples, then to her neck and lower abdomen. She checked her reflection in the mirror one last time. Satisfied with the sight of the gorgeous, naked beauty looking back at her, she grabbed a purple, silk gown and wrapped it around her body, tying the wide sateen sash with a bow.

She went back into the living room, feeling the same chill at the mere sight of Crystal's bedroom door. With pleading eyes, she looked at the clock on the wall. It was ten past eleven.

"Please, don't be late tonight," she whispered, as she sat in an armchair by the window, looking outside restlessly.

A few minutes later, the familiar shape of the black BMW coupe with deeply tinted windows appeared and stopped at the curb.

Paul was here. Everything was going to be just fine.

Relieved, she let a long breath of air escape her lungs and rushed to open the door.

15

PROFILE

After spending the night on the downstairs sofa, I left Anne sleeping soundly in the master bedroom and snuck out of the house with the light of dawn. I'd spent a restless night, tossing and turning, trying to make sense of the little information I had. At about five-thirty in the morning my eyes popped wide open and the notion of sleep seemed like an impossible endeavor. It made more sense to get an early start to my day.

First thing I did was request a squad car in front of my house, in the odd case that Anne was still a target. When I pulled out of the garage, I saw Holt's unmarked Interceptor SUV across the street a few numbers down but pretended I didn't, unwilling to start an argument, especially with the squad car already there.

I made my first stop at Starbucks, where I bought everyone's favorite form of liquid life support in a venti size: a black coffee for Holt, a Frappuccino with lots of whipped cream and everything on it for Fletcher, and a green tea for me. While I stopped for coffee, Holt had the time to get to the office before I did, so he could pretend he didn't spend the night on an unnecessary protection detail.

I parked my white Toyota in a visitor spot at the precinct, took the beverages upstairs and didn't stop until I set them on Fletcher's desk. As expected, Holt was already there, wearing yesterday's shirt and a tired smile. My heart swelled a little, but I hid it behind a frown and feigned ignorance like a pro.

"Hey, what happened to you? An adventurous night?"

He shook his head slowly, only once, wondering if I was for real or something. I couldn't help it; I burst into laughter.

"What's with the girl drink?" he asked, pointing at the Frappuccino as I handed it to Fletcher.

The young tech rubbed the sleep from his eyes and the shirt he wore could've served as his pajama top the night before; I wasn't entirely sure he'd changed after getting out of bed.

"Excuse me?" Fletch reacted, stifling a yawn. "This ain't a girl drink, and even if it were, so what? It's awesome. It'll wake me up and that takes a miracle."

Holt smiled but didn't reply; it was his turn to swallow a yawn, a long one.

"Want some?" Fletcher offered, pushing his venti cup toward me.

"No, thanks," I replied, thinking I'd probably have to give up dinner to make up for such an indulgence.

"Wait 'til you see what I got," he said playfully. "You'll be sorry you didn't take me up on that sugar rush."

"Did you find him?" I asked, referring to the mysterious man who, by several witness accounts, had interacted with Crystal minutes before her death.

"Did I find him on the video? Yes," Fletcher replied pedantically, stopping long enough to suck some caramel-coated whipped cream through the thick, colorful straw. "Did I find out who he is? Not yet."

He put up the surveillance video on one of his wide monitors. It was already cued to the right spot. Mr. Cline, the witness who'd stated the man had approached Crystal at about three in the morning had been unusually accurate for a witness. The time code read 03:04:17 when the unknown man entered the view of the camera.

I held my breath.

The silent video was showing both of them from their sides, at a distance, and only the profile of the man was visible, not a frontal view of his face. The camera, installed on a nearby wall, was to Crystal's right as she faced the stranger, and all we could see was the left profile of his face. And yet he seemed familiar somehow.

Their interaction was brimming with intense emotion. I let the recording run uninterrupted at full speed, taking in all that emotion conveyed clearly through their body language. I watched him approach the elevated stage, as the girl recognized him and came closer to the edge of the stage, hesitant, worried. He shoved what could've been a casino chip between her breasts with a forceful, angry gesture of his hand. She didn't react; she seemed petrified, stunned. He grabbed the thin strap of her bra and pulled her down closer to him, his face now mere inches away from hers. He said something to her while she looked at him with eyes rounded in fear and a slacked jaw. She put both her hands on his forearm, pushing him away, but he didn't budge. After saying what he had to say, he let go of her and left, walking quickly out of the frame.

The entire interaction had lasted fifty-five seconds.

"Were you able to run facial recognition against this?" Holt asked.

"Not enough markers in this view," Fletcher replied. "But I believe I have an idea about learning what he said, that we couldn't hear. There's a new girl in Human Resources, she just started a few months ago. She's deaf; I wonder if she could lip-read what this guy says."

"From the side?" Holt reacted. "I doubt it, but sure, why not give it a try? See what she says. But we need him identified, Fletch. His mug must be on video somewhere else. Let's request the rest of the video surveillance, the entire floor, the lobby, the exits."

"You got it," Fletcher replied, typing quickly with his long fingers.

"Okay, now go back to where he first approaches the girl and play it in slow motion," I asked.

Fletcher executed.

I watched again the expression on Crystal's face as it changed from the jaded smile she wore while she was dancing to the incontestable fear when she recognized the approaching man. As he spoke, that fear intensified, and, at some point, she looked around to see if anyone would help her. No one did.

"Freeze frame," I asked, and the video paused. "Let's see who else was there. Here's Farley, who sees the man grabbing her but doesn't intervene." I pushed play and watched the rest of the interaction again, this time focusing on the players at the blackjack tables. "These guys, they don't seem to notice, but the woman, she's watching the whole thing with amusement," I said, almost touching the LED screen next to the woman's entertained smile and raised eyebrow.

"She didn't intervene though," Holt said.

"Let's face it, guys," Fletcher said, "there's no real reason to interfere. He didn't hit her; he gave her a tip, right?"

"Yes, the chip we didn't find," I said. "Let's rewind and watch again, in slow motion, and watch for that chip. See if you can catch a frame where you can zoom in."

The recording was dark and the many club lights made it difficult to distinguish details about anything in the video, but Fletcher managed to catch a particular frame where the chip was visible, held between the man's right thumb and index finger.

"Magnify that, will you?" Holt asked impatiently.

"Hold your caffeine-fueled horses, it doesn't work like that. I have to augment it, apply some filters, otherwise all you'll see will be a blur of pixels."

He worked quickly and with every click of the mouse, the image became a little clearer. Holt and I approached the screen until we could see each grain in the enhanced image.

"That's as good as it gets," Fletcher announced.

The remaining blurriness made it difficult, but I could distinguish a white and purple chip bearing the insignia of the Scala Hotel and Casino. The value of the chip was hidden by the man's thumb, but we could easily determine that; every casino had its own color scheme for each chip denomination, and all we had to do was ask what value the white and purple ones were.

"Okay, so that chip was gone by the time we got there," I said for Fletcher's benefit, although my guess was he already knew. "Let's find it."

He played the video at an accelerated speed, and we watched Crystal resume dancing immediately after the man walked away. The only sign of distress she'd shown was to run her hand over her forehead and hesitate a little, looking around. Then Farley looked at her and she immediately grabbed the pole and let herself bend backward until her long hair touched the floor.

"Then nothing happens until here," Fletcher announced, "when I think she started to feel sick."

I watched the video with a strange feeling of powerlessness, as if I somehow could've rushed and saved Crystal's life, forgetting for a moment she was already dead. The time code showed 04:09:24 when she slowed her dance and tripped but managed to grab on to the pole and stand on her feet. She looked around, probably for Farley, but he wasn't in the frame, so we couldn't be sure where he was. It was just my assumption; that's what I'd do if I were sick while working, while dancing on a stage: I'd ask someone for help.

Seconds passed, and she continued to dance, moving slower and slower, out of rhythm, but that too was an assumption, because the video didn't carry any sound. She slipped to the floor, letting herself slide against the pole in a clumsy manner, and holding on to it for as long as she could. When she let go, her head bounced as it landed on her extended right arm, and her hair settled around her like an ethereal veil.

The time code read, 04:12:07, marking the exact moment of Crystal Tillman's death.

"There it is," Holt said, pointing at the screen excitedly. "Rewind a little and play it slow, okay?"

Fletcher obliged and played frame by frame the seconds before she died. As her body hit the ground, the chip dropped out of her bra and rolled onto the stage. It fell off onto the floor and disappeared from view.

"The damn thing might still be on that floor somewhere," I said, while Holt grabbed his car keys.

"You better hurry, guys," Fletcher said, "they're about to release the crime scene."

16

THE CHIP

We rushed all the way to the Scala, eager to get our hands on the missing gambling chip that could still carry the mysterious man's fingerprints and DNA. It was a stretch, I knew that, considering Crystal had danced for a while with it tucked inside her bra, but we still needed to find that piece of critical evidence.

While Holt drove us there, going at least twenty miles over the speed limit, I called the crime scene techs and found out the scene hadn't been released yet, but they'd finished collecting evidence and they were about to sign off on the release, under the continuous pressure coming from the hotel's pushy legal department. Unfortunately, no white and purple chip had been found, and they usually did a thorough job combing through a crime scene.

Holt parked right in front of the main hotel entrance and left his flashers on. We rushed all the way upstairs to the high-limit gambling room, afraid we'd see it already swarming with staff and patrons; it wouldn't've been the first time a powerful, connected organization like the Scala cut a few corners and didn't wait for the official release. Instead, we found the wide doors closed, and a hotel security employee standing in front of them with his arms crossed at his chest. The uniformed officer who should've been guarding the crime scene was slouched comfortably on a nearby red, plush settee, texting away on his phone, completely unaware of our presence.

I glanced quickly toward Holt, but he was already standing in front of the officer. His furrowed brow wasn't predicting a friendly conversation. He slid his badge between the officer's eyes and his phone, startling the young man.

"Officer Jarvis, is that correct?" Holt asked, reading the man's nametag.

The uni jumped to his feet, visibly flustered. "Y—yes, sir."

"Where's the police line and the seal that were supposed to block access to the crime scene?"

"Um, an official removed them," he replied, avoiding Holt's inquisitive glance like the plague.

"A police official?" he asked calmly.

"Um, no, sir, a casino official."

"Since when do we allow civilians unrestricted access to active crime scenes?"

Officer Jarvis shifted his weight from one foot to the other, nervous. "Nobody's got access, sir, the room is locked."

Holt nodded a little sideways. "Good. Now let's have the key, please," he asked, extending his hand.

"I don't have it, sir, the, uh, official has it."

"What the hell, Jarvis? You're going on report. You've handed over the control of an active crime scene on a damn silver platter."

"They said they can't have crime scene tape and stuff in plain sight to scare their clients away. I had no choice." His pitch was higher, conveying his frustration mixed with anxiety over having screwed up at his new job.

"How about calling a supervisor? Did you think of that?"

"I did, sir, I called him," Jarvis replied, red as a beet. "He said it was okay, as long as those doors stayed locked."

I almost felt sorry for him; I'd been just as young once, although I liked to think I'd demonstrated more street smarts than Jarvis. But whatever trace of compassion I had for the inexperienced Officer Jarvis would immediately vanish if we failed to find the missing casino chip.

A familiar figure appeared at a brisk pace from around the corner and headed straight for us. Joe Deason, the casino security manager, had been hailed by the guard he'd posted at the door. I was willing to bet the intimidating, never-smiling man was the official who'd talked his way out of the crime scene tape and seal being displayed at the door.

"We need to go inside, Mr. Deason," Holt announced in an uncompromising tone.

Deason took out a key from his pocket and unlocked the doors, then hit some light switches and flooded the room with bright white service lights. A faint smell of deodorizer and cigar smoke still lingered in the air, but at least that air was breathable without much effort, unlike the day before.

We rushed to the stage where Crystal had performed her last dance and turned on the flashlights, scanning the floor for that chip.

"May I ask what you're looking for?" Deason probed, seemingly a little concerned, uneasy.

"We'll know when we find it," Holt replied dryly, without even looking at the man.

I kneeled on the plush carpet and shone the flashlight beam in all directions, but still nothing. Then I had an idea.

I got up on my feet and searched for the camera whose feed we'd been reviewing earlier on Fletcher's monitors. It was on a wall behind us, about seven feet up from the floor. I positioned myself right underneath the camera, making sure what I saw now had the same vantage point as the recording, with the exception of height. Immediately, I could visualize where Crystal's body had fallen on the stage, and where the chip had rolled off and disappeared.

"It should be under those table legs," I said, pointing at the two blackjack tables on the right.

The tables around the stage were relatively close to one another, their legs only a few feet apart. The carved legs were thick, at least five by five inches, and seemed firmly set on the thick carpet, apparently leaving no room for anything to slide underneath.

"Are these tables riveted to the floor?" Holt asked, crouched down, trying to look under the thick table legs and not seeing much.

"No, they're on recessed casters," Deason replied. "I'll get someone to move them if you'd like."

I glared at him. Really? He couldn't be bothered to push over a table on casters? Good thing Holt and I could.

Before I could offer a hand, Holt had easily pushed the first one out of the way by himself. The casters supported the legs leaving a one-inch clearance between the floor and the wood, nearly invisible in the dim light and against the thick, dark carpet. There was nothing trapped under the legs of the first table, except for some dirt the vacuum cleaners couldn't get to.

Holt pushed the second table in the opposite direction from where the chip would've rolled under the leg.

"Jackpot," he said, when he saw the small, purple-and-white plastic disc. He slid a glove on and picked it up carefully, then whistled in surprise and showed it to me.

"Jackpot indeed," I said, stunned.

The chip had a face value of five hundred thousand dollars. I didn't even know they made them that large.

I looked at Deason, whose anxiety had picked up a notch or two.

"Anything you could tell me about this chip, Mr. Deason?" I asked, firing nothing but a shot in the dark.

"Um, I'm not sure how that got there," he replied, taking a step back and running his hand over his goatee a couple of times. He was distancing himself, and his face and nose tickled under the attack of increased blood flow, a direct consequence of lying.

Our Mr. Deason was definitely hiding something. But what?

He stood a few feet away from us, his back straight and his face immobile, forcing himself to project calm and composure, while he was visibly riled up by something.

I stared intently at him until he lowered his eyes, just to make him aware I knew he was hiding something. Then I turned to Holt and grabbed his arm, turning our backs to the nosy Mr. Deason.

"I want to question him," I whispered. "Did you see his reaction when he saw that chip? The man knows something and is not willing to share. I don't think these chips are that common."

"Yeah, no kidding. But my question is why would a str— um, dancer who just made half a million dollars, continue to perform as if nothing happened?" Holt asked. "That's more than enough money to put her through school and last her until she could graduate and get a decent job."

His question brought up a valid point, just as important as finding out what that money actually paid for. She might have been a good dancer, but no one is that good to be worth a half-a-million-dollar tip. And, why didn't she step down and walk away?

I looked around, trying to put myself in her high-heeled shoes. What would I have done? Let's assume a man, who's visibly terrifying me, came and shoved half a mil down my bra, then said something presumably nasty and walked away. Why would I still be there, when all my instincts told me to get the hell out? There could be one simple explanation: I didn't know I could afford to do that yet.

"Mr. Deason," I called, "please switch the lights to typical business mode."

He frowned, confused. With some people, if I didn't use the exact terminology that they expected to hear, they couldn't understand one iota, nor were they willing to make the extra effort and think.

I refrained from letting out a long sigh of frustration. "When you're open for business, what lights are typically on? It seemed much darker on the video."

He didn't bother to reply; he walked with offended dignity to the wall by the door and opened a switchbox hidden behind the lush paneling. He touched a few buttons, and the white light dimmed and veered toward yellow. The colorful club lights came on, some fixed, some dynamic yet immobile in the absence of music to synchronize with. Deason understood my next request before I had a chance to voice it and turned on the music. The lights started moving with the rhythm, flickering, dancing, occasionally blinding me when my eyes caught one of the numerous laser glimmers projecting fast-moving, geometric shapes on the walls.

"Perfect," I said. "Now, could we please have someone bring us a few chips of various denominations? We wouldn't dream of bothering you personally with this menial request," I added seriously, unable to refrain from poking a needle dipped in sarcasm at the man's overinflated ego.

Holt turned his head away to hide his grin.

"Sure," Deason replied, with a look of infinite disdain in his beady eyes, then disappeared for a few moments.

"What are you thinking?" Holt asked.

I looked at the chip, already sealed in a transparent evidence pouch. "Just testing a hunch," I replied.

Deason walked back in carrying a tray filled with assorted chips and laid it on a blackjack table. I picked one of each denomination and set them face up under the colorful lights, then set the half-million one next to them. In the dim kaleidoscope of moving lights, I couldn't tell the difference between the light-purple and white, one-thousand-dollar chip, and the dark-purple and white, five-hundred-thousand-dollar chip.

I pushed the two similar chips toward Holt. "There's your answer. That's why Crystal didn't walk away."

17

POSTMORTEM

Anne thanked the chief pathologist at the University Medical Center of Southern Nevada for lending her two fully equipped rooms in his lab and sat on a stool the moment the man left the room. She refrained from letting out a sigh of relief; if she breathed shallowly, her cracked ribs didn't hurt much at all.

For anyone in her condition, she would've prescribed at least one week of bed rest, but she couldn't afford that luxury, not after someone had killed Erika and blown up the morgue in what seemed to have been an attempt to thwart the investigation into Crystal Tillman's murder.

She had work to do. There would be time to lick her wounds later, after the killer was behind bars.

The van, bringing whatever could be salvaged from the morgue fire, was still a few minutes out. She picked up the phone and dialed a number from memory.

"Crime Lab, this is Shawn speaking," a man's voice announced.

"This is Dr. St. Clair," she said, her throat a little raspy. She still suffered from the smoke inhalation.

"Ah, our own warrior coroner," he greeted her, his words making her smile. Was that what they called her? "What can I do for you, Doc?" he asked.

"Just a heads-up, please be extra careful with how you use the blood in the Tillman case tox screens, in case we might need to run more tests. What you have on hand right now is all the blood we have left."

"We figured that much," the technician replied coldly, the earlier friendliness gone from his voice. "We have enough for several iterations. Anything else?"

"No, that's it," Anne replied, wondering what in her polite request had caused the young technician to go ice-cold on her. He must've felt insulted she needed to say what he already knew, after the news of the morgue explosion had propagated throughout the Vegas law enforcement community. Maybe he was offended by her thoroughness; if that was the case, tough luck. She couldn't afford any slipups.

The Clark County coroner's van pulled up at the door and her technicians started unloading what they'd salvaged from the rubble. Within the hour, she had Crystal's charred remains laid on an exam table, her organs and tissue samples in specimen jars filled with formalin neatly labeled and placed on shelves inside the refrigerator, and all the evidence they could recover, stored in individual pouches stacked in the refrigerated chest by the door.

She was ready to resume her duties.

While her two assistants laid out the instruments and equipment she typically used with silent efficiency, she put on a protective gown and goggles and approached Crystal's body.

First, she walked around the table slowly, paying attention to every detail she could see. Then she slipped on a new pair of gloves and grabbed a scalpel from the instrument tray.

The explosion and the subsequent fire-extinguishing efforts had done massive damage to her remains, and looking at her corpse brought back unwanted memories from Afghanistan, from a time when another charred body had landed on her examination table with the goal of establishing the man's identity: was he the most-wanted terrorist they'd been hunting for?

Under dim lights and with the thunder of artillery fire not that far away, she'd examined the badly burned body and had concluded he was the man they'd been looking for. And she'd made a costly mistake. In the absence of DNA forensics, dental records, and all the modern paraphernalia conveniently placed at the discretion of Western medical examiners, she'd failed to ascertain that the man lying on her table was not that terrorist, but his brother. That unpreventable error cost her unit two precious lives, two Marines whose deaths weighed terribly on her conscience. Hence, the young Johns Hopkins graduate and honorably discharged Marine and doctor, who could've had her choice of glamorous residency programs with prestigious medical institutions, had chosen to spend her life atoning for that one fateful night; she became Clark County's youngest coroner.

But this time, she knew better. Every word that was going on her autopsy report would have to be verified time and again, and everything science and technology had to offer would be utilized in the service of finding justice for Crystal and Erika. This time she would be sure, and she would be right.

With the help of an assistant she'd beckoned silently, she turned Crystal's body face down and resumed her examination. During the blaze, the thick, metallic exam table had shielded her body from the flames in several places. Gesturing for specimen jars, she started collecting tissue samples from all the areas where charring had occurred superficially or not at all. Crystal's lower back and buttocks. A small area around the nape of her neck that had been protected by the head rest. The back of her thighs and calves. A small area on the back of her left arm, right above the elbow.

She pulled out of refrigeration the specimen jars containing Crystal's organs floating in formalin. Careful, taking her time with each organ, she examined them thoroughly, then collected tissue samples she put in smaller jars, ready for tox screening. As soon as she had the toxin that had killed Crystal identified, testing all those specimens for that particular toxin's concentration would give some indication as to how the poison had been delivered into Crystal's bloodstream. Had she ingested it? Had she been injected with it?

Anne closed the last of the specimen jars and put the one containing Crystal's heart back into the refrigerator. It was a healthy heart, one that should've pounded strongly, exhilarated by love, thrilled to be alive, not sit on a cold shelf waiting for answers. But that healthy, anatomically perfect heart had told Anne she'd been correct in guessing Crystal had been poisoned; there wasn't a single finding to support the theory that Crystal's death had been a natural occurrence.

She stared at the jars for a long moment, hesitant to close the refrigerator door. For some reason, Anne's ghosts still haunted her. Was she forgetting something? If Crystal had been poisoned with something powerful enough and quick enough to stop her heart in mid-dance, how did she become exposed to that toxin?

She finally closed the door to the cold storage box, getting ready to go over her notes once again, when the wheels of a gurney reminded her she had another autopsy to do, this one even more painful.

Her assistants wheeled in Erika's corpse sealed in a black body bag and looked at her for direction. Not a word was spoken; it was as if disrupting the cold silence of the morgue would somehow offend the two girls who waited for her to bring them justice.

She pointed toward the empty exam table and proceeded to remove her tainted gloves and gown she'd used in the previous examination. She scrubbed her hands vigorously at the sink, as if preparing to perform surgery and splashed some cold water on her face. She patted her eyes gently, thankful for the water droplets that hid her tears.

She unzipped the body bag slowly and opened it, revealing Erika's pale, bluish features. With trembling fingers, Anne moved a strand of hair off her face, tucking it behind her ear as she would with a child. "I'm so sorry, Erika," she whispered.

She turned on the powerful exam lights above the table and pressed the pedal that started recording her voice notes. She was ready to begin.

18

ENTANGLED LEADS

I carried the chip, sealed in its plastic evidence pouch like a trophy, feeling more confident about our chances to untangle the web of leads and lies that surrounded Crystal's untimely death. We headed straight to the Crime Lab from there, and as we peeled away from the Scala's curved driveway I started to notice my partner's increasingly sullen mood. Whatever I said, he acknowledged monosyllabically or with a grunted interjection, enough to tell me he'd heard me, but had nothing to say.

Something was eating at him and I had no idea what it was, which strangely reminded me that almost two days had already passed from the week Steenstra had given me to provide the evidence that would put an end to Holt's career. What the hell was I going to do about that?

One thing I could do, given more time: I could reopen, unofficially of course, the case that ended with the cocaine bust where seven kilos were seized but only six made it to the evidence locker. Given more time... Most people involved in that case were already behind bars, a couple were dead, and several more had fled the country. One of them had to have taken that kilo, if Holt was indeed innocent. But, unless I found the real perp bang to rights holding the missing cocaine and offered them both on the sacred, bloodthirsty altar of internal investigations, come next Monday, I'd be out of a job. Duffers, all those incompetent, stupid people, didn't leave me any other options.

Maybe I should do the only thing I should've done a long time ago.

Ask Holt about it.

As soon as we dropped the chip with the Crime Lab, I would ask him straight up, with the honesty and openness he deserved. Until then, I wanted to know what was eating at him.

"Funny how we have so many leads in this case," I started casually.

"Uh-huh," he muttered, keeping his eyes on the road.

"We have this mysterious, rich man, who must've paid her for a reason," I said, holding my thumb in the air to keep count. "Then there's Roxanne, who might be hiding something," I added, raising another finger, "these two casino schmucks, Deason and Farley, who are definitely not telling the truth, whatever secret Crystal's sister wants to unveil, and then there's Crystal's boyfriend."

"Him, yeah," Holt replied, the frown on his forehead not relenting.

"Is he your favorite lead?"

"Uh-huh, they're usually the ones who do this kind of deed."

"What, kill?"

"Uh-huh."

I studied him for a moment and noticed the tension line in his jaw, the slightly raised shoulders, another sign of nervous tension, and the strong grip he had on the steering wheel, white-knuckled. Something was going on.

"Okay, partner, spill it. What's up with you?"

He shot me a quick glance, then focused on the thick traffic. "Nothing. Why?"

"You're not your usual self, that's why."

I gave him a few moments, in case he decided to talk to me, but he didn't. He pulled into the parking lot at the precinct and I sighed, reluctantly letting the subject go.

"We're here," he announced, as if I couldn't see for myself. It was his way of answering my question without really answering it, a polite way to say he refused to tell me what was on his mind.

I touched his sleeve, holding him back. "Listen, whatever it is, I have your back, all right?"

He looked straight at me for a moment, a loaded gaze filled with a mix of emotions. Then he looked away and muttered, "Uh-huh, thanks."

I found myself standing, riveted to the middle of the parking lot, frozen in place by a single, troubling thought. Was he using again? *Bollocks, Holt... This is so not the time to relapse*, I thought, knowing that the IAB could ask for a urine test at any time.

He'd walked ahead, and he was almost at the door when he stopped and turned toward me. "Are you coming?"

I rushed to catch up and we shared a silent ride on the elevator up to the Crime Lab level. We signed the chain of evidence paperwork and handed over the chip, the same stunned glances thrown among the lab technicians as Holt and I had exchanged earlier. Probably, none of them had seen one of those before, but I knew that if there was any DNA, fingerprints, or traces of poison on that chip they would find it and let us know.

The next stop was Fletcher's desk, who met us with a high-five without getting off his chair. The empty cup of the earlier Frappuccino had been all but licked clean, and he was working on a sweaty Coke bottle now. The man mainlined sugar and caffeine, and he could pull it off without adding any pounds around his waist. Wasn't life fair, like that? I couldn't even remember the last time a sugary dessert made it on my menu; if I so much as looked at a cookie I could feel my waist line growing a few fractions of an inch, and I liked myself the way I was. Who needed sugar, after all? But I couldn't keep myself from envying Fletcher's metabolism, just a little bit.

"We got it," I announced happily. "Now we need to find that boyfriend of hers. Any way you could identify him? Track that helo? Phone records maybe?"

Holt leaned against a nearby desk, visibly distracted.

"Nope, I already tried the phone," Fletcher replied. "The only number that was calling Crystal frequently came from a burn phone."

"Smart bastard," I muttered. Those married men getting into affairs with young girls had a world of technology to keep them at a safe distance from trouble, making our job more and more difficult with each hurdle we had to go through to identify them.

"But I think I solved the mystery," Fletcher announced proudly.

I smiled, inviting him to tell us already.

"Roxanne's statement mentioned he's rich and somewhat famous, and his name is Ellis. Well, turns out there's only one rich, filthy rich by the way, and somewhat famous man named Ellis in the entire state of Nevada."

He touched a few buttons and displayed the photo of a charming, thirty-eight-year-old man. He seemed familiar, but, just like with the man who'd given Crystal the chip, I couldn't place him.

"I give you Ellis MacPherson, no priors, clean as a whistle. As a diamond-encrusted gold whistle, I might add. He's the husband of Celeste Bennett MacPherson, of Bene—"

"BeneFoods?" I reacted, recognizing the name that was commonly referred to as Nevada's royal family. Celeste Bennett's ancestors had started a grocery chain in 1939 that was now worth several billion dollars, with thousands of stores across the country.

"Yup, none other," Fletcher replied. "This man could be the helicopter owner. It fits."

"How is he famous?" I asked. "I remember reading about them in *People* magazine; isn't he some kind of musician?" Roxanne had said that too.

"He's a cellist," Fletcher replied, shooting Holt an intrigued look, picking up on the detective's distracted mind. "He plays with the Las Vegas Philharmonic, but also has his own shows on the Strip. He's darn good, they say."

"Okay," I replied with a slight frown, thinking, *Where there's smoke there's always money,* my own personal motto. Fire too, but always money. The best part of that motto is that it seemed to work both ways. In this case, where there's so much money, there has to be some smoke. Maybe fire too.

Maybe Holt was right about the boyfriend. Homicide case statistics definitely seemed to agree with that scenario. "Push his photo to our devices, I want to run it by Roxanne, make sure we have the right man."

"Done," Fletcher replied after tapping on a few keys. "What else do you need?"

"The photo of the other guy, the one who gave Crystal the chip. Maybe Roxanne knows who he is?"

"And... done."

"Did your friend in HR figure out what he's saying on that recording?"

"No, but it's not an exact science. Some people are better at lip reading than others. She has a friend, and she'll ask her."

I sighed, waiting for him to conclude his long-winded response.

"Long story short, I'm still working on it, but it's not looking all that good." He paused for a moment, giving me time to ask for anything else, but my mind was already in a different place: Crystal's freckled sister and whatever her mom's boyfriend was hiding.

"Did you dig into Crystal's social media yet? Please look at Roxanne also."

"On it," Fletcher replied, already typing commands on his system.

I turned to Holt, who still seemed to be miles away, in whatever realm preoccupied him that much. "Crystal's sister hasn't called yet. Let's swing by her school on our way to Roxanne's."

Holt snapped out of his absentmindedness and grabbed his keys. "Sure. I'll need to stop by my house and change clothes first. I have somewhere I have to be later today."

"No problem," I replied, walking quickly by his side toward the exit.

On the front steps, we ran into Detective Nieblas. I squinted, seeing the glare he shot Holt. The two men measured each other from head to toe like fighters do before raining lethal blows on each other at the sound of the gong.

"Are you ready to testify?" Nieblas asked Holt. "They want you in at four, sharp."

"Yeah, I'm ready."

"Dressed like this?" Nieblas asked, his voice filled with contempt.

Holt's clothes were wrinkled, and his tie loosened, a memento of the night he'd spent parked on my street, watching over Anne and me. I felt a wave of anger creeping up on me, bubbling, ready to burst.

"Back off, Nieblas, don't be a knob," I said, but the detective completely ignored me, fueling my irritation.

Instead, he continued to glare at Holt. "Don't screw this up," he urged Holt. "Don't jam us up. If anyone's going down for this, it's going to be you, not me."

Holt made a dismissive gesture with his hand, but his frown deepened. "It will be fine," he said coldly. "Everything was done by the book."

"Which damn book would that be, Holt? I can't believe you're dragging me down into your filth with you," Nieblas said, raising his voice and taking one step closer to Holt, who didn't back up one bit. They were in each other's face, a mere few inches between them, Holt steady and calm, unyielding.

Whatever was going on, it was serious. I had to know.

"What's happening here, Nieblas?" I asked, pushing Holt to the side a little to make some room for myself in the conversation. Any additional distance between the two men could only prove beneficial.

"This bonehead is testifying today. Remember TwoCent, the cop killer he collared, although it was my case? He's on trial for murder."

I felt a pang of anxiety ripping through my gut. That testimony could go badly in many ways. I'd had my own unorthodox role in the arrest of that cop killer, nothing I wanted to hear about again.

"It's routine," Holt intervened. "I was the arresting officer, that's all. Why are you so worked up about it?"

Nieblas stared at Holt in disbelief, then turned to leave. "Just don't screw this up, Holt."

The anxiety unfurling in my gut dried my mouth and brought up my heart rate. Nieblas was right; nothing had been routine about that arrest.

Not a single, bloody thing.

19

SCHOOLYARD

We drove in silence all the way to Cashman Middle School, the same sense of gloom that had engulfed Holt earlier now extending its unwanted cloud over me. Only last week I'd heard of TwoCent for the first time. The day Holt and I met, he was dragging the thug in cuffs, collared for the murder of Detective Park. A few days later, I had become more acquainted to the cop killer than I would've wanted, maybe just because I have difficulties knowing when to draw the line, to know where the pursuit of justice stops being lawful and starts being fueled by a sense of right and wrong that supersedes any other rational thought.

All in all, a bloody mess.

TwoCent was facing a trial by his peers because I'd made it possible, and no one knew about it except those creeps in the rat squad; not even Holt. I hoped with all my heart it would stay that way.

Triggered by an unrelenting wave of anxiety, unwanted thoughts started whirling in my head. What was going to happen, once Holt took the stand? Did he really break protocol when he'd collared TwoCent? Was that going to come up during his testimony?

Ultimately, what did I really know about Detective Jack Holt?

I looked at him with scrutinizing eyes, noticing every detail. But it wasn't the tall forehead, the kind, hazel eyes, or the dark hair that held all the answers, nor were the warmth and the friendship I'd felt whenever I'd allowed him to get near; it was his record.

I found myself wondering if I could run a full background search on my partner. I didn't expect my user profile to have the necessary access levels to display information on fellow cops, but, because the IAB had asked me to investigate him in the first place, at least I had a good cover story in case I got caught trying to nose around.

I opened my newly assigned work laptop and, keeping an eye on Holt while he was driving, I started a database search. I waited for the data to load while dealing with an overwhelming feeling of guilt. What had he ever done to me to deserve my suspicion? Only last week he'd saved my life, for crying out loud. He said he was going clean, he said he'd done nothing wrong, and I owed him as much as to believe him.

On the other hand, he was a drug addict suspected of stealing a kilo of cocaine. And yeah, I'd demonstrated precisely zero common sense by shagging him. Twice.

Ah... Whatever, I thought, shrugging off whatever guilt I still carried for the mistake I'd made when I crossed the line by inviting him into my bed. It wasn't going to happen again, and that was that.

The screen displayed his background, and I started reading, hungry to know more about my new partner.

He was forty-one years old and not really showing his age, I concluded, after shooting him a side glance. Not a single gray hair that I could see, not even on his temples. Former Navy, he'd served two years on an aircraft carrier, then four more with a Special Warfare Group, aka SEALs. That much I already knew; he'd told me.

I had no idea he'd been decorated as many times as his record showed. He'd been awarded the Navy Cross and Navy Expeditionary Medal for acts of valor in combat. There weren't any more details on the subject; most likely classified, but one thing came across loud and clear from his record: the man was a hero.

After his honorable discharge fourteen years ago, he'd joined the Las Vegas Metro PD.

He'd started his new career on the streets, but even as a patrol officer he had an excellent performance record, except for the occasional issue dealing with red tape or specific partners. I'd heard personally the day I'd transferred in from Henderson that he was on the hook for not being much of a team player. There were multiple reports on that kind of behavior, some with warning letters, others just notes on his file from his commanding officers. If I were to read between the lines, he was a brave, dedicated cop with an outstanding solve rate and a strong sense of urgency that translated into impatience, especially when he had to deal with slow thinkers, and specifically when those slow thinkers were other cops.

Then, I asked myself, closing the lid on my laptop, why the hell did the IAB want him buried?

"Got everything you were looking for?" he asked, giving me a start.

Ah, yes, and apparently, he was also psychic. Either that, or he had an incredible peripheral vision augmented by an uncanny ability to draw the right conclusions. Excellent qualities in a cop, nothing a Navy SEAL wouldn't master.

"What do you mean?" I replied candidly, although my throat was dry.

He shot me a side glance and flashed his crooked grin. "Really?" he asked, but the smile didn't touch his eyes or color his voice.

He pulled over in front of the school, across from the entrance. We didn't have to wait long before the bell rang, and the doors opened, the peaceful neighborhood flooded with hundreds of chipper voices filled with laughter, celebrating their freedom. A long line of cars waited at the pickup curb, but we crossed the street and made our way between them, heading straight for the entrance.

I looked everywhere for Tina, but she was nowhere in sight.

Focused on scanning every kid who ran by me, when my phone rang I took the call without checking the display.

"Hi," a young voice said, whispering. "It's me, Tina."

I stopped and got Holt's attention and put the phone on speaker.

"I see you coming, Detective," she said, and I heard fear in her voice. "He's here already, and he can't see me talk to you. He'll kill me if he finds out."

"Listen, if you're afraid of something," I said, speaking as gently as possible, "we can take care of you. You'll be safe."

"No," Tina replied firmly. "Just leave, and don't let him see you. Please," she added, her voice almost a whimper. "I promise I'll call you today."

"Does he usually pick you up from school?" Holt asked.

There was a moment of silence before she replied. "Yes. Every day when Mom's at work. But I'd rather take the bus."

"All right, Tina," I replied, "we'll do as you wish, but we'll follow you from a distance, just to make sure you're safe."

"Okay, but don't get caught," she added, and I laughed, but that laughter died on my lips when I thought of the reasons she must've had to be so terrified of that man.

"We won't get caught, I promise," Holt replied seriously, his furrowed brow expressing the same concern as I did.

The line went dead and I put the phone in my pocket. We walked back to Holt's unmarked car keeping our heads down.

"Prison tat, huh?" I asked as soon as I climbed in his SUV.

"Yup," he replied, keeping his eyes riveted on the street, looking at every driver who'd picked up kids from that school, searching for Norm Chaney. "He's done serious time, and I don't care what his record says; I'm willing to bet on it."

We both waited while the long line of cars started and stopped in a never-ending ritual. Then Holt saw Chaney and pointed him out discreetly. He was driving a beige Honda minivan and barely stopped his wheels in place when he opened the door for Tina. She climbed in, and he took off in a hurry before she'd had time to click in her safety belt.

Holt let a couple of cars slide through and joined the traffic, following the minivan from a safe distance. He didn't want to take any chances with Chaney; I would've done exactly the same.

Chaney went straight home and dropped Tina in front of her house, then drove off, going at least ten miles over the speed limit. The kid looked around carefully, then went inside, while we waited at a safe distance, tucked neatly out of sight behind a utilities truck.

"We need fingerprints for this guy," I said, stating something Holt knew just as well as I did. "If he's done time, he'll be in the system. No way he can beat that."

"Uh-huh," he acknowledged.

It didn't take long and my phone rang again. This time, the display had Elaine Tillman's name on it.

"Do you see the house with the green garage doors on your left?"

I shook my head, smiling. The kid had made us. Unbelievable. "Yeah, I see it."

"Meet me in that yard in ten minutes," she said. "They're not at home, and the dog is friendly. They don't mind when I visit."

"Okay," I said, but she'd already hung up.

"Feel like breaking and entering?" Holt asked.

"We were invited," I replied.

"Absolutely," he replied, laughing. "We were invited to collude in the perpetration of a B&E. Let's go."

20

SISTER

I entered the backyard holding my hand on my weapon's holster, ready to pull it out at the slightest sign of trouble. Tina was already there, sitting on the grass with her legs folded under her and scratching a Shetland Sheepdog behind the ears. The Sheltie sensed our approach and rushed to us wagging its tail, without as much as a single bark.

"Great guard dog they have here," Holt muttered, relaxing a little.

"How did you get in?" I asked Tina. There's no way she could've entered the backyard through the gate, like we'd done. We would've seen her, and that meant she must've jumped a few fences.

The Sheltie curled next to her and laid its head on its front paws. Only the eyes moved, looking at us, then at her and back, sending ripples into its long, shiny coat. Tina seemed pale and frail in her dark clothes, and kept her eyes riveted on the dog, while petting it with long, soft strokes.

She didn't reply; she sat silent, looking down. She sniffled quietly, and I crouched next to her, gently lifting her chin with my fingers.

"What's going on?" I asked, although I suspected I already knew the answer.

She still didn't reply, but then Holt kneeled next to the dog and scratched its head.

"What's his name?" he asked.

"It's a she," Tina replied. "Bella," she added, and the dog promptly perked her ears and wagged her tail.

"She seems to love you very much," Holt said, and the girl lowered her head again, hiding her tears from us.

I wanted to ask her what she wanted to talk to us about, but Holt signaled discreetly, and I clammed up. He seemed to have a natural talent with kids, and I couldn't help but wonder how that came to be. He'd never mentioned a family.

"I know Norm killed Crystal," she said as she looked me straight in the eye through a veil of tears. Then she turned toward Holt, grabbing at his forearm. "I know he did, I know it."

"Why is that?" Holt asked calmly. He spoke with her as if she were an adult, and Tina responded well to his approach.

"Because she'd told him to stay the hell away from me," she replied, lowering her eyes and dropping her voice to a whisper, as if ashamed. "She told him if he ever came near me again she'd send him right back to jail." She sighed, the loaded breath of air lingering on her lips as it left her chest, filled with the promise of more tears. "I don't know why she said that, because Norm said he never went to jail."

I exchanged a quick glance with Holt. We both had the same question on our minds, by the looks of it. If Chaney was indeed living under a false identity, how did Crystal find out about it? Maybe she'd spied on him and overheard a conversation he'd had with a former cellmate. And that was motive, spelled with a capital M in large, bold font.

But, beyond that, I wanted to know what Chaney had done to Tina to earn such attention from Crystal, including the threats she'd made.

"Why did your sister tell him that, sweetie?" I asked, doing a mediocre job at hiding the sudden surge of anger coursing through my veins.

Tina patted Bella's side, and the dog immediately turned on her back, welcoming the belly rub. The kid's shoulders heaved, burdened with sadness and shame, maybe even guilt.

"He looked at me funny," she whispered, while her cheeks flushed with embarrassment. "Two days after he moved in with us, the bathroom lock broke and it's still not fixed. He never knocks when he finds the door closed. He just barges in, then apologizes and leaves, but there's this weird smirk on his face."

I looked at Holt and saw his jaws clenched tightly, and a threatening glimmer in his eyes. If he would've had Chaney in his sights right that moment, he would've killed him with his bare hands.

"Have you told your mom about it?" Holt asked, his gentle voice revealing nothing of his internal anguish.

Tina sniffled and quickly wiped her nose against her sleeve. The dog fidgeted a little but settled again under her soothing hand.

"Yes," she eventually replied, barely a whisper. "She's always at work, doing twelve-hour shifts. She wants to believe me, but he's a great liar, and when she's at home he never does these things."

I exchanged another look with Holt.

"We'll bring him in, sweetie," I said, and rose to my feet. "Will you be okay?"

She looked at me for the first time in several minutes. There was a glimmer of unspoken courage, of resilience in that little girl's eyes. "I have to be, don't I? Because if I'm not, you'll take me away and I lose my mom too."

"You won't lose your mom," Holt said. "It's a promise," he added, crossing his heart in a gesture I hadn't seen since elementary school.

Tina's lips fluttered in a tiny, shy smile and she straightened her shoulders. "It's just me and Mom now. Crystal's gone, and she was the strong one," she said, and as she talked about Crystal, her smile widened a bit, fueling new tears. She stood, and the dog followed suit, weaving patterns around her ankles. "She was fierce, my sister. You should've seen her, getting in that asshole's face."

"Watch your language, kiddo," Holt admonished her gently, patting her shoulder.

I grabbed her hand and she held on tight.

"What's she supposed to call him if he's an arse?" I asked seriously. "An arse is an arse, right?"

"Right," Tina replied, while Holt looked at me with an indecipherable expression on his face.

"We'll make sure to call him that when we catch him," I said, and Tina giggled, but her quick laughter soon was smothered in tears.

"I miss her," she whispered, squeezing my hand. "It's my fault she's gone, isn't it?"

I had to bite my lip hard to keep from crying myself. I ran my fingers through her hair and bent forward a little, to put our misty eyes on the same level. "Never ever think that, okay? It wasn't your fault." I silently pleaded, looking at her intensely until she nodded, barely noticeable. "Call me anytime, okay? You don't need a reason."

She nodded, this time with enough enthusiasm to loosen a few curly, red strands of hair from her scrunchie.

"Shall we?" I asked, showing her the gate.

Behind us, Holt was calling Fletcher.

"I need a BOLO on Norm Chaney. Get a warrant going, he's a suspect in Crystal Tillman's murder. He's driving a beige Honda minivan, Nevada plates—"

"He's gone," Tina interrupted. "Like, really gone. He always talked about going back to California one day. Maybe he went there."

Holt showed her a thumbs up.

"And set up traffic cam screening on I-15 south," he added. "We have reasons to believe the perp's on his merry way to LA."

21

THREATS

We parted ways with Tina, and I watched her walk quickly toward her house, her silhouette, clad in black, vulnerable and thin, disappearing in the distance. I kept my eyes on her until she was safely inside her home and took my seat in Holt's SUV.

"I struggle with this whole thing," I said, blurting out uncensored, disorganized thoughts. "Why did Chaney bother to pick up Tina from school, if he was going to skip town?"

"You got a point," Holt replied, frowning while he started the engine. "Maybe he wanted to make sure no one missed him before he could be gone already?"

"Then, why not beat it in the morning, after he'd dropped her off? That would've given him a good six hours head start."

Holt unscrewed the cap off a new bottle of water and offered it to me. I passed, and he took a few thirsty gulps. "What if he wasn't planning to run, not until he came to pick her up?" he asked, still holding the bottle as if he wanted to drink some more. "It's the only logical explanation I can think of."

"That means he made us at the school," I replied. "It's either that, or he's not skipping town, and we'll find him at his place of employment."

I looked at the time displayed in LED digits on the dashboard. It was almost three, and Holt needed to be in court by four.

He followed my glance and hesitated a little, while screwing the cap back on the water bottle and placing it in the cup holder. "It's not a big detour. Didn't he say he worked at that new hotel construction site, the one on East Sahara?"

"Yes, that's correct," I replied, after checking my notes.

"That's minutes away from the courthouse."

He floored it, flashers on, while I called for a patrol car to keep an eye on the Tillman residence. As I instructed dispatch to make sure the officers didn't let Tina Tillman out of their sight, I caught the glance Holt threw me, the same indecipherable, loaded look. It was as if mixed, conflicting emotions swirled and fermented, threatening to come out.

I ended the call to Dispatch and looked at him. "Okay, what's going on?"

"Nothing," he replied, a little too quickly. "Why do you ask?"

I groaned. It wasn't as if he didn't know I could spot a lie from a mile out; he knew, but still preferred to lie to me nevertheless instead of telling me the truth, sending me a message of unavailability, of cold distance.

"What were you thinking of, just now?" I asked, rephrasing the question in the odd chance he'd misunderstood.

"Just wondering if we're drawing the right conclusions here, that's all."

Another lie.

He pulled in front of the gate marked, "Sun Builders." He parked and both of us rushed beyond the fence, with no concern for the sign that warned, "Hard hat required beyond this point."

There was always something being built in Vegas, and construction jobs were available throughout the year, for qualified workers and day laborers equally. A good place to start for someone living under a false identity, trying to cover their tracks and establish a "legitimate" paper trail under a new name. It made sense.

A bulky worker in a yellow hat and protective goggles approached, and we flashed our badges.

"We're looking for Norm Chaney," Holt said, as soon as the man was close enough to hear over the loud, banging noises coming from the structure above.

"Who?" he asked, putting his hand at his ear. His hearing must've been shot, if he'd spent his days working in such ambient noise without ear protection.

"Norm Chaney," Holt repeated, "he's a foreman here."

The man's sweat-beaded eyebrows lifted, disappearing under the rim of his hat. He removed his glove and rubbed his chin between his index finger and thumb for a moment. "N— no, I'm sure we don't have anyone here by that name. Definitely not a foreman; I know all the foremen and none of them is your, um, what was it? Norm Chaney?"

"Yes," I replied, exchanging a quick glance with Holt.

"Yeah, definitely not a foreman. I can check the computer to see if he's one of the day laborers, maybe."

I checked the time. It was getting late for court, especially because Holt had to stop by his place to change.

"That won't be necessary," Holt replied, before I could say anything. He wasn't as surprised as I was that Chaney had lied about his job; my partner seemed to have a better perception of the man's shady past than I did. I wondered why; it wasn't as if Chaney had fooled me for one minute with the display of fake concern and empathy he'd demonstrated when we broke the news of Crystal's death to her mother. After witnessing the previous moments of his uncensored, angry reaction, I knew exactly who he was. And yes, Holt seemed to have a point with him being an ex-con; he definitely looked and acted like one. But did any of that make him a killer?

He had plenty of motive; we'd already established that. But poison? I still believed he was too butch for poison, even if he was now in the wind. People had a lot of things to hide from police other than murder. Like being in violation of one's parole, or a fugitive on an open warrant for who knows what.

One thing was clear; the more I thought about Norm Chaney, the more certain I was he wasn't Crystal's killer. He seemed to be a well-versed pedophile, a rotter I wouldn't mind locking up and throwing the key so far away he'd never see daylight again.

Once we arrived at Holt's place, he went inside to get changed, while I waited in the Interceptor with the air conditioning on, checking my email, eagerly anticipating any updates from Fletcher. There were none.

I started looking around; Holt lived on a quiet street, in a two-car garage, single-story home that seemed a little old, maybe creeping up on forty years since it had been built. I made a note of the address, just in case I'd need it at some point. Remembering how well he interacted with Tina, and my thoughts as I watched them together, I looked for any sign of a family living at his address, as opposed to a bachelor. There were none. The tiny garden was dying, uncared for, most likely because the sprinkler had broken, and no one had noticed. There were no toys scattered anywhere, and no sheers at the windows, something only a woman would think of using.

Frustrated, I let a long, loud sigh escape my chest. If only the man would open up a little, everything would be much easier, and I wouldn't have to chew on my own guilt-ridden paranoia. It wouldn't change my decision about him, but still, it would make sense.

As if I'd told him the truth about anything lately. Who was I to judge, right?

He took less than ten minutes to emerge dressed neatly in a charcoal suit, white shirt, and burgundy tie, his hair still wet from a shower that couldn't've taken him more than two minutes. I watched him tighten his tie as he rushed toward the SUV and couldn't refrain from smiling. He was easy on the eyes, every single bit of him. I remembered his strong arms wrapped around my body and blushed; I bit my lip and thought I'd contained my smile before he got a chance to see it.

"See anything you like?" he asked in a serious tone of voice, and I almost choked.

I managed to frown. "What are you talking about?"

He didn't reply; he drove fast, leaving the residential neighborhood with all flashers on, but took the wrong turn, heading south instead of north. He wasn't headed to the federal court building.

"Where are you going?"

"Dropping you off at the precinct. I should've done that before going home to change, I'm sorry."

"No, I'm coming with you," I said in a firm voice, hoping I was conveying clearly enough I wasn't going to take no for an answer.

"There's no need for that," he replied, continuing to head for the precinct at top speed. "This TwoCent character was collared before your transfer. Not worth wasting your time with it."

Bollocks... He was wrong about that.

I couldn't tell him how I'd become wrapped up in the TwoCent case, just because I couldn't stand seeing a cop killer go free. I couldn't tell him what I'd done after I'd learned that the murder weapon had been stolen from evidence. He could never find out I'd gone and made it appear as if it had been misplaced, not stolen to begin with. Holt could never know, just as much as he could never know what I sometimes did after hours, when taking the lawful way to justice was too bloody convoluted and filled with obstacles for me to follow anymore.

Sometimes, I just cut to the chase. It might not be what a cop was supposed to do, but I did it only when there were no other options left but do what was right, what was just.

Unfortunately, the IAB had me on tape visiting the evidence locker around that time and held that over my head right next to the punches I'd delivered up close and personal to my husband's killer while the odd-eyed wanker was in my custody.

And now this... Holt being called to the stand to testify.

I swallowed with difficulty, as if a noose was tightening around my neck.

Holt's testimony could take a wrong turn and expose what I'd done or invite more attention. It didn't make sense; the moment TwoCent's defense would challenge the chain of evidence on the murder weapon used to kill Detective Park, it would implicitly incriminate TwoCent for the theft of that piece of evidence.

Even so, it wasn't as if I were going to be able to do anything else but sit in the courtroom pretending I was calm and relaxed, without a care in the world, while my partner was being cross-examined on the stand.

I had to go. I had to be there.

"Turn this vehicle around right now," I said firmly, "I'm coming with you. End of story."

He shot me a short, intense glance from underneath his furrowed brow, flipped a U-turn, then resumed his high-speed driving. "Why?"

I laughed quietly. "It's not out of curiosity, you know. Testimony given in court is public information, and I could find it online while doing my nails," I said, cringing a little because I'd just used a negation evasive technique, blatantly deflecting, which, at least to talented investigators like Holt was a huge, red flag. "No, I'm hoping it will mean something to have me by your side, that's all," I added, continuing to lie, but doing it slightly better the second time around, because it was only a partial lie. I did want to have his back, to show everyone my support. Screw the rat squad and their ultimatums.

He drove quietly for a couple of minutes, not taking his eyes off the road. "Thank you," he eventually said.

Anxiety twisted a knot in my gut, as I recalled the events surrounding TwoCent's arrest. I couldn't help thinking how much I needed that entire case to be over and done with, and how much I was willing to bet that TwoCent wouldn't say a word about what had happened that night.

Unless...

No. It could never happen.

I had already bet my career on that, and Holt's too.

We pulled into a police-reserved parking spot near the Lloyd D. George US Courthouse entrance and rushed up the stairs leading to the majestic, modern building in glass, concrete, and steel.

Once on the fourth floor, as soon as the elevator doors opened, we ran into an old acquaintance of mine, Frederick Volo Jr., attorney at law for the richest and sleaziest of Sin City's scum. He and I had crossed paths many times before, and I still remembered how it felt having him cross-examine me on the stand, and how many stiff drinks I usually required after breaking free from his deathly grip. He had a knack for taking facts out of context, for pushing witnesses to give answers that he then cut short, stripping them of their intended meaning and twisting them around, bending them into tools that would set free the criminal elite he represented, one murderer at a time.

I nodded curtly in lieu of greeting, hoping he wasn't there to represent TwoCent.

Volo completely ignored me and focused on Holt instead.

"Ah, Detective Holt," he stated theatrically, "you're almost late."

My heart sunk. He *was* defending that piece of scum, cop killer.

Holt frowned but didn't reply. It wasn't four o'clock yet; there were seven more minutes left before anyone could accuse Holt of lateness. Volo was such a jerk, nothing but a bully dressed in an overpriced suit.

"Have you rehearsed all your lies for today, Detective?" Volo asked, and that accusation lit my fuse.

"Really, Mr. Volo?" I snapped, getting two steps closer to the man. "Are you attempting to intimidate a witness in front of law enforcement, a cop, no less? Are you really that naïve?"

Volo grinned and walked away, lifting two fingers at his temple in a mock salute. What an arse.

When I turned to Holt, I saw he was smiling, a smile that touched his eyes.

"Focus, will you?" I said. "This man's fierce; I've dealt with him before."

"I know the bastard well enough," Holt replied calmly, a trace of his smile still lingering in his eyes. "I'm wearing a cup."

22

TESTIMONY

"Do you solemnly swear that you will tell the truth, the whole truth, and nothing but the truth, so help you God?"

"I do," Holt replied, his voice strong and unwavering, his steady hand touching the Bible firmly, without a trace of hesitation.

I smiled encouragingly from my second-row seat, although he didn't seem to need any encouragement, nor was he looking elsewhere but in the court clerk's eyes. My partner's demeanor was textbook power witness, instilling credibility and respect.

"You may be seated," the clerk said, and Holt obliged, unbuttoning his jacket and arranging his tie.

ADA Gulewicz, a bright, young man, whom everyone he knew personally referred to as Gully, stood and nodded briefly to the judge, and then, with a polite smile, to the jury. He wore his favorite tie, a bright, orange one that complemented his youth and brought a nice contrast with his dark navy suit and white shirt.

He approached the stand, greeting Holt with a head gesture.

"Detective," he said, "let's go back to the day you arrested Marcus Jones, aka TwoCent, for the murder of Detective Park."

Holt remained silent; no question had been asked of him.

"Walk me through how that arrest took place, Detective."

Holt touched his tie briefly, then his hands settled neatly in his lap. I could tell he was getting a little nervous; thankfully, no one else could.

"I was driving on East Carey Avenue, on my way to interview a witness in one of my cases, when I stopped to yield at a pedestrian crossing."

"What time was that?" Gully asked.

"Precisely, seven-oh-nine in the morning," Holt replied impassibly. "Shall I...?" he gestured with his hand, asking permission to proceed.

"Please continue, Detective," Gully said.

"As I was saying, I was driving on East Carey Avenue, when I stopped to yield at a pedestrian crossing. While I waited for pedestrians to cross, I noticed the convertible parked at the curb, right next to mine. The car's top was down, and the suspect was behind the wheel, fast asleep. On the passenger seat, I saw a handgun."

He stopped talking for a brief moment, but Gully encouraged him to continue with a hand gesture.

"I pulled over in front of the suspect's Mercedes, approached the vehicle on the right side, and, while keeping the suspect at gunpoint, I secured the weapon found on the passenger seat. I circled the vehicle and approached on the driver's side. When I had the suspect in my sights, I tapped the barrel of my weapon against his window, to wake him up."

"Then?" Gully prompted, when Holt stopped talking.

"He woke up and surrendered without resisting, if you disregard his verbal attack. I instructed him to exit the vehicle with his hands up, and cuffed him and read him his rights. I proceeded with the suspect to the precinct, more precisely to Central Booking."

"Why do you think the defendant, against all logic, was sleeping soundly in his car, by the side of the road, with a gun in plain view and the car top down?"

"It's not about what I think," Holt replied politely. "It is my understanding that the lab found the defendant to have been intoxicated, under the influence of alcohol and several opioid narcotics."

"Meaning?" Gully asked.

"Meaning he was sleeping it off. People with those levels of drugs in their system don't exactly think logically."

"Objection," Volo said, raising his hand holding a gold pen. "Witness is not an expert in psychiatry."

"Sustained," the judge said. "Jury will disregard the last remark."

"Thank you, Detective. What can you tell us about the gun you recovered from the defendant's car?"

"The weapon was covered in the defendant's fingerprints, as later proven by the Crime Lab. Furthermore, ballistics demonstrated it was the weapon used to murder Detective Park."

"Was this your case?"

"No, it was not. There was a BOLO out on Marcus Jones. I happened to be the one who saw him and executed the arrest."

Gully smiled briefly. "No further questions, Your Honor. Your witness," he said to the opposing counsel, then walked to his desk and took a seat.

Frederick Volo Jr. shuffled through some papers, then stood and walked slowly with a calculated gait, until he was only a few feet away from the stand. For a long moment, he stared at Holt, but the detective didn't budge, didn't blink, didn't lower his gaze.

"Detective Holt," Volo eventually said, just as the judge was starting to glare at him. "Were you assigned the investigation into Detective Park's murder?"

"No, I was not," Holt replied calmly.

"Who was the case assigned to?"

"It was assigned to my colleagues, Detectives Nieblas and Crocker."

I looked briefly over my shoulder and saw Nieblas shamelessly grinning, satisfied to have his vindication in open court. The only thing that seemed to matter for Nieblas was to even the score with Holt, whatever the damage. As for Crocker, he seemed detached, dispassionate, absentminded.

The defendant, a bulky man I knew better than I cared to remember, seemed uncomfortably dressed in a suit his attorney must've forced him to wear under severe threats. Although he'd been trying to clean up his appearance for the court, he hadn't given up on wearing at least half a pound of jewelry, assorted in the poorest taste possible, a must have for twenty-nine-year-old, semi-famous rappers like him. As for his demeanor, once a thug, always a thug. His head on a swivel, he kept looking back and forth, from Volo to Holt to the public and back to the jurors, with a fresh smirk on his face and a hip-hop hand gesture whenever anyone said anything that went his way, as if expecting the public to cheer for him.

By contrast, thin and tall at his six-foot-five stature, Volo wore with class a silver gray Armani suit that lent the fifty-year-old litigator a youthful look, enhanced by dark-rimmed, designer glasses and side-parted blond hair. His white shirt shone like silk, and he wore it with gold cufflinks, in all probability embossed with his initials. I liked his physical appearance up to a point; what worried me specifically were the tension in his jaw and around his chin, the fierce look of determination in his blue gray eyes, and the overall predator demeanor. I'd seen all that before, not something I'd easily forget.

Volo paced the room for a moment and stopped in front of the stand again. "Tell me, Detective, is it a common occurrence to arrest other detectives' suspects? To take over their cases?"

I cringed; the answer wasn't at all favorable.

"Which question would you like answered, Counselor? If it's common to arrest other detectives' suspects? Or if it's common to take over their cases? You should know these are two different situations," he said casually, in an attempt to throw Volo off his game.

His back tensed; I couldn't see his eyes, but I could've placed a relatively high bet he was glaring at Holt.

"How so? Please elaborate, Detective."

"As a law enforcement officer, I am sworn to uphold the law, regardless of case number. Therefore, if I see a known suspect at large, I will apprehend him or her, because it is my sworn duty."

"How about taking over another detective's case?"

"That I will not do in the absence of a direct order from my superiors. It's against regulations."

"I see," Volo said in a low voice. "This wasn't your case, Detective, I believe we established that?"

"No, it wasn't my case. But there was—"

"Thank you," Volo interrupted, putting both his hands in the air, palms facing Holt, in the universal, unspoken message to stop. "Did you think, at any time, to call the two detectives on the case?"

"There was no reason to waste police resources. There was a BOLO out for Marcus Jones; every police officer in Las Vegas was looking for him."

"You want the jury to believe that Mr. Jones, despite being asleep in plain sight with a weapon by his side as you keep claiming, was found by you, entirely by accident?"

"That's the truth," Holt replied with a slight shrug.

"Let's talk about my client's car," Volo said, turning to face the jury for a quick moment. "What kind of car are you alleging my client was asleep in when you found him?"

"A Mercedes S-Class convertible, white."

"Was the top down, Detective?"

"The car top was down, yes."

"So, you could easily see the gun on the passenger seat, correct?"

"Yes, that is correct."

"Was the gun packaged in anything?"

"No, it was just the gun, directly on the seat. That gun was later proven to be—"

"Thank you," Volo cut him off again.

I remembered his tactics from the times I had to take the stand and be interrupted every two phrases. But Holt was handling it much better than I had. He was a cool customer, my partner.

"Is it possible," Volo continued, "that someone else could've dropped that gun onto the car seat, because the top was down, and my client was asleep?"

Holt frowned. "Yes, but—"

"Yes or no answers, please," Volo said. "Is it possible, then?"

"Yes," Holt admitted, letting out a sigh of frustration, the first emotional reaction he'd shown that far.

I glanced at ADA Gulewicz, wondering how he felt about Volo's cross. He seemed to sense my look, because he turned briefly in my direction. We locked eyes for a moment, and he nodded, almost imperceptibly. He was too smart to let Volo have the last word.

"Isn't it a fact that *you* planted that gun on the passenger seat of my client's car, Detective?"

The courtroom reacted with a collective gasp, followed by a wave of whispers.

"No, absolutely not."

"Isn't it a fact that my client, startled out of his sleep and shocked to find a gun by his side, a gun that wasn't his, touched it out of reflex?"

Holt looked at Volo inquisitively. "What reflex is that you're talking about?"

"It's a proven scientific fact that humans use their sense of touch to investigate things that are new to them, especially under duress. Is it possible that my client touched the gun *after* you woke him up?"

"Absolutely not," Holt replied calmly. "If you recall, I was holding my service weapon in my hand at the time I approached the vehicle and had the defendant in my sights. If your client would've touched that gun, he would've been in the morgue right now with two in his chest, not here, in this courtroom."

"So, you admit to wanting to kill my client, Detective?" Volo asked serenely.

"Objection," Gully said.

"I'll rephrase, Your Honor," Volo said quickly, before the judge could rule. "Are you a good cop, Detective?"

"Define good," Holt replied calmly.

"Abiding by the law in everything you do, upholding the law at all costs, following procedure?"

"Yes, all that."

"Have you ever broken the law, Detective?"

"No, I have not."

"How about bent it?" Volo said with a smile filled with contempt. "Just a little, to get your man?"

"No, I have not."

"Have you ever engaged in any illegal activities while on duty or off duty?"

"Objection, Your Honor," Gully said promptly. "Asked and answered."

"Sustained," the judge said. "Are you going somewhere with this, Mr. Volo?"

"I am, Your Honor." He cleared his throat again and arranged his tie, smoothing it down with both his hands, while smiling at the jury. "You claimed the defendant was under the influence of drugs and alcohol when you arrested him, is that correct?"

"I did not claim anything; the Crime Lab ran those tests. They are the experts who said that."

"But you know a thing or two about drugs and alcohol impairing judgment, don't you, Detective?"

My blood froze. Volo's tone as he'd asked that loaded question had been eerily calm, but I knew better than to be fooled by that.

"It comes with the job," Holt replied calmly, although color had drained from his face.

"Is that the only experience you have with impairing levels of drugs and alcohol, Detective? Through your job?"

"I believe so," Holt replied, still calm.

"You *believe* so?" Volo reacted. "Have you ever been impaired while on the job, Detective?"

"No, I have not," he replied.

"Are you sure about that, Detective?"

"Positive."

"Are you a fame seeker, Detective?"

"What do you mean by that?" Holt asked.

"Are you actively hunting for collars, looking to score as many as possible, to look good to your superiors and gain access to promotions and raises, maybe even media attention?"

Holt grinned, that asymmetrical grin of his that meant he had the upper hand and only he knew it. "I'm not seeking fame more than anyone else, Counselor. Not more than you do."

I couldn't contain a smile. Bravo, Holt!

But Volo seemed unfazed. Instead, he made a gesture of theatrical frustration for the jury, then turned to Holt. "Are you asking the jury to believe that my client decided to have a nap with the top down and he just left his gun—according to you, the murder weapon—for all to see?"

"Yes, that is the truth."

"Because I can't understand why my client would be so stupid as to fall asleep in his convertible, a gun next to him, and wait for someone like you to slap the handcuffs on him. This is incredible, as a matter of law. Unless you're omitting something, Detective. What are you omitting?"

"I'm not omitting anything," Holt replied. "My testimony includes all the details pertaining to the arrest of Marcus Jones, a suspect in the case of Detective Park's murder."

"But you do affirm that someone could have planted that gun on the passenger seat of his car, while he was asleep."

"With his fingerprints already on it?"

"Yes or no, please?"

"Yes, I believe it's possible, if they'd—"

"Thank you, no more questions," Volo said. "Defense rests."

"Redirect, Your Honor?" Gully asked.

ADA Gulewicz stood and smiled at the jury. The twelve men and women lined up on the two rows of chairs fidgeted in place after having held their breaths during Holt's cross-examination. I could easily relate, because I'd barely drawn air myself.

"Detective," Gully said, approaching the stand, "do you believe someone else planted that weapon in the defendant's car?"

"No, I don't."

"Why is that?"

"As previously stated, the weapon was covered in the defendant's fingerprints, as later proven by the Crime Lab.

Furthermore, ballistics demonstrated it was the weapon used to murder Detective Park."

"Has it ever happened before to collar another detective's suspect? On your own?"

"No, never. This was haphazard; he was in the right place at the right time to make my day."

Holt ended his statement with an infectious smile. I saw several jurors smile also, and Gully used the opportunity to end the redirect.

"Recross, Your Honor?" Volo asked.

"I'll allow it," the judge replied, looking at his watch. "Make it quick."

I felt a new, stronger bout of anxiety grab my insides and twist them in a knot. I'd thought we were done, over with it. I'd been wrong.

"Detective," Volo asked, "where were you last Wednesday at nine PM?"

My breath caught. Last Wednesday night he'd attended an AA meeting, giving into my insistence. Somehow, Volo had found out about Holt's cocaine addiction and was using it to discredit him. How the hell did that happen? Anonymous, my arse... He was totally screwed. I suddenly understood why the IAB wanted him gone, as in gone for good, without the faintest possibility of him carrying a badge again in his life.

I sought his eyes, but he was looking straight at Volo, unfazed. "I'm afraid I can't recall, exactly."

"You must have some idea, Detective."

"Objection," Gully finally sprung to his feet. "Relevance? The detective's private life is his own."

"I believe it's relevant to my client's defense," Volo argued.

"I'll allow it, but watch it, Mr. Volo. If you're fishing, we're done here." The judge turned to Holt. "You may answer, Detective."

"I'm sorry, Your Honor, I really can't recall."

"Approach, Your Honor?" Volo asked, and I felt as if I were going to faint, right there, on that crappy courtroom bench.

The judge beckoned with a bored and rather irritated expression on his face. Volo started saying something in a low, rushed whisper I couldn't comprehend, but I thought I'd heard my name and I froze. I wasn't sure at first, but then I saw alarm in Holt's eyes as he looked at me. Still on the stand, he was close enough to the bench to hear what was going on.

My head started spinning.

In a daze, I saw Gully and Volo take their seats, and the judge picked up the gavel.

"Mr. Volo?"

"Yes," he replied, standing again. "Defense would like to call two new witnesses, Detective Laura Baxter and Internal Affairs Lieutenant Steenstra."

"Grounds?"

"Given Detective Holt's memory problems and his inability to recall his whereabouts last Wednesday at nine PM, we have reasons to believe the two witnesses will bring relevant information pertaining to the professionalism and credibility of the arresting officer."

"Granted, Mr. Volo. Have your witnesses ready to testify at nine o'clock tomorrow morning."

"Request for continuance, Your Honor?" Gully said, his voice a little unsure. "This is last minute. We need time to prepare the witnesses."

"It's five in the afternoon, Mr. Gulewicz. You have enough time until tomorrow morning. I won't hold the jury for one more day, so you can enjoy your work-life balance. Request denied."

"Your Honor," Gully said, "respectfully, we don't—"

"We're adjourned for today."

The gavel fell, and with that sound, my entire world collapsed at my feet.

23

PLANS

I walked by Holt's side without saying a word, while thoughts raced through my mind in a desperate search for a solution, for a way out. I couldn't help but think that was exactly what happened when the lines were blurred or stepped over, when corners were cut just to bring a perp to justice. The scumbag could walk free, and there would be no justice for the death of a good cop. Not to mention, our careers ruined, our lives completely finished.

I knew I'd be going down with Holt the moment it came out I'd been aware of Holt's addiction and failed to report it. One thing bothered me more than anything else; was last Wednesday the night I waited just outside of the Community Center, working on Holt's laptop, while he attended his AA meeting? How many people, some of which had records and could've been TwoCent's old cellmates for all I knew, had seen me there? There was no way I could claim ignorance and avoid a perjury charge.

I'd been a reckless fool.

Bloody hell.

I couldn't sit and watch our lives destroyed, but I also had no idea how to dig us out of the hole we'd landed in. I hated admitting that I also had no clue whether Holt had done anything he wasn't willing to share during TwoCent's arrest. Was it possible he found the gun in a different location, maybe surrendered by a confidential informant, and had decided to conveniently "find" it in TwoCent's car?

There was no doubt in my mind that TwoCent was Detective Park's killer. He'd been picked out of a lineup by a witness, but that witness had since disappeared. Knowing the thug's background and methods, that poor bloke was now fish food somewhere at the bottom of Lake Mead.

The more I thought about it, the more things crystalized, came into focus. I couldn't let TwoCent walk free, and I couldn't let our lives be ruined. I needed to do something, and fast.

But what?

We were at Holt's SUV when we heard Gully calling us, and we stopped and waited. Holt was grim, the frown that landed on his forehead a permanent fixture since he'd heard I was being called to testify. He avoided looking at me, preferring to keep his eyes riveted on the horizon instead.

When Gully caught up with us, he was out of breath.

"This is bad," he said, between panting breaths. "We're an inch away from having the judge dismiss the case, and even if he doesn't, there's no way they'll convict. That means Jones walks. And now, this," he added, gesturing toward me as if I carried the blame for the state of the prosecution's case against TwoCent.

"Yeah, I'm not that bloody thrilled either," I said coldly.

"Baxter doesn't belong on the stand, Gully," Holt pleaded. "She wasn't my partner when I collared that piece of scum."

"It's not my call, Holt," he replied. "I did my best in there, and she'll have to testify tomorrow morning, first thing."

"Fantastic," I mumbled. "You know the perp's guilty as sin, right?"

"Yes, I know that, and you know that, but the justice system has checks and balances in place for a reason," he reacted, bitterness tinging his voice. "What we know isn't worth much if we can't prove any of it. Next time, Detective, let the perp sleep and call the lead detective on the case, all right? It would make everyone's life easier, especially considering your... issues."

"What, you're saying it's my fault, now?" Holt snapped.

"Whoa, guys, we're all after the same thing," I intervened. "We want TwoCent to pay for what he did. Let's find a way to get us there."

They both agreed; Gully with a rather hopeless undertone, and Holt still visibly fuming.

"Detective, I need to prep you for tomorrow. Please come by my office in about two hours," Gully said, looking straight at me, and then he walked away.

We drove back to the precinct in silence, a grim, loaded silence that neither of us dared to break. I was afraid of the questions that could arise, the truths that I wasn't prepared to share, the suspicions I was harboring myself. As he pulled over in his parking spot and cut the engine, he let out a sigh and turned toward me.

"Thanks for everything, for having my back," he said. "I'm really sorry for all this."

Bollocks... Bloody, hairy bollocks the size of Volkswagens. We're still in the game, partner.

I wasn't ready to lay down and die, not yet. I wasn't defeated, and if I wasn't, neither was Holt. I still had plenty of fight left in me, and that infatuated arse, Volo, was going to regret the day he ever put my name on a bloody witness list. And I knew, right then and there, that whatever I chose to do, Holt would be right there with me, fighting all the way. But he'd better not ask me what I was planning to do; some things are better left unsaid.

"Nothing to be sorry about, Holt. We haven't lost the war; we just saw the enemy draw closer and shoot one across the bow, that's all."

I felt a strange wave of excitement as I kept thinking of the challenge ahead. Instead of being afraid of the looming testimony scheduled for the next day, I was exhilarated, crazy as it seemed, because I knew one thing for sure: I could never take that stand.

The corner of Holt's mouth stretched in a tentative smile, but a phone call interrupted it.

He took the call on the car's media center. It was Fletcher. It was about bloody time we heard from him.

"Hey, guys, have I got some news," he said in a chipper voice. "Guess what the cat dragged in? The piece of work is waiting for you in Interrogation Two."

A few minutes later, we found Norm Chaney cuffed to the scratched table, cussing and kicking like a blabbering plonker when he saw us walk in. The small room reeked with the smell of his sweat, of his fear.

I laughed and propped my hands on my hips. "Well, hello, Mr. Chaney."

Holt requested a Crime Scene tech with a mobile fingerprint scanner and then he leaned against the wall.

"Want to do us all a favor and give us your real name?" Holt asked, but he only got grunts and oaths in response. Chaney, or whatever his real name was, had stopped trying to fool anyone about his true colors.

"We know you've done hard time," Holt continued calmly, "only we don't know for what. We'll know in about ten minutes, when the tech gets here and scans you in. But that's when I'll also mark your file as 'noncooperative.' You know what that does for perps like you?

Chaney glared at Holt with murder in his eyes, his mouth gaped open, frozen in a snarl.

"Nothing much for now. That will only come into play at sentencing. The judges tend to give noncooperative felons the maximum sentence, for each item on their list of charges. Concurrent, huh, partner? Or...?"

"It's *consecutive* sentences for noncoops, always consecutive," I replied with feigned indifference. "Come on, let's get out of here. Crime Lab will sort this out. I'm hungry."

I wasn't even lying. The events of the afternoon had made lunch impossible and the adrenaline jolt I got during Holt's testimony had left me ravenous.

Holt smiled and opened the door for me. As I stepped outside, the perp made a guttural noise and we stopped.

"Kemsley," he muttered, spraying saliva between his chipped front teeth as he spoke. "Bill Kemsley."

"What were you nailed for, Bill?" Holt asked.

He chewed on a dirty, stained fingertip for a second or two. "Sex with a minor," he finally said, mumbling the words so badly we could barely understand what he was saying.

"How old was the minor?" Holt asked with a certain dark intensity in his voice. Kemsley lowered his gaze under his scrutiny.

"She was eleven, but she looked—"

"Don't even bother," I snapped at him just as the Crime Lab technician walked in.

His nametag read, "Shawn," no last name. He didn't smile, barely acknowledged us, and proceeded immediately to scan the perp's right index finger with his device. A few moments later, a chime announced the record had been found.

Shawn looked at Holt and me, waiting for permission before sharing his findings in the presence of the suspect.

"By all means, go ahead, I'm sure he knows everything you're about to share," I said.

"William Kemsley, forty-two. Long rap sheet, starting with a couple of B&Es and drug charges to aggravated sexual assault. Early release after three years served on the last sentence. Active warrant; wanted for skipping parole."

"See? I told you," Holt said cheerfully. "I can smell a con a mile out."

The technician gathered his stuff quietly and disappeared.

"Thank you, Shawn," I said while he was closing the door behind him. "So, Mr. Kemsley, why did you kill Crystal Tillman? She made you, didn't she? She was threatening to drop a dime on you, is that it?"

A look of pure terror appeared in his eyes. "What? I didn't kill Crystal, I swear!"

"Then why were you fleeing the state?" Holt asked. "And why did you lie to us about your job?"

Kemsley had been constantly shaking his head, as if to repel a resilient nightmare.

"I saw the way you looked at me last night," he said, wringing his hands. The movement made his cuffs rattle.

"Then why not run last night?"

"I thought maybe I'd pulled it off, you know, thrown you off my scent. But I saw you at school."

"What were you doing at that school, anyway? You don't strike me as the concerned guardian of a minor," Holt asked.

Kemsley lowered his eyes, mumbling something I couldn't understand. I slammed my hand against the table's surface. "Louder."

He didn't say another word, his lips pressed closely together, and his fists clenched, white-knuckled.

"I see," I said, "you like hanging around schoolyards, don't you?"

He didn't reply; he just shot me a glare filled with hatred and curled his lip in a snarl.

Holt grabbed a pen and paper and slammed them on the table, in front of him.

"Start writing," he ordered, while Kemsley still stared at his handcuffs, shaking his head.

"What?"

"Everything," Holt replied. "The entire story of your miserable, good-for-nothing life. Who sold you the fake ID. Everything you did, said, or thought of doing to Tina. All your interactions with Crystal, and how you killed her."

Then he opened the door and invited me to go ahead. "Come on, partner, we're late for dinner."

"Hey, wait a minute," Kemsley shouted, tugging violently at his restraints. "I didn't kill anyone! I swear I didn't."

I waited for Holt out in the hallway, while he turned and said to Kemsley in a conspirative whisper accompanied by a wink, "Go ahead, write. Convince me."

24

SUGGESTION

We didn't have the time to grab dinner, or lunch for that matter. I was due in the ADA's office for court prep, and it was already past six. In passing, I swiped an apple from a fruit basket neatly wrapped with a silk bow and a card that had been delivered to the attention of our sheriff, knowing he wouldn't mind. Holt followed suit and helped himself to a pear.

Wolfing that crispy apple in front of Holt's desk, I read quickly through my emails. A note advised me I now had my own desk, only a few feet away from Holt's.

"I've got to run; Gully's waiting for me," I said, talking with my mouth full. My mother, a formally educated British woman, would've slapped me right there, in front of a bullpen full of cops, if she saw me do that. Embarrassed, I swallowed the half-chewed bite and smiled apologetically.

"Are you coming back here after court prep?"

"Probably not," I replied, knowing I absolutely wasn't going to come back. I had other things to do, like making sure I didn't have to take that damn stand the next morning.

"I'll follow up with Fletcher then, see where he's at with his lip-reading friends."

"Sounds good, see you tomorrow," I said, then rushed out.

The Clark County District Attorney's office was located in the Regional Justice Center building on Lewis Avenue, a short drive away. When I entered Gully's office, I was still chewing on the last bite of apple, but I made sure I didn't speak with my mouth full again.

The ADA seemed tired, drawn, and had a deep ridge across his forehead, all explicable after the turn of events during the earlier court proceedings. A box of Papa John's pizza was open on his desk, atop file folders and scattered paperwork, a couple of slices untouched. The smell of stale pizza filled the room with the promise of artery-popping, empty calories, and I could think of nothing tastier I'd rather eat, but my stomach had already twisted in a knot, anticipating the ADA's questions.

He lifted his eyes from the multipage document he was revising with a red pen in his hand. He barely sketched a smile.

"Thanks for coming in, Detective. Please give me a few seconds here."

I nodded and sat in one of the two chairs in front of his desk. "Sure, take your time."

He continued reading, while I observed the details of the small office: the family photos pushed to the side of his desk to make room for case files with archive date stamps on the covers, his jacket thrown casually over the back of a chair by the window, his shoes discarded next to his desk. He'd probably been working sixteen-hour days for a while.

It was already dark outside, and, in the distance, the colorful world of the Las Vegas Strip barely lit the sky, although the heart of South Las Vegas Boulevard was only a couple of miles away from there. I kept my eyes riveted on the dark, winter sky, wishing I was out there, free, over and done with the ADA and court prep, wishing it were tomorrow and all the nightmare safely behind me.

I wondered whether Lieutenant Steenstra had already visited with Gully, and if she'd been there, what exactly did she find suitable to share. It occurred to me I could be the one asking questions, at least some of the questions that weighed on my mind, in the hope of avoiding having to share too much with the ADA.

Because, if my plan was going to work, no one would have to hear my testimony in open court, nor Steenstra's.

Gully set aside the document he'd been reading and buried his face in his hands for a moment, massaging his forehead. Classical sign of migraine onset.

"Hey, do you know what this is about?" I asked. "I wasn't involved in the case, nor in the arrest. I actually met Holt after he'd collared TwoCent; I'm sure you knew that already."

"Yeah," he replied, while his frown deepened, putting the seed of early wrinkles on the man's brow. "Chances are you're being called as a character witness for Detective Holt."

"Did you already speak with Lieutenant Steenstra? I'm curious what she—"

"Let's focus on you, Detective," he replied, and that trace of a tired smile disappeared from his lips, replaced by a hint of tension in his jaw.

"All right," I replied calmly, crossing my hands neatly in my lap, while the familiar pang of anxiety wreaked havoc in my gut. What the hell had the woman said? Had she filled his ear with her witch hunt suspicions about Holt and the missing kilo of cocaine? She probably did, that twat!

"Are you aware of any information about Detective Holt that could come out during tomorrow's proceedings and jeopardize this case?" the ADA asked, pulling me into the present moment.

There it was, the million-dollar question. But I wasn't under oath yet, so I gave the answer I'd carefully rehearsed on my short drive over. "No, I am not. I only met the man last week, Gully."

He sighed and ran his hands through his thinning hair. If I were anywhere else, and the man in front of me were anyone other than the Clark County ADA, I would've sworn he seemed relieved. It was in his body language: in the softened line of his jaw where I'd seen the ripples of tension just moments earlier, in the slouched shoulders, in the relaxed line of his eyebrows.

I breathed. Okay, that was unexpected. I had an ally I didn't anticipate I'd find, even if he didn't know it yet.

"For tomorrow, Detective, do as you always do when you take the stand. Give short answers to the point, don't speculate, don't assume, don't be emotional, and definitely don't argue."

"Understood," I replied with a bit of a smile, loaded with all the charm I could throw behind it.

"Have you been cross-examined by Volo before?"

"Once or twice," I admitted, trying to retain my innocent smile when nasty memories invaded my brain.

"So, you're familiar with his antics. That's good." He leaned back in his chair and seemed to think for a while. "Don't sweat this, Detective. If you don't know anything, they're just wasting the court's time and yours."

I allowed my smile to bloom a little. It was time to make my move, the move that my entire plan hinged on.

"Hey, Gully, I just had a crazy idea."

His eyebrows popped, and a glimmer of interest lit his pupils. "Shoot."

"This case barely stands, right? We'll probably lose?"

He pressed his lips together for a moment, avoiding my eyes, but then said, "Thank you for the vote of confidence, but yeah, pretty much."

"What would be the plea deal you'd offer, if you had all the aces in hand?"

"First degree homicide, twenty-five to life. He gets to avoid the death penalty."

"What if you made TwoCent a plea offer? I mean, tonight? It almost certainly won't work after tomorrow."

"What... now? He'll laugh in my face, moments after my boss will doubt my sanity and have me committed. I know you want this cop killer behind bars for good, Detective, but he's not stupid."

"Exactly."

"I'm not following."

"They know what you're doing tonight, right? Prepping the witnesses that *they* called to the stand, not you? That's the norm, isn't it?"

"Yeah, and?"

"What if, when seeing the plea deal, they assume you've uncovered something during witness prep that gives you the upper hand? TwoCent *knows* he's guilty."

"Then why would I offer them the deal, instead of crucifying them in court tomorrow?"

That was an excellent question. I knew the answer from my point of view, but that wasn't going to do the ADA any good.

"Why do you normally offer plea deals, and how do you sell them?"

"We horse trade to get suspects to testify and help us catch bigger fish, or because it saves the state a lot of money. And we like playing the risk down. The sale is quite easy if our case is strong and the death penalty is an option."

"All of the above apply here," I said, thinking hard. "Plus, this is Vegas."

"Meaning?"

"Sometimes, when your hand is crap, all you need is a decent poker face and a good bluff."

He scratched his head while mulling over the idea. I could see it in his eyes, he was starting to like it.

"What do you have to lose?" I asked serenely. "Worst that can happen is they'll say no."

He took a deep breath and rubbed his palms together, energized. "Okay, I'll do it."

"Make sure it expires at eight tomorrow morning, and good luck!"

I rushed out of there in such a hurry, I didn't bother to close the door behind me. My work was far from done for the evening, and the tricky part was just starting.

25

RECON

From Gully's office, I stopped briefly by a convenience store and picked up a few items, including some life support in the form of a caffeine-heavy chocolate bar that set me back several hundred calories. I swung by the Scala and left my car somewhere on the busy, third-floor parking garage. Wearing oversized shades and my hair in a loose ponytail under a baseball cap, I exited the hotel and hailed a cab.

While waiting for the driver to make his way through the tourist-heavy traffic jam, I turned off my LVMPD-issued cell phone, then my personal one. A few minutes later, I was staring at the second-story windows of a mid-rise apartment building in Spring Valley that the smartest geek I've ever worked with called home. There was a flicker of TV lights coming from the living room window. I was in luck; Fletcher was home.

Moments later, I rang the doorbell and was invited in by the surprised techie, dressed casually in shorts and a loose T-shirt; the man likely didn't own a single clothing item in his own dress size.

He stood there in the doorway, scratching his head and pushing his thick, unruly curls to the side so he could see where he was walking.

"May I come in?" I asked, although technically I was already in. He nodded and closed the door behind me. "Oh, I thought that was the TV," I reacted, noticing a layout that included four immense monitors hooked up to a huge computer lit with colorful LEDs.

"Nah, that's just my gaming station."

"Could you spare one of those?" I asked, pointing at the empty bottle of Bud Light guilty of leaving wet circles on his desk. "I need to ask a favor."

He popped the cap off a cold, sweaty bottle and handed it over. "Shoot," he said, straddling the side of an armchair.

I gulped down half of it. After a day like this, it was exactly what I needed.

"It's late, so I hope you don't mind if I skip straight to the point," I asked, but my hesitation made him frown. "Okay, I need everything there is to know about the TwoCent household."

"Like, now?" he asked, tugging at the side of his T-shirt for some reason, seemingly uncomfortable.

"Right this moment, while I finish this," I said, holding the beer bottle in the air before taking another couple of swigs.

"I'm assuming I shouldn't ask certain questions right now," he said, sitting behind his desk and cracking his interlaced fingers before starting to type.

"It's better you don't," I replied. "I need to know if TwoCent has a dog. See if you can locate any vet bills, pet store credit card charges, anything that would indicate the presence of a dog. Cats, I don't care about; just dogs."

"This will take a while, you know. More than finishing up that dying beer you're holding."

"That's not all," I said, entertained by his metaphor. "I need to know who else lives there. Who sleeps in what he likes to call his crib? Any permanent residents? Anyone tonight? Not only do I need to know, but I need to be sure."

He looked at me from underneath thick, corkscrew-like locks of unruly hair and squinted slightly. "That will take some doing," he said in a low, thoughtful voice. "Not any kind of doing I could testify or sign an affidavit about, if you know what I mean."

"That's fine, you'll never have to. This never happened," I said, putting the empty bottle of beer on his desk, "and I was never here."

"Anything else?"

"I need to know if TwoCent is at home tonight, and the moment he goes to sleep."

He nodded, then glanced at me briefly before looking at his monitors. "I'll try to gain access into the—"

"The least I know, the better," I smiled and patted him on the shoulder. "Just dig deep, and all on the QT."

"You got it," he said, typing commands in white font on a dark blue screen. "How do I tell you?"

"Use this," I said, handing him a burner I'd picked up earlier from the convenience store together with some snacks and a bottle of water. "There's only one number stored on it, and that is also temporary. After tonight, they'll both stop working." I started toward the door, but came back and caught his eyes. "Thank you. It means a lot."

He stood, his skinny legs appearing even thinner by contrast with the XXL-sized gym shorts. He tilted his head a little and frowned, then avoided my eyes, looking at his bare feet instead.

I waited patiently for him to collect his thoughts.

"Are you sure TwoCent did it?" he asked eventually. "I mean, how sure are you?"

I looked at him intently until he lifted his eyes from the ground and met mine. "I'm one hundred percent positive," I said, in the most reassuring tone I could muster. "And, by the end of tomorrow, I promise you'll be too."

He shrugged with the gesture that teenagers use as an expression of semi-confidence mixed in with the right amount of "whatever."

"Okay," he said with a half-smile.

"Good," I said, smiling widely. "I'll also need to know if his former cell mate is still doing time. If he is, please make sure he's on a no-contact order for forty-eight hours. No calls, no visitors."

"That will leave a trace in the system," he said, seeming a little worried.

"For that piece of business, we'll use the official channels. I'll send you a formal request as soon as I get home. Chances are it will never come out anyway."

I was at the door, but his hand lingered over the deadbolt before unlocking it. I waited, smiling patiently. If he had concerns, I was better off addressing every one of them while I was still there.

"Good luck, Detective," he eventually said, looking straight at me with an intrigued smile. "Whatever it is you need all this info for, I hope it works out well and we still have our jobs tomorrow."

26

SUSPICIONS

After leaving Fletcher's place, I walked out of the residential area and flagged down a cab, then went to pick up my car at the Scala. I played the exact same steps, but in reverse. I asked the driver to drop me off in front of the hotel, as if I were just another tourist with an itch for a good time. I walked across the vast casino floor toward the parking structure, wearing large shades and a baseball cap. For anyone watching, for any of the hundreds of security cameras, I was just another girl, an anonymous figure in the crowd.

I turned on my official cell phones, while still in the parking structure of the Scala, after having reached my car. As such, to anyone thinking of tracking my movements using the GPS function of my work or personal cell phones, it would appear I had been at the Scala the entire time; the massive hotel and casino was notorious for its unreliable cellular coverage, due to the high concentration of users trying to make calls or browse at the same time.

Finally, I was ready to go home and prepare for the next stage. It was still early, not even eight-thirty. I needed time to think, to prepare, to eat, to rest, and to get ready for what could easily turn into a long, challenging night.

I drove my white Toyota all the way home well within the speed limits, obeying every stop sign as if my life depended on it, because it did. If I was going to be pulled over by another cop, even if I'd only have to show my ID and get away with rolling a stop sign or speeding, I'd leave a trace in the system, and that absolutely could not happen. Not now, not later, at any given moment during the following few hours.

As I turned onto my street, I realized I was smiling widely, a sense of exhilaration within me, still injecting adrenaline into every fiber of my body, anticipating the hours to come. I loved every moment of it. The thrill of the hunt, the challenge to lay down and execute a bold plan, all in the service of justice and with a dually noble purpose: to put a cop killer behind bars, and to help a friend, a partner, a good cop.

"Hello, Baxter," I heard a man's voice coming from the darkness of my front lawn, and it gave me an instant start. Instinctively, my hand jolted to the grip of my gun. "Whoa, there, partner, it's me," the man said, and I instantly recognized Holt.

I breathed, swallowing a long and detailed oath. "What the hell are you doing here?" I blurted, before I could remember to play it cool. I was irritated as hell; I needed time alone to think.

"You're that happy to see me, huh?" Holt said, traces of dark sarcasm tingeing his voice.

"Come on in," I said, unlocking the front door.

I stepped in, cringing as I recalled how I'd left my living room earlier that day after having slept on the couch: a bloody mess of scattered clothing, dirty dishes, and empty bottles of beer. I turned on the light and took in the disaster with one quick look around the room, then rushed and collected some of the items littering the furniture. "Take a seat," I said. "Can I get you anything?"

"Just water for me, thanks." He paced the room nervously, not granting the couch a single thought.

Something was on his mind, and I believed I knew what. The sooner I'd deal with it, the sooner he'd leave, and I'd have the time to prepare, to do what I needed to do to save us both.

I grabbed a couple of small bottles of Perrier from the fridge and handed one to him. "What's on your mind, Holt?"

He threw me a side glance. "You know what; tomorrow's testimonies. What do you think they'll ask you about? What did Gully say?"

"He said it's most likely a character reference for you, because TwoCent was already collared when I became your partner."

"And Steenstra? How does she come into play? Why the hell are they calling the rat squad to the stand? I'm not on their radar, am I? And, if I was, how would *you* even know about it?"

He asked the questions in rapid fire, not giving me a chance to squeeze in an answer, unloading a heavy burden off his chest.

I sat on an armchair, leaning forward, getting ready for what was going to be a difficult conversation. But I'd put things off long enough; my partner, good or bad, had done nothing but been loyal and honest with me, and he deserved to know what was going on. I owed him that much.

"Please, sit," I insisted, and he obliged, a deeper frown marking his brow. "This entire thing has to do with the case you worked before you and I met, before you collared TwoCent. You closed that case with a drug bust, remember? A cocaine seizure?"

"Yes, and?" he probed impatiently, turning a little pale. "How do you even know about that case?"

"The IAB believes you took one kilo of cocaine from that bust. The seizure was for seven kilos, but only six made it to the evidence locker."

He sprung to his feet before I even finished talking. "What? I didn't take any of that damn cocaine," he shouted, pacing the room angrily with his fists clenched. "You've got to be kidding me!"

"Unfortunately, that's what's going on," I said, pausing briefly to take a deep breath before continuing. I needed to know for sure before I jeopardized my career for him. "I'm inclined to believe them," I added.

He stopped in his tracks as if hit by lightning, his eyes open wide in shock, then blurred by the cloud of deep disappointment. "How could you possibly believe them, Baxter?" he asked, his voice low, no longer thunderous but hurt.

I repressed a long sigh. *Forgive me, Holt*, I thought, *but I really have to know.*

"Because you're an addict, that's why," I said gently, feeling his pain like a knife in my chest. "Because that brick of dope is your supply for how long, two, three years, maybe?"

"Yeah, it would be, if I were still snorting, and if I'd taken it to begin with, but I swear to you, I didn't touch that coke."

I looked at him steadily, and he withstood my scrutiny without flinching or looking away. I believed him. For a long moment, I wondered why I believed him: had I really noticed the microexpressions of truthfulness? Or were my own feelings clouding my judgment? A lot was riding on my decision whether to trust my partner or not: my career, my next conversation with Lieutenant Steenstra, that night's actions. I could not afford to be wrong.

Then why did my eyes linger on his strong arms, and why did I yearn so badly for his touch? Why did I want so desperately to end his turmoil, to tell him that everything would be all right?

Because cops shouldn't be shagging their partners for a damn good reason, that's why. I had been a complete idiot, but it was over. Now, at least in theory, I was lucid, letting the voice of reason make the decisions that needed to be made.

I gave myself one more chance to notice any signs of deception in Holt's reactions. I asked, "Then, what do you think happened to that kilo?"

He shrugged, buried his hands in his pockets, and shook his head a couple of times, slowly, as if trying to remember what had happened during the commotion of the drug bust. "I don't know. No one's ever questioned me about it. I didn't even know it was missing until you told me."

"They never asked?"

That seemed strange, to say the least. More and more like a setup. But why? And who would have an interest to frame Holt?

Now that the cat was out of the bag, I wondered what options I really had to find out what had happened to that coke and clear Holt's name. He could make the investigation really easy for me. Maybe together we'd find who really took that brick and sort things out with the IAB once and for all. Although I could easily anticipate Steenstra would be less than thrilled with that outcome. She just wanted Holt gone. Period.

"No, they never bothered to ask," he replied coldly. "I could've accounted for every moment of my time during that drug bust, because I wasn't alone for one single minute the entire evening."

"Okay, I believe you," I replied in a pacifying tone. "And you can count on me tomorrow, when I take the stand."

"Can I?" he retorted, back to pacing the room, keeping his hands buried inside his pockets. "Can I really trust you, Baxter?"

"What the hell do you mean?" I asked, although I already knew the answer.

"How do you know what the IAB has to say about me? How could you possibly know, unless you—"

"They came to me," I said softly, feeling ashamed as if I'd done something wrong.

"You ratted on me?" he shouted, stopping firmly in front of me, mad as hell. His eyes threw flashes of anger mixed with disappointment.

I held his gaze firmly as I said, "No, I didn't, and I never will."

He let a loaded breath of air out of his lungs and stepped away, breaking eye contact for a moment. He probably didn't know what to believe anymore.

"But they got stuff on me, that perp I beat while he was in my custody," I continued calmly, knowing it was the time he knew everything. "So, I have to talk to them when they call me upstairs, and pretend I want to play ball."

He turned and looked at me with a different expression in his eyes; all his rage was gone, but the disappointment and the hurt were still there.

"They want me to confirm you took that kilo of coke," I continued, pretending I didn't see his anguish. "My guess is that the info leaked somehow, and TwoCent's lawyer wants to put the IAB on the stand to show that you're a crooked cop who'll bend the rules to get what he wants."

"Jeez," he reacted, letting himself drop on the couch. "Someone in the IAB is on that thug's payroll?"

"Maybe, maybe not," I replied. I'd been thinking about that the entire afternoon, trying to figure things out. "Maybe someone recognized you at one of the AA meetings and called TwoCent; one of his fans, possibly. From there, all they had to do was ask questions of people who could, in their turn, ask more questions."

He nodded, his jaws clenched tightly and his pallor clearly noticeable. I'd stopped short of telling him that the IAB had given me only until Monday to prove he'd taken the cocaine, or that Frederick Volo Jr. could ask some other questions of me while on the stand, infinitely more damaging. There would've been zero benefit in sharing that information with Holt, all things considered.

I watched him as he sat on my couch, leaning into elbows rested against his thighs, his shoulders tense, his brow deeply furrowed, and his eyes riveted to the floor. I knew I could share what I was about to do, but then again, I couldn't, not really. Instead, I stood and approached him and laid a comforting hand on his shoulder.

"Hey, we're the good guys in this, remember? Things could still go our way, you know."

"You think so?" he retorted sarcastically. "With our kind of luggage?"

I laughed quietly, willing myself to believe what I'd just said, now that the earlier exhilaration had dissipated, and Holt's worries had contaminated me, running through my blood like sharp icicles of fear. "I know so. Now, why are you here, again?" I asked, my way of telling him life moved on, despite the following morning's scheduled testimony. We still had a killer to catch.

"I thought we could drop by Roxanne's tonight. We were going to talk to her again, show her those photos?"

I looked at the time. "It's nine-thirty, Holt. Really late for a house call."

"She's working tonight; I already checked. Her night is just beginning."

I grabbed my keys with a frustrated sigh, then I laughed quietly.

Yeah... Mine too.

27

IDENTITY

We drove to the Scala in Holt's Interceptor, and his dark mood lingered in there with us, heavy, an ominous cloud of silence and tension. I wasn't too talkative either, my mind preoccupied with the many things I still had to do to prevent the night from turning into a fiasco.

An unfamiliar ring tone resounded; I didn't react at first, not recognizing it, but then I remembered the burner I'd tucked into my pocket before leaving the house. Only one person had that number: Fletcher. I took the call promptly.

"Yeah," I said, holding the phone pressed tightly against my right ear, as far away from Holt as possible.

"There's no trace of a canine companion at the TwoCent residence," Fletcher said, cutting to the chase in his typical, direct style. "The man hasn't spent a single dollar on vets or pet supplies in the past two years. I believe I went far enough on this one, yes?"

"Absolutely," I replied. "Anything else?"

"It's anyone's guess how many people sleep over on any given night," he continued. "I had to tap into the security system at his house. Believe it or not, our thug has fully monitored security with multipoint video surveillance, and thankfully it connects via Wi-Fi."

"I see," I replied, careful not to say anything that could trigger Holt's insatiable curiosity. He'd already shot me a long glance when I'd pulled out the flip phone from my pocket, a phone he'd never seen before.

"I went back a few days," Fletcher continued. "Last Wednesday he had a party. Girls, booze, snow, the works. It ended at about four in the morning; some of the folks crashed, some left."

"And tonight?"

"All is peaceful at the TwoCent crib," he replied, and I sighed with relief. "He's killing time on TV, getting drunk and high by his lonesome. I have eyes on him."

"Keep me posted with any changes," I said, afraid I'd already said too much in Holt's presence. Every now and then he shot me curious glances, and I could expect a flurry of questions as soon as I ended the call.

"You got it," Fletcher replied. "And you owe me one, a big, fat one, if you're up to what I think you are."

I smiled. "Yes, I do owe you one, but I have no idea what you're talking about."

"Uh-huh, sure, Detective," he said, then the line went dead.

I flipped the phone shut and slid it in my pocket as Holt took a right turn onto South Las Vegas Boulevard. From there, the majestic silhouette of the Scala stood out from the rest of the skyline, its contour highlighted in blue neon lights.

"New phone, Baxter?" he asked, a crooked grin stretching his lip. But there was no humor in his smile, and not a trace of his boyish charm.

"You noticed," I replied casually. "You a detective or something?" I asked, and we both laughed, a little tense and insincere, but the ice was definitely starting to crack. It was about bloody time; I hated his coldness, his distance, his distrust.

Moments later, we entered the high-limit gaming room on the upper level of the Scala Casino. It was open for business as if nothing had happened, with the same lights, the same music, and two of the same players as the day before. Only five players were there that night, not surprising for a Tuesday evening when business was slow.

No one had taken Crystal's place yet, although Brandi was most likely eager to leave the world of craps and retake her old spot. Roxanne danced on her usual stage, near the roulette tables, and we approached quickly. I looked around and saw Farley across the room, in the lounge, talking to a woman in a strapless, sequined lavender gown.

Roxanne stopped dancing when she saw us approach and climbed off the stage. She arranged the straps of her top and smiled shyly. "Hello," she said, not loud enough to cover the music, although it wasn't exactly blaring. She seemed faint, tired, and dark circles surrounded her eyes despite generous amounts of pro grade concealer.

I took out my work phone and showed her Ellis MacPherson's photo. "Is this the man Crystal was dating?" I asked.

"Yes, that's him," she replied.

"Have you seen him since, um, when's the last time you saw him?" Holt asked.

"I haven't seen him in a couple of weeks, but I know for sure Crystal was meeting with him Sunday night. The chopper was here for her, remember?"

"Yes, exactly, that's right," I replied. Then I flipped to the next photo attached to the email from Fletcher. The image was a screenshot taken from the video surveillance showing the unknown man approaching Crystal, moments before he'd shoved that chip in her bra. "How about him?"

When she saw the photo her eyes turned dark, an illusion given by the dilation of her pupils, an unmistakable sign of intense emotion. Then her gaze veered away from the photo, and she instinctively hugged herself, without realizing. She took a small step back, seemingly a bit unsure on her feet, and leaned against the edge of the elevated stage.

"How about this one?" I said, shifting to another screenshot showing the unknown man grabbing Crystal. "Maybe you can recognize him in this photo?"

She looked with wide-open eyes but didn't say a word. I flipped to the next file, the video of the fifty-five second interaction between the man and Crystal. She watched the entire clip without breathing, without moving, without making a single sound. When the video ended, she continued to stare at the screen for a while, as if stunned.

"I'm sorry, but I don't know who that is," she said, barely above a whisper. "Is there anything else?"

Her lips were pale under the lip gloss and she seemed to tremble slightly, as if she were in shock.

I thanked her for her help, and she excused herself and vanished behind a curtain hiding the "Authorized Personnel Only" door leading to the dressing rooms.

"She's lying," I told Holt as soon as she was gone.

"You think?" he asked with a short laugh. "Hey, I got an idea," he added, grabbing my elbow. "Isn't that our friend, Mr. Farley?"

"The one and only," I replied, walking toward the lounge area.

The woman in the lavender gown was still there, her long, tan legs crossed artistically, allowing her skirt to part generously, showing a lot of skin. I found myself envying her, everything about her, almost. I was younger and more attractive than her, but it had been a while since I wore a decent outfit, not the shirt-and-slacks-with-flats that had become my unofficial uniform, dictated by common sense, reason, and the detective Code of Conduct. The woman's heels were to die for, in the exact same shade of lavender as her gown. I missed going out, having men fawn all over me, size me up, trying to hit on me. Yeah, I knew that was shallow of me, but still, I so needed to get out more.

The moment we approached Farley, the woman stood and quickly disappeared, and Farley shot us a disappointed glance that spoke volumes of his recent luck with the ladies.

"Detectives," he greeted us with a professional smile he forced on his lips. "What can I do for you now?" he added, emphasis on the word "now" as if he'd constantly been doing things for us in the past two days.

I put my phone under his eyes and showed him the screenshot of Crystal and the unknown male. "Do you know this man, Mr. Farley?"

He looked at the screen for a brief moment, then at me, while his eyebrows curved in disbelief.

"What, are you kidding me?" he asked.

"Do you see me laughing?" I snapped. It was late, and I wasn't in the mood for wiseass humor.

"Sorry," he said quickly, checking the surroundings with quick, fearful glances. "That's Paul Steele," he clarified, lowering his voice.

"And that should mean something to us?" Holt asked.

"Yeah," he replied, "it should. He owns this joint."

"The Scala?" I reacted, while countless more questions flooded my brain.

"Precisely," he replied, still keeping his voice low. "Now, if you'll excuse me, I have to go back to work."

He disappeared without waiting for our reply. Holt and I headed for the exit, walking quickly, me half a step ahead of him. I was the one pressed for time, thinking of everything else I still had to do that night. But I also couldn't help thinking about Crystal.

"Why would the owner of a billion-dollar hotel give a stripper half a million bucks wrapped in wrath?" I asked, and to my surprise, Holt laughed quietly.

"You said stripper, not dancer," he explained.

I rolled my eyes. "Force of habit, I guess. I do resent the word, though."

"I don't find it offensive," Holt replied. "To me, it's like a dance specialty. There are carpenters out there, but only some are cabinet makers."

"Yes, but exotic dancing comes with social stigma, which doesn't happen with cabinet making. Society doesn't respect these girls, although most of them are honest, decent, and work really hard for the money. I just feel I convey that stigma by using the word stripper, especially when I think of Crystal."

"Because she's dead?"

"Yeah, maybe because she's dead I'm more sensitive, more keenly aware of that undeserved stigma. But I don't like to use that label with anyone, dead or alive, especially with a smart, ambitious kid like Crystal. In any case, how would this hot shot Paul Steele know her, anyway? They don't exactly belong to the same country club."

"That's the million-dollar question, or half a mil," he said, grinning. "My guess is it's hush money. That would explain the tension on his face as he delivered the threat or whatever it was he said to Crystal."

"No news on that yet?"

"Nope. Fletcher's friends seem to agree it was some kind of threat, more from the body language than from reading any actual words on the man's lips. They're still trying to figure it out. There's an expert in lip-reading out there; one of the girls knows him personally. They'll show him the tape tonight."

We exited the hotel and I stopped at the curb, stepping to the side to avoid the constant flow of tourists.

"Perhaps she saw something she wasn't supposed to," I offered.

"Maybe she was sleeping with him?"

"With Paul Steele *and* with Ellis MacPherson?" I asked, the pitch of my voice climbing to a higher tone. "What was this chick, a billionaire magnet?"

"Or a high-end escort?"

"People like Paul Steele and Ellis MacPherson don't use escorts," I replied. "They're too smart for it, and they don't need the service either. That kind of money gets them all the companionship they need, and more."

"I don't agree," Holt said. "I've seen worse lapses in judgment with the Vegas wealthy elite, enough to make me think anything is possible. Especially if the client is into, um, unusual stuff, if you catch my drift."

I shrugged and signaled a parking valet to get me a cab. He was right; we couldn't assume we had the two billionaires figured out.

"I can drive you," Holt offered.

"No need," I replied, eager to get rid of him. "We're due in court first thing tomorrow, and we both need rest and time to think."

A taxi pulled up at the curb moments later, and I climbed in the back of the white sedan wearing the insignia of Ace Cab. I waved at Holt, but he just stood there, watching me leave without saying a word.

***

As soon as Baxter's cab turned the corner and joined the heavy traffic on South Las Vegas Boulevard, Holt peeled off in his Interceptor. After fourteen years on the force, he didn't need any fancy Scotland Yard training to know his partner was lying. Every other word she'd said all night had been a lie.

He followed the white cab from a safe distance, a little closer on the highway and falling carefully behind on smaller streets. It seemed that Baxter was going home after all, but his gut told him that her day wasn't over yet.

"She needs time to think, my ass," he muttered, as he pulled over short of turning onto Baxter's street. "Not buying a single, damn word the woman is saying."

28

READY

With the growing distance between Holt and me, the effect of his grim, anxious mood on my spirits seemed to fade away, making room for some excitement, although I had to admit I hated leaving Holt like that, in front of the Scala; it just felt wrong, and I could see the dismay in his eyes, even the lack of trust blooming in there. If I were in his shoes, I'd probably feel the same, unable to trust the partner who had been sitting on that IAB investigation information for a while without so much as giving me a heads-up. If he didn't trust me anymore, I'd earned that.

It still made me feel bad, though.

We made a great team together, but no two cops can really function as a team in the absence of trust. Something to think about later, after the looming threat of tomorrow's testimony would become a thing of the past.

I unlocked the door but felt the urge to look around me before stepping inside. I felt a little paranoid, my instincts riled up, as if there was someone watching me from the darkness, from behind the shrubs that marked the edge of my property. Maybe it was the residual memory from the day's earlier scare Holt had given me, right there on my lawn.

I finally entered and locked the door behind me and set the chain. I kicked off my shoes and got undressed while speed-dialing Anne. I hadn't heard a word from her the entire day. Her phone went to voicemail. I left her a quick message, apologizing for the late hour, then went straight to the shower.

I let the water run over me for a few minutes, not moving, not doing anything, just enjoying the relaxing drops of warmth, feeling my sore muscles soothed, refreshed. I washed my hair thoroughly, although I was painfully aware of how late it was. By the time I was finished with the shower and my hair was dry and shiny, it was eleven thirty.

Bollocks… Time to hustle.

I chose my bra carefully, being that I needed to clip on an underbra holster. I slipped on Fleur du Mal lingerie, one of my favorites, smiling to myself at the soft touch of the exquisite fabric. While the cop dress code had limited what I could wear at work, it had left my passion for sexy lingerie untouched, unrestricted. Half my colleagues would be shocked to see what I normally wore underneath the boring, buttoned-up shirts and Anne Klein slacks; the other half would either be envious or aroused, depending on gender, mostly.

I applied makeup, hesitating for a moment between two styles, then I proceeded with a slightly darker-than-usual eyeshadow, in harmony with the part I was going to play. Eyeliner and mascara completed the job, but the final touches were the deep red, shiny lip gloss and the silk spray I applied generously on my hair, glad to see its natural shine enhanced to a shimmer.

I checked my image in the mirror and smiled. I might've been a thirty-something cop, but I could still make myself look like a drop-dead, gorgeous, twenty-something lady of the night.

The first stop after that was the master bedroom closet, where I pulled all the hangers to the side and accessed the rear panel. The fake back wall slid open and exposed a hidden storage compartment, one that held all the goodies I needed to get the job done.

First, I had to take care of my fingerprints. Standing in front of the shelves stocked with everything a cop could ever dream of, I hesitated between two small plastic containers, one white and one blue, then finally opted for the white one. It didn't contain fake fingerprints, like the blue one did; it contained silicone fingerprint prosthetics that left no marks whatsoever except for some carefully designed smudges. I took a small bottle of adhesive from a drawer and took the two items to the dining room table. Before doing anything else, I checked to make sure all curtains were shut, all windows and doors completely covered. I applied the glue and, one finger at a time, put the layers of silicone on the tips of my fingers, thus making sure I'd leave no usable prints, no matter what I touched.

I moved to choose my weapons. Because of the little black dress I was planning to wear, I had to settle for two subcompact weapons. I chose a Smith & Wesson Bodyguard to go in my bra holster, and a Sig 365 for my purse. I made sure both weapons were loaded and had one in the pipe, then put the Smith & Wesson in its holster and clipped it to the middle of my bra, so it hung down below the cups. I could easily slide my hand in the deep cowl neckline of my dress and pull my backup weapon in case of trouble.

I chose a lock picking kit and closed the panel. I arranged the hangers back as they normally were and grabbed the dress I was wearing, suitable for what I had in mind for the night: a black, metallic, shiny, spandex number that covered my butt by a measly two to three inches, showing my long legs and making me look just a tad slutty, the exact look I was aiming for. The rich, cowl décolletage with its many folds showed the promise of my curvy breasts but hid the Smith & Wesson impeccably.

Shoes came next, and I opted for a pair of Zanotti open-toe heels I rarely got to wear. I pondered a little before slipping those on, unsure what kind of terrain I'd have to deal with while trying to gain access to Marcus Jones, aka TwoCent, but my longing for wearing sassy, four-inch heels sealed the deal. Worst that could happen, I would kick them off and do the job barefooted.

Finally, I added jewelry to the overall look, also hinting toward the high-end call girl appearance. The generous folds of the cowl neckline didn't tolerate a necklace, but I added long, shimmering earrings in sterling silver and matching bracelets. I smiled at myself again, ran another brush through my hair, touched up my lip gloss, and applied a generous amount of hairspray.

I was ready.

I pulled my work and personal cell phones from my bag and put them in the microwave and took the burner and texted Fletcher's phone.

"Still no guests at the crib?" my message said.

"None. Our man is sawing wood."

I locked the door behind me, having the same uneasy feeling that I wasn't alone, although not a single light was on at the neighboring homes and the night was as quiet as could be. I shrugged it off and climbed behind the wheel of my Toyota, while the smile on my face continued to bloom, fueled by the anticipation of the hunt and mumbling curses mixed with solemn promises to deliver justice for a dead cop and deliverance for two live ones.

"I'll get you this time, you bag o' shite, cop-killing wanker."

29

ROULETTE

Roxanne climbed off the stage with a long sigh of relief; her shift was finally over. She'd had the hardest time keeping a smile on her lips the entire night and the appearance of dancing nonchalantly, while she was dying inside. She wanted to hide somewhere and cry bitter tears of jealousy, of betrayal, of the deepest grief she'd ever felt.

She made her way quickly to the dressing room, and let another sigh escape her trembling lips when she saw the room was empty. Brandi was still working, and Crystal... She was gone.

Roxanne threw her tips on the counter and sat in front of her vanity. She buried her face in her hands, letting the sobs she'd been stifling for hours finally come out. Her shoulders heaved with every shattered breath carrying cries that resounded and echoed in the empty room.

"You lying, cheating bastard," she shouted, lifting her eyes and looking at herself in the mirror as if she were the one responsible for her heartbreak. "You son of a bitch... I'll make you pay," she threatened, "if it's the last thing I do on this earth."

As she spoke the words loaded with venom, her eyes dried under the flame of anger, of a pure, unfiltered desire for vengeance. She stared at her image for a minute and made her decision.

Quickly, without hesitation, she wiped the stained makeup off her face, removing every last trace of her stage persona. She treated her skin with a high-end serum to enhance the smoothness of its appearance and started applying fresh makeup slowly, deliberately.

Thinking.

Planning.

A smudged eyeliner contour later, she had to admit she was still rattled; she needed some time for herself before she could decide what to do with the two-bit piece of lying, cheating shit she'd fallen in love with. She corrected the smudge and reapplied eyeshadow discreetly, to enhance the color of her eyes and make her look sophisticated, wealthy, self-assured, like one of the high-limit gamblers she saw every night.

That was who she wanted to be, if even for an hour.

The door opened, and Brandi stumbled in, out of breath.

"There you are," she said, "want to grab some drinks tonight?"

"Leave me the hell alone," Roxanne replied.

She wasn't in the mood for company. She wanted to be by herself, so she could drop her mask for a few minutes and be who she really was, who she wanted to be.

"All right," Brandi replied defensively. "Didn't mean to upset you. Just tell me what I can do for you. I know she was your closest friend; it can't be easy."

Roxanne shook her head as if to get rid of a bad memory. "Just leave me alone. Please."

Brandi looked at her for a moment, then grabbed her purse, jeans, and a T-shirt and left without saying another word.

Roxanne breathed again as the look in her eyes became steeled, vicious, and bloodthirsty. If Crystal weren't dead already, she'd gladly put two bullets in that lying, two-faced heart of hers. Hell, if her rotting corpse were there, she'd still put two bullets in her chest. No, she'd unload the entire magazine, slowly, feeling the weapon's recoil soothe her rage, the sound of every shot an echo of her heartbeat.

She got rid of her stage outfit, ripping it off her body, and put on fresh lingerie. She put on a long, red, backless dress and matching pumps with three-inch heels. She combed her long, blonde hair until it crackled, then parted it low on one side so it would fall over her shoulder in waves.

She counted her tips for the evening. It had been a slow night; not even four thousand dollars.

Cheap bastards.

She stuffed the bills and chips in her purse and threw herself another look in the mirror. She looked just like one of them; she'd belong and be treated with respect, even if stupid Farley would recognize her immediately. But he couldn't touch her on her time off, because her money was just as good as anyone else's at the green table.

Roulette was her game.

Not because she happened to dance on the stage between the roulette tables and she wanted a different perspective on life; no.

Roulette was exotic, with the croupier making announcements in French, with the high payouts, and the spinning wheel that crushed more dreams than she could count, right there at her feet, night after night.

Roulette had charm, had a little *je ne sais quoi*, something indescribable that drew her in again and again. Before she'd met Paul, she gambled most of the money she made, knowing one day Lady Luck would smile her way and she'd finally be free. Rich, to live a life of plenty, without a care in the world.

Then Paul came into her life.

The lying son of a bitch.

When she exited the dressing room, she was someone else. She walked straight, slowly, with dignity and class. No one could tell, by looking at her, that she was just another casino girl, one who wiggled her butt for a living when she wasn't waiting on gaming tables.

After making a stop at the cashier, where she got three-thousand dollars' worth of chips, she sat at one of the roulette tables, ignoring Farley's mockful smirk. Screw that filthy asshole; he'd never be more than an idiot who had to threaten women to get laid, and even so, he wasn't scoring much. But undoubtedly his right hand worked wonders for him in his lonely moments, in the staff men's room.

"Madame?" the croupier called her elegantly to attention, although he knew her well. He was respectful and kind. Otherwise, she would've been tempted to take her gambling elsewhere, to another casino where people didn't know who she was.

She put some chips on the table.

"One thousand, thirteen, black," the croupier announced.

Another gambler placed a chip on the table.

"Five hundred, twenty-one, red. *Les jeux sont faits, rien ne va plus,*" he announced, no more bets, and the ball started spinning against the wheel. As it slowed, it bounced around a little, then settled on the number thirteen.

"Thirteen. Madame wins," he announced, his smile genuine. "Payout is thirty-five thousand dollars," he added, pushing a small tray filled with chips her way.

That was more like it. Lady Luck was beginning to smile her way. As for Paul... screw him too. He'd soon be sorry, the cheating son of a bitch. She smiled, a smile loaded with the promise of vengeance, of ending the game her way.

From across the room, a man stared at her intensely, seated casually in a lounge chair. She caught his heated gaze right when she was thinking of him, of how to make him pay, and that startled her, as if the man had read her mind.

Paul.

She held his fiery stare, feeling the electricity in the air, seeing it sparkle. She bit her lower lip provocatively and batted her long eyelashes a couple of times. He clenched his jaw and her smile bloomed, while her teeth still pressed against her lower lip, her head tilted forward, studying her effect on him.

He fidgeted in his seat, a sure sign her charms were starting to have a physical effect on him. Good.

"Seven. Red wins," she heard the croupier announce in the background, but she didn't care anymore, her eyes locked in a remote seduction game with Paul. She eventually nodded, smiled once more in his direction, then collected her chips and headed for the cashier, while Paul left the gaming room using the main entrance.

While she waited for the cashier to count the chips, a man approached her in a brisk walk, and then grabbed her arm, forcing her to turn and face him. She barely recognized him dressed like that, in simple jeans and a golf shirt, and wearing a fifties Fedora.

"Why?" the man asked, and she winced under his strong grip.

"Ellis, let me go," she said, trying to free her arm from the man's grip.

"Why did you kill her? What did she ever do to you?" he said in a tearful voice, pulling her to the side, where the cashier couldn't hear them. "She only meant to help you, to keep you safe. Do you know what someone like Paul could do to you if he found out what you're doing?"

"I didn't kill her, I swear," she said between tears of frustration and pain.

Great... Now Ellis knew everything, because stupid, self-righteous Crystal couldn't keep her big mouth shut. She should've known better; those billionaires stuck together and helped one another, no matter what. Girls like her meant nothing when the big boys closed ranks. What if Ellis told Paul about it?

A wave of weakness rippled through her body as fear turned her blood into frozen sludge. "I didn't do it, Ellis," she repeated, her words weak, carried on a trembling breath.

"I don't believe you," he replied, letting go of her arm with a shove. "Who else? There was no one else in her life; just you and me."

"And I swear I didn't kill her," she said, looking him straight in the eye. "You have to believe me. She was my friend."

"Is there a problem here?" one of the floor security officers asked, approaching them quickly. They must've seen the loaded interaction on video, or maybe the cashier had called him. The cashiers hated any sign of turbulence next to their windows, especially when customers carried large amounts of cash on them.

"No, there's no problem," Ellis replied and quickly walked away, keeping his head down under the brown Fedora.

She breathed, leaning against the cashier's counter for support, because her knees were unexpectedly weak. She thought of sitting in one of those large armchairs for a while until she felt better, but she couldn't be late. Paul was waiting for her outside, and she couldn't afford to make him angry. Not now, when she realized he might know what she'd done, courtesy of that dead, rotting bitch and her big mouth.

Ripping through her gut with renewed anxiety, memories flooded her mind. She recalled Paul's burning look, his intensity, the gazes she'd assumed were only loaded with desire. From that distance, could she be sure it wasn't something else? If he knew what she'd done, she was as good as dead.

She somehow found the strength to breathe deeply and walk toward the exit, shoving the thirty-five-thousand-dollar check in her purse. When she stepped onto the porte-cochère, gripping the skirt of the floor-length gown in her hand, a long, black, deeply tinted limo pulled up at the curb. She opened the door and climbed in.

Before she could close the heavy limo door behind her, one of the parking valets grinned when he heard a man's sultry voice saying to her, "You drive me crazy, baby... What the hell are you doing to me?"

30

EXTRACURRICULAR

As I usually did on such occasions, I was a little concerned TwoCent might recognize me. Earlier that day, we were in the same courtroom together, albeit I was dressed as any of the thousands of cops out there: light-blue shirt, navy slacks, my hair in a tight bun, a pair of Ray-Ban Aviators on my face. A far cry from the hot chick in the little black dress and Zanottis who walked down TwoCent's street, carefully casing the place. Chances were he wouldn't recognize me, not tonight, after our conversation, not even tomorrow, if we happened to run into each other at the courthouse. I looked nothing like the cop I was during the daytime and, on nights like these, I almost didn't recognize myself.

Okay, the heels were a mistake, but they went well with the part I had to play.

I didn't want to approach TwoCent's house from the street, risk tripping a sensor and have emergency lights go on, while I was in plain view. Instead, I entered the backyard of the house behind TwoCent's crib and spent some time observing. Not a sound from anywhere, not a light turned on, not a single movement. I'd walked barefoot the entire distance from where I'd left my car, on a parallel street where the sodium lamp was broken and under a big tree it was pitch black. There, my white Toyota didn't stand out one bit, tucked between the usual residents who parked at the curb, its rear plate safely shielded from view.

Now, staring at a six-foot concrete wall I had to climb to get inside TwoCent's backyard, I didn't have many options. If my plan failed, in a few short hours I'd have to take the stand and, with a few fateful words, bring my career and Holt's to an abrupt end, or go to prison for perjury. Neither scenario worked well for me.

I threw the Zanottis over the wall and they landed without making noise, most likely on a patch of grass. I tied my hair in a loose knot, to keep it from getting caught in the rugged masonry, then I lifted my skirt all the way up, so I could move freely. Good thing no one was watching, or they'd have a show to remember.

I tried to grab the upper edge of the wall to pull myself up, but I couldn't reach it without doing some real damage to my dress, the fine fabric an easy prey for the rough, gritty finish of the wall.

"Bollocks," I whispered, letting go of the wall's edge and rubbing my hands together to clear the dust and the rubble that had stuck to my skin. "Infinite, endless, massive, bloody bollocks."

I looked around, trying to find another solution to get over the wall, some object I could use as a stepladder, anything. The perfectly maintained yard didn't offer such opportunities, unless I was willing to leave the shaded areas behind the trees and step into the lights surrounding the pool, to grab one of the lounge chairs. A bad idea.

I stopped for a moment, thinking hard. Sure, I could take the main street and approach the property directly, but even if Fletcher could somehow cut the proximity lights on TwoCent's home, there was no guarantee I wouldn't trip a neighbor's lights, maybe get caught on their surveillance camera, and that would be a disaster, especially if things went south and an investigation followed.

I heard a sound, nothing other than some leaves rustling in the yard next door, but I froze. I looked hard but couldn't see anything, and I wanted to kick myself for leaving my thermal imaging camera at home, a tiny device that worked with my phone and found the heat signature of any warm-blooded creature in the dark.

After a few seconds of silence and not seeing anything, I breathed; maybe it was some animal, a cat, or maybe a rat. The thought of a rat made me smile; maybe that would help me get over the wall quicker. If I saw one at my feet, I'd fly over without so much as touching the edge.

One option was to ruin the dress I was wearing, damage it beyond repair. Another option was to risk a few scratches and bruises, but it seemed like the logical thing to do. I drew air into my lungs to conjure some courage and took off my dress with one quick move, pulling it over my head. Then I hung it over the wall as gently as I could, concerned that any inch of contact with the coarse surface would cause irreparable pilling to the fine fabric.

I heard a dog barking angrily in the house behind me. A light went on and a man's voice saying groggily, "All right, shut up already, we're going. Good boy, yeah, let's go."

I didn't have much time, nor could I back away anymore. I was trapped.

I grabbed the edge of the wall and pulled myself up, pushing with my toes and the soles of my feet against the rugged surface, and managed to throw myself over the barrier just as the dog was let outside. It came rushing toward me, raising hell, but by the time it reached the wall, I'd already taken my dress from the ledge and put it back on.

"What the hell are you chasing?" the man muttered, his low, raspy voice so close to me I was startled.

I stayed in place, not breathing, standing close against the cold wall, and listened to the dog bark angrily, inches away from me, on the other side. Eventually, the owner got tired of the noise and took the dog inside while it still barked, desperately trying to get at me.

It took a few minutes for my heart rate to drop back to a relatively normal level after the dog went away. I listened some more, and the neighborhood seemed as fast asleep as it had been before Cujo had done its number.

It was three in the morning, when sleep is the sweetest. It was time to move.

I picked up my shoes from the grass and put them on. I pulled out the burner phone from my bra and texted Fletcher.

"Still no guests for tonight?" my message said.

A quiet vibration alerted me of his reply. "No, he's sound asleep, and so was I." A sad-faced emoji ended the message.

"You got access to the security system?" I asked.

"Taking the fifth," came the answer.

"Is the system armed right now?"

"Yup."

"Could you please change that?"

I held my breath, hoping, praying, willing it to happen. Last thing I needed was an alarm going off and cops showing up.

Finally, the phone vibrated. "It's done. Ping me when you need me to arm it again."

"You're the best," I texted back and slid the phone back inside the left cup of my bra.

I sneaked carefully alongside the house and found the side entrance. I tried it gently, but it was locked. Without skipping a beat, I pulled out the lock picking kit from my right cup and worked the lock in under twenty seconds; not a personal best, but still impressive.

I took one last look around and listened intently for a few seconds, still having an uneasy feeling that I wasn't alone, that someone was watching. I pulled out my Sig and went inside.

31

BACKFIRE

Roxanne let Paul's hands guide her body and she sat on the bed, smiling with her mouth slightly open while he kneeled in front of her, inhaling her fresh scent. She'd put a touch of pheromone perfume on her body, and it seemed to work well. She wore a silk, burgundy nightdress she'd put on earlier, while she had him wait for her to get into something more comfortable, as she liked to call it, when she was getting him taut, ready, eager with anticipation, burning with desire.

She'd tied the satin sash around her waist with a double knot, knowing it would give him trouble untying it and increase his eagerness. She'd kept on her high heels, although she'd made him wait while she took a shower, getting ready for the night ahead, but he didn't seem to mind, seeing how he caressed her tense calves.

She relaxed under his warm hands, relishing their exploration of her body, while her eyes stayed firmly open and locked on his. Waves of memories came crushing in and for a moment she looked away, as if afraid he'd see into the depths of her dark soul.

She'd met him only three months ago, after having tried to cross his path for a while. At first, she didn't like him too much, despite his strong appearance, his elegant, attractive features, and his raven black hair. She had to force herself to keep her eyes open when they were making love. He was but a stranger, a powerful, intimidating, fierce stranger with such intensity in everything he did or said that she was afraid of him, although he never hurt her nor said a harsh word to her. But she'd seen him in the presence of others and knew what he was capable of. She knew how his staff trembled in front of him, and for good reason; Paul Steele wasn't a forgiving man. He was passionate in everything he did, ambitious, a fighter who'd never lost a battle in his entire existence.

Before she'd taken him to bed the first time, she'd researched him thoroughly, afraid of what she might discover. Although his father had built the Scala, Paul was a self-made billionaire. When he took over the hotel from his dad, the place was in shambles, about to file for bankruptcy, and his father fighting for his life after a heart attack. But then the recent MBA graduate took the reins and turned the place around swiftly, merciless with anyone who didn't obey his orders, didn't do their jobs, or didn't give their absolute best every day.

By the time he'd turned thirty-five, the hotel was debt-free. When he celebrated his fortieth birthday, Forbes listed his assets as exceeding one billion dollars. But he didn't stop there; he always wanted more, because what he had was never enough.

Merciless.

That was the word that best described Paul's disposition if anyone did wrong by him, as substantiated by the famous team of enforcers he kept on payroll, tasked to beat the thought of cheating, counting cards, or stealing out of anyone thinking it in any way, shape, or form. Since Paul had taken over the Scala, card-counting gamblers, pickpockets, and crooks of all flavors had moved their business elsewhere, afraid for their lives and limbs.

That was the man she loved, the man who'd easily kill her if he ever found out what she'd done.

She remembered their first night together like it was yesterday. Although she'd known exactly what she was doing, she was also afraid of him, afraid he'd see right through her, and then the enforcers would come calling. She had to fight the urge to close her eyes during the most intimate moments of their first encounter. Back then she didn't care; she wanted their eyes to connect during his climax so that their souls would connect, so that his ecstasy would forever be associated with her blue irises, looking at her, feeling, absorbing her love.

It had been a great strategy; it had worked wonders. Before long, Paul Steele was in love with her, craving her body like the drugs she was covered in, addicted to her in more ways than he knew.

Only her strategy had backfired; she had fallen for him hard, with everything she had, with every fiber of her being. There was no turning back from that ledge, and no closing her eyes now, during their torrid nights, because she couldn't dream of not looking into the dark abysses of his black irises while she found her bliss in his arms.

But now her elation was poisoned with the green venom of jealousy. His hands had touched Crystal's breast, had grabbed the straps of her bra as if he'd done it many times before, and maybe he had. Despite looking at Paul's elegant features and aquiline nose as he caressed her heated body, all Roxanne could see were the images she'd witnessed on that horrible video, forever burned into her memory.

Her so-called best friend hadn't shied away from his touch, the conniving, little bitch.

If she could grab Crystal and shake her, beat her to a pulp or whatever she needed to do to make her tell the truth, she'd do it. If only she could bring her back, now that she needed answers so badly, before losing her mind completely. But Crystal was gone forever, and the thought of her death no longer brought relief to her scarred, guilty soul.

How long had their relationship been going on? How did it start? Did he see Crystal dance when he'd come looking for her, like he'd done earlier? Had his lustful eyes touched and craved Crystal's body? He was a power freak used to taking what he wanted, and once he wanted something, there was no stopping him.

Her mind kept spinning, descending farther and farther into the bottomless, poisoned well of doubt. She was losing her mind, one moment at a time, one unanswered question after another.

Paul kissed her lips hungrily, tasting her, possessing her in ways that dissolved her anger, leaving her molten, desperate for his touch. Then he nuzzled her hair and whispered in her ear, "I love you, baby. I'm crazy about you."

If she could only believe those words again.

The thought of confronting him was appealing, a dire need, like the thought of cold water after a stroll through the desert, and for a moment she pulled herself away from him, ready to pounce with her first question. But her body and mind betrayed her; she was too weak, too much in love, too afraid she was going to lose him. What if she made him angry with her suspicions, and he just up and left? There would be a time for the truth, maybe, but that time wasn't now. Not when her heart thumped, fueled by her deep desire for his touch, not when she craved him just as badly as he did her.

He wrapped his arms around her, kissing every inch of her neck, then peeled off the smooth silk and let it fall at their feet. Then she lay on the bed, waiting, her eyes half open, fixated on his.

She was ready for him.

He made quick work of getting rid of his clothes and dropped to his knees in front of her. He drew close to her with an impulsive move and a smile filled with promises and anticipation, but the sharp heel of her shoe scraped against his thigh, leaving blood in its trail.

She cringed, afraid she'd hurt him, terrified she'd made him angry. Instead, he moaned and closed his eyes for a moment, lost in the feeling. She opened her eyes widely, surprised, frowning a little, while her rage for his betrayal rekindled, set off by the sight and smell of blood. Her nostrils flared.

Maybe there was another way he could pay for what he'd done.

Aroused like never before, she squealed with delight as she thrust both her heels against his thighs, arching her body to meet his.

32

CONVERSATION

I entered TwoCent's home feeling my way in the dark, then turned on a small flashlight as soon as I closed the door behind me. The house was huge, a monument to the worst taste money can buy, where rapper décor met traditional, conservative architecture in a deathly collision where common sense had succumbed.

Wrought iron chandeliers with Bohemian crystal fringes hung over vaulted rooms furnished in contemporary, lounge-style couches and armchairs in fine Italian leather, while the walls hosted a vast array of street-quality prints of naked women. One wall featured a couple of platinum records. Most of the furniture had been picked up as separate pieces in different styles, colors, and finishes, and no room had a theme of any kind, other than lots of money paying for lots of things.

In the living room, on the coffee table, I found a gun and some dope, lined up nicely and ready to be snorted. I grabbed the gun with two fingers and slid it under the sofa, out of reach if things got ugly and we'd end up downstairs, clenched in some fight.

Then I continued my search.

His poor taste had stopped short of his digital equipment. His electronics were top shelf, all well-chosen, only brand names I recognized. His TV was the biggest I'd ever seen, complemented by a surround sound system, a seven-speaker Bose. It could've easily been used in a small theater, and I had to get closer to see the brand, a name I'd only heard of before, because none of the things in that house were affordable on a cop's salary, especially one who was a closet fashionista like myself.

I walked slowly, careful not to let my heels clack on the shiny marble of his floors, and checked every room, weapon in hand, making sure no one was there to surprise me. I laughed quietly seeing that he had a relatively large, octagonal room dedicated entirely to a fish tank; other than the custom-made vessel filled with many colorful, exotic fish and the Pirates of the Caribbean décor, the room had only leather benches along the walls and LED projectors on the ceiling, sending colored beams of lights to showcase the aquarium.

After all, TwoCent was, first and foremost, a bachelor and a kid who happened to have more money than he knew what to do with.

Satisfied that the ground floor held no surprises, I made for the bar and mixed Alizé and cognac in equal parts, then found a rocks glass in one of the many cupboards. Extracting some ice silently posed some issues and gave me a start, because I had to open the massive fridge door and it chimed. The alternative was to use the door ice dispenser, but those usually made more noise than a compacting garbage truck.

Satisfied with the drink in my hand, I holstered my weapon and climbed up the stairs, heading for TwoCent's bedroom. It wasn't difficult to find, although the second floor was as vast as the ground floor, but his snoring guided me like some kind of thunderous beacon.

Even before I reached the bedroom where the throated snorts were coming from, I sensed the smell, a terrible stench of metabolized alcohol, sweat, and junkie grime.

"Ugh," I whispered with disgust, covering my mouth and stopping for a moment, trying to give my nose time to get used to the foul odor before I had to fake a big, wide smile.

I entered the bedroom and found TwoCent lying on his back, fast asleep. He'd fallen over the covers, still wearing his baggy jeans and an unbuttoned shirt over a sleeveless undershirt. The bed had been made neatly and the bedroom was unexpectedly tidy; he probably had house help.

I stepped out in the hallway and turned on the light, so only an indirect light came into the bedroom. It was all for the best if he couldn't see me that clearly. I was planning to stand against the light, the contour of my body clearly visible and appetizing, but my face completely in the dark.

I breathed, getting ready for what I was about to do, putting myself in character, as I'd learn ages ago, in the acting classes I took in London. Then I pushed his foot with the tip of my shoe.

He didn't even stop snoring or skip the beat of it. I pushed again, harder, and called out. "Hey."

He stopped snoring and started turning on his side, but I called again, shouting, "Yo, wake up. I got something for you."

It worked. He nearly jumped out of his skin, scrambling to sit on the side of the bed, squinting and rubbing his eyes amid a slew of curses that had one overused word in common.

"Wha—? Who the fuck are you?"

"Care for some hair of the dog?" I asked as I handed him the drink. "Thug Passion, yeah?"

"Uh-huh," he said, taking a couple of thirsty gulps. He was dehydrated from the solo party he'd pulled the night before. "How d'ya know?" he asked, mumbling the words and setting the glass down on his night table.

"I know things, gangsta'," I replied, smiling widely and shifting my weight from one foot to the other, an opportunity to sway my hips a little and make him drool.

"How come you're in here? I got an alarm," he said, sounding more and more lucid as he continued to wake up, but at the same time, more confused.

I laughed, a quick laugh that didn't promise anything good. I let that laugh disappear and replaced it with an expression of seriousness. "Digger sent me," I said, hoping the well-documented grip that his former, more experienced cell mate had over him was still a fact.

"Digger? Why? What's up?"

His reaction told me I wasn't wrong. When he said Digger's name, his voice climbed at least two tones higher, and an expression of concern, fear, took over his alcohol-swollen features.

"He's hearing that you're about to take the fall for a murder you haven't done," I said calmly, as if I were there as his best friend. "He sent me to help. Take care of things, if you know what I mean."

"You?" he reacted, licking his dry, cracked lips. "How the hell can a broad like you help?"

"I got skills. That's why Digger sent me and not some sorry-ass homie," I said seriously, then I stayed quiet, leaving him enough time to process.

"What do you mean, I'm about to take the fall?" he finally asked the right question. "*They're about* to drop the case, that's what *they're about* to do. Tomorrow we'll bury the pig who busted me, and then I'm out. Something about the gun, and how they won't be able to use it in the trial."

"That's not what Digger's hearing," I said just as calmly, although hearing the references to the upcoming testimony sent shivers down my spine.

The name I was so casually throwing around was that of a man serving multiple life sentences, mainly for burying people while they still drew breath. His reach, even outside the prison walls, was incontestable, worthy of all respect among those who walked on the wrong side of the line, whether they walked on the inside or outside, on the streets. No one who'd ever crossed him had lived to tell the story; most of them vanished without a trace, believed to be rotting in a shallow grave somewhere.

Through a touch of fate, Digger had been TwoCent's cellmate and protector, taking the singer under his wing during his first stint behind bars. Now all I needed to do was convince that hungover moron he was in danger of being found guilty in court, and that only Digger could bail him out, like he'd done countless times while he was on the inside.

He didn't disappoint.

"What's he hearing?" he asked, wringing his hands. His forehead was scrunched together under the pressure of fear bordering on panic, elevated by alcohol fumes and the remnants of who knows what white powder was on his downstairs coffee table.

I looked at him seriously, as if terribly concerned. "The word out there is that tomorrow's testimony will bring some new evidence about that gun. That they'll have enough to fry you." I let that fact sink for a moment, then added, "All that for a deed you didn't even do. Digger isn't too happy about that."

"About what?" he said in a raspy, strangled voice.

"You stole cred for wasting that cop, Park, and it was some other cat's street cred. You know how Digger is, he hates a liar, but he and you go way back, and he's willing to forgive you. He still wants to whup your ass, though."

TwoCent scratched his shaved scalp, then ran his fingers over his stubble.

"What other cat? Who's sayin' shit about me?"

I shrugged, keeping on with the act. I'd started living it, breathing it, feeling as if I really were Digger's envoy. "He isn't talking about you, man. I don't believe he knows you exist," I said casually, looking to poke his oversized ego. "He's saying *he* killed that cop, and Digger believes him."

"Why would Digger believe that piece of shit?" TwoCent asked, then quickly downed all the booze left in his glass. "He knows me, he knows I ain't lyin' about important things like that."

"He thinks you don't have the stones, man," I said, then smiled and raised my hands to pacify him. "Don't get me wrong, I believe you do have them, but Digger... well, you know Digger. It takes some real stones to impress him."

TwoCent sprung to his feet and walked right past me, on his way to the living room. I didn't want to move to a better lit area. I needed him unable to recognize me in the future, and for that, he had to stay put.

Calmly, I dove my hand inside my cleavage and pulled my gun, aiming it at his chest. "Sit your ass down, homie."

"Whoa," he said, freezing in place. Then he reached behind his back, but his hand came empty. He'd left his gun downstairs, on the coffee table, right next to the partially snorted lines of snow. "You crazy or something, bitch?"

"Think of me as Digger's extension on the outside, doing his bidding. I'm to decide whether to believe you and help you beat the rap tomorrow or rid the world of a spineless liar who takes other people's street cred."

He sat back on the bed, his eyes rounded in disbelief. "How did you get in here, again?"

"I'm asking the questions," I replied. "Why should Digger believe you, and not his new best bud?"

"I never lied to Digger in, like, never, I swear to God," he said, and I smiled with condescension. "*I* popped that cop, Detective Park. It was me, no one else. He was circling my act, looking to bust me and my homies for possession and some other shit. I didn't want to go back to the joint, not now, when I'm making shitloads of money."

I paused for a moment, then sighed. "I don't believe you. Tell me how you did it."

"He came by the club, asking questions. I had my homies yap with him until he went to the can, then I cornered him in there, popped two in his chest. No one else knows he got offed in the toilet, with his dick in his hand. That proves it, doesn't it?"

I paused again, a good second. "I don't know, man, I still don't see you doing all that. I think you're just talking the talk."

"Really?" he snapped, wanting to get on his feet again, but I gestured with the gun and he cursed, resigned to continue sitting where he was told. "That cop wasn't even the first pig I whacked. I offed two more, two dumb patrolmen three years ago, near the Owens overpass."

"So you say," I laughed in disbelief. "Who can say that it's true, after all this time?"

"I didn't use the same gun, 'cause I ain't stupid, but I used the same *brand* of gun, you feel me? I'm a sucker for a nine mil Smith & Wesson M2.0. Digger can ask around; he'll see I'm telling the truth."

"Well, I don't know, really," I said, shaking my head for effect. "I'll have to ask Digger what he thinks."

"Ask Digger? What do you mean, ask Digger, when I'm due in court in five hours, bitch?"

"I don't know that I can believe you, man, that's all. No hard feelings, nothing personal."

"I swear I popped them, all three of them, I swear it on my life!"

There it was, everything I'd come to hear from TwoCent's own lips. I was convinced; now I could pull the curtain on our little show.

"Okay, all right, I believe you," I said, and he stood again. I took a step back, gun still in hand.

"So? What are you going to do for me, huh?"

"Oh, I'll put your lights out," I said, then whacked him in the head with my gun.

He fell with a loud thud, but then squirmed a little. He was massive and thick-skulled, while my piece was a subcompact, light and small. I hit him again with the butt of the weapon, and he stopped moving.

I killed all the lights and mostly left everything just the way I'd found it. Downstairs, I fished his gun from under the sofa and put it back on the table, next to the dope, then left the same way I'd come in, through the side door.

As soon as I got to my car, I drove out of that neighborhood, still under that strange feeling that someone was watching every move I made. But who? I frequently checked my rearview mirror and changed direction and saw no one. Eventually, I pulled into the parking lot of a nonstop pharmacy and got down to business.

First, I texted Fletcher to tell him he could arm TwoCent's alarm system, then I fired up my personal laptop; it was time for some sound editing.

The recording wasn't top notch; I could've done better with more expensive equipment. But what I had would serve its purpose, and the pauses I took each time before speaking made it easy for me to edit my voice out of the conversation, leaving only the interesting parts.

His confession sounded natural, uncoerced, albeit a little emotional, but it was still going to work. As for my voice, I laughed a little hearing myself talk in street lingo with my sophisticated British accent, a clash of cultures. Good thing I got to cut those pieces off, although I was quite proud of myself and my performance; a solid eight and a half, maybe a nine.

When I was done editing the recording, I listened to it again to make sure it didn't include a single hint of my voice, then sent it as a text message attachment to all the players: TwoCent; his son-of-a-bitch attorney, Volo; and Gully, the ADA.

Then I went straight home; it had been a long day, and another one was about to start, just as long. I needed to get some sleep.

33

DEAL

When I woke, the sun was up, sending darts of light between the seams of the thick, opaque curtains of my living room. I'd never made it upstairs the night before; I'd kicked my shoes off and dropped on the couch, just like the previous night when Anne was sleeping in the master bedroom.

I wasn't sure, but it must've been a noise that woke me. I jumped to my feet, abruptly immersed in anxiety; was I already late for court? Why hadn't anyone called yet? Then I heard knocks on the door, loud, persistent. I pulled open a curtain and peeked through the sheers, immediately recognizing the man carrying a Starbucks tray with two large cups.

Holt.

In a frenzy, I looked around, evaluating the room. I rushed to get rid of the two weapons I'd abandoned on my kitchen counter, unceremoniously sliding them in the cutlery drawer.

"In a minute," I shouted, as I rushed to grab the shoes and dress from the floor and shove them into the pantry. I put on a shirt and some pants, whatever was handy, not really caring I'd worn them the entire day before.

I unlocked the door, a little out of breath but smiling. Holt came in, sizing me up from head to toe, unspoken questions in his eyes. It took every ounce of willpower I had not to avoid his scrutinizing glance.

"Come on, we're going to be late for court," he said, still looking at me as if I were one of his suspects.

I smiled, looking at him straight as if nothing was wrong. It wasn't difficult to smile, because I liked what I saw.

He was dressed sharply in a navy suit and light-blue shirt, matched with a pinstriped navy and white tie. By contrast, I needed work, and lots of it. My hair was a mess, and yesterday's makeup was smudged badly after staining the couch pillows.

He looked at me with laughter in his eyes, but also something else I'd seen before but couldn't pinpoint, then he veered his eyes toward the sofa. It was visibly slept on; he didn't need to ask.

"Anne still with you?"

"Nah," I replied, fidgeting, looking for my phone. I remembered I'd left both my phones in the microwave the night before; that was going to raise an eyebrow. Casually, I opened the oven and took them both out.

"That's where you keep 'em?" he asked, his grin wider.

"Not always. Only when they piss me off and won't let me sleep."

"Uh-huh," he said, in the tone of voice a parent uses when he hears his child tell a lie.

Damn him… he was good, and he was always there, not leaving me much room to maneuver. Not at all ideal, considering my after-hours hobby.

I checked the time; it was seven-forty-five, and I needed to start getting ready for court. I was hoping I wouldn't have to testify, but unless I heard otherwise, I had to assume I was still due to take the stand at precisely nine AM. Feeling anxious and wondering why I had no news yet, I grabbed the cup he'd placed on the dining room table for me and tasted the green tea; it was just right, and the hot liquid soothed my taut nerves as it made its way down my parched, constricted throat.

Had something gone wrong? Was I about to step into a trap, once I took that stand? Did TwoCent recognize me? Maybe he had video surveillance at the house, recordings that Fletcher couldn't remove, and he knew who I was by now. Maybe I was going to hear police sirens coming to pick me up in a few minutes. Maybe I'd totally screwed up and was about to take my partner down with me.

I managed to smile and thank him without a word, then set the cup down. "Will you be okay by yourself until I get dressed?"

"Sure," he replied, taking a seat on the couch. "I could always come upstairs and keep you company while you do that," he added in a sultry voice that sent instant butterflies to my abdomen. Against all logic I was tempted, but I found the strength to say no.

I went upstairs and took a quick shower, while anxiety did a number on me, swirling millions of questions in my head, making me relive every moment of the night before, analyzing it, wondering what could've gone wrong. I'd expected to find a voicemail canceling my court appearance, but there was no message.

Only moments after running the water, I heard music playing downstairs, possibly coming from the TV. I finished the shower as fast as I could, put on fresh makeup and got dressed, choosing a spiffy, black pantsuit with a light-beige, silk blouse and a fine, gold necklace with matching studs.

I rushed downstairs, black pumps in one hand and a matching purse in the other, but halfway through the steps the smell of fresh omelet and toast filled my nostrils. I heard my stomach growling; the night before I'd been too tired to eat. But then I remembered where I'd hid the guns, a fraction of a second before I saw them neatly laid on the counter.

Ah, bloody hell.

I stopped midstep, short of climbing down the last two steps.

"That's where you keep them?" Holt gestured to the guns, smiling innocently.

The bastard.

"Anne was staying here, remember?" I replied calmly, but then I saw my dress folded carefully on the armchair and the Zanottis by the door. Of course, he'd run into those when he took the toaster out of the pantry.

Damn. I wasn't going to explain that away.

Fortunately, he didn't ask, although he noticed my unguarded stare when I was gawking at the dress. He just pretended to focus on setting the table for us, and I was grateful for that, trying really hard to ignore the obvious question that gnawed at the corners of my mind. How much did Holt really know, if anything, about last night? Why was he here today?

I'd only taken a couple of mouthfuls of what had to be the world's best omelet, when Holt's phone rang.

"Ah, it's Gully," he said to me and took the call on speaker.

"Good morning," Holt said, "what's up?"

"Something weird happened," Gully said, and I breathed with ease as I could hear the excitement in his voice. "TwoCent took the plea, and we have a taped confession too."

"What plea? What do you mean, we have a taped confession?" Holt asked frowning, but shot me a quick glance I could've sworn was filled with admiration. Somehow, that only made me worry more.

"Someone sent it anonymously to my cell phone," Gully replied, "from a burner phone that's no longer pinging active."

Holt's lips stretched into a wide grin that brought warmth to his eyes while looking at me. "So, no court today?"

"Nope, you got your day back, Detective. Just thank Baxter for me, will you?"

I froze, while Holt's frown rematerialized.

"What for?" he asked.

"For her idea to put a plea on the table," the ADA replied. "I didn't expect it to, but it worked. Makes me wonder, with that confession coming into play when it did, how come she…"

He let his words trail off, while I stopped breathing.

"Yes?" Holt said, encouraging him to continue, while his frown deepened.

"No, it's nothing, it must be a coincidence," Gully replied. "I guess sometimes we win these things because we're the good guys, right?"

"That you are, Gully, great job putting that slime bag away for good," I heard Holt say, while I walked to the window and stared outside at the sunshine-filled street, letting my thoughts run free. At some point Gully could start asking some uncomfortable questions. At some point I could be asked to explain why I had suggested the plea, and my previous answer would not hold anymore. And maybe TwoCent, after rejoining his old friend Digger in prison and exchanging notes, might start putting two and two together and come after me. But neither of those things were going to happen today.

Today I had a killer to catch.

And if any of those things were ever going to happen, I'd deal with them then, just as I'd dealt with good, old TwoCent.

When I turned around, I caught Holt's eyes on me, a mix of worry and desire that made me uncomfortable. It was as if he was able to read into the depths of my mind and resonate with me in everything I did and thought and felt, although he didn't know half of what was going on.

I smiled at him from across the room and said jokingly, "Whew, we're off the hook."

"Yeah," he said, pushing my plate across the counter toward me. "Come on, finish your food."

I didn't need another invitation. I grabbed the fork and wolfed the food while standing and washed it down with the rest of the green tea, while trying to force the persistent smile off my face. After the exhilaration of the previous day, after the thrill of the hunt, now I was so relieved I felt like celebrating. Having Holt just two feet away made me smile incessantly, while he surely wondered what was going on in my head. I knew I couldn't make the same mistake again and shag my partner, but I could at least think about it, right? Dream about it just a little?

Wrong. In my personal history there were plenty of mistakes made just because I'd been thinking of things. It was time to get busy and wipe that smirk off my face.

"Let's catch us a killer," I challenged Holt, cleaning my plate with the last piece of toast. "What do you say?"

"As we're all dressed up with nowhere to go," Holt offered, "let's talk to this Paul Steele, and then we can ask Ellis MacPherson a few questions. It's time to meet the men in Crystal's life. We have an opportunity to rub elbows with Las Vegas royalty, and you sure look the part," he added with one of his boyish grins.

I laughed. "Dream on. Do you think they'll talk to us?"

34

PAUL

The corporate office of the Scala Hotel and Casino was located in the downtown business district, a short drive north from the hotel on South Las Vegas Boulevard, then east on Fremont. The building, elegant and modern in glass and steel, had borrowed nothing from the hotel's curved elegance; a rectangular parallelepiped, four stories of blue, tinted glass and white concrete, reminding me of the colors of rural Greek architecture, there, in the heart of the desert, thousands of miles away from the Mediterranean Sea. The windows on the top level were visibly taller, and I pointed them out to Holt.

"Penthouse, most likely. That's where we'll find our Mr. Steele."

He looked up and nodded but didn't say anything while we made a beeline for the entrance.

The vast lobby bore the Scala logo in large, silver brushed metal, slightly elevated from the wall behind and artistically emphasized with Persian blue lighting.

We showed our badges at the front desk, and the receptionist picked up the phone immediately and called upstairs.

"Mr. Steele's personal assistant will be with you shortly," she said in a professional tone of voice, displaying the whitest teeth I'd ever seen. "Please, take a seat."

Both Holt and I ignored her invitation and explored the immense lobby. The walls were decorated with framed photos illustrating the history of the Scala. A black-and-white image taken when it was being built. The founder, the old Mr. Steele, John, when he signed the incorporation documents, more than thirty years ago. An image of the Strip taken back then, barely recognizable today. The first neon sign that was installed on top of the building, during times when LED lighting wasn't even someone's dream.

"Hello," I heard a woman's voice behind me, and I turned around.

She was a short-haired, natural blonde in her mid-thirties with high cheekbones and excellent skin tone, and her smile was textbook professional. She extended her hand and I shook it, appreciating the woman's strong, no-bull grip.

"I'm Miss Gentry, Mr. Steele's personal assistant," she said. "How can I be of assistance?"

Holt shook her hand and I frowned, seeing how Miss Gentry's eyes lingered on Holt's body longer than they had on mine.

"We need to speak with Mr. Steele immediately," I said, my tone colder than I had intended, raising an eyebrow on Holt's forehead.

"Is this in regard to, um, Miss Tillman?" she asked, lowering her voice.

"Yes."

"Follow me, please," she said, leading the way to the elevators without looking behind. I had the opportunity to admire her perfect legs stepping without a trace of hesitation on her three-inch heels, despite the lobby's marble floor, glass-like shine. How did she manage that? Practice, probably, that's what it was.

She used a key to call an elevator, and one opened its doors promptly, as if it had been waiting there for her the entire time. Or maybe it had been, I had no idea.

Just as I'd suspected from the windows outside, we landed on the fourth floor and she led us straight into Mr. Steele's office, without stopping to announce his visitors; by all appearances she'd already done that, and he'd already agreed to see us.

I entered the vast, corner office expecting to find two people, Steele and one of his overpriced attorneys. Instead, it was just Paul Steele sitting behind a huge, mahogany desk, working. The windows closest to him were shaded, so that the desert sun wouldn't reflect off his two monitors. He typed quickly, an expression of deep focus on his brow, and barely acknowledged us with a wave of his hand that Miss Gentry quickly translated.

"Please, take a seat, he'll be right with you."

This time, we complied.

"Can I get you anything, coffee, water?" she offered, but I declined, while Holt didn't seem to hear her. He was studying the bookcase lining the wall behind Steele's desk, where many framed photos lined the shelves. Reading the story those photos told, Mr. Steele was a family man, a father, a dedicated son, a passionate horseback rider.

Meanwhile, I studied Paul Steele, a man worth one billion and a half. Dollars. My mind couldn't comprehend what life would be like if I had that kind of money. *Probably that's why I don't have it*, I thought, my lips twitching with the urge to laugh at myself a little.

He was intense; that was the first adjective that came to mind. He was handsome in a dangerous kind of way, emphasized by a black shirt he wore unbuttoned at the neck. When he finally looked at me, then at Holt, his gaze was dark and penetrating, ferocious. I couldn't tell what my partner was thinking, but I felt the need to challenge him, just to prove he wasn't in control, he couldn't intimidate me.

I smiled. "Thank you for seeing us on such short notice, Mr. Steele."

He turned his attention to me for a moment, then stood, plunged his hands inside his pockets and walked to the window, effectively turning his back to us. "What can I do for you, Detective?"

We stood and joined him by the window, while I recognized how easily he'd controlled our moves, our attitude. How he made us feel who was in charge without as much as a single word. That spelled power. So much for my challenge; I stood defeated.

"We need to ask you a few questions about Crystal Tillman," Holt said. "Are you familiar with that name?"

"Absolutely," he replied, looking straight at us. "I was fortunate enough not to have this kind of tragedy take place in my hotel before. As you can easily imagine, we're all stunned something like this could happen. As her employer, I've taken steps to ensure her family will have our assistance to cope with the practical aspects of this senseless tragedy."

All the right words, with the right intonation, a perfect recital of horse manure. I was starting to feel nauseated; the man was wasting our time. But I knew better than to snap at him or call him a liar to his face.

"What was your relationship with Crystal, Mr. Steele?" I asked in a neutral tone.

"I was her employer, of course," the reply came promptly.

"Nothing more?" Holt probed.

Steele frowned, an unspoken question filling the air. "Nothing more, no."

"And yet you gave her five-hundred-thousand dollars in the form of a gambling chip, Mr. Steele," I stated. "May we know why?"

He glared at me, his eyes even darker than before, even more intense. "Because I can, that's why. Do you have a problem with that?"

"Have you ever given your employees such sizeable amounts before?" Holt asked unperturbed.

He shrugged, but the gesture wasn't one of indifference; it was more violent than that. "I don't know, maybe, yeah. Why?"

He was definitely hiding something, and we were not hitting the nail on the head, not yet. I decided to change the course of my questioning and be more direct, more in his style, from what I could gather his style was.

"Were you having an affair with Crystal Tillman, sir?" I asked, the tone of my voice accusatory, not neutral.

"What? No, I wasn't," he replied, and I couldn't see any signs of deception. He was telling the truth for a change.

"She was pregnant," Holt said, then paused for a moment, waiting for a reaction that didn't come. "Did you know that?"

"N—no, I'm sorry," he replied.

This time, I wasn't so sure he'd told the truth.

"Could you please give us a sample of your DNA, to rule you out as the father?" I asked with a tiny smile.

He took two steps toward me and stopped only a few feet away, just as Holt was touching the holster of his gun. "Let me be clear here," Steele said, "hell, no."

I pressed my lips together and nodded once, my head a little tilted. "Okay, then."

"I can't believe you had the nerve to ask," he added.

"Here's what we believed happened," Holt intervened. "You got her pregnant, then paid her off to keep quiet and disappear. That's why you were threatening her."

He straightened his back and stepped behind his desk, where he picked up the receiver of his desk phone, holding it in his hand, not to his ear.

"I believe this has gone on long enough. It's time for me to call my lawyer."

"It's your right, sir," I replied coldly. "Please inform your attorney we will come back with a warrant for your DNA, and we have no interest to ask your whereabouts the night Crystal Tillman was killed."

That statement got his attention. He frowned and put the receiver back in its cradle, then sat in his chair, tilting it back slightly.

"Why is that?" he asked.

"We have video that already puts you at the scene," Holt said casually. "You had motive, you had means, and plenty of opportunity."

He didn't say anything; the way his lips pressed together told me he had a lot to say but knew better than to speak without his lawyer present.

"How did she die?" he eventually asked, still frowning.

"Ha, nice try," Holt reacted. "Please have your lawyer call us, Mr. Steele. Today." ·

He nodded once, then pressed a button on his desk phone.

Miss Gentry appeared immediately, charming and efficient and smiling.

"Please escort the detectives out of the building, and have Dennis see me ASAP."

Miss Gentry's smile died the moment she closed the door to her boss's office. Her demeanor had stiffened, and her disposition had dropped about sixty degrees in temperature. Patient and diligent, she waited until we left the building and watched us cross the street to our car from the lobby window.

"Great," I said with a long sigh as I climbed into the SUV. "He's lying, but I still don't think he's behind this whole thing, threats or no threats."

"Why? Because of that, 'poison is a woman's weapon' rule you have?" he asked, making quote signs with his fingers.

"Maybe," I replied, taking a moment to think. What was it about Steele's well-rehearsed lies that led me to believe he might be innocent? And what was he hiding? As far as I was concerned, he was still a lead, a person of interest in Crystal Tillman's death. First impressions could be deceiving, even if they were my own first impressions.

"I happen to agree," Holt said. "I don't think he'd poison someone, even if he were homicidal. He seems to be more of a straight shooter, calm, methodical. Men shoot their victims, or stab them, or strangle them if their rage is of a more personal nature."

"People with his kind of money don't kill with their own hands," I said, thinking of the pro who'd blown up the morgue and killed Erika. "I've heard of contract killers who poison their targets and are quite good at it. Might be the same guy who committed both murders, a contract killer on someone's payroll."

"The poison rule doesn't apply to them, does it?"

"A tool is a tool, right?" I said, then looked outside the window as Holt started the engine, getting ready to leave. "But Steele is definitely hiding something serious. A man like him doesn't lose it that easily."

"Lose it? He seemed in perfect control," Holt replied, turning to me, seemingly confused.

"No, not now. On the video, here," I said, pulling up the video on my phone and showing it to him.

We put our heads together to look at the small screen and Holt's proximity stirred me a little. I inhaled his scent, aftershave and a tinge of something else, maybe shower gel, all too familiar.

Baxter, get a bloody grip, I thought as I swallowed a curse and focused on the video.

"See here?" I said, and froze the recording. "See how his hand clutches Crystal's strap? See the tension in his arm, in the tendons on his neck, in his knuckles? He could've strangled Crystal right there, on that stage. That's rage, or maybe deep resentment. He definitely doesn't appear that cool-headed."

"Okay, shifting gears," he said, actually shifting into gear and peeling away from the curb. "Who would use poison?"

"The majority of deaths by poisoning have been linked to women perpetrators," I said, quoting from memory. "Anne can tell you specifics and numbers. It's in a woman's psychology to use indirect methods to achieve her goals. That's why women prefer poison, because it doesn't put actual blood on their hands. That makes them more difficult to catch."

"Huh," he reacted. "I don't know about that."

"Well, at least that was the case before the age of modern forensics and trace evidence analysis," I added with a light laugh. "Don't worry, we'll catch Crystal's killer; I promised Tina." I turned to look at Holt again. "What next? Ellis MacPherson?"

"Yes. He's my bet, you know. The lover is always your best shot. I'm thinking she cheated on him, or she broke up with him, or something. You have a rule with women killers and poison, I have a rule with sex partners. It's always the partner somehow, or the cheated wife. You'll see."

"Do you think Crystal dumped Ellis for Paul Steele? Or, the other way around?"

It wasn't the first time we'd asked that question. Questions we had plenty. Answers, not that many.

35

ELLIS

Visiting with Ellis MacPherson was not as simple as ringing the bell and showing some ID. His home, a sprawling estate on the northeast boundary of the Anthem Country Club in Henderson, had a gate meant to keep all unannounced visitors away. Holt pulled up next to the intercom and pressed the button.

"Detectives Holt and Baxter to see Mr. MacPherson," he said, holding his badge close to the camera lens pointed straight at us.

"Do you have an appointment?" a man's voice asked.

"No, we don't, but it is imperative we see Mr. MacPherson immediately."

"Please wait," the man said. The intercom crackled a bit and turned silent.

Less than a minute later, the massive gates opened, and we drove inside the property.

I'd never before had the opportunity to see one of these properties from within, and I was embarrassed at how slack-jawed I'd turned in mere seconds. The house had to be more than twelve thousand square feet, surrounded by acres of perfectly kept lawn, apparently immune to the desiccating touch of the desert. The building, a single-story contemporary design in stone and glass, took my breath away.

Holt pulled up at the main entrance and offered me a tissue.

"What's this for?" I asked as I took it hesitantly.

"You're drooling," he replied with a wink.

I punched him in the shoulder unceremoniously, then put on a straight face and approached the door, already opened by a uniformed butler.

"Please, come in, Detectives," he said, and his wasn't the same voice I'd heard on the intercom. "Mr. MacPherson will see you in the study."

He led the way and I kept up, a little distracted by the lavish décor. Even the interior walls were stacked stone, and the furniture wasn't anything I'd seen in any store. Apparently, the MacPhersons and I shopped different venues.

We entered the study, a vast room decorated with wall-to-wall bookcases and leather seating in small clusters around coffee tables. Next to the fireplace, a cello was placed on a stand with the bow neatly by its side.

Ellis MacPherson sat by the window, his forehead leaning into his left hand while his elbow rested on the windowsill. He didn't look at us when the butler announced our names.

I approached, clearing my throat quietly. "Detectives Baxter and Holt, Mr. MacPherson. Thank you for seeing us."

When he finally looked at me, I could see his eyes were hollow, as if the life that had once lit them was now extinguished, a faint memory of the past. I instantly recognized the look of unbearable grief, the aftermath of death ripping someone's heart apart.

He was a handsome, dark-haired man with sensitive, slightly feminine features and the fine, long fingers of a virtuoso. I recognized him from adverts I'd seen for his concerts, but in person he seemed fragile, distraught. It was as if I was looking at myself in the mirror after Andrew had died.

"We won't take too much of your time, Mr. MacPherson," I said in a low tone of voice. "We're investigating the murder of Crystal Tillman, whom I believe you knew?"

He nodded a couple of times, then clasped his mouth in his hand, as if stifling a sob.

"Were you having an affair with Miss Tillman?" I asked.

"Yes... no," he replied, "I was in love with Miss Tillman, not... having an affair." He stood and turned to us with that same hollow look in his eyes. "To say we were having an affair is trivial, demeaning, an insult to her memory, and I won't have it."

"Yes, but you are also a married man, aren't you, Mr. MacPherson?" Holt asked.

He turned his back to us and looked out the window, at the idyllic landscape featuring an infinity pool with green water and a rose garden surrounding the pool deck, laid out with lounge chairs covered in white and blue canvas cushions.

"Yes, I am," he eventually said, only a whisper.

"Does your wife know about your affair?" I asked, knowing that Holt was statistically correct when it came to the most common motive behind the murder of people involved in extramarital affairs. When jealousy and scorn collided, nothing seemed impossible, including homicide. Add money to that, and you've got a winner.

"I don't think she does," Mr. MacPherson replied. "I've been discreet."

I searched for something to indicate he was uneasy talking about his affair and his wife in the same sentence but saw absolutely nothing. There was nothing other than grief on Mr. MacPherson's mind; no fear, no concern, no shame.

"Were you planning to leave your wife and start a new family?" Holt asked. His voice was tense, and I couldn't tell why. He seemed irritated with Mr. MacPherson's demeanor.

"No, I wasn't," Mr. MacPherson replied. "I would never do that to my wife. She deserves better than to be dragged all over the tabloids because of me. Can you imagine the filth they'd print?"

"But you knew Crystal was pregnant, didn't you?" Holt asked.

MacPherson closed his eyes, and a tear rolled down his check. "Yes. We were going to have the baby."

"I am sorry for your losses," I said.

"Thank you," he replied so faintly I could barely hear him.

"How did you and Crystal meet?" Holt asked.

A shadow of a smile fluttered on his lips. "It was after one of my concerts at the Scala. I stopped to get a cup of coffee in the lobby café and heard this girl saying she hated my music. She spoke passionately about how classical music was doomed, finished, and people needed to freshen up. Her girlfriends spotted me and they found it amusing to let Crystal continue her negative critique, as I listened from the sideline, aghast. But when our eyes met, I stood there, mesmerized. She was the most beautiful woman I'd ever seen; I couldn't walk away. She apologized, and then she gave me the honor of accepting an invitation to dinner, where I did my best to plead the cause of classical music."

"When was that?" I asked, trying to put together a timeline in my mind, wondering how soon after Crystal had started working at the Scala she'd met him. Was she targeting him? She wouldn't be the first ambitious, beautiful girl who'd do anything to land the right sugar daddy.

"Six months and four days ago," he said with a sad smile that quickly vanished. "We celebrated last Saturday."

"Was that the last time you saw her?"

"Yes."

"How about Sunday, before she died?"

He frowned, as if wondering why I was insisting. "No. I had a concert last Sunday at the Philharmonic."

"Your wife, she must've suspected something, right?" I asked. "Women have an instinct for that kind of thing."

"Maybe," he replied, "I don't know."

How could someone be so unfazed about their affair being exposed to their spouse? Not something I'd seen before. I'd encountered threats with force if I were to disclose liaisons uncovered during murder investigations. I'd run into screaming, sobbing wives, imploring, groveling men, even a couple of bribe attempts, not to tell the spouse. But I'd never encountered a complete and transparent indifference.

It was time to change the approach.

"Do you know of anyone who might have killed Crystal? Someone with an axe to grind?"

He stared out the window for another moment before he spoke. "She had a roommate, Roxanne."

"Yes," I encouraged him.

"The two of them got into a fight recently, and things were turning sour between them. I thought it was just girls being girls, but Crystal told me she wanted to move out of the house they shared."

"When was that?" I asked. Finally, a piece of information that could resemble a lead.

"Um, about two weeks ago, I think," he said, and I nodded, waiting for him to continue.

But he didn't; he stopped talking as if saying even that much had taken all the strength from him.

"Then, what happened?" I asked gently, after exchanging a quick glance with Holt.

"Nothing," he replied, one bitter word carried on a long sigh filled with pain. "I offered to help, to put her in one of our corporate apartments, but she wouldn't hear of it. She was proud, an honest girl. If only she'd listened to me."

He paused a little, and I gave him time to collect his thoughts. By the turmoil in his features, he had more to say.

"She wanted her own place, and I respected that," he eventually added, still staring out the window. He turned and approached us, looking first at me, then at Holt with pleading eyes, wringing his hands clutched in front of his chest. "It was her, Roxanne, I know it was her. Only I can't prove it."

I touched his forearm gently. "It's not your job to prove anything, Mr. MacPherson, it's ours."

"Okay," he whispered, "but do you believe me?"

I didn't know what to believe. Roxanne didn't seem like the type to hire a contract killer, but she had been untruthful more than once. She definitely had something to hide.

"We will follow this lead diligently, Mr. MacPherson, I can promise you that. Do you know what it was the girls fought about?"

He looked away and to the left for a brief second, then touched his ear in passing, quickly. He was about to tell a lie, the first one I could spot on the day's repertoire of answers.

"Something to do with Roxanne's boyfriend, I believe."

"Was there, um, jealousy?" I asked, treading lightly.

"No, none of that. But you'll have to ask Roxanne about their argument."

I looked at Holt, who'd stayed unusually silent during the interview, then turned to MacPherson again. "One more thing, Mr. MacPherson. We might have to ask your wife a few questions," I said, as gently as I could. "We don't want to create issues for you, but this is a murder investigation. I hope you'll understand."

He shrugged, completely unfazed. "She's at the office all day today. Do what you have to do. Please find who killed my Crystal and make them pay."

"We will, Mr. MacPherson," Holt said, but the man was back in his seat by the window, staring outside.

We let ourselves out of the study without another word, and the butler was quick to appear and escort us to the exit.

Something didn't add up. Irked by our lack of progress, I tied my hair in a loose knot as soon as I got inside the SUV and let out a groan filled with half-articulated oaths.

"What's on your mind?" Holt asked, turning from the MacPherson driveway onto the cozy street.

"It's like we entered a parallel universe or something," I blurted. "You can't bloody have billions of dollars, affairs, and pregnant eighteen-year-old mistresses all mashed-up together and see this level of indifference, of absolutely no emotional response. This isn't human. It can't be real."

"Maybe we didn't speak with the right human, that's all," Holt replied.

"You mean, the scorned wife?"

"Yeah, let's see if she's just as calm about her husband having an affair. I seriously doubt that."

36

TENNIS

"You were tense in there," I mentioned, the moment Holt set the vehicle in motion. "What was that about?"

"Something's bothering me with this entire arrangement," he replied, after mulling it over for a moment. "You have this girl, Crystal, smart, pretty, determined, and she finds herself a rich boyfriend just like that? These people are jaded by women's attention; they don't fall in love that easily, you know, and risk jeopardizing what they have."

"Are you saying it can't happen?" I reacted, a little surprised by his perception.

"I wasn't finished yet," he said with a quick chuckle. "I was about to say, now that you see just how improbable that is, go ahead and multiply it by two, because another loaded, married man in his forties was having some kind of deal going on with the same eighteen-year-old dancer. She was beautiful, okay, but what the hell?"

He had a point, a big one, blooming right before our eyes in the form of an emerging pattern. My Scotland Yard instructor would've said, "Two data points don't establish a pattern," but there was something going on with that girl's life that we needed to uncover, and fast.

"Roxanne might be able to shed some light," I said. "We should speak with her again. MacPherson's accusation was quite interesting," I said, unwrapping a protein bar. "Want some?"

"Uh-huh," he said, turning his face slightly toward me without taking his eyes off the road.

I broke the bar in half and held a piece out for him. Instead of grabbing it with his hand, he bit into it with a satisfied groan.

"This is Vegas," he continued. "When I see stuff like this, I can't help thinking she was an escort of sorts. Maybe Roxanne is our best lead yet; they might've been in it together."

"I'm thinking of that pro who killed Erika at the morgue," I said. "Someone hired him, and I don't think that's Roxanne; I just don't see it happening. But I can think of at least two people who wouldn't hesitate to pay for murder."

"Who? Ellis and Paul?" Holt asked, still chewing.

"No, Paul Steele and his wife. As for Mrs. Celeste Bennett MacPherson, we haven't met her yet, but she probably makes three."

"Why Mrs. Steele? You haven't met her yet."

"I'm not sure," I replied, wondering the same thing myself, moments after I'd offered her name in an unfiltered, spontaneous thought. "My gut is telling me Paul Steele didn't marry a ninny, and there was something going on between the two of them, between Crystal and Paul. A secret worth at least half a million dollars to Paul Steele, maybe more to the missus. The only thing is, if Paul had ordered Crystal dead, why waste half a mil on her? Why risk being seen with her moments before she died?"

"Agreed," Holt said, unscrewing the water bottle. He drank a few gulps, emptying it after I'd declined his offer. He screwed the cap back on and put it in the cup holder. "Let's go see Mrs. Bennett MacPherson first, then we'll pick up Roxanne."

"Pick her up? Why?"

"I think it's time we turned up the heat. She might remember more if she's—"

His phone started ringing through the SUV's media center, displaying the name of our commanding officer, Captain Morales.

"Captain," Holt said, the moment he accepted the call with a tap on the screen.

"Holt," the captain's voice came across loudly, "is Baxter there with you?"

"I'm here, Captain," I replied, frowning a little.

"Great, that saves me a second phone call. Is it true you banged on Paul Steele's door this morning?"

"Yes," I replied cautiously. I'd been expecting some whiplash from that but not nearly so soon. "Anything wrong?"

"The governor called," Morales said. "He said this was a delicate matter, and he would personally appreciate if you treaded lightly."

"You mean, back off?" I asked, looking for a straight answer. My British background still had me at a disadvantage when reading between the lines of my boss's orders. I grew up in a country where people were direct, blunt almost to a fault, not at all concerned with the feathers they'd ruffle, especially in boss-to-employee communication. But I found that to be quite different in the states, where everyone seemed so preoccupied with not offending anyone, that communication was ambiguous if not indecipherable, albeit politically correct and mostly not usable in court.

"No, I mean work it with kid gloves, but follow the evidence nevertheless. And lay off that DNA request, unless you can't close the case without it. I won't be signing off on that warrant request for now."

I exchanged a quick glance with Holt, his frustration just as visible as mine. "Yes, Captain, understood."

"Call me with updates," he said, hanging up before I could acknowledge the order.

"And that's a bloody load of bollocks," I muttered.

"It's just politics," Holt said reassuringly, as if I were a child who needed to be appeased. The thought made me smile.

I didn't reply; I rested my head against the window, feeling a bit tired after last night's adventures. I needed to catch up on sleep, but that wasn't going to happen anytime soon. Even if we hit the jackpot with Crystal's murder, I still had the hairy issue of the IAB investigation into Holt and the missing kilo of cocaine. That entire situation was a dark cloud that followed me everywhere I went. It wasn't as if the IAB wanted the missing cocaine found and the thief apprehended; no, they'd just made up their minds that Holt was guilty, and I wasn't sure that proving them wrong was going to help either of us a single bit.

Holt pulled into a visitor parking spot at BeneFoods headquarters. Three identical, high-rise buildings placed at different angles surged at least twenty stories against the blue sky, flanking a courtyard where employees gathered around picnic tables shielded from the sun by colorful sail canopies. I stopped for a moment, hesitating between the three buildings, but then I noticed a Bentley limousine pulled up at the curb in front of the middle tower.

Reception informed us that Mrs. Bennett was playing tennis on the rooftop of the building. I'd noticed during the exchange with the receptionist, and later the executive assistant, that although we'd referred to Ellis MacPherson's wife as Mrs. Bennett MacPherson, her full legal name, everyone else called her Mrs. Bennett. Maybe there were reasons for Ellis MacPherson's indifference with being found out by the missus.

We were immediately escorted upstairs by another executive assistant, who could've been Miss Gentry's twin. Waiting for the modern elevator to climb all the way to the roof, I wondered if there was a special school or training program that taught these girls how to smile, how to act, and how to dress for these jobs, in addition to typing a gazillion words per minute and perfect diction when answering the phone.

The elevator dropped us in a lounge area with large windows overseeing the tennis court. It was surrounded by tall glass panels, to keep the high winds from ruining the game, and equipped with outdoor air conditioners. The assistant had us wait while she went to get Mrs. Bennett, then excused herself and disappeared.

Mrs. Bennett's tennis partner, a young, good-looking man in his late twenties, stayed behind on the court, practicing his swings in the air, pretending poorly that he didn't see us, while at the same time showing off his moves, his perfect body.

As Mrs. Bennett approached, I had to admit she was stunning. Per my earlier research, she'd just turned thirty-nine, but looked at least ten years younger. Slim and tan, with a pleasant smile and the reassured demeanor of a woman who'd never wanted for anything in her life, she greeted us warmly.

"Detectives," she said, extending her hand. "Celeste Bennett," she introduced herself, as if that was needed.

I liked that about her; she wasn't blatantly arrogant about her wealth; she was pleasant.

"Thank you for seeing us," I said, shaking her hand.

"What can I do for you?"

Holt and I looked at each other, hesitant. We needed to break some news to her that normally wreaked havoc in people's lives. Holt took a small step back, inviting me to take the lead. He was most likely thinking a woman might be the best one to break the news of her husband's infidelity.

I decided to cut right into it, albeit as delicately as I possibly could.

"We're investigating the murder of Crystal Tillman," I said, watching closely for any recognition, any reaction on her face. There was none. Her perfect smile endured, unfazed. "Are you familiar with that name?"

"Yes, I am," she replied, taking us both by surprise. "She knew my husband."

Bloody hell, I thought to myself, shooting Holt a quick glance, enough to notice his raised eyebrows.

I cleared my throat quietly and breathed. "Are you aware your husband was having an affair with her?"

She nodded, and her smile waned a little, replaced by sadness, feigned or real, I couldn't tell. "Yes, I am. He's devastated by her death, poor darling."

I felt my jaw drop. "I must confess, I am surprised by your reaction," I said, wondering if she was truthful about the whole thing or if she was that good an actress. I looked at her intently, noticing every minute detail of her facial expression, of her demeanor. Her shoulders were lowered, her arms folded in front of her body yet relaxed, her fingers steady and calm. Her gaze was direct, forthcoming, seemingly sincere. Despite all that, to me her reactions appeared paradoxical.

Her smile widened somewhat. "I understand how unusual this might seem to you, Detectives. Ellis and I have a different kind of relationship." She laughed quietly as her eyes turned toward the tennis court, where her partner was stretching his long, muscular legs. "After a few years of marriage, my husband and I recognized that we both have needs the other can't fulfill. We care deeply for each other; our friendship is the glue that will hold us together 'til death do us part. Such friendship is a rare gift that cannot be wasted, a real partnership for life. But the passion… Let's just say I don't like tennis enough to justify having a tennis pro on speed dial," she added, lowering her eyelids shyly and blushing under her impeccable makeup.

I looked at Holt again, stifling the smile that threatened to bloom, seeing the disbelief in his eyes. My partner was appalled.

"Do you have children?" I asked.

Her smile widened, touching her azure eyes. "A daughter," she replied. "She started college this year. Brown," she added, her voice filled with maternal pride.

"Did you know Crystal Tillman was pregnant with your husband's child?" I asked, watching for a reaction. And again, nothing.

"Yes," she replied, "what a tragedy, two lives ended so soon."

"And you were okay with that?"

"With the pregnancy? It's not the first time it's happened," she replied. "Ellis is great about these things, always so considerate."

I frowned, thinking whether I should tell her the considerate Ellis had planned to keep Crystal's baby and play Daddy, unlike other times when he'd dealt away with the problem, throwing money at the pregnant mistresses until they went away.

"Mrs. Bennett," Holt said, "do you know—"

"Call me Celeste, please," she invited, giving Holt an appreciative look.

"Um, Celeste," he said, his voice a little strangled. "Do you know if Crystal had any enemies, or anything—"

The elevator doors whooshed open and chimed, and an older woman stepped out. I recognized her; I'd seen her photo on many magazine covers, and just as many times on television, being interviewed at charity events and the Governor's Ball.

The old Mrs. Bennett.

She was Nevada royalty more than anyone else. Her father had created BeneFoods in 1939, when war was looming, bringing cheaper food options to struggling neighborhoods. As a young girl, she'd worked side by side with her father to turn the already successful stores into the network of supermarkets they were today. When her father died, she took over the company with talent and ambition, making it into a giant. Rumor had it she was semiretired, still involved in many executive decisions, although she'd taken the company public fifteen years ago and Celeste was the president and CEO.

Elegant and distinguished in a cream-colored pantsuit with a burgundy, chiffon blouse, she made me wish I'd look as good as she did when I'd get to her age; only a few wrinkles hinted to that number, which I believed was about seventy. I was in awe, feeling small in the presence of such legendary greatness.

"There you are, my dear," she said, smiling at us as if she were greeting us at some formal event. "You're needed downstairs, in the boardroom. They have some kind of emergency."

We thanked Celeste and parted ways, not seeing a reason to hold her back with more questions. I'd seen nothing to cause a single concern. Ellis MacPherson had all the reasons not to be worried about his wife's reaction to his affair.

Our strongest lead had just dissolved in thin, perfectly conditioned, Nevada air.

"Are you buying it?" Holt asked the moment we climbed inside his Ford.

"Could be true," I replied, although I failed to comprehend it. I was the jealous type myself, more likely to scratch the other woman's eyes out for just looking at my man. I couldn't see myself accepting an open marriage, but not everyone was like me. "There was no emotional response, no pain markers, no stress," I said, summarizing my earlier observations.

"Do you think it was rehearsed?"

"Great question, but no, I don't think so. If you feel strongly enough about your husband's affair to put a contract out on his mistress, that passion won't disappear in a few days, just by rehearsing your responses. Your body needs more time to adjust, to learn the new reality, to process the rejection, the hurt."

The phone rang, and I saw Fletcher's name on the display. I let Holt answer.

"Hey guys," he said in a cheerful tone. "There's a surprise in your inbox."

Holt pulled over as I opened my email and looked at the images attached to Fletcher's message. It showed Paul and Roxanne climbing in the same elevator together, holding hands and undressing each other with their eyes.

"Whoa," Holt reacted.

"She lied," I snapped. "When she said she didn't recognize him in those video screenshots, the little bitch lied."

"There's more," Fletcher said. "Play the video," he instructed, and I executed, holding my breath.

The video, grainy and distant, yet clear enough for us to recognize the players, showed Roxanne talking with Ellis in front of the high-limit gaming room cashier's desk. The conversation was intense, judging by the firm grip Ellis seemed to have on Roxanne's arm, her unsuccessful attempts to free herself, and their overall body language. Just like with other surveillance videos, there was no sound.

"I think I know what that's about," Holt said. "If Ellis suspects Roxanne of killing Crystal, and we know he does, he must be confronting her. What's the time code on that video?"

"Last night, well, technically today, one-thirty in the morning," Fletcher replied.

"What did she do after that conversation?" I asked, seeing that the video ended with Ellis leaving.

"She climbed into Paul Steele's limo and drove off," Fletcher said.

The brazen, perfidious little shite had lied to us about everything.

37

FINDINGS

I was fuming.

It wasn't like I'd never been lied to before, during an investigation. That's what all perps do, all the time: they lie. That's what most witnesses do most of the time, with intent or by omission: they deceive, misrepresent, exaggerate, fudge, or invent. In other words, they lie.

But Roxanne? I'd sensed she was hiding something, but I felt bad for her; I sympathized with her loss, I resonated with her heartbreak.

And she'd played me. With her vulnerable little girl act, with her sobs and her batting eyelashes dripping lacrimal droplets, with her feigned every-bloody-thing.

She'd been shagging this Paul guy, but didn't recognize him? The hell she didn't. Her lying arse belonged in jail.

"I want her charged," I said coldly, as if getting ready to fight Holt over it.

"Yup," he replied. "You think she's the doer?"

"She had means, motive, and plenty of opportunity. These girls were practically together twenty-four-seven," I replied. "But how do you explain the contract killer?"

"I can't," Holt replied. "I've been thinking about it, while you've been busy mumbling incoherent British words that make me doubt I speak the language."

"And?"

He didn't get to answer; my phone rang. It was Anne. I took the call on speaker, glad to hear from her.

"Hey," I said, "I've been worried about you."

"I'm fine," she said with a long, bone-tired sigh. "Why don't you swing by? I've got some news for you."

"Swing by, as in...?"

"The University Medical Center Morgue."

Holt pulled a tire-squealing one-eighty as soon as he heard the address, then floored it.

"We're on our way," I said and ended the call.

I looked at Holt, waiting for him to continue sharing his thoughts, but he drove in silence.

"You were saying?" I prodded.

"I was saying maybe there could be two perps. One killer, and another one who wanted to clean up after the killer. Let's say, Roxanne poisoned Crystal, but then Paul, assuming he cares about her, paid that muscle to bomb the morgue and burn all the evidence."

I frowned and pressed my lips together, thinking, trying my best to shoot holes into his theory. It was airtight; it could work. It could explain why we had two entirely different kinds of suspects: people with money, but apparently without motive or opportunity, and Roxanne, who had all those, but no money to hire a killer.

As far as we knew. Note to self: let's pore over that girl's financials, with gusto.

We entered the morgue quickly, practically running. It was starting to get dark outside, on our third day of chasing Crystal's killer through a maze of entangled leads woven among thick webs of lies and deceit. Statistics said that if a killer wasn't caught in the first forty-eight hours after the homicide was committed, the chances to clear the case dropped by a factor of five. We needed whatever information Anne could give us.

We needed a miracle.

The makeshift setup she'd organized was functional, albeit every other piece of equipment was temporarily installed on a table on wheels, some even on stretchers borrowed from the Medical Center. Anne looked pale, exhausted, her eyes surrounded by black circles. She didn't smile when she saw us, but that wasn't unusual when she was working.

"Why aren't you in bed?" I asked, knowing how useless my question was.

She swatted my concern away with a hand gesture, then opened a folder and pulled out a report. "The preliminary tox screen was negative. That's the basic one, screening for most commonly encountered drugs and poisons, alcohol, narcotics."

"Great," I mumbled, letting myself drop on a backless lab stool.

"She was negative for any recreational drugs and had only small amounts of alcohol in her bloodstream. She'd had a glass of wine at dinner, but other than that, she was sober."

"You said you had something?" I asked, instantly regretting my lack of patience. She'd dragged herself out of bed to work, to wrap up Crystal's postmortem; the least I could do was give her the time she needed.

She shot me a quick, amused glance, then continued. "We have enough blood left to continue testing. I've narrowed down a list of alkaloids they should be testing for."

"What kind of poison is that?" Holt asked.

"Like I mentioned before, a plant extract. There are a few concoctions out there that could kill by stopping the victim's heart or impairing the respiratory function."

"Who could make extracts like these?" Holt asked.

"Anyone with knowledge, a small garden, and a pot of boiling water. No luck narrowing suspects down this way, Detective." She breathed deeply, and broke down in a coughing spell that ended with a few inhalations from her oxygen mask. "Once I have it identified, we'll be able to determine how it entered her bloodstream."

She needed to be in bed, not here, in a makeshift morgue, inhaling chemicals. "Are you all right?" I asked. "Let's get you home."

"Nah, I'll be fine," she replied in a raspy, choked voice. "I have to wrap this up today; we can't wait any longer. You need to know exactly what toxin was used."

"How long?" I asked, cringing at the thought of pushing her any further than she'd already pushed herself.

I needed that information quickly; a killer could always get a panic attack and decide to disappear for good. Plus, I didn't know how much time I had before the IAB decided I hadn't kept my end of the bargain and terminated me. For some reason, it was important for me to catch Crystal's killer before being kicked to the curb, even if it was the last thing I did as a cop.

Especially because it would be the last thing I did as a cop.

Anne rubbed her eyes, filled with tears after the coughing spell, and continued, "I inspected Crystal's stomach lining again, looking for chemical burns, lesions, or other signs she might've ingested the poison. There's nothing probative. However, I have her last meal documented, if you're interested. It was exquisite, to say the least. Maybe it will help you map her last twenty-four hours."

"Shoot," Holt said, ready to take notes.

"She had king crab with remoulade and toast, veal with rice and fine herbs, raspberry mousse, champagne wafers, and a glass of wine."

"Who eats like that?" Holt mumbled. "When was this fancy schmancy dinner?"

"Sometime between eight and ten, the night she died," Anne replied.

"Wait, she ate all that before going to work?"

"The quantities were small," Anne replied. "She barely tasted the foods, but she was somewhere where they served all that, and I can't think of a single place that has all those items on the menu."

"Anything else?" I asked, sounding a little discouraged. It would take some doing to call the many high-end restaurants in Vegas to narrow it down.

"Nothing more on Crystal for now, but the DNA came back for Erika's killer," she said, her voice tinged with sadness as she threw a quick glance at the cold storage shelves lining the back wall. "Ronnie Sanford, forty-two."

She walked to the computer and typed a few commands. A man's rap sheet displayed on the wall-mounted TV. Seeing how bulky and muscular his throat was, and the expression of sheer evil in his face, I was surprised that Anne had survived the attack and had managed to dent him at all. Andrew would've been proud; I knew for sure, because I was.

"He served six months for an illegal firearms charge; that's what landed him in the system," she continued. "He was also tried and acquitted for a homicide that was suspected to have been a murder for hire."

"Could you please send this to Fletcher?" I asked, but Holt was already on it.

"Done. He'll put the BOLO out. I asked Fletch to pull Sanford's financials, but don't hold your breath."

38

TRUTH INTO LIES

I walked quickly across the vast Scala lobby, then up the stairs, Holt by my side, in a weird déjà vu moment, a snapshot of last night's visit to the high-end gaming room. It was nine, peak hour in Sin City, and the foot traffic was heavy everywhere in the hotel, the gaming room no exception; I counted eight gamblers losing money elegantly under the direct supervision of our friend, Mr. Farley.

I beckoned him, and he rushed toward us, in an attempt to keep any police talk as far from his clients' earshot as possible.

"We need to speak with Rox—Devine again," I said, remembering at the last minute she used that name for anything work-related.

"You mean, Roxanne Omelas, Detective?" he smiled sarcastically. "We're required by law to check ID before hiring anyone."

"Yeah, right," I said, thinking of Crystal's fake ID. Farley had been really diligent with that.

"Where is she?" Holt asked impatiently. "We don't have all night."

"In her dressing room, I think; her shift's about to start," he replied with a slight frown, shooting a worried glance toward the gamblers. "I'd rather you talked with her there; I'll walk you over."

"We know the way, thanks," I said over my shoulder, already rushing toward the door marked, "Authorized Personnel Only."

Roxanne opened the dressing room door herself after we knocked. I thought I saw color leave her face when she recognized us, but the yellowish hallway light was dim, and I couldn't be sure.

"Come on in," she said, "it's just me in here."

She waited for us to come in, then closed the door. Her fingers trembled slightly, and she knew it, because she quickly hid them behind her back. She was already dressed for the stage, wearing a strappy, lace bra with tiny, narrow bands connected to a thick, leather choker. When she turned around, a V-shaped keyhole in the back of her cheeky panties left little to the imagination.

"We're taking you in," I broke the news, pulling zip ties from my pocket.

She took a few steps back, until she hit the wall behind her, sending the clothes on a hanging rack into a heap on the floor. "Why? What have I done?"

"You lied to police during a murder investigation, and that will cost you an obstruction charge."

"I didn't... I don't know what you mean," she stuttered, while her eyes filled with tears.

"This," Holt said, putting his phone in front of her. "Yesterday, we showed you this photo, taken from a video surveillance camera on the night of Crystal's murder, and you said you didn't recognize the man." He paused for a moment, giving her time to process. "We know you lied. We have you dead to rights holding hands with Paul Steele, climbing into his limo. Turn around, hands behind your back."

She grabbed Holt's forearm with both her hands, sobbing. "Listen, I didn't mean to lie, I was in shock. You have to believe me," she pleaded, her voice shattered, sounding sincere to me.

"Explain," I said, putting the zip ties back in my pocket.

She turned toward me and let go of Holt's arm. "I didn't recognize him at first, I swear I didn't. It made no sense that Paul would be talking to Crystal, would... rough her up. They barely knew each other, there was nothing going on between them. Then I realized who he was, saw how he grabbed her bra, all that anger, and I froze. Please..."

"Jealous?" Holt asked.

"No... confused, lost. The two most important people in my life were having such a heated conversation, and I knew nothing of it. My mind went crazy, spinning with questions."

"Did you kill Crystal, Roxanne?" I asked, looking at her intently, ready to catch the tiniest flinch.

"No," she shouted, clasping her hands in front of her chest in a pleading gesture. "I swear to you, I didn't."

There was no sign of deception that I could see. Was she a true psychopath? Those were the only individuals who didn't display the typical microexpressions of deceit, because they had no conscience to trigger them.

"You lied to us before," Holt said angrily. "Are you lying now?"

"No," she replied, sniffling. "This is the truth."

"We know you had some kind of an argument with Crystal before she died," I said, and I saw a flicker of emotion, pupils dilating, her hands pulling away from me, her eyelids dropping to cover her eyes. Jackpot. "What were you two arguing about?"

"I have n—no idea," she said, wringing her hands while her shoulders tightened. "I thought we were good, like sisters, like we'd always been." She avoided my scrutiny, keeping her eyes riveted to the floor, shooting quick, guarded glances at me or Holt, as if to see if she was getting away with her lies.

"Cut the shite, all right?" I snapped, getting in her face, so close she had to lift her eyes and look at me. "We know she was moving out, that's how bad a fight you two had. Don't tell me you still can't remember."

There it was again, the pupils dilating, her eyes looking anywhere but at me, as if tracing the movements of a fly buzzing around the ceiling fixture.

"I'm really sorry," she bawled, "I don't know what you're talking about!"

I looked at Holt and shrugged. "Take her in."

Holt took out his zip ties and grabbed Roxanne's shoulder. "Roxanne Omelas, you have the right to remain—"

"No!" she shouted, trying to pull herself away from Holt. "I'll tell you, all right?"

I nodded, and Holt released his grip on her arm, rolling his eyes. It seemed we had to do this dance with her every time we needed a tiny morsel of information. She didn't demonstrate too much logic, or good memory for that matter.

"I'm listening," I snapped, "and it better be the truth, the whole truth, and nothing but the truth, or I'll throw the book at you."

She sniffled and wiped her nose on a Kleenex she picked from a box on her vanity, then nodded a few times. "We were fighting over Paul," she admitted in a weak, defeated voice.

"I thought you said she didn't know him that well?" Holt asked.

"She wanted me to dump him, threatened me she'd talk to him about it."

What she said made absolutely no sense. "Why? Why did she care? Was she into him?"

"No," she replied, sniffling again. "She didn't like him that much."

"Then what?" I insisted, sitting on a vanity chair, my eyes riveted to her face as she spoke, looking to catch that precise fraction of a second when truth turned into lies. Holt paced the room impatiently, fed up with her act.

"It was because he's married, and I was pushing him to leave his wife," she continued, her voice just as weak.

"More," I asked, inviting her to continue with a demanding hand gesture.

She lowered her head again, giving herself time to think on how to best wrap up her serving up a pile of crap, so she could dish it to us. I glanced quickly at Holt, drawing his attention to her demeanor. He nodded discreetly with a hint of a smile; she wasn't fooling him either.

"I got drunk one night," she finally said, raising her eyes and facing mine directly, openly. "I told her I was after Paul for money, at first, that I'd hunted for him, made it possible for us to cross paths."

"How exactly did you cross paths, by the way?"

She covered her mouth with her hand and shook her head, wondering if she really had to answer. She saw my glare and made the right call. "I, um, stalked him for a while, until I learned his schedule, his patterns, which way he took to leave the casino at night, and so on."

"And?" Holt asked the moment she stopped.

"I, um, arranged it so that some guy grabbed me and attacked me right there, on the casino floor, just as he was coming by."

Holt whistled, while I thought to myself, *Bloody unbelievable, the little twat. Maybe she does have what it takes to hire a contract killer.*

"Paul intervened, saved me, and so we met," she said blushing, visibly embarrassed, as if that were the worst thing she'd ever done. "He felt responsible, because I was attacked in his hotel, and took me to dinner, gave me the opportunity to... seduce him."

Holt and I exchanged a quick glance. Paul Steele should've been smarter, but he was almost certainly thinking how to best avoid legal liability and bad press for his hotel after that incident.

One thing was certain; Roxanne Omelas was a predator. But was she a killer?

"What happened with your so-called attacker?"

"Paul was nice about it," Roxanne replied, smiling warmly. "He asked whether I wanted to file a complaint with the cops, and when I said no, he said he'd take care of him personally."

"Okay, what do you *think* happened to your attacker?"

She shrugged with indifference. "He was beat up by Paul's guys, but we expected that, and he'd been paid good money for it. He had no complaints."

How lovely. The girl was an angel, no less. She did, however, look bloody fantastic in that stage outfit.

"Then what happened? How did Crystal get entangled in all this?"

She shifted and fidgeted for a few seconds before speaking, and when she did, her voice was different, transformed. "I was in it for the money at first, all right, but that changed; I'd fallen in love with Paul. Crystal called me a homewrecker and told me to dump him."

"Wasn't she sleeping with a married man also?"

"Yes, but she wasn't pushing Ellis to divorce his wife, and she'd never been in it for the money."

"No offense, but you two girls don't exactly strike me as saints," I said, still not completely grasping what Crystal's issue had been. "There's something you're not telling me."

Roxanne stood silently, staring at the floor.

"Was Crystal threatening to tell Paul he'd been manipulated, if you didn't dump him?"

"Yes," she whispered, not lifting her eyes from the stained cement.

"Why? Was she afraid Paul Steele would kill you if he found out? Would break your legs, like he does to cheaters and cons caught screwing around in his casino?"

She nodded, sending rippling waves into her long, silky hair.

"Do you realize this means you had one hell of a motive to kill Crystal?"

"Yes," she whispered, lifting her eyes and looking at me, then at Holt. "But I didn't do it, I swear."

39

MONEY TALKS

"Why isn't Roxanne in jail already?" Fletcher asked between slurps from a half-pint coffee mug.

"We hung a tail on her," I replied. "We lit a fire under her already burning, liar pants, and we hope she'll feel compelled to take some action. So far, nothing."

"She's a cool customer, that one," Holt laughed.

"Not sure she's our killer, though," I said as I took another bite from my breakfast bagel, covered generously in Philly spread, trying to ignore the nine grams of fat per ounce. "I'm getting all sorts of bad vibes from her, but she seemed truthful when she said she didn't do it."

"She pulled off some nasty crap," Fletcher commented. "Good thing she isn't on my case."

We burst into laughter, and I wondered if I should tell him that could never happen, considering how much a technical analyst made each paycheck. Roxanne most likely scored that much from one night's tips. No good could've come from telling him that, so I changed the subject.

"We need you badly," I said, and he looked at me from underneath thick, entangled curls, his eyes still sleepy, reminiscent of a teenager's, despite the soon approaching noon hour. "We need financials on all these people."

"How do you think that's going to work?" Holt asked. "We're dealing with smart, educated, and ridiculously rich people who can private jet it to the Caymans or Grand Bahama easier than you and I can get refills on our morning joes."

"Yeah, yeah, I know," I said, raising my hands in a pacifying gesture. "That doesn't mean we're not going to try."

"They could move fortunes by pretending they lost it in a card game, and we'd have no way to prove that isn't true," Holt insisted. "Why do you think Steele gave Crystal a chip, instead of cash?"

He was right; it was a long shot, at best. If we couldn't track the money, we needed something else to work with.

Anything.

Something to help us catch Crystal's killer, to point us in the right direction. And for an eighteen-year-old, Crystal had made a lot of enemies.

"Let's be methodical about this whole thing," Fletcher said. "Paul Steele's net worth is one point six billion dollars."

"By the way, when is our appointment with Steele and his lawyer?" I asked, mulling over a fresh idea. What if Roxanne had started her pursuit of Paul Steele for the money, as in thousands, maybe more, maybe even a million, but then realized she could be in it for the whole shebang? Well, technically, for a part of it, but still, a nice, round chunk of change she could sink her acrylic claws into.

Holt checked his phone email, mumbling something I didn't catch. "Um, a week from next Tuesday, the smug son of a bitch."

"Are you serious?" I asked, and Fletcher chuckled, without taking his eyes off his computer screens, scrolling over endless rows of data. "We're investigating a murder, for Pete's sake."

"He knows that very well," Holt replied, "and he's doing his best to stall us. Ideas?"

"Oh, I got one," I said. "Fletch, what's Steele's office phone number?"

He dictated the digits and I dialed on my phone, then initiated the call on speaker.

"Mr. Steele's office, how may I assist you?"

I recognized the voice of the efficient Miss Gentry.

"Miss Gentry, this is Detective Baxter, Homicide."

"Yes, Detective, what can I do for you?"

"I need you to bring forward our meeting with Paul Steele and his lawyer."

"Let me see," she said, her voice trailing off as she typed something on her keyboard. "I'm afraid Mr. Steele is completely booked for the next week."

"And I'm afraid that makes no difference whatsoever in a murder investigation, Miss Gentry." I paused, letting my words sink.

"I—I'm afraid I don't follow."

"It's simple. He either makes time for us today, or we bring a warrant at five PM sharp. However, we might have media trailing in with us. We really can't tell; those people are awful, like vultures; they always follow us around, hoping to get a juicy piece of news to slap on the first page of their tabloids."

Fletcher extended his hand for a fist bump, and Holt gave me a high-five and an appreciative smile. I bowed my head as if I were accepting ovations at open stage.

A moment of perfect silence on the line; Gentry was undoubtedly consulting with Steele.

"I believe I could squeeze you in at lunch, Detective," she replied, her tone turned to ice.

"Wonderful," I said, smiling widely, then hung up. "One bastard down."

"Speaking of this particular bastard, I just got word from the lip-reading expert," Fletcher said, reading from an email. "They really can't be sure, it says here, because the video doesn't have a frontal view of his lips. They conducted several reviews, including one where they analyzed both the lip movements and the emotional conveyance through stance and gestures, and, if they were to guesstimate—"

"Okay, what did he say, already?" I asked, tapping my foot impatiently.

"Apparently, Steele told Crystal, 'Not one single word about this, not ever, you hear me?'"

"Oh," I said, deflated. I'd expected more than a confirmation of my earlier suspicions. I already knew Steele had threatened Crystal about something; it was in his body language. I shook my head, disappointed. I needed hard evidence to point us at the killer, not more of this circumstantial, entangled stuff. *Bollocks...* I wanted names, addresses, social security numbers.

"Steele's financials are going to take a while; the dude's got a lot of accounts," Fletcher continued, shooting me a side glance. "Moving on to our next contestant, Roxanne. First of all, she's using a fake ID too. She's nineteen, not twenty-two. The doer fixed her driver's license but forgot her birth certificate."

I stomped my foot against the thick carpet. "Where do these bloody fakes keep coming from, huh? Now everyone's got one?"

"Remember that piece of scum, Kemsley?"

"Him, I will never forget," I replied, my voice caustic. "Pedophiles hold a place close to my heart."

"His statement said that he got his fake ID from the Dark Web. The feds showed up and grilled him on that," Holt said. "Per his statement, he went online and used an automated site where he gave a scan of his legitimate ID and a photo, then paid two bitcoins for it. That's about thirteen grand."

"Not bad, considering how well it was done. But who makes them?"

"The licenses?" Holt asked. "Apparently, a certain DMV worker who was busted this morning."

"That's why they look so real," I replied. "Because, from the manufacturing process perspective, they *are* real." Then I remembered we were talking about Roxanne, who was growing on me by the minute. "You're saying Roxanne has one too?"

"*Has* is the operating keyword here," Fletch said, peeling the wrapper off a stick of chewing gum and throwing it in his mouth.

"This chick is aiming for a world record, the longest rap sheet before legal drinking age," I muttered. "Okay, what else do you have on her?"

"Her accounts were the easiest to access," Fletcher replied. "A checking and a savings account, nothing unusual until eight months ago, when she made an out-of-cycle deposit, fifteen thousand in cash."

"And that's unusual for someone who makes thousands per week in cash, if not more?" Holt asked.

"Tips that aren't declared on income tax usually get spent outside of the banking system, as cash. Jewelry, vacations, cars, you name it. You'd have to be a complete idiot to not report the tips, then leave a paper trail."

"Got it," I said. "Where did the fifteen grand come from?"

"That I can't say, but I can tell you what else happened the same week. She bought herself a brand-new Mustang, paid in full, color blue. That retails for about thirty grand; with the fifteen deposited and five more I'd guess she killed on clothes, shoes, and whatever else these peelers buy, I'd say she came into an unexpected windfall of—"

"Fifty grand, I got it."

"Happy to see your neurons still work with little sleep, Detective," he said, grinning widely.

Holt shot me a long look, but I said nothing.

"With a rich boyfriend like Paul, are we even considering that relevant? Why? He could be shoving chips in her bra too," I said, thinking that fifty grand wasn't much to go on.

"I'm still convinced these girls were running a high-end escort service," Holt said. "Both of them are teenage strippers using fake IDs and hanging out with married, rich men in their forties? I'm not buying the coincidence."

"We'll figure it out. I don't believe Crystal was a prostitute; she was a good kid, working hard to get her degree as quickly as possible. Maybe she made some wrong choices, but I just don't see her turning tricks. Roxanne, on the other hand, anything is possible with that girl," I said, grabbing my stuff from Fletcher's desk. "Let's get going, we don't want to be late for our meeting with Mr. Steele and his lawyer."

"Do I keep digging through these accounts?" Fletcher asked.

"If anyone can find those fifty large ones, that's you," I replied. "Look at everyone involved; the men and their wives."

"You got it," he replied morosely. "Expect my call in about two years from now."

"Oh, and please dig up her closest college friends; we need to talk to some people at the university. Who knows what else she was up to?"

Instead of replying, Fletcher mock-saluted with two fingers raised at his temple.

We arrived a little early for our appointment and decided to cross the street and get some refills of coffee. I felt good, positive about the outcome of the case; I didn't have a clear suspect yet, but we were peeling the onion, uncovering the truth layer after layer, and soon we'd get to the core.

I walked by Holt's side toward the coffee shop across the street, mulling things over in my mind, falling behind with every distracted step I took. Had Crystal told Paul Steele he'd been had? What kind of game had she been playing? Why didn't she mind her own business? She was doing quite well for herself with Ellis wrapped around her little finger.

I heard the screeching tires before I saw the SUV coming, then I heard Holt shouting, "Laura!" For a split second, I thought something must be wrong; he'd only called me by my given name once, in my bedroom.

He sprinted and swept me out of the way, and we both fell to the ground between two parked cars, while the black Suburban sped by, mere inches from running us over.

Holt jumped to his feet, still holding my arm in a tight grip, pulling his gun with the other. I quickly found my own balance and shot a few rounds in rapid fire, alternating with Holt's. The rear windshield exploded, but the black Suburban turned the corner and disappeared.

I holstered my gun, wondering if we should give chase. I was tempted, but the meeting with Steele was more important, and Holt was already calling it in.

"All units, black Chevy Suburban, no plates, has a couple of bullet holes in the rear panel and a smashed rear window." He turned toward me and grazed my face, his gaze intense, his fingers sending shivers down my spine. "Are you all right?"

"Uh-huh," I replied, straightening my clothes and arranging my shirt. For a long moment, I focused on brushing every speck of dust off my sleeve, real or imaginary, only to avoid Holt's gaze. I wasn't ready for what I was seeing. I wasn't ready for him, for us, for whatever all of it meant, if anything other than a terrible mistake. "Yeah, let's go. You think it was him?"

"Who? Sanford, the contract killer who blew up the morgue?"

As he spoke, a couple of patrol cars appeared at the scene, sirens blaring.

"Who else? Maybe he's being paid to keep us from having this meeting."

40

QUESTIONING

When we made it inside the Scala corporate headquarters lobby I had the feeling that all chatter subsided instantly. Receptionists, security officers, employees drinking coffee on their breaks, all stopped interacting and pretended they had something to do. After all, through the huge windows facing Fremont, anyone present in that lobby had witnessed the earlier incident from a safe distance. I was willing to bet that many days, even years went by without shots being fired just outside their doorstep; Holt and I had provided excitement, prime time entertainment, good gossip material for years to come. No one asked us any questions though, as if waiting patiently for us to disappear so they could resume commenting on the adrenaline-pumping event.

Miss Gentry escorted us up, not a smile on her face, and a stiffness in her gait that spoke volumes, as if her giving us the cold shoulder could've had any chance of changing the direction of our murder investigation. Once on the top floor, she led us to a conference room with opaque glass walls, labeled "Boardroom." She opened the door and we stepped in.

I was expecting Mr. Steele and his attorney, but there was a third man there. Him, I recognized from the photos I'd seen in the downstairs lobby, adorning the walls. It was Paul's father, the man who'd built the Scala, John Steele.

Holt pulled out his ID, and I followed suit.

"Detectives Holt and Baxter," he announced, then pulled out a chair and sat across the table from our reluctant hosts.

"Dennis Byers, attorney for Paul Steele," the third man said, extending his hand to shake Holt's, then mine.

"Thank you for agreeing to speak with us, Mr. Steele," I said, pulling out a leather chair on casters and taking my seat.

Paul nodded, but didn't say word.

"My client has agreed to answer your questions at this time," Byers said. "As to be expected, in his capacity as Miss Tillman's employer, he is heartbroken about what happened and would like to do whatever he can to ensure the perpetrator of this senseless act is brought to justice. But please be advised, Detectives, we will not tolerate any fishing expeditions."

"Thank you," I replied candidly. I could play that game too.

I took my time opening my notepad, where earlier I'd jotted some points I wanted to touch during the conversation. Holt sat calmly, looking at Paul, not smiling, just sizing him up, building up his discomfort, fueling his anxiety.

During all this time, John Steele looked at me, then at my partner with eyes loaded with contempt. He was about seventy years old, from what I could remember; he sat leaning forward into his elbows, his bony hands clasped together and raised in front of his mouth; he was making heroic efforts to follow legal advice and keep quiet.

"Mr. Steele, did you know Crystal Tillman's roommate, Roxanne Omelas?" I asked.

Paul exchanged a quick glance with his attorney, who nodded.

"Yes, I know her."

"Are you dating Miss Omelas?"

The same thing happened; a quick exchange between client and attorney, but this time the attorney shook his head only slightly.

"I thought we were here to discuss Crystal Tillman's unfortunate demise," Byers said. "How is my client's alleged relationship with Miss Omelas relevant to your investigation?"

"We're not at liberty to divulge at this time, unfortunately," Holt replied. "Typical procedure for active investigations; I hope you'll understand."

"Then let's move on," Byers said, his stare uncompromising.

"You gave Miss Tillman a five-hundred-thousand-dollar chip on the night of her murder," I started. "Is that correct?"

Byers nodded.

"Yes," Paul said.

His father fidgeted in place and looked at his son from underneath ruffled, salt-and pepper eyebrows. The frown brought out two vertical ridges at the root of his nose. He visibly condemned his son's largesse.

"Could we ask why?"

Another quick, silent exchange between attorney and client. This time, Byers replied.

"It is my client's prerogative to gift his money as he sees fit, with or without reason."

I pressed on. "Is it possible it was hush money?"

Byers put his hand in the air, palm facing me across the shiny lacquer of the mahogany boardroom table. "You're fishing, Detective. If you have direct questions, we'll answer; if not, this meeting is over."

I repressed a frustrated sigh. "All right, then. Is your wife aware of your affair, Mr. Steele?"

He frowned, deeply displeased, then pressed his lips together and didn't look at his attorney, nor at his father. "No, she is not," he eventually said. His attorney steepled his hands on top of a folder and clenched his jaws. He seemed tense, a change from the earlier self-assured calm.

"When did you start seeing Miss Omelas?" I asked, pretending I didn't hear Byers tell me earlier his client wasn't going to answer that. This time, he allowed Paul to answer.

"About six months ago."

"Mr. Steele, are you in love with Miss Omelas?" I asked, and I saw him reel from the question. He lowered his eyes and two deep ridges flanked the corners of his mouth.

"You don't have to answer that," Byers said quickly, as if afraid Paul would start talking. "My client's feelings are not the concern of the police."

I smiled, pretending to be unfazed, when instead I was fuming. Yes, I'd forced Mr. Steele's hand to meet with us today, but what good did it do? Nothing... I wasn't getting a single, bloody thing out of him. I looked at Holt, inviting him to take over if he wanted, but he sat back with a hint of a smile. I didn't mind one bit; I loved the thrill of the hunt.

"Mr. Steele, did you kill Crystal Tillman?" I asked, and John Steele slammed his hand against the table.

"No, I did not," Paul replied calmly, although I could see a darkness in his eyes.

"Do you know who did?"

"No, I do not."

"We have reason to believe Crystal was threatening to inform your wife about your affair. That's motive to me. Half of your net worth is a lot of motive, Mr. Steele, and you seemed really angry on that video, threatening her before you shoved that chip in her bra."

"Your question, Detective?" Byers asked.

"My question is, did you pay her off to—"

"You should be ashamed of yourselves," John Steele erupted, cutting me off. "You know nothing about this man, my son. Nothing!"

Byers tried to pacify old Mr. Steele, but the man yanked his sleeve out of the lawyer's grip and slammed his fist against the table, making all the coffee cups and water glasses rattle against the silver trays.

"He's a talented, hardworking businessman. He saved my hotel, by himself, with no help from anyone! Vultures were circling back then, just like you are right now, but he didn't care. He just did what he had to do and look at it now! The biggest, best hotel and casino in Las Vegas!"

"Mr. Steele," I said, "we mean no disrespect. Asking such questions is the typical—"

"You shut your mouth, woman!" he bellowed, and Holt stood abruptly, pushing his chair so forcefully behind him that it slammed against the wall. He glared at Mr. Steele, taking him aback for a moment.

I touched Holt's arm, but he didn't back down; he stood right in front of John Steele, ready to pounce.

"Listen, I believe we've been forthcoming enough," Byers said, but old Mr. Steele didn't let him finish either.

"I will not allow you to drag my son's name through the mud, you hear me? That girl, God rest her soul, had nothing to do with my son, and that's the end of it. Go catch the real killer and leave us alone."

"Dad," Paul said, grabbing his hand. "I'll take care of this."

But John Steele didn't break eye contact with me; he was staring me down and I resisted, entertained to see him power tripping the way he was, and wondering if I had, at least by accident, hit a nerve. Paul Steele was one of our suspects; I'd never before considered his father might've been one too.

"I wonder what the mayor will have to say about all this," John Steele continued. "He and I play golf every Friday. That's tomorrow, by the way. Now, go eat your doughnuts or whatever the hell you do with your time at the taxpayers' expense."

He scoffed at me and I smiled, unperturbed.

But the meeting was over, and the only morsel of valuable information we'd gathered this entire time was that Mrs. Steele wasn't aware of Paul's philandering. I was willing to bet millions of dollars I never had and never will have, that Mrs. Steele was not going to be as indifferent to her husband's cheating as Mrs. Bennett had been.

41

POISON

My disappointment with the results of Paul Steele's questioning soon dissipated at the news that they'd collared Ronnie Sanford. If given enough incentive, because I didn't assume he'd be the kind of man to easily yield under the pressure of a police interrogation, he'd probably be willing to name his employer.

I smiled, enjoying the afternoon sun on my face and knowing that Crystal's killer was about to be brought to justice.

"You were awfully quiet in there," I said, giving Holt a quick, side look.

"Seemed to me you were doing just fine on your own," Holt replied, a bit on the glum side.

I decided to let that go, as we only had a couple of minutes left until we reached the precinct. "You know, I'm really itching to have a sit-down with Mrs. Steele and see her reaction when we break some news to her."

"Uh-huh," Holt replied, turning left on Swenson Street.

"Strange thing, they didn't think to warn us to not approach her without counsel present."

"Well, that's a given, knowing who she is."

"Given or not, they didn't say, and that means we're going to try, right?"

"Uh-huh," he replied, pulling into the precinct's parking garage.

Moments later, we found Ronnie Sanford was waiting in an interrogation room, while the arresting officer filled out paperwork in the adjacent observation room.

"Officer Reilly?" I said, reading his name tag, "thanks for bringing him in."

"Sure," the young man replied. "He was trying to board a flight when we nabbed him."

"Where to?" Holt asked. "His flight?"

The officer consulted his notes. "Um, Armenia, by way of Los Angeles, then Moscow. The tickets were purchased at the airport, with cash, only thirty minutes ago."

The timeline worked; if he'd been the one who tried to run us over in front of the Scala corporate HQ, considering he failed and had raised all that heat, he must've taken I-15 straight for the airport.

"Armenia is a nonextradition country," Holt commented. "Makes sense."

"Did he say anything during or after the arrest?" I asked.

"Not a single word. He didn't resist either; he could barely walk. There's something wrong with his knee."

I smiled. Anne was what was wrong with the perp's knee.

"Officer Reilly, see if you can't locate a black Suburban with a shattered rear window and a couple of bullet holes in it, somewhere at McCarran International. I believe we'll find this man's fingerprints in that SUV. I'd be happy to add two counts of attempted murder of a police officer to his rap sheet."

"If it's there, we'll find it," he replied.

"Okay, let's have it," I said, rubbing my hands together excitedly as I entered the interrogation room followed by Holt.

The first thing I noticed about him were the scratches, deep and ragged under his right eye and on the side of his neck. His eye was bloodshot and half-closed. The man's breathing was accelerated and shallow; he panted due to the pain in his knee. Sooner rather than later we had to get him medical attention; last thing I needed was another issue with a perp in my custody landing in surgery.

Not that it mattered, anyway. By Monday, when I'd have nothing to show to the IAB, they'd fire me; hell of a way to start a new week.

I didn't bother to pull out a chair; I leaned across the table and grinned in his face.

"You're going down hard, Mr. Sanford."

He glared at me without a word.

"Who did that to you, Mr. Sanford?" I asked, pointing a finger at the lacerations underneath his right eye, so close he flinched.

"My cat scratched me," he replied, showing his teeth in a smirk loaded with hatred. "What's it to you, bitch?"

"Well, the cat who did that to you has lived to tell the story and had your DNA under her claws."

He stared at me in disbelief, then looked at Holt briefly.

"Uh-huh," Holt said, with an exaggerated nod. "What she said."

"That cat will testify; she's brave like that," I continued. "But you already know that, Mr. Sanford. A tough guy like you, floored by a chick," I said, then chuckled lightly. "Who hired you?"

"Lawyer," Sanford said quietly.

Bollocks... There it went, down the drain, just when I thought we were getting somewhere.

I looked at Holt and saw the same disappointment in his eyes.

"If we catch the killer before this dude names his employer, we're going to fry his arse," I told Holt, as if Sanford wasn't even in the room. "He'll have nothing valuable left to trade for his sorry life."

"Lawyer," he repeated, raising his voice.

"All right, sweetie," I said, "but you don't have to say anything, okay? We still have the right to talk among ourselves, even if your lawyer isn't present. We aren't asking you any questions; you had your chance to talk, now use your rights and shut up."

"L-A-W-Y-E-R," he spelled out, driving me nuts.

"Good thing they still have capital punishment in Nevada," I said to Holt calmly, turning my back to Sanford. "He tried to kill us; he doesn't deserve to live."

Holt looked briefly at his buzzing phone, and then at me with a smile on his face. "We have the ME's final report. We know the poison used in Crystal's murder."

"You know what that means, right?" I said, looking only at Holt, ignoring the perp completely. "It means we'll nail the killer today, and tomorrow I will sleep the whole day through."

"That also means this poor schmuck only has a couple of hours to spill his guts, or he gets toasted," Holt replied.

"Lawyer, now!" he shouted. "Get me a lawyer and a reasonable deal on the table, and maybe I'll talk."

"What's a reasonable deal to you, honey?" I asked, tilting my head as if I were a Southern belle flirting with him.

"No jail time, nothing; I'll leave the country and never come back."

Holt and I looked at each other and burst into laughter at the same time.

We were still laughing when we left the room and closed the door behind us. The moment we reached the observation room, I grabbed Holt's arm.

"I just realized I never got a chance to thank you," I said, searching his eyes.

"What for?" he replied, a little uneasy.

"For saving my life. Again."

He looked at me for a moment, a mix of emotions on his face. Then his usual, lopsided grin reappeared. "Should I hope for the same reward as last time?"

"Ah," I reacted, then shoved my elbow in his side. "I was being serious… Thank you, I mean it."

"You're welcome," he replied simply. "Now let's call Anne."

"That was for real? She's got the poison?"

"Uh-huh," he replied, his grin evolving into a full-blown smile. "Your bestie came through."

I dialed Anne, frowning at Holt's last remark. He was doing it again, sprinkling words that were meant to trigger a response and give him the information he believed he had to have, like the full story with Anne and me.

"Detective," Anne said, the moment she picked up.

"I got Holt with me, and we're all ears."

"The toxin used to kill Crystal Tillman was an alkaloid called pseudoaconitine, extracted from aconitum, a perennial plant you might know as monkshood."

That didn't mean a thing to me, one name or the other, and, by his reaction, Holt hadn't heard of it either.

"How does one find this plant?" Holt asked. "Is it local, here, or exotic?"

"It grows in mountain meadows, in moist, well-drained soil," Anne replied. "You could find it if you hike Mount Charleston, I presume, but you have to know what you're looking for. Or, some people might grow it, although I can't think of a nonhomicidal reason to do so."

"What does this plant look like?" I asked, thinking I'd hiked Charleston many times and hadn't worried about any poisonous plants. Ignorance, apparently, is bliss.

"It's two feet tall, with dark green leaves and inflorescences of purple flowers that look like the hoods that monks wear."

"How toxic is it?" Holt asked.

"Very. You can't even touch it without gloves. If you run into anything like it, steer clear and leave it to the experts to collect samples."

"How did Crystal get exposed to it?"

"I still don't know that," Anne replied with a sigh of frustration. "But now that I know what to test for, and I have samples of her organs, skin, and hair, I'll be able to tell you shortly."

"Skin? Why skin?" Holt asked.

"The first thing I did was test the stomach lining, but, as I had initially suspected, there's no indication she ingested the poison. The only other alternatives are inhalation, and I will test her lungs for it, and direct dermal contact. I'll test the hair for the odd scenario she had long-term exposure to minute quantities of the toxin, although the symptoms preceding death would've been different."

"Anne, you're awesome," I said, then turned to Holt. "Now let's send CSI to pore over Roxanne's house and her personal belongings, to look for traces of this monkshood extract."

"Already done, and the warrant includes the Scala dressing room too," he said, showing me his phone. "If she's our killer, we've got her."

42

MORE MONEY

Next stop was Fletcher's desk. It felt like we'd left there only minutes earlier, and yet a lot had happened during that short time. I almost got killed. We'd discovered critical pieces of information regarding Paul Steele and his potential reason for making threats. We knew the name of the poison that killed Crystal.

We still didn't know who killed her.

I couldn't remember a single case I'd worked on in my entire career, when my gut couldn't decide and favor a certain suspect, or at least give me a hint as to which door to pound on next. It seemed that the person I'd thought had the strongest motive to kill Crystal, Ellis MacPherson's wife Celeste, actually didn't have a motive, but everyone else did.

Paul was still a suspect in my mind, although he couldn't've been so stupid to kill her immediately after having threatened her, paid her off, and been caught on camera with her.

Roxanne had the best motive, full-time opportunity, and means because anyone can climb a mountain and pick some flowers; she was the strongest suspect, yet my gut disagreed, but not wholeheartedly. As for Mrs. Steele, she was next on our list to visit and evaluate.

Instead of narrowing a list of suspects, we kept adding to it.

"You two again," Fletcher greeted us with mock disappointment. "You should know better than to come empty-handed. This," he pointed at his head, "works on caffeine and refined carbs."

"I'm willing to sign an IOU," I said.

He shrugged, the universal gesture for, "Whatever."

"What have you got?" Holt asked.

"Who told you I got anything?" he reacted, scratching his stubble. "I didn't call you, did I?"

"Don't be a wiseass," Holt replied harshly, to my surprise. "Give."

"Okay," he said, shifting through some database screens. "I will give, only because you can't wait a little longer, but please be advised some of my information is incomplete, and I'm doing this under protest."

"And no caffeine," I added, smiling.

"That's insult to the injury," he muttered. "So, you asked me to see if the two happy couples, the Steeles and the MacPhersons, had prenups in place."

"Do they?"

"Prenuptial agreements are not public information; they don't have to be registered anywhere, and they can be kept in the family safe for eternity. That said, I will assume both couples did, because Paul Steele and Celeste Bennett brought fortunes of over one billion dollars into their respective marriages, and when people do that, they prenup the crap out of it."

"That's your deduction, not evidence-based fact, is that correct?" Holt asked.

"Entirely, with some circumstantial facts to support my conclusions."

"Such as?"

Fletcher ran another search and some IRS reports displayed on one of his monitors. "Ellis MacPherson only made three hundred thousand a year before marrying Celeste Bennett. He wasn't rich. Maybe, considering whatever prenup might be in place, he's not really that rich now."

"That's still almost five times what I make," I grumbled, throwing that tidbit of frustration out there although it brought no value; it just made me feel better for exactly one second.

"What I mean is, he's not 'unmarked helicopter' rich. The Bennett fortune is huge compared to what he makes from sawing that chunk of wood."

"I heard he's really good," I said. "How much is he making now?"

"About half a million a year, and that's including his shows."

"Yeah, I see what you mean. He's in a different world. Maybe that's why he wasn't considering a divorce, no matter how much he loved Crystal," I said. "He's got one hell of an incentive to stay married to Celeste."

"Speaking of that helo—" Holt started to say, but Fletcher groaned and cut him off.

"I was just getting there, all right?" He threw a mint into his mouth and cracked it between his teeth with a loud noise, then flipped through some screens until it displayed the photo of a black helicopter. "The helo is a Eurocopter EC145, and it's not completely unmarked."

"What do you mean?"

"All aircraft have to display a tail number starting with the letter N, if it's an American registration. This helicopter is no exception, only someone pasted the N-number on it with dark-gray characters, making it almost illegible. I spent hours looking at videos of the thing landing and taking off in the dark at the Scala heliport, then I called the security office and talked to them. They double as flight control for that pad, and they were able to find an older recording where the N-number was visible enough for me to track it."

"And?" I asked, impatiently, although I kind of knew what was coming.

"I tracked it using the FAA database, and the bird belongs to Bennett Holdings, also known as BeneFoods. No surprise there."

"What kind of traffic does the Scala see from that helo?" Holt asked.

"Just pick up and drop off, mostly undocumented, once or twice a week. They don't announce arrivals ahead of time, and they never talk to them. Last time it was there," he added, pulling on the screen a video recording cued to a certain time code, "was the night Crystal died." He started playback, and we saw the helo landing and dropping off someone we recognized immediately: Crystal Tillman, wearing a lace cocktail dress over above-knee, black boots, the same ones she danced in later that night. The time code confirmed Roxanne's statement, that Crystal had been out that night before her shift, and that the helo was there to pick her up, and drop her off a couple of hours later.

"Now there's a surprise," I reacted. "We asked Ellis if he'd seen Crystal on Sunday night, and he said no. He has a confirmed alibi for that night, playing in front of hundreds of people. If Ellis wasn't the one picking her up in that helo, then who was?"

No one answered.

"Fletcher," I said, a tad above whispering, "find me that pilot, please. We need to have a conversation."

"We'll likely need a subpoena for that," Holt said, grabbing his phone. "I'll ask Gully."

"Nah," Fletcher said. "How many licensed helicopter pilots work for BeneFoods, do you think? It can't be that many; once I have that list, I'll run it against active and recent flight plans and give you the name. Let sleeping ADAs lie," he snickered.

Holt laughed, a hearty laugh like I'd rarely seen from him. "You really don't feel the need to complicate your life with legal documents, huh?"

Fletcher's smile widened, showing impeccable white teeth, despite their daily exposure to caffeine. "Just a waste of time; no need for that."

Holt pulled himself off the desk he'd been leaning against, halfway sitting on, and beckoned me. "Thanks, Fletch, you rock."

"And I'll rock some more; I'm not done yet."

Holt sat back against the desk, intrigued.

"No restaurant in this town serves all the items the coroner found in Crystal's stomach contents. The closest I could find was one place that had the crab and the veal with rice, but nothing else. My guess, comparing the timeline of her dinner with the incoming and outgoing helo flights, is that she was taken for that dinner to an unknown location, probably not commercial."

"Like what?"

"Like someone's home, equipped with a helipad and personal chefs who cook those kinds of fancy menus."

I nodded. It made sense, but then again, it didn't. Maybe Ellis had some property close by where he could've flown Crystal? I couldn't believe he'd taken Crystal home, to the mansion he shared with his wife. Maybe we should ask Ellis where they went that night. Or maybe we should just find out for ourselves.

"I'll need a list of all real estate holdings Ellis has access to, that are within reasonable flight distance. Or better yet, scratch that last order, and get me that pilot," I asked, then grabbed my stuff, ready to go.

"Already on it," he replied. "One more thing, quite surprising, because I'd never, in my wildest pipe dreams, expected to find a paper trail for this, but here goes: Mrs. Steele had some interesting cash withdrawal activities eight months ago."

"What? Mrs. Steele? How much?" Holt asked before I could say a word.

"Fifty grand. One withdrawal out of her personal brokerage account, made to cash, two days before Roxanne registered a brand new, blue, Ford Mustang with the DMV."

43

TERMS

Driving to the Steele mansion burned a bit of daylight; we took I-515 south, then the Lake Mead Parkway exit going east. The Steeles owned waterfront property on Lake Las Vegas, nothing short of amazing, but different in many ways from the Bennett MacPherson homestead.

The house wasn't secluded in its own park; rather, it was part of a community of high-end mansions nestled between the waterfront and the golf course, on Rue Mediterra Drive. I found myself wondering why I hadn't, in all my years of being a Las Vegan, ventured to explore that neighborhood. Andrew and I liked to look at homes we couldn't afford and dream of better times, of a different life. But here, on the shores of Lake Las Vegas, we'd never ventured.

We rang the bell and were immediately let in by a housekeeper with a friendly smile. She led us to a living room with black-and-white marble floors so shiny I was afraid I'd slip and fall. We were invited to take seats on the curved, white, leather sofa, but we declined, preferring to stand.

I ambled through the vast, two-story space, so neat and clean it seemed unlived in. After my initial awe subsided, I realized the room was cold, unfriendly, albeit worthy of the cover of *Unique Homes* magazine.

I focused my attention, trying to ascertain what exactly in the décor conveyed the chill I felt in the air. Maybe it was the colors, brightest white contrasting with matte black, those two colors present in the flooring, the furniture, even the table setting in the dining room. Or perhaps it was the crisp, winter-cold, blue sky visible through the tall, wide windows facing the lake.

Footsteps broke my train of thought; I turned and saw Mrs. Steele approaching, elegantly dressed in a cashmere suit in dark green with a black turtleneck and matching pumps. But it was difficult to see past the giant Hermes Porosus Birkin bag on her arm; crocodile skin in such a dark green it was almost black but shone in the bright light. I stopped myself from whistling; that bag had worn a fifty-thousand-dollar price tag. That simple factoid changed the way I thought about the fifty grand she'd apparently given Roxanne. To her, it must've been peanuts.

"How can I help you, Detectives?"

She sat on the edge of a white leather armchair and invited us to take a seat with a charming gesture of her hand and a matching smile. She removed her Chanel sunglasses and placed them on the glass-top coffee table, keeping the bag in her lap.

The housekeeper appeared with a tray and served coffee with fascinating efficiency. I took a sip from a cup she'd poured, without adding sugar or milk, curious to taste the flavor; it was amazing.

"Thank you for seeing us, Mrs. Steele," Holt said, and she smiled at him, a friendly, open smile filled with class and sex appeal at the same time. "We won't be long."

A pang of jealousy reminded me I was alive; she was a beautiful brunette, her shoulder-length hair styled in a sophisticated bob, and her hazel eyes glimmering with gold when the light reflected in them.

"This is in regard to the young woman who was killed at your husband's casino," Holt continued. "I'm sure you must've heard about it by now?"

"Yes," she replied calmly. "Such an unfortunate situation. How can I help?"

I looked at Holt briefly, inviting him to continue, while I studied her reactions in detail. Money had changed hands between her and her husband's mistress; that made her more than a person of interest.

Holt cleared his throat quietly, seemingly uncomfortable. "This is probably going to upset you, Mrs. Steele, and I apologize for having to ask this question, but are you aware your husband was having an affair?"

She breathed; not gasped, like I would've done in her place. No, just breathed and straightened her back, then looked away, seemingly embarrassed.

"Was he sleeping with the girl who died?" she asked, just a whisper I barely caught.

"No, with her roommate, Roxanne Omelas," Holt replied. He paused for a moment, giving her time to react, but other than her hand clasping her handbag spasmodically, nothing happened. "But you already knew that, Mrs. Steele," Holt continued in a gentle tone of voice, "because you met her. In person."

Deliberately, as if it were a movie in slow motion, she turned toward Holt and looked straight at him, then at me. She wasn't shocked; not even surprised.

"Yes, we know you met Roxanne Omelas, and we know how much money you gave her," Holt pressed on, his voice still gentle, friendly. "The only thing we can't figure out is why."

She pressed her lips together with the gesture women make after applying lipstick. A slight frown put minimal lines on her perfect forehead. "Do I need an attorney present?"

"Do you believe you've done something wrong?" Holt asked. "We're not arresting you, if that's your question, nor do we believe you've done anything wrong."

He was smooth, my partner, I thought while I watched Mrs. Steele drop her shoulders just a tiny bit, a sign that his demeanor was helping her relax and trust.

But she didn't say anything for a long moment, and I had to summon my will to keep from fidgeting and asking questions; we didn't have all day. When she finally spoke, it wasn't what I'd expected.

"I need to get out of this marriage," she said, lowering her voice and looking briefly toward the kitchen, but the housekeeper wasn't there anymore.

Holt caught the hint and pulled his chair closer to her, and I did the same.

"You don't know Paul like I do," she continued, weakly. "No one does. All people see is this powerhouse man, an ambitious overachiever, who rebuilt the Scala from the smoldering remnants of his father's bad management. He pulled the company from the brink of bankruptcy, and look where he is now. Right?"

I nodded, and Holt whispered, "Yes."

"But Paul Steele is also a distant, harsh man who expects me to stay locked in here every day, alone, doing nothing but prepare his next gala, organize another reception for the mayor, or create a birthday party for the governor's daughter. To him, I'm a resource, little more than an employee."

Just like that, I understood why I'd felt coldness in that house; because it was there, expressed through visual cues that the rational mind doesn't consciously interpret and acknowledge, but the subconscious analyzes and delivers a result in the form of gut feelings. It was in the fabulous pool, silently still, no laughter and no splashing of water to ripple its perfect surface. It was in the complete absence of anything that suggested people lived there; a book left open on a coffee table, a TV on, some music, or anything to break that terrible silence.

I felt sorry for Mrs. Steele, despite her high-end handbag and fabulous looks.

"Do you have children, Mrs. Steele?" I asked, thinking of another thing that seemed to be missing from that house.

She smiled, that smile touching her eyes with a hint of sadness, of longing. "Yes, two boys, both of them gone to college now." She interpreted my look correctly, because she immediately added, "I had them young."

Then she stopped talking again, her eyes lost in the distance, focused on something on the horizon line, far beyond the massive windows overlooking the lake.

"Please continue," Holt said.

"I wanted to continue my career, once the boys were old enough, but Paul wouldn't hear of it. I have a master's degree in advertising, but practicing, even if it meant a job at our hotel, was out of the question for my husband." Her voice had turned fraught, with hidden tears threatening to break the floodgates open. She fell silent again, her gaze turned away from us and lost in that serene distance.

"Have you thought of divorcing him?" I asked gently.

"There's a prenuptial agreement in place," she replied, her voice tinged with embarrassment. "If I initiate the separation, I get nothing, and that's after twenty-two years of working with my husband to make the Scala into what it is today."

She stopped for a moment and breathed, a long breath of air inhaled, then exhaled slowly, presumably an attempt to control her emotions.

"But if he initiates the separation, if he wants to get rid of me, I get what's rightfully mine. It wasn't only Paul who built this empire. I worked side by side with him, day after day, year after year," she added, reiterating what she'd said before, only more bitterly.

"Or, if he dies or goes away for murder, you get it all, don't you, Mrs. Steele?" Holt asked, his tone harsh, all his previous sympathy and understanding gone and replaced by something I couldn't exactly name. Was that one of his interrogation tactics? He had great talent across the table from a suspect, playing at the suspect's emotions, but I believed I discerned more than that in the tone of his voice.

"Oh, no, absolutely not," Mrs. Steele reacted, "I'd never do that to the father of my sons."

"Then what did fifty grand buy you, Mrs. Steele?" Holt asked coldly.

"It was two hundred and fifty, Detective, and it bought me his indiscretions, my freedom. Nothing else."

"Walk us through the details of your arrangement," he asked, increasingly aggressive with her. I glanced at him, trying to get him to put a lid on whatever was crawling up his arse, but he veered his eyes away from mine, pretending he didn't see me.

Mrs. Steele stared at the shiny, marble floor for a while, then cleared her throat, keeping her hand pressed against her chest. "Roxanne was paid to seduce my husband. I paid her fifty thousand to start. I was going to pay fifty thousand more when she brought me evidence they were sleeping together, then fifty more when he filed for divorce, and the final hundred thousand when the divorce papers were signed and sealed."

"How is that deal going for you, Mrs. Steele?" Holt snapped harshly.

"Pardon my partner, Mrs. Steele," I intervened. "Sometimes men have issues understanding that we women have to get creative to break the chains of our slavery."

"Or men just hate it when the women they trust manipulate and lie to them," Holt reacted, turning toward me, as if I were the source of his anger. "Have you thought of that?" He drilled his dilated pupils into my eyes, making me wonder what he was so riled up about. Was he really having a problem with me? Was it that IAB issue?

I pushed that thought to the side and turned to Mrs. Steele with a sympathetic smile.

"Has Roxanne told you anything recently, about how this arrangement was going?"

Mrs. Steele frowned and fidgeted in place, tucking her bag to the side and taking a sip of coffee.

"I know Paul's been sleeping with her, and I know since when; I could see the signs. I don't know why she hasn't contacted me for her next payment. I hope she's not backing out on our deal."

"You know what I believe?" Holt snapped. "That you heard Crystal was threatening to tell Paul about it, and you decided to eliminate the risk."

She gasped, then quickly covered her mouth with her hand.

"Roxanne didn't tell you of that little wrinkle in your plan?" Holt added coldly.

"No... I didn't even know that other girl existed." She looked around panicked, as if searching for someone who could help her. "You mean, someone out there knows of this, um, arrangement? Oh, no..." she whispered, starting to whimper quietly.

"Well, someone else out there *knew* about it, and I find it hard to believe it wasn't you who eliminated the threat that Crystal posed," Holt added. He stood and started pacing the floor in wide, measured steps, circling the armchair Mrs. Steele took. "Eight hundred million dollars is a hefty motive, Mrs. Steele."

"I—I didn't," she replied, her words shattered as she struggled to breathe. "I don't know what you're talking about."

I stood, ready to leave, and grabbed Holt's sleeve before he could throw another stone. Guilty or not, the woman had talked to us without a lawyer present and that could change anytime. At that moment, I couldn't wrap my head around Mrs. Steele's guilt or innocence; all I could think of was that sniveling, conniving, little bitch, Roxanne. She'd lied to us again.

"We'll be in touch, Mrs. Steele. Thank you for your time," I said, turning toward the exit.

But Holt was standing by the kitchen counter, drawing my attention to where a silver tray held a few, fresh-cut, long-stem roses, pruning shears, and a small pair of fancy gardening gloves.

Our Mrs. Steele was a gardener.

44

SUSPECTS

"Come on," Holt said, leaving Rue Mediterra with a tire-squealing turn, "the woman had eight hundred million reasons to poison Crystal, and she gardens!"

"Just admit you hate her guts," I replied. "I saw you in there, all nice and friendly, and then you lost it. What's crawling up your rear, partner?"

He clenched his jaws and muttered an oath under his breath, then took his anger on the car, slamming his hand against the steering wheel. "Nothing."

"Nothing, my arse!" I'd raised my voice and I wasn't proud of it. I took a deep breath and felt a tad better. "Listen, the woman buys what she needs. I just can't picture her brewing monkshood leaves to make the tea of death, then sneaking out to murder Crystal; I just didn't get that vibe from her. But Roxanne, she lied to us again."

"She kind of lied," he pushed back. "She admitted she'd started dating Paul for money but omitted to say *whose* money. We didn't know to ask, and she wasn't under any legal obligation to volunteer that information."

"So, now you're on that harlot's side?"

"Harlot?" he laughed. "Can you hear yourself?"

"Yeah, it means—"

"I know what it damn means," he shouted, and I looked at him surprised. I'd never seen him so angry. "One of our lockup guests tonight is a contractor, a killer for hire. Mrs. Steele could've easily contracted him, just as she'd contracted Roxanne."

"But why hire both? It makes no sense, admit it," I said, putting a bit of humor in my words.

"It makes sense, if you think of what she said. Roxanne was sleeping with her husband and wasn't coming up with evidence of the adultery to get her next installment. What if Mrs. Steele was afraid Roxanne had changed sides? That's motive, clear as day."

"Listen, Fletcher is working on tracking down the money paid to Ronnie Sanford. We'll find out who paid him. That will put an end to the story; we'll have our killer."

"People like him don't leave paper trails. I'm not going to sit on my hands and wait for that, because it ain't going to happen," he pushed back, still angry.

"I wasn't suggesting that... Jeez, Holt, what the hell is wrong with you today?"

"Fletcher's never going to find out who paid Sanford," he said, avoiding the answer I was looking to get. "The likes of Sanford are careful not to leave any evidence behind. I'm willing to bet you a nice dinner in the most expensive joint in Vegas he got caught by accident last time, and he'll never let that happen again."

"What do you mean, he won't let that happen? He's in lockup right now, you know that. It happened already."

"He's beat the court system once before," he replied. "I saw something in his eyes; I saw determination, skill, and self-confidence. He knows there's no evidence."

My partner, whose impeccable deductive reasoning I'd always respected, was not making too much sense. I studied him briefly, ashamed of thinking he might've been high. But he seemed fine, articulate, his hands stable, his grip on the wheel firm. Only his logic was off.

Maybe he was tired; he wasn't the only one.

"Holt, you're forgetting about the DNA under Anne's fingernails and her testimony. No way Sanford doesn't go down for blowing up the morgue, for killing Erika. He's toast, and he knows it. That's what *I* saw in his eyes; panic, despair, the acknowledgment that his journey was over."

Holt drove silently for a while, the tension in his jaws still visible as knotted muscles danced under his skin.

"If I didn't know better," I said gently, "I'd say you're trying to gaslight me."

He turned toward me for a brief moment, enough for me to catch a glimpse of that crooked grin I knew too well.

"Is that so, Baxter?" All his anger was gone, as if it never existed.

I frowned, "Yes, that's exactly how it feels."

"And you hate that, don't you?"

"Yes, I prefer logic to this mumbo jumbo of partial facts and misinterpreted evidence, of dust in my eyes you keep throwing."

His phone rang through the Ford's media center and Fletcher's name displayed on the screen.

"Keep that in mind for a while, how much you hate being gaslighted, all right?" he said to me before accepting the call. "What do you have, Fletch?"

"The special of the day is one helicopter pilot," he said, and I could hear the smile in his voice. "Mack Eggers, twenty-nine, clean record. He flew choppers for the Army, eight years, honorable discharge. Has been working for BeneFoods for two years."

"Where is Mack Eggers now?"

"I knew you'd ask me that," Fletch replied. "His phone pings at the corporate headquarters, but you better hurry. He's filed a flight plan for later this afternoon, going to Los Angeles with one passenger."

"You're the man, Fletch," I said, feeling the excitement sizzling in my body.

"Don't I know it," Fletcher laughed, and ended the call.

Holt fired up the lights and siren and floored it.

"That's it, Holt, now we'll know."

"Know what?"

"Where Ellis took Crystal the night she died," I replied.

"I thought you liked Roxanne for the murderer," he replied, not a trace of his earlier angst left in his voice.

"And I thought you said it's always the lover or the jilted spouse," I replied smiling.

"Okay, stop this," he reacted. "You used to talk to me, Baxter. What the hell happened?"

He was right. I'd grown so preoccupied with trying to hide my many secrets from him that I'd forgotten how to share, to collaborate, how to brainstorm with him. He was smart, perceptive; he'd seen that change the moment it crept up on me.

"I'm sorry; you're right," I said, but he didn't reply. "I honestly believe Roxanne belongs in jail, but I don't think she killed Crystal. If this makes any sense at all, it's like I can feel her motive was there, her intention to kill her was there, but someone else beat her to the punch. How about you? Do you really think it was Mrs. Steele?"

He mulled the question over for a long moment. "She didn't have the opportunity. From what we were able to figure out, she and Crystal never crossed paths. It's difficult to murder someone remotely, right? She also didn't seem to know Crystal existed. That surprise, when we told her someone else knew about the arrangement she had with Roxanne, was genuine."

"I agree," I replied. "Then let's go back to the basics and finish mapping Crystal's last twenty-four hours. Sometime during this past Sunday, someone got close enough to poison her."

"Deal," Holt replied, pulling into the BeneFoods corporate parking lot.

"I still want to bust Roxanne, though."

"For what? I don't believe the DA will be able to bring criminal charges against her for duping Mr. Steele, even if she got paid to do it."

"She still lied."

45

THE PILOT

I stopped short of entering the BeneFoods lobby, and Holt let go of the door, so it would close. We'd rushed there, driving as fast as we could through the thick traffic, but now I hesitated, thinking it would only be a minute or less after we entered that building before the alarms sounded and lawyers were asked to intervene. Although both Ellis MacPherson and his wife, Celeste Bennett, had been more than forthcoming with us, I doubted that they'd be thrilled to know we were interviewing their employees.

We needed to be smart about things if we wanted to have a fruitful conversation with the pilot.

I took a few steps back and studied the three towers again; the tower in the middle had the rooftop tennis court we'd visited yesterday. The one on the left had a pool, and the one on the right, the helipad. I could tell for sure by the windsleeve blown out all the way at the corner of the roof, sustained by high winds.

We were about to enter the wrong tower.

"That one," I pointed at the right tower, and rushed toward the entry. "Listen," I said between raspy breaths of air, "it's your turn to play a game. Keep the receptionist busy, work your charm, while I find the pilot and talk to him. Otherwise, security will escort us out in thirty seconds or less."

"What do you mean, it's my turn?" Holt asked.

I stopped, panting heavily after rushing up the stairs, and contemplated kicking myself a couple of times. A slip of the tongue, but he'd caught it, and knowing Holt, he wasn't going to let it go anytime soon.

I swallowed with difficulty, feeling my throat constricting, and managed to put a smile on my face, hoping it would seem genuine enough to hoodwink the talented cop standing next to me. "Just joking," I said. "What, you can't handle a sexy receptionist?"

"Uh-huh," he said, giving me a long stare that screamed I wasn't fooling him for one single second.

Bollocks. That mistake would end up costing me dearly, like any other mistake I've made with Holt.

We entered the right tower lobby and Holt went straight for the reception desk, while I pretended to be studying the stunning architecture, trying to get my bearings and locate the elevator that led to the roof. From considerations of symmetry, I had every reason to believe that the elevator I was looking for would be the matching pair of the one in the central tower we took the day before to get to the tennis court.

I had no idea if the pilot would be at the helipad, but I was counting on that; it seemed a safe bet to assume, considering he had filed a flight plan for that afternoon. If he wasn't there, maybe the security officer on that floor would know where to find him.

Walking casually toward the elevator bank I saw Holt leaning against the massive, custom-built reception desk, smiling and looking at the beautiful, young woman sideways, shamelessly flirting. She was an attractive, twenty-something redhead who was about to rip her clothes off right there, in the middle of the crowded lobby. She wasn't taking calls anymore, and she'd removed her headset, then ran her perfectly manicured fingers through her hair to restore the styling and put more of her female scent in the air.

I waited for the elevator to arrive, aware I'd been holding my breath, suffocated by jealousy. I was losing my marbles; that was the only explanation. *I'd* sent Holt to keep her occupied; it was me, no one else. I knew that, but still, seeing him deploying his power smile for another woman and noticing her response to his attention brought my blood to an instant simmer.

Bloody hell, why? I asked myself. If he was just my partner, and the mistake I'd made shagging him was never supposed to happen again, why did I feel like I could easily go over there and bitch-slap that redhead?

Because I was being an idiot, that's why.

I breathed deeply and forced myself to focus on the elevator digits counting down, ignoring the happenings at the reception desk. When the doors finally opened, I stepped inside the cabin and pressed the top floor, glad no one else was sharing my ride.

I gave myself a long look in the wall-sized mirror and sighed. Instead of feeling reassured, I felt the obsessive need to compare myself with the redhead downstairs. Nevertheless, I undid the top two buttons of my shirt and lifted the collar to deepen the V.

Bloody stupid, undecided, irrational, I complimented myself as the doors opened on the top floor. Then my eyes locked with those of a young security guard seated behind a small desk.

Swaying my hips, I approached and caressed his cheek with the tips of my fingers. "Where's Mack, sweetie?"

Slack-jawed and turned into a mute, he pointed toward the helipad, while his eyes stayed riveted to the tip of that V.

I thanked him and went outside, where the pilot, in full gear minus the helmet, was busying himself detaching red covers marked, "Remove before flight" from the black, unmarked helicopter's air intakes. Even standing so close to it, it was almost impossible for me to read the N-number on its tail.

Keeping my back turned toward the security guard I'd just dazzled, I approached Mack and discreetly showed him my badge.

"Mack Eggers?"

"Yes," he said, approaching hesitantly.

"We have a few questions regarding the death of Crystal Tillman. I believe you knew her?"

He ran his fingers through his hair. He reminded me of Andrew; maybe there was something about helicopter pilots that created a certain air about them. Just like doctors have a recognizable demeanor when they walk the hallways of a hospital, pilots share a specific mien, a discernible gait, a particular facial expression, especially when they fret over their flying machines.

"I'd flown her a few times," he replied. "I'm sorry to hear what happened to her, but I signed an NDA with BeneFoods. There's nothing I can share."

"Nondisclosure agreements don't apply to law enforcement during the investigation of a murder, Mr. Eggers," I lied without skipping a beat. In reality, only a subpoena would've counteracted the NDA from a legal point of view, but I was planning to do right by him and get one issued, just in case someone at BeneFoods would decide to hold his feet to the coals.

"Oh, I see," he replied. "What do you need to know?"

"Do you fly this helo to the Scala Casino?"

"Yes, every time one of the Bennetts goes there. Both of them go, usually not together."

"Who's your most frequent flyer?"

"Mr. MacPherson, of course. He's got concerts, and, um, girlfriends," he added, after lowering his voice a little. In the brisk winds up on that rooftop, it was difficult to hear what he was saying.

"And Mrs. Bennett?"

"She gambles sometimes, plays high-limit blackjack."

Ah, there it was, maybe that's how she'd met Crystal; she must've seen her dancing near her blackjack table. Maybe she'd watched her husband interact with her from the lounge, unnoticed by the two lovers.

"Four days ago, on Sunday night, you picked up Crystal from the hotel at about nine PM; is that correct?"

"Yes, ma'am," he replied.

"Where did you take her?"

"To the house."

"Ellis MacPherson took his mistress home?"

"No, ma'am. Mr. MacPherson didn't fly in with me that night to pick her up. I flew alone, under orders from Mrs. Bennett."

That piece of information was so unexpected I had to think for a few seconds, trying to understand what it meant. The fancy dinner Crystal had eaten before she died was served at the Bennett mansion. Only that food wasn't poisoned.

"Then what happened?" I asked, while a deep frown started to take up real estate on my forehead.

Had I been so wrong? Was Mrs. Bennett the murderer, despite her perfectly calm demeanor and her apparent indifference toward her husband's infidelities? How could I have been so blind?

"Nothing, as far as I could tell," he replied, a little pensive. "I took her back to the casino, I dropped her off at about eleven, and that's the last time I saw her."

"Did she say anything during the flight?"

"No, not really. She was smiling at times, but wouldn't say what that was about, and I know my place, ma'am. I don't ask questions."

I nodded a couple of times, mulling things over. Why would Mrs. Bennett want to talk to Crystal? I didn't recall Mrs. Bennett sharing that tidbit of information when we'd spoken with her.

"One more question, Mr. Eggers," I said.

"Shoot."

"I heard you filed a flight plan for Los Angeles for this afternoon. Who are you taking and where?"

"That would be the old Mrs. Bennett," he replied with a smile. "It's her annual vacation with the Legacy Ladies; they're all going to the Dominican, flying out of LAX. That's where the corporate jet is today."

"Who are these Legacy Ladies?"

"They're the surviving spouses of the Bennett Corporation founders—the first executive team. A bunch of old women."

I thanked Mack Eggers and left, and while waiting for the elevator to arrive, I threw a smile at the security officer and entertained myself, seeing him flush then spill some of his coffee on his shirt. *Eat your heart out, redheaded receptionist; I got the goods better than you do.*

Then I texted Holt.

"Meet me in the lobby. We need to speak with Mrs. Bennett again."

46

MRS. BENNETT

We waited for a few minutes outside Mrs. Bennett's office, under the annoyed gaze of her executive assistant. At first, she'd invited us to make an appointment she would've been happy to schedule. When we declined, she invited us to take a seat on one of the plush sofas and wait, but I preferred to look out the window; I'd never had the opportunity to see the Las Vegas business district from that vantage point.

I'd have expected Mrs. Bennett's office to be on the top floor of the center tower, where we found her the day before playing tennis. However, after riding the elevator all the way down to the lobby and meeting with Holt, we learned from his new, redheaded friend we had to ride it back up again; her office was in close proximity to the heliport, which, in practicality, made a lot of sense.

The door to Mrs. Bennett's office swung open and a man, dressed impeccably in an expensive suit, rushed out, carrying an armful of large-size prints and a thick portfolio.

"Detectives," Celeste Bennett called, before I saw her amazing figure appear in the doorway, inviting us in. She wore a black and beige combo, with a black blouse and a beige and black pencil skirt with an asymmetrical gold zipper running down her thigh. I didn't recognize the label of the attire, but it was to die for.

We entered her office, and her assistant followed us in with a tray filled with espressos in tiny cups, and cold, sweaty glasses of water. The room was huge, decorated with impeccable style. The desk was a massive piece in dark-hued wood, matched with the bookcases that lined the wall behind her, the coffee table, and the fireplace mantle. At the side of her desk, toward the window, a Bohemian crystal vase held an intricate arrangement of rare orchids.

Cream-colored leather chairs were placed in front of the desk, and we followed her invitation to take a seat, while she walked briskly and elegantly behind her desk and sat in her massive executive chair.

She leaned forward, waiting for her assistant to finish serving the coffee, making small talk.

"Pardon the wait, Detectives, I was in the middle of a marketing review. We're rebranding our stores starting next year."

"No problem," I replied, amazed at how calm and detached she seemed. "Thank you for seeing us again."

"Tell me, what can I do for you?"

"We're aware you invited Crystal Tillman to your home on Sunday evening; your helicopter flew her in from the Scala."

She didn't skip a beat, and her perfect smile stayed perfect. "Yes, and?"

"You omitted to share that piece of information with us yesterday, Mrs. Bennett," I said, putting a tinge of accusatory disappointment in my voice. "You must understand, when we're investigating a murder, the whereabouts of the victim before she died represents a critical piece of information. I believe you deliberately withheld that from us."

She lowered her eyes for a moment, as if embarrassed with her omission. "You didn't ask, Detective, and I didn't think to volunteer that information. I didn't think of it because our meeting had nothing to do with her murder. What would you like to know?"

Again, I was stunned, disarmed seeing her candor, her flawless composure when dealing with matters that couldn't've been easy for any wife to discuss, no matter how open her marriage was.

"Why did you have Crystal over for dinner?" Holt asked. "What did you two talk about?"

She sighed and veered her eyes for a moment, but straightened her back and looked straight at Holt, then at me.

"I offered her money to disappear, Detectives, but she wouldn't take it. She was pregnant," she added, hiding her eyes for a split second.

"But you said you and your husband have an open relationship," I reacted. "I'm not sure I understand."

"Open, yes," she replied, and I thought I heard a vein of repressed emotion coming across in her voice. "Open to fleeting passions and insignificant flings, but Crystal was becoming more than significant. Ellis had fallen in love with her. He'd fathered her child, for goodness' sake, and wanted to, um, keep it." She stopped talking for a moment, aware her emotions were bubbling up too close to the surface. "I was losing him..." she continued after a while. "I was willing to pay anything to make her go away."

"And when she wouldn't take the money, you poisoned her?" I asked harshly. Her calm had been a façade, and I'd been had; she was just like the rest of us, a jilted, jealous woman, and that meant she had motive. "Is that what you did?"

"No, Detectives, I didn't," she replied calmly, but tears started flooding her eyes. "Listen, I've been forthcoming answering your questions, but if you have accusations against me, then this conversation needs to come to an end."

Her fancy talk stepped on my nerves. I kept thinking of Crystal, of how she collapsed on that stage where she worked night after night to keep herself in school, eager to start making enough money to help her family. She didn't deserve to die because she'd fallen in love and gotten pregnant and wouldn't put a price tag on her feelings for the man she loved.

"I don't know what you're talking about," she added. "What poison? How did she die, exactly?"

"A plant extract," Holt replied. "Monkshood. Stopped that poor girl's heart and paralyzed her lungs. But don't worry," he said, standing up and pulling out zip ties, "you'll learn all the details you're pretending not to know during defense discovery for your murder trial."

He walked around the desk toward Mrs. Bennett, whose mouth gaped open in shock. I looked at her face and had to admit that, based solely on her microexpressions, she was truly surprised. No one can fake the pupils dilating upon the delivery of a shocking blow, the tiny beads of sweat breaking at the roots of one's hair, pallor spreading like a white shroud over one's features.

"A plant extract?" she asked quietly, letting herself be handled and handcuffed without opposing the tiniest resistance.

"Celeste Bennett, you're under arrest for the murder of Crystal Tillman," Holt started to say, when I noticed her shooting a lightning-fast glance at a framed photo on the wall before she lowered her eyelids.

I followed her glance and approached the photo. It was a framed cover of *TIME* magazine dated fifteen years ago, titled, "Vegas Royalty Blooms." The woman on the cover was the old Mrs. Bennett, Patricia, younger then, photographed against a mountain landscape backdrop I recognized from my hikes on Mount Charleston. The subtitle referenced BeneFoods stock being traded on the New York Stock Exchange, the company's successful initial public offering making its owner a billion dollars richer overnight. But that wasn't what caught my attention; in the photo, Patricia Bennett wore gloves, despite it being summer, as proven by numerous flowers in bloom surrounding where she stood, in the middle of a small, sun-filled meadow. Among those flowers, some were purple and could've been described as resembling a monk's hood.

"Holt," I said, and beckoned him over.

I felt a strange, ominous vibration, at first in the rattling of the windows, then as if the entire building resonated. I shot Mrs. Bennett an inquisitive, worried look.

She smiled, a smile touched by sadness, as she looked up at the ceiling. "That's our helicopter getting ready to take off. Nothing to worry about, Detective, we don't have earthquakes here in Vegas."

47

THAT NIGHT

Crystal's heart was pounding with excitement after reading the text message advising her of the pickup time at the Scala heliport. Sure, she would've preferred Ellis had texted her and not the pilot, but she was thrilled nevertheless, as she always was when Ellis could spend any time with her.

She devoted twenty frenzied minutes wondering what she should wear, rummaging through the hangers in her closet in an exhilarated rush. She had no idea where they were going to go, but she didn't assume it would be a public place; after all, Ellis was married, and quite discreet about their affair.

With that thought in mind, she decided to wear something sexy, something that would remind him of the day they met. She still blushed when she recalled how she was running her big mouth in the café, for the immense amusement of Roxanne and Brandi who, bitches that they were, let her continue ranting even after they'd noticed Ellis MacPherson standing there, petrified to hear her go on and on about how awful his music was, and how he should be prohibited from torturing people's ears with those squeaky sounds.

However, her world stood still when their eyes met. At first, she didn't recognize him, but when she did, she wanted the earth to gape open and swallow her whole. She remembered turning around and taking two steps back, as if to distance herself from the man who should've been, by all measures, beyond angry. But he wasn't... he seemed mesmerized, looking at her as if she were someone he'd been waiting for his entire life. Hesitant, he introduced himself.

"I'm, um, Ellis MacPherson," he said, his voice strangled by emotions she didn't understand.

"Crystal," she replied, offering her hand while her cowardly girlfriends vanished. "I'm really sorry about what I said—"

"No, please don't apologize," he replied, his eyes still fixed onto hers. "Can I take you to dinner and plead my case?"

That's how it all started, her affair with a married man, with her soul mate.

The night of their first dinner she'd worn black boots and a see-through sheer dress on top of a skin-colored camisole, turning many heads on the Scala's floor. She smiled at the memory she held dear in her heart and chose to make him relive it on this occasion. She picked a Self-Portrait navy, off the shoulder, guipure lace, mini-cocktail dress, and paired it with over-the-knee stiletto sock boots. As such, if she was tired when her shift started, she could keep the boots on; they were gentle on her ankles, offering support while she danced, and making it easier for her to endure the long hours on her feet.

She added extensions to her hair, and braided it in a loose fishtail, leaving a few strands free to float on her shoulders and around her face in wispy waves. She put on evening makeup but elegant, not loud like she wore on stage, and grabbed a black, Saint Laurent clutch purse in embossed leather, one of her recent extravagances she felt guilty about. She would've preferred to give more of her money to her family, but if she did that, they'd have questions she couldn't answer. After all, they knew she waited on tables at the Scala and went to college on a financial aid program. But soon, when she graduated, she could leave the world of lies and deceit behind her and start building a life for herself she wouldn't be ashamed of anymore.

She drove to the Scala, barely making it in time for the helicopter pickup. She rushed through the lobby, took the elevator all the way up, and climbed the last flight of stairs in a rush to get outside.

The security guard stopped her before she got to the door leading to the helipad. He knew her; at first, the guards had been mean to her, throwing insulting words in barely intelligible comments behind her back or double entendre phrases they believed she wouldn't understand. But that soon came to an end *after Ellis heard them talking about her like that. She didn't know what he'd done, but since then they'd been polite and respectful.*

"He's not here yet," the security guard said, but she decided to step outside on the heliport nevertheless. She loved the cold, windy air swirling above the Strip and she loved looking at the night sky, waiting for the helicopter's strobes to appear in the distance.

Soon it was there, and she climbed in, a little disappointed to see only the pilot had come to pick her up.

"Hey, Mack," she said as soon as she put her headset on.

"Hello, Miss Crystal, how's it going?"

She didn't reply for a while; she tried to stay positive and understanding, but sometimes it was difficult for her to deal with all that. The fact that Ellis was not only married, but an easily recognizable public figure. His wealth and her poverty. His prestige and her demeaning job.

"Where are we going?" she eventually asked, a few minutes after takeoff. Mack was already losing altitude, preparing to land somewhere she didn't recognize.

"I was told to bring you over to the house," he replied after a brief hesitation.

An alarm bell rang loudly in her head. "At the house? Are you sure? We never—I mean, I've never been there before. I don't want to cause trouble."

"No trouble at all, Miss Crystal; you were invited."

Mack touched down the helicopter on the helipad behind a stone mansion, lit with yellowish lights in a postcard-beautiful layout. Hesitant, she waited for him to power down the rotors and walk her to the house, afraid she'd do the wrong thing, or run into the wrong people.

Mack was understanding; he smiled and offered his arm, and walked her to the patio entrance, then to a study overlooking the pool with massive windows behind thick sheers.

"I have Miss Crystal for you," he announced, and he quickly disappeared, closing the door behind him.

"Come in, my dear," she heard a woman's voice. Her blood froze, while sheer panic gripped her galloping heart. Where was Ellis?

The woman stood from the armchair by the fireplace and approached her with a wide smile. Suddenly, her idea to dress provocatively for Ellis that night didn't seem like such a good one; she wished she would've worn a burlap sack instead.

"I'm Ellis's wife," she explained, still smiling kindly at her. But Crystal couldn't think of a word to say. "Come, let's sit outside, by the pool. I had them start a nice fire for us."

She stood there, frozen, panic holding her throat in a tight grip. She couldn't move, although she wanted desperately to unglue her feet from the marble floor and run the hell out of there, wherever she could go.

Ellis's wife sized her up from head to toe, but her smile didn't disappear, nor did it get tainted with hatred or jealousy.

"Why don't you take off those boots and put on some fuzzy slippers to keep your feet warm and comfy? I'll ask for a blanket for you; we don't want you catching a cold."

A maid materialized without being called, holding a soft blanket and a pair of pink faux-fur slippers, and remained standing by her side, waiting. As if hypnotized, Crystal took off her boots, and the maid took them and placed them by the entrance, in a small closet. Crystal put on the slippers, feeling like a child, and followed Celeste to the large patio, where she took a seat next to a burning firepit, wrapping herself in the soft blanket. She was shivering, struggling to keep her teeth from clattering, but she wasn't sure it was the cold air to blame.

Another maid brought wine in tall glasses, set them on the stone table, then vanished.

"I thought we'd have dinner together," she said, but all Crystal could do was nod. "You do speak, don't you?"

"Yes," she managed to whisper, feeling her throat parched dry, but not touching the wine.

"Cheers," Celeste said, raising her glass in the air, but Crystal didn't touch hers.

"Could I have some water, please?" she asked, her voice trembling.

Celeste nodded, her eyes focused on something behind Crystal, most likely on one of her maids. "Why not a hot cup of tea, my dear? You're shivering."

Crystal nodded again, keeping her eyes lowered. She wanted to get out of there... she wanted to cry, to scream. She wanted Ellis to hold her and tell her everything was going to be all right.

"It was reckless of me to offer you wine, and I apologize," Celeste said. "In your condition, you shouldn't touch any alcohol."

A new wave of fear froze her blood. Ellis had told his wife about their baby? Why? What kind of screwed-up marriage did those two have?

She didn't say anything; she couldn't think of an appropriate thing to articulate.

The maid set the table with impeccable efficiency, setting a platter of king crab legs between the two women, a small bowl of remoulade, and a plate with several slices of fresh toast.

Celeste took a bite of toast, then used her utensils with elegance to get a piece of crab meat on her fork and into her mouth.

"This is delicious," she said, as if they were best friends with nothing to do but enjoy gourmet food. "Here, try some," she said, offering her a piece of crabmeat.

Too ashamed to refuse, she took it, dipped it in remoulade, and forced herself to swallow it, together with a tiny piece of toast.

Celeste gestured with her hand and soon the king crab was gone, replaced by veal with rice, served directly on their plates. The smell was delicious, but Crystal couldn't bring herself to unclench her jaws. Her stomach had turned into a stone, and she felt like throwing up.

Unwilling to insult her host, she nibbled at the fantastic-tasting veal and ate a little bit of the rice. She just wanted the entire thing to be over and done with, she wanted Mack to take her back to the Scala, where she could climb on the stage and lose herself in the music.

Where was Ellis? How could he leave her to go through this alone?

The question sent a new wave of anxiety throughout her body. She listened to Celeste making small talk with elegant mannerisms, *first discussing the weather, then the new layout of her patio furniture, and asking Crystal about her plans for the holidays.*

"No plans," she managed to say. "Work and study; nothing much."

The maid collected the barely touched plates and replaced them with tiny cups of raspberry foam and champagne wafers, then brought two champagne flutes, half filled.

"This barely has any alcohol in it," Celeste said, raising the glass.

Crystal hesitated, thinking of her baby, but she raised her glass making the briefest of eye contact with the woman, and took a sip.

Warmth started spreading through her body and she welcomed it. Soon her trembling dissipated, leaving her exhausted, yet the adrenaline kept her anxious, alert.

What did the woman want?

"Why am I here?" she finally summoned the courage to ask.

"I wanted to meet you in person and offer you a life few can only dream of."

Crystal frowned; she could sense a trap opening in front of her, but she didn't know where.

"I don't understand," she replied, looking at Celeste with a slight frown on her forehead.

"I'm saying you could leave here a rich woman, richer than you'd ever have the chance of becoming by yourself."

"And all I have to do is…?" Crystal asked, her voice loaded with sarcasm. She'd realized what was going on. Celeste Bennett was trying to make her disappear.

"Stop seeing my husband, nothing else." The kindness in Celeste's voice had vanished, as if a velvet curtain had been pulled to expose the wrought iron behind it.

A sad smile stretched Crystal's lips. "I'm sorry, but I can't do that."

"You haven't heard the amount, my dear," Celeste replied. "You get to name it."

Crystal stood, feeling ridiculous wrapped in a blanket and wearing fuzzy slippers. "Stop calling me 'my dear'."

"All right, my apologies," Celeste agreed, her voice back to being kind and warm.

It was all a façade, phonier than Crystal's blonde extensions and her stained mascara.

"I think I should leave," Crystal said.

"Please, take a seat," Celeste invited her. "Have another sip of champagne and let us talk, woman to woman."

She sat, realizing she wasn't going to run barefooted through the yard to get out of there. She needed Mack to take her back, or at least someone to call her a cab. She also had her pride, and she wanted so badly not to embarrass Ellis, to behave like a sophisticated woman, the kind he was used to.

In the study, from behind the heavy curtains, the old Mrs. Bennett listened, her frown deepening with every word she heard.

Crystal took another tiny sip of champagne and smiled coldly. "I'm sorry, but what Ellis and I have is not for sale."

"Twenty-five million dollars," Celeste blurted.

"No."

"More?" she asked, in an incredulous and sarcastic tone of voice, as if she thought Crystal was nothing but a scammer.

"Absolutely nothing," Crystal said. "I've never asked for, nor accepted anything from Ellis. I don't want your money, Celeste, and I don't want your wine. As you know, I'm pregnant, and that could hurt my baby." She ended her statement by throwing the remaining wine in the fire. She locked eyes with Celeste and, for once, didn't back down under the woman's loaded gaze.

In the studio, Patricia Bennett gasped when she heard the word, "pregnant." She hesitated for a minute, then rushed to her bedroom upstairs, careful not to make any noise. Moments later she came back downstairs, hiding her gloved hands and a small bottle inside the pockets of an oversized cardigan.

She looked around briefly and rushed to the closet by the entrance. She opened the door, looked around one more time, and slipped inside, pulling the door behind her. Under the dim light of a small flashlight, she found the girl's boots. Using the eyedropper, she was careful not to spill a droplet of poison on anything else. She dripped a few globules of the clear liquid inside the boots, on the *lining of the calves and on the cushioned insoles. She left everything exactly as she'd found it and vanished, unseen and unheard by any of the housemaids or by Celeste and her unwilling guest.*

Outside, on the patio by the fire, the two women still stared at each other, neither willing to back down.

"I'd like to leave now," Crystal eventually said.

"Let me know if you change your mind," Celeste said with a long, bitter sigh, doing a poor job at hiding her tears.

"I won't," Crystal replied, standing. "Not now, not ever."

Celeste beckoned a maid who listened to instructions and disappeared, probably to get Mack.

Crystal realized she was looking at a woman who was afraid she'd lose her husband to another, a woman who was trying to fix something in her life that was badly broken. She felt a wave of sympathy for her, despite Celeste's offer to buy her off.

"Listen," Crystal said, "Ellis and I never discussed marriage, or divorce, or anything. It's not like that. I'm just happy to see him every now and then, and I understand there are limitations to what he can offer me."

Celeste stared at her in disbelief, which Crystal misinterpreted and continued. "I know Ellis loves you and would never do anything to hurt you. That's why I'm surprised we're doing... this," she added, gesturing toward the table, where dishes were being cleared away quickly and quietly by the help.

Mack appeared and looked at Celeste, who nodded discreetly. He rushed toward the helicopter, not waiting for Crystal.

Back in the foyer, Crystal put on her boots and shivered. They seemed cold and damp. It would feel good to keep them on the entire evening, to warm her up after that dreadful dinner. Before heading out toward the helipad, she turned to Celeste and extended her hand.

"I'm really sorry for the hurt we must've caused."

She walked away, holding her head up high, bracing the cold without that blanket and painfully aware of how inappropriately she'd dressed for the unexpected occasion.

Once the helicopter took off, a smile bloomed on her lips, thinking of the real meaning of what had just happened. If Celeste was that worried about her marriage, that meant Ellis really loved her. And soon she'd be in his arms, where she belonged.

48

TAKEOFF

Holt and I rushed out of Celeste Bennett's office and ran up a flight of stairs behind a door marked, "Heliport." Holt climbed two steps at a time, and I wasn't far behind. As we approached, the vibrations coming from the helicopter's rotors intensified. We entered the neatly furnished departure lounge that overlooked the heliport, and I breathed, seeing the aircraft still there.

Holt opened the door and stepped on the helipad, while I was quick to catch up. We both struggled to close the door against the strong gusts coming from the main rotor blades. The noise was unbearable; the EC145 had two jet engines and they were already revved up, ready for takeoff.

We approached the helo as close as we dared, keeping our heads down, and, when the pilot looked at us, I made a clear, imperative gesture running my fingers across my throat a few times, the universal request to kill the engines. Holt made wide gestures with his hands, palms facing down, demanding the same thing.

Yet Mack Eggers didn't obey the request; instead, he turned and looked at old Mrs. Bennett, installed comfortably on the rear seat. I saw her gesticulating, talking agitatedly; although I couldn't hear what she was saying, I believed it safe to assume she was pressing him to take off.

"Hey," I yelled against all reason, as my voice couldn't possibly be heard over the sound of the helicopter's jet engines. I repeated my hand gesture over and over again, squinting to discern what the pilot was doing in there, why he wasn't cutting the engines.

He seemed to argue with Mrs. Bennett, keeping his head turned away from us and toward her. But, after a long moment, he looked straight at us, seemingly regretting what he was about to do. That's when I knew he was going to take off after all.

"No," I yelled, as I pulled out my gun. I didn't want to risk injuring him or Mrs. Bennett, so I stepped toward the side of the helo, followed closely by Holt, who'd also pulled his weapon, holding Mack in his sights.

I took aim at the axle of the tail rotor and squeezed the trigger, the shot barely audible under the loud engine noise. I was about to fire a second shot when the rotor started to wobble and it flew off its damaged axle, coming straight at us.

"Down," I shouted, as I grabbed Holt's arm, throwing him to the ground under my weight.

The spinning rotor missed us by a few inches and, after ricocheting against the helipad's surface, became lodged into the departure lounge wall. The pilot cut the engine and soon silence ensued, although the high winds kept roaring.

We picked ourselves up from the ground, grunting and cursing, while I felt uncomfortable under Holt's frowning scrutiny. Holding my gun in one hand and my loose hair off my face with the other, I gestured to the occupants of the helicopter to climb down. Mack Eggers was the first one to obey. I cuffed him and read him his rights, while Holt opened the door for Mrs. Bennett.

But, instead of dragging her out of the helo, as if he'd remembered something, Holt came toward me and asked, "How did you know to shoot the stabilizing rotor?"

"It's a helicopter's most vulnerable spot, right?" I asked, panting, unable to breathe in the strong winds.

"Yes, exactly, but how did you know?"

I avoided his glance. He drove me crazy with his questions, all coming at the most inappropriate times. "Doesn't matter, Holt. I just knew, all right?"

"It does matter, damn it," he shouted. "You and I have to talk. You don't trust me worth a damn," he shouted over his shoulder, while grabbing Mrs. Bennett's arm and supporting her as she climbed out of the helicopter. "That's a serious problem we're having, Baxter."

"Holt, please," I said, but he'd already turned his back at me. Moments later, I heard his voice rushing through the Miranda rights.

"Patricia Bennett, you're under arrest for the murder of Crystal Tillman. You have the right—"

"I want my lawyer," the old woman said, standing proud and unfazed while being restrained by Holt.

"Of course, you do," he muttered, as he resumed Mirandizing her.

As I watched him take her into the departure lounge, I had the strong feeling I was losing something important, something I couldn't afford to let go.

My partner.

49

EMPATHY

Booking Mack Eggers and Patricia Bennett wasn't routine, because nothing about Patricia Bennett was banal, or had ever been. When we arrived at the precinct, a fire-eating lawyer who'd identified himself as Salvatore Lucio, attorney at law representing Mrs. Bennett, met us on the doorstep, running his mouth on how we could've had the decency of not dragging such a respected pillar of the community in cuffs like a regular hoodlum. Yes, we could've, but we didn't, and I, for one, couldn't care less, after the old hag had potentially cost a good pilot his license, maybe his freedom.

Instead of apologizing, which I really didn't feel like doing, I grinned cynically at Lucio and told him, "Be thankful the media isn't here yet. We could've also dragged our feet, so they could catch up with us and give us all our moment of fame."

That shut him up promptly, but by the look in his eyes he wasn't done with me yet.

However, Mr. Lucio had already started to put the wheels of justice in motion; he'd secured an appearance in front of a judge that same evening, even if it was seven-thirty and any other arrestees brought in that late would've looked at spending the night behind bars, waiting to be arraigned the next morning. Due to Lucio's influence, the rotation judge was willing to hear the parties on bail within the hour.

Gully appeared, out of breath and flustered, and stopped next to us, shooting Lucio side glances filled with worry. "Thanks for the heads-up," he said to me, referring to the call I'd made the moment Holt snapped the cuffs on Mrs. Bennett. "I better not screw this up," he added, apprehension seeping into his voice as his eyes veered to the left again, where the imposing Mr. Lucio stood by his client's side.

"If I may offer some advice?" I asked, and he nodded quickly. "Shoot for the stars and land on the moon with this one. No amount of bail will make her a safe bet, but, being who she is, she won't be remanded either. Just point out to the judge that she tried to run from the police in her eight-million-dollar helicopter, one of the many resources at her disposal, in an attempt to flee to the Dominican Republic, a nonextradition country."

Gully smiled widely, a little embarrassed. "I owe you big on this one, Baxter. You too, Holt," he said, and Holt showed him a thumbs up. "What's with him?" he asked, pointing at Mack Eggers.

I took a deep breath, hoping I was about to do the right thing. "This guy's more a victim than a perp," I said, and Holt shot me an inquisitive glance.

"How come?" Gully asked. "Didn't you have to shoot that helicopter to get him to comply?"

I looked briefly at Holt, and he approached, his curiosity piqued.

"Yes, and no," I replied, hesitantly at first, then gaining momentum under Holt's supportive look. "He seemed under duress from his employer, who was making threats at the time. The way I see it, a mere pilot can't afford to make an enemy out of a person of this caliber of power and wealth. I know, in his shoes, I would've hesitated a little myself."

"So, you're saying he shouldn't be indicted?"

I looked at Holt again, and the corner of his mouth flinched imperceptibly in the faintest hint of a smile.

"That's exactly what I'm saying," I replied calmly, ignoring the pilot's stunned stare. He was within earshot, and I'd done nothing to lower my voice to keep him from overhearing what I had to say. Later, my words might serve to get him out of his jam. "I'm saying he could've taken off five times already in the time it took us to get there and shoot the rotor. I'm saying Mrs. Bennett is the real villain here."

"Is that your perspective too, Holt?" Gully asked.

"Word for word," he replied without a trace of hesitation.

Gully nodded a few times. "Noted. I'll review the circumstances and decide if the state will prosecute." He scratched his head and looked at Mrs. Bennett, then at Salvatore Lucio. Mrs. Bennett had been fingerprinted and processed, and now was waiting for the database searches to complete before proceeding to the arraignment. Lucio had negotiated for his client to wait in the Central Booking area, instead of a holding cell.

I watched Mrs. Bennett closely, looking for any sign of emotion on the distinguished face I had, until mere hours ago, regarded with such admiration. She sat on a backless bench, holding her spine straight and her head high, as if she were there to discuss adding a new wing to the police department building. No trace of concern in her eyes, no worry, and no guilt.

"By the way, the CSI report came back on Roxanne's house," Holt said, reading from his email. "Not a trace of poison was found at the house, but they found her fake ID right next to her real one. And guess what? She had hashish-laced, edible body gel. That's possession."

"Did anyone collar her yet?" I asked, but no one answered because everyone was distracted by the drama unfolding before us. I was unable to take my eyes off the sophisticated Mrs. Bennett, impassible in the face of adversity like no other woman I'd ever seen.

Gully drew near me, looking at her with the same intensity as I was, only with different thoughts on his mind.

"She's big fish, this one," he muttered, careful not to be overheard by Lucio. The attorney was engulfed in a spirited conversation with one of his aides, standing only a few feet away from Mrs. Bennett, but with their backs turned toward her, shuffling through the papers in a file.

"She's a bloody blue whale," I said. "How are you going to handle her?"

He shrugged, letting a quick and raspy breath of air out of his lungs. "It's not that easy."

"Why? This is an open-and-shut case, right?" I asked. "As soon as the search warrant is executed, and the poison is found, your case will be even tighter."

"Not really, no," Gully replied, and Holt approached us, frowning. "We need strong evidence linking her to the poison, or a confession. Even if the poison is found in the house, we can't tie her to it beyond a reasonable doubt. Tons of people are in that house every day."

"What about the *TIME* cover?" Holt asked. "That proves access, knowledge."

"That magazine cover is circumstantial at best. That shark over there will claim she didn't even know what plants were growing in the background," he said in a low tone of voice, shooting Lucio another worried look.

"You know she did it, right?" I asked, looking first at Gully, then at Holt. "Well, I'm willing to bet my next paycheck they'll find the poison hidden in one of her drawers."

"And if they don't? Then what do we have, really?" Gully asked. "A harmless, old woman who wanted to take her annual trip to the Dominican, and you arrested her for no valid reason after destroying her property and endangering her life, because that's how they'll spin it. The mayor's friend and the governor's daughter's godmother, a Fortune 500 personality without access to the victim, without any proof of premeditation. All in all, a bad arrest that we'll be hearing about for the rest of our short careers. Did you know the DA wouldn't hear of showing up tonight, and the Nevada Attorney General won't take my calls?"

But I'd moved away already, leaving Gully in Holt's charge; my partner was a good listener for ADAs with thin career cases and cold feet.

After making sure Mr. Lucio was still busy with his aide, I walked casually toward the bench where Mrs. Bennett was and sat next to her, maybe one foot away, not more. She gave me a long, cold stare, but didn't say anything. After a few moments, I drew closer to her.

"I understand, you know," I said in a low voice. "I do, I completely understand."

She threw me an intrigued look, but still didn't say anything. However, there was a glimmer in her eyes that told me I was welcome to carry on.

I shook my head slowly, dramatically, drawing even closer to her. "Just the thought of having a stripper's bastard stake claim to your father's legacy, that must've driven you crazy. I know what it would've done to me."

She was silent, but words were fighting to come out, judging by her lips, pressed tightly together as if it took all her willpower to keep her mouth shut.

"I'll do my best to help you," I added, lowering my voice even more. "We, decent women, have to have some measure of defense against these gold-digging harlots. Believe me when I say, I would've done the same."

I locked eyes with her and held her gaze without budging, trying to convey empathy, not judgment. I'd entered in character, and my script called for a mean, selfish, despicable woman who'd do anything to protect her fortune. It wasn't all that difficult to act; all I had to do was emulate what I saw before my eyes.

"There are ways I can help you, and you can count on me," I added, knowing the truth was about to burst free from the prison of her mind. "I'll speak with the DA and put the seed in his mind that you were under extreme duress."

"I had to," she finally said, looking at her lawyer as if she were afraid he'd hear her talking to me and give her a hard time for that. "There was no way I was going to let that shame stain our family's impeccable reputation," she continued, clasping my hand with her bony fingers.

"Why didn't your daughter divorce the cheating bastard?"

She slapped her hands against her thighs in a gesture of frustration. "Because my daughter was stupid, reckless, a complete fool."

"Ah, there was no prenup?" I asked, my voice filled with a warm understanding I was feigning quite well.

"Not one that matters," she replied bitterly. "It only excluded assets predating the marriage." She bit her lip in an angry gesture. "When Celeste married Ellis, the company was worth under a billion dollars. Now it's worth five!" She turned halfway to me, to look at me directly. "Now tell me that piece of scum and his whore are worth two billion dollars."

"But, I thought you owned most of the company," I said, confused as to how all the assets were distributed in their family.

"When Celeste's father died I was sick for a long time, so I put most of it under my daughter's name, for tax purposes. You know, in case I died prematurely. That was before she got married. But afterward the business grew like a weed."

"Oh, I see," I replied, "then there wasn't really anything you could've done."

"Can you believe it, this Ellis nobody ripping the company to shreds over a stripper?"

The word never sounded so demeaning until that moment.

"I understand, I really do," I said, patting her gently on her hand while the tone of my voice changed, turning cold, unforgiving. "She was a dancer, that's true, but she was also a daughter, a sister, a loyal friend, a woman in love, a young, soon-to-be mother."

Her jaw dropped, as she watched me take my phone out of my shirt pocket and stop the recording. Then I stood and bowed my head with mock respect. "Thank you for this," I said, gesturing with the phone in my hand.

"Mr. Lucio," she called out in a loud, commanding voice.

The attorney approached, his brow furrowed and his thinning, combed-over hair in disarray. He listened to what she whispered in his ear, then turned on me like a lion going after a gazelle.

"I'll have your badge for this," he shouted. "You questioned my client without her attorney present, after she'd retained counsel. Whatever you think you have is inadmissible."

Huh, you and everyone else who wants my badge, I thought, unimpressed. "What do you mean?" I asked candidly. "You were present during our conversation. You were right there, inches away. Wait, aren't you her counsel?"

"Yes, but—"

"Yes, and you were present," I interrupted him rudely, thankful my mother wasn't there to hear me and slap me silly. "The fact that you became distracted and didn't feel necessary to do your job doesn't make the evidence inadmissible."

My phone chimed, and I briefly turned my attention to my inbox, seeing Anne's name pop up on the screen. Her message was short; she'd found increased concentrations of the toxin in the skin samples taken from Crystal's calves and feet. She confirmed that the poison had entered Crystal's bloodstream through her skin. Then she'd tested the boots she'd kept in cold storage and could ascertain the killer had murdered Crystal by tainting the linings of her boots.

Without a word, I showed the email to Holt, then he and I smiled. We had her dead to rights; Patricia Bennett had gained access to Crystal's boots during her visit at the Bennett mansion. We still needed Patricia's fingerprints found on the actual poison, or at least for her confession to be admissible in court, but, in any case, our job was mostly done.

Satisfied, I turned to Gully, whose slightly gaping mouth gave him a comical appearance. Behind him, Holt smiled with a look of amazement on his face, the kind you give a child when she jumps out of a second-story window but manages to land on her feet without breaking a single bone.

"The confession is in your inbox," I told Gully. "I'm not sure you're going to be able to use it, but at least now we all know where we stand, and Anne's got the medico-legal report to back it."

He stared at me, then at Lucio who kept on spewing all sorts of threats and had started making phone calls to influential people who'd soon want my badge too.

"So that's how you did it," he muttered, running both his hands through his hair in a gesture of despair.

Thinking of TwoCent's confession, I looked him straight in the eye without skipping a beat. "Did what?"

50

ONE QUESTION

The heated banter had turned into an annoying ruckus, after Lucio's threats had escalated to a unilateral shouting match that the ADA was taking unexpectedly well. Captain Morales had appeared in the meantime, summoned back to the precinct due to the unusual circumstances that we'd created.

Morales had already debriefed us in his office, then dismissed us without showing much regard for the successful conclusion of our case; for him it was a political pitfall, and I could easily imagine he'd waited for us to close the door to speed dial the sheriff and ask for instructions on how to proceed with the hot potato making noise in Central Booking. Not even the fact that Fletcher had been able to track the money paid to Ronnie Sanford to an account in the Bahamas, paid at the exact time that Patricia Bennett was vacationing there had removed the deep ridges marking his brow.

Thankfully, to defuse the situation and avoid other involvement from my part, he ordered us off the premises, pending an investigation into the way we'd handled the case. I was finished anyway; little did Morales know that, even if I survived said investigation, I wasn't going to survive the IAB's noose tightening around my neck. Because there was no way in hell I'd jam up Holt, even if I believed he'd done something less than kosher with that bloody brick of cocaine. The man had saved my life twice; I owed him that much.

I felt a strange exhilaration at the thought of leaving the precinct, now that the case was technically closed. I'd get a chance to eat, to enjoy a meal without rushing through it, without feeding myself stale, greasy food from paper wrappers in Holt's speeding Interceptor. But there were two loose ends still gnawing at my mind, threatening to ruin the dinner I was planning to share with Holt.

There had been something weighing on his mind over the past few days; gradually, he'd turned more and more distant, less engaged in our investigation, and there was a certain look in his eyes I needed to understand better.

"Want to celebrate?" I asked my partner, flashing my megawatt smile.

"What, being suspended?" he reacted, laughing quietly, but that laughter didn't touch his eyes. "Sure, why not?"

"Okay, you pick the place, I pick the tab," I offered. "I got one more thing to take care of, all right?"

"Make it quick," he said, throwing a frowning glance toward the closed door to Morales' office. Our boss had told us to leave; he wasn't going to take it lightly if we disobeyed that order.

I rushed back toward Central Booking and found Gully. He was still in the middle of a series of heated exchanges in thick legalese, out of which I didn't understand anything other than the fact that I'd started it all and I deserved to be hanged for it. Unwilling to wait for Lucio to stop his verbal attack, I grabbed Gully's sleeve and dragged him out of there.

"He'll be back in thirty seconds, I promise," I said to Lucio, whose eyes threw darts at me while he muttered something I pretended I didn't catch.

"What's up?" Gully asked in a low voice.

"Hey, I need a favor," I said. "Remember that five-hundred-thousand-dollar chip that Paul Steele had given to Crystal before she died?"

"Yes, that's locked in evidence. What about it?"

"Crystal earned that money before she died, right?"

"Technically, she—"

"Great," I cut him off, unwilling to hear anything else but a loud yes articulated with conviction. "Please see that her family cashes that after the trial, okay? That's what Crystal would've wanted."

Gully stared at me for a brief moment, his eyebrows ruffled and slightly raised. "I'll see what I can do," he replied cautiously. "But why ask me this today? Won't you be able to make sure that happens just the way you want it, later on down the road?"

"Hey, you never know," I said, avoiding the direct answer he was looking for. "Good luck with this mess," I said. I gave him a quick peck on the cheek and rushed toward the exit, where Holt was waiting, leaning against the wall with a strange expression on his face.

Once outside, I stopped and breathed in the cold, evening air, feeling it oxygenate my brain and dissipate my weariness. I still had one annoying question on my mind and, no matter how hard I tried, I kept going back to it, again and again.

How did Celeste find out about Crystal? Did Ellis share with his wife all the sordid details of his affairs? I understood, to some extent, the concept of an open marriage, but I couldn't imagine the two of them having dinner and talking leisurely about who else they'd slept with that day, who was pregnant, or how good in bed the tennis pro really was.

Something didn't add up.

As we walked across the visitor parking lot toward the garage, a black limousine pulled up at the curb, and I saw Celeste Bennett step out, looking cautiously around her, fearing the media storm that was about to start. She saw me approaching quickly and stopped in her tracks.

"Detective," she said, her voice barely a whisper.

I looked at her and saw her pale lips, the weariness in her eyes, the hopelessness that engulfed her like a shroud. Maybe she feared I would change my mind and arrest her, like I'd started doing a few hours earlier, before I found out her mother liked purple mountain flowers. Or maybe there was something else going on.

"What happened?" I asked, instead of asking what I really wanted to know.

"I lost my mother tonight, and my husband too. He left... he blames me for everything."

"How did you know, Mrs. Bennett? How did you find out Crystal had become significant? Did your husband tell you?"

"I sensed something was different, but he didn't tell me, and I didn't know for sure," she replied. "Not until I got that letter and I learned her name. Then I went there, to the Scala. I watched her dance, I saw how Ellis looked at her."

"What letter?"

She smiled sadly, as she opened her purse and pulled out a handwritten letter folded in thirds. I took it using a latex glove, then waited until Holt pulled out a see-through evidence bag and slipped it inside.

There, in the yellow sodium lights of the parking lot, I read the words that had sealed Crystal's fate.

Dear Mrs. Bennett,

I'm hoping you will forgive the sender of this note, knowing that my intentions are pure. I am deeply concerned for the future of my dearest friend, a young, talented girl by the name of Crystal Tillman. She's everything I have in this world, and I am scared for her.

She's in love with a married man, and she's carrying his child. I've urged her to give this man up, to walk away, knowing that her actions are breaking someone else's heart, and that her happiness is based on someone else's misery.

Yours.

She wouldn't listen; she wouldn't let him go, and I'm terrified that you'll feel the need to seek retribution for the damage she and her lover have done to your life.

Therefore, from the bottom of my heart I am begging you, Mrs. Bennett, please find the strength and the kindness to forgive, to understand. Someone as powerful as you can easily crush a young girl like her, but she doesn't deserve that. She never wanted to be a homewrecker; she's just a naïve girl with a heart of gold, who made the mistake of falling in love with the wrong man.

Please, Mrs. Bennett, she's all that I have.

The letter wasn't signed, but it didn't have to be. Even if the Crime Lab wouldn't find any fingerprints on it, I still knew who sent it.

"Roxanne," I said to Holt. "That little—"

I thanked Mrs. Bennett, cringing when I thought of what she'd think of me as soon as she'd learn about my role in taping her mother's confession. Thankfully, she hadn't heard about that yet, or she wouldn't've shared that letter with me. She walked back to the waiting limousine, got in, and we watched as it pulled away.

"What do you say we have dinner at the Scala?" Holt said with a crooked grin.

"It's a deal," I replied.

I spent the entire drive to the Scala mulling over Roxanne's letter, a murder weapon just as deadly as the monkshood extract had been. That apparently unsophisticated epistle contained one poisonous dart after another, seemingly innocent words aimed at ripping Celeste's heart apart like the deadly claws of a monster lurking in the shadows.

It made sense... Roxanne was the one with the strongest motive to kill Crystal, the person she saw as a threat in her move to have and to hold Paul Steele and his fortune. Yet in the eyes of the law, she wouldn't be found guilty of Crystal's murder. In my eyes though, she was guilty as sin.

And she was about to pay.

A few minutes later, we dashed across the plush carpet in the high-limit gaming room toward the stage where Roxanne danced, paying no attention to the gamblers lining the tables. When she saw us, she stopped dancing and climbed down, color draining from her face, while Farley rushed over from the lounge area, his oversized jowls bouncing over his shirt collar like a bulldog's.

I held out my zip tie cuffs and beckoned Roxanne to approach.

"Not here, please," Farley urged me, but I ignored him.

She didn't move, so I yanked her arm, folding it behind her back. She instantly started to cry.

"No, please," she whimpered, pulling away from me and hiding her hands behind her back as if that was going to stop me from cuffing her. I grabbed her shoulder and propped her against the side of the stage, then cuffed her wrists behind her back.

"Roxanne Omelas, you're under arrest for obstruction of justice and the use of false identification. That's all we can think of right now, but I promise you there will be more," I said, as I recited the list of her Miranda rights.

"Call Paul," she urged Farley, who obeyed without question.

"Great, we have something to discuss with him too," I said to Roxanne and winked.

"No," she screamed, "no, why are you doing this to me?"

I stopped and stood in front of her, my eyes drilling into hers. "You killed that girl just as if you'd poisoned her yourself. That letter you sent was a brilliant move."

She stopped whimpering for a brief moment, staring at me in disbelief. Then, as she understood the consequences of what I'd said to her, she started shaking, while a deathly pallor overtook her face.

I grinned. "Yes, it was brilliant, and I will make sure you pay for what you've done."

I resumed walking her toward the door, holding her arm tightly in my grip, not really concerned if I left any marks on her alabaster skin.

When Paul Steele rushed in, she started sobbing louder, pleading with him, but Holt intercepted the man before he could reach her.

"Mr. Steele, there's something I think you should know," Holt said, as he pulled him aside for a private conversation.

He whispered something inaudible in Paul's ear, then the two men shook hands and the magnate turned to leave. The only sign that his world had just been shattered was in his shoulders, in the tension that gripped them and brought them higher up.

"No, Paul, no, don't leave me, please," Roxanne cried, and the echoes of her cries accompanied Paul Steele who looked back and stared at her blankly on his way to the door, his pupils dark, menacing.

"Please carry on, Detectives. I have no idea who this person is."

INTERROGATION

I managed to persuade Holt to accept dinner at the HEXX as soon as Roxanne was taken to Central Booking by a patrol crew we radioed for. I loved the HEXX, and it was probably going to be a while until I could afford to set foot in there again, as I was about to become unemployed. In a repeat of Monday night's outing, I chose to sit outside in the cold but fresh air of the patio, enjoying the warmth coming from a space heater the hostess had pushed next to our table.

I looked at my partner and felt a knot in my throat. He looked grim, sitting silently across from me, his shoulders hunched forward, barely looking at the menu.

"Hey, do you—" I started to ask, but he cut me off before I could continue.

"Excuse me just a second, Baxter, I need to wash my hands," he said with a humor in his voice I wasn't buying. "I handled too much scum today."

He stood and disappeared inside the restaurant, while I watched the thinning flow of tourists on the Strip and the water show across the street, at the Bellagio fountains.

He was taking a while, so I figured I might as well get that pesky IAB business off my mind, so I could enjoy the evening. I pulled out my work phone and typed an email to Lieutenant Steenstra.

Lieutenant,
Please be advised there isn't a single shred of evidence I could find to prove that Detective Jack Holt has mishandled evidence or has stolen the missing kilo of cocaine.

That said, bearing in mind our recent conversation, should you find it necessary to terminate my employment as a consequence of my failure to deliver said evidence, please feel free to do so, and communicate your decision at your earliest convenience.

Best regards,

(Barely, but still) Detective Laura Baxter

I chuckled at the bit of humor I'd embedded into my signature and clicked send. The rat twat at least would see she hadn't brought me to my knees, and she could go screw herself for all I cared.

When I looked up from my phone, Holt was there, pulling out his chair and taking his seat. He looked just as sullen as before; washing his hands hadn't worked any wonders for his mood. I forced a smile on my face.

"Come on, partner, we're not really suspended, you know. We can have adult beverages and celebrate closing one hell of a case."

"Trust me, we're suspended. We still have our badges and weapons, but we're busted."

"No, we're not, you'll see. Come Monday morning, worst that will happen is modified duty for a week, until they sort things out. The brass have got to cover their arses somehow. We dropped them quite the bombshell, didn't we? What a perp walk that will make," I laughed, imagining Patricia Bennett shielding her face from the media flashes gone crazy, when the sharks would gather for a feeding frenzy.

Then my smile withered, and my eyes veered away from his; I'd omitted telling him he was also looking at being assigned a new partner come next Monday; there was no reason to ruin a perfectly good dinner.

Michelle, our old acquaintance approached, and her professional smile wavered a little when she recognized us. But I was hungry and aching for some alcohol to warm my blood, so I smiled back at her as I ordered a stiff drink. Holt settled for a beer, and just the thought of holding a cold beer in that late-night chill made me shiver.

As soon as Michelle brought our drinks and took our orders, I raised my glass. "To closing one hell of a case, partner," I said, and a tinge of sadness touched my heart when I recalled Crystal's body on that stage where she had fallen, her beauty untouched yet by death's grip. We'd brought justice for her, but we were never going to bring her back to her loved ones.

"Speaking of cases, what the hell was that stunt you pulled out there with old Mrs. Bennett?" Holt asked, dissipating my sadness.

"Nothing," I said, smiling serenely above my French 75 cocktail, double the gin. "Just an interrogation technique."

For some reason, my casual answer brought another shade of gloom to Holt's face. Maybe it was time to have the conversation I'd been avoiding for a while.

As Michelle placed mouthwatering appetizers on the table, I heard my phone chime. I had a new email. Curious as to who might be emailing me from work that late at night, I took a peek.

The email from Steenstra was only a few words in length. "Please report to duty as scheduled."

Hey, I still have a job, I wanted to cheer, but I couldn't, not without sharing lots of information I wasn't ready to with my sullen partner. Instead, I stabbed a piece of crispy broccolini with my fork and chewed it with my eyes half-closed.

I looked straight at Holt and asked, "What's eating you up?"

He let a long breath of air leave his lungs and clenched his jaws for a moment.

"I'm putting in for reassignment," he eventually said, avoiding my look.

"What?" I reacted, feeling my stomach turn into a tight knot. I couldn't lose him, not now, not knowing I still had a job to go to come Monday. Not when my entire being screamed for him. "But you can't," I said pleadingly. "Didn't the boss say you've had too many partners, and you couldn't be reassigned?"

He still didn't look at me. "I'll put in for a transfer if I have to, but you and I can't work together anymore." When he finally looked at me, I saw a determination in his eyes that left me breathless, hurting inside like I'd never thought possible.

"Why?" I whispered, clasping my freezing hands together to hide the tremble in my fingers. "We're darn good at it, aren't we?"

His jaws clenched again, and he muttered a long oath. "Do you trust me, Baxter?"

"With my life," I replied immediately. I believed those words with all my heart.

"Maybe that's true," he admitted, seemingly reluctant to do so.

"I lied to the IAB for you," I said, lowering my voice, "I covered for you, and still do."

"Yeah, all that," he said, speaking slowly, as if still thinking things over, still trying to reach a decision.

I held my breath for a long, tense moment. *Please, Holt, don't leave me*, I thought, unable to articulate the words out loud.

"How did you know where to shoot that helo to incapacitate it?" he suddenly asked, riveting his eyes into mine, the way I did when trying to catch a suspect in a lie.

I closed my eyes for a moment, feeling a wave of pain catching up with me and crushing me. *Damn you for forcing me to do this… damn you.*

When I opened my eyes, a flare of anger lit them up and I didn't try to hide it.

"I was married to a helicopter pilot. A passionate one... he talked about his missions a lot, about flying, about maneuverability, agility, endurance, yawing ability, all that fun stuff." I struggled speaking, as sadness choked me when I said the words Andrew used to say to me; in my mind, his voice resonated with mine, like an echo only I could hear. I pushed the pain aside, feeling anger bubbling up in my chest and swelling it, making my heart thump harder, faster. "But you knew that already, didn't you?" I said, looking straight at him, unyielding.

"What?" he replied, feigning surprise, but he didn't fool me for a minute. The flicker I saw in his dark pupils when I'd asked the question, the tiny twitch of his mouth, and the barely noticeable flutter of his eyebrows told me he was lying.

"Yeah, you knew," I said calmly. "You did a full background on me, because you're a good cop, and that's what a good cop would do." He didn't say anything, but he lowered his eyes and played with his food absentmindedly. "Because that's what *you* would do."

"Yes," he whispered, and looked at me again, this time with sadness and shame in his eyes.

"Then you know he's dead, you know how and where he died. Not overseas, but here, in Vegas, at the hands of an odd-eyed drug dealer—"

"That you pummeled to a pulp a year later," Holt intervened.

I took a sip of alcohol, hoping it would quench my all-consuming anger; instead, it fueled it.

"Yeah, and if you know all that, you must know how painful it still is for me to talk about it, but you keep pressing and pressing," I said, raising my voice with every word that stirred up the pain I'd been carrying with me for so long. "Why? Is this some kind of screwed-up mating ritual you're trying to pull off? 'Cause it sure as hell ain't working."

He was taken aback by the violence in my outburst, but then he pushed the plate aside and leaned closer to me. "Because I want you to trust me," he said quietly, his voice filled with soothing warmth.

My anger was too strong. "I trust you, Holt, I already told you. Not bringing up my late husband as a conversation topic doesn't mean I don't trust you," I reacted, exasperated with him for bringing me to the brink of tears.

"Sending me away two nights ago so you could pay a nocturnal visit to TwoCent means you don't trust me as your partner," he said, speaking just as calmly as before.

I gasped, covering my mouth with my trembling hand. When I spoke, my voice was shattered, as if air wouldn't want to leave my lungs. "You knew about that?" I managed to ask.

"Yes, I did."

"How?" I asked, swallowing hard, feeling my throat constricted, dry as parchment.

"I was there, having your back, in case things didn't go your way," he replied casually, as if we were talking about routine aspects of our jobs. But that warmth in his voice was still there, speaking more than his words were able to.

I felt tears burning my eyes, tears of gratitude, of guilt, of shame, and no effort I made to hold on to my anger and dry them away yielded anything but rolling droplets of salty water down my cheeks. "Thank you," I eventually whispered, touching his hand over the table. "Thank you for being there for me, for caring. No one's ever done that for me, not since Andrew."

Holt didn't pull back his hand, but he didn't reciprocate the gesture either. He looked at me for a moment, his eyes loaded with that blend of emotions I sometimes saw when he thought I wasn't paying attention.

"I'll always have your back, Baxter," he eventually said.

I frowned, confused. "But you said you're putting in for reassignment?"

"Nah," he reacted, while the familiar, crooked grin pulled at the corner of his mouth. "Just an interrogation technique."

I gasped again, recognizing the words I'd previously said, and felt another wave of heated anger coursing through my blood. My face scrunched, and my hands trembled with the urge of breaking something, of throwing something at him. Out of options, I grabbed the napkin off my lap and slammed it on the table.

"Detective Jack Holt, I swear to you, I could kill you right now. I could make you scream and bloody enjoy it," I said, making a scratching gesture with my fingernails, as if I were about to reach over the table and leave long, bloody marks across his smirking face.

He leaned back against his chair while his grin widened, his eyes not leaving mine, his gaze intense, searing, melting my anger and turning it into overwhelming, urgent desire, equally intense, only far more dangerous.

Michelle appeared, bringing strawberries and whipped cream, but we didn't break our loaded eye contact. She dropped them on the table and disappeared without a word, wondering if her two customers were sane, considering how they stared at each other.

Holt interlaced his fingers behind his head and said in a low, sultry voice, "Tell me in detail, how exactly are you planning to make me scream?"

~~ The End ~~

If *Casino Girl* had you totally immersed and gasping at every twist and turn, then you have to read more unputdownable page-turners by Leslie Wolfe!

Read on for a preview from:

Las Vegas Crime

In Las Vegas, secrets can kill.

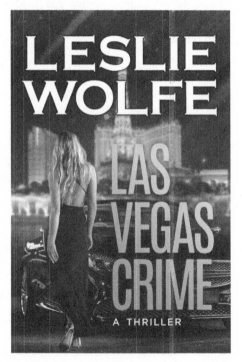

~~~~~~~~

THANK YOU!

A big, heartfelt thank you for choosing to read my book. If you enjoyed it, please take a moment to leave me a four or five-star review; I would be very grateful. It doesn't need to be more than a couple of words, and it makes a huge difference.

Join my mailing list to receive special offers, exclusive bonus content, and news about upcoming new releases. Use the button below, visit www.LeslieWolfe.com to sign up, or email me at LW@WolfeNovels.com.

Did you enjoy Baxter and Holt? Would you like to see them again in another Las Vegas crime story? Your thoughts and feedback are very valuable to me. Please contact me directly through one of the channels listed below. Email works best: LW@WolfeNovels.com or use the button below:

CONNECT WITH ME!

Email: LW@WolfeNovels.com
Facebook: https://www.facebook.com/wolfenovels
Follow Leslie on Amazon: http://bit.ly/WolfeAuthor
Follow Leslie on BookBub: http://bit.ly/wolfebb
Website: www.LeslieWolfe.com
Visit Leslie's Amazon store: http://bit.ly/WolfeAll

PREVIEW: *LAS VEGAS CRIME*

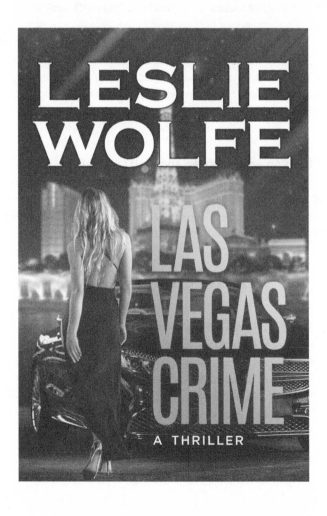

1

SILENT SCREAMS

She struggled to control her sobs but failed miserably. With every mile the man drove into the dark desert, her fear grew, panic overtaking her sense of reason, making it impossible for her to sit still and be quiet like the man had ordered.

"No, please," she whimpered, "I'll disappear. I won't say a word to anyone. I swear," she added in a high-pitched plea, her voice trembling badly.

She stared through a blur of tears at the man's intense eyes, reflected in the rearview mirror. He rarely looked at her, not even when he spoke to her, but when he did, his eyes were ice cold, feral.

She couldn't tell how long they'd been on the road, or how far away from the city they'd traveled. Far enough for darkness to engulf the dazzling lights of Las Vegas, left behind at their brightest and now gone from view. Far enough to know that no matter how loud she'd scream, no one would hear her desperate cries for help. She sat silently, petrified, unable to fight anymore, knowing what Homeboy did to those who disobeyed him.

They had entered the desolate vastness of the Mojave Desert, cold and bleak at night.

Her breath shattered as raw memories swirled in her head, repeating over and over like a broken record.

"Get rid of her," that terrible man had said, "this bitch ain't good for nothin'." The one they called Snowman had curled his lip in disgust and ran his fingers across his throat in a clear gesture, sealing her fate.

She was to be killed.

She remembered how her knees gave and she folded onto the cold, grimy floor, half-naked and barefoot, shaking, sobbing uncontrollably, while the other man, a brute she got to know only as Homeboy, smiled and licked his lips. Then he'd grabbed her arm and dragged her out of that place, mumbling, "Sure, boss, whatever you say."

She'd seen that look on Homeboy's face before.

Maybe she was better off dead than having that animal's hands on her again. Her body still ached from the hours she'd endured at his pleasure. The thought of peace soon to be found, even if in death, calmed her taut nerves. Soon she'd be free, one way or another.

No one dared defy Snowman's orders.

Her mind wandered, numb and absent for a while, as Homeboy drove fast into the night, mile after mile, without saying a word.

A slight chime came from the GPS and he braked, although there was no intersecting road crossing the highway, no available turn to take, just desert dunes, covered in shrubs and cacti, and trolled by scorpions, snakes, and coyotes.

He turned off-road and drove carefully into the desert, climbing over a hill then descending behind it. He didn't immediately stop; he kept on going, putting more and more distance between them and the road, eliminating any chances that someone could see her, could hear her screams.

She felt her heart thumping against her chest, the sound of its terrified beats deafening against the deathly silence of the desert. Fresh tears started rolling down her cheeks and her pleas were left unanswered.

She gasped when he cut the engine, bringing the SUV to a stop. Trembling, she didn't fight back when he grabbed her arm and pulled her out of the vehicle.

"Please," she mumbled, "I'll do whatever you want. Please let me go."

"Can't do that," he replied, his lips stretched in an evil smile that exposed crooked, yellow teeth. "You heard the boss man."

He let go of her arm and reached inside his pocket. Panicked, she bolted in a desperate attempt to save herself. She ran toward the highway, now hidden behind a hill, not feeling the cactus thorns tearing at her flesh, not minding the sharp edges of the desert stones bloodying the soles of her feet.

She'd run a few yards and he hadn't caught up with her yet; hope gave her wings, and she sprung uphill clawing at the stones with her bare hands, desperate to put more distance between the two of them.

She was almost at the top of the hill when his steeled grip bore into her arm, stopping her in place so abruptly that her bleeding feet sent pebbles and sand in the air. Angered, he dragged her back to the SUV and slammed her against the cold metal.

"Nice try, bitch. There's nowhere to go."

She was starting to understand that, to accept it, although every fiber in her body screamed its fear, urged her to fight, to run, to survive. She drew breath hastily and let out a blood-curdling shriek.

Homeboy laughed. "Sure, go ahead, scream. You're giving me a hard-on."

Her scream died, stifled by a sob.

He dug into his pocket and pulled out a small bottle fitted with an eyedropper. With a lewd, sickening smile, he took his time unscrewing the cap and carefully extracted two drops of the clear liquid. Then he grabbed her jaw and forced her lips open.

"No, no," she whimpered, fighting desperately to free herself.

Homeboy just smirked, ignoring her feeble kicks, and squeezed the eyedropper, releasing the liquid into her mouth. Then he held her lips sealed under his heavy hand, forcing her to swallow.

She couldn't detect any strange taste; he'd barely used a drop or two. It couldn't be too bad, she thought, gasping desperately for air as soon as he released his grip.

She felt her tongue becoming numb, then her lips. Panic opened her eyes widely and made her lungs scream for more air. She gasped, feeling an evil numbness taking over her body, reaching her extremities, weakening her knees. A strange sense of dizziness overtook her, making her reach for support, finding none until her body hit the ground. No matter how much she willed herself to move, she lay still on the cold desert dirt, feeling every stab of pain where sharp-edged rocks cut into her flesh.

Homeboy crouched near her body with a satisfied grin. He pushed aside a few locks of her hair, clearing her face, touching her frozen lips.

"You won't die," he said, while his hand fumbled with his belt buckle. "Not now, anyway. Not until I'm bored with you."

She forced her lungs to draw air and screamed, then drew another raspy breath and screamed again.

She listened but couldn't hear her own screams. The desert was completely silent, except for the brute's rhythmic grunts.

~~~End Preview~~~

Like *Las Vegas Crime*?

Buy It now!

ABOUT THE AUTHOR

Leslie Wolfe is a bestselling author whose novels break the mold of traditional thrillers. She creates unforgettable, brilliant, strong women heroes who deliver fast-paced, satisfying suspense, backed up by extensive background research in technology and psychology.

Leslie released the first novel, *Executive*, in October 2011. Since then, she has written many more, continuing to break down barriers of traditional thrillers. Her style of fast-paced suspense, backed up by extensive background research in technology and psychology, has made Leslie one of the most read authors in the genre and she has created an array of unforgettable, brilliant and strong women heroes along the way.

Reminiscent of the television drama *Criminal Minds*, her series of books featuring the fierce and relentless FBI Agent **Tess Winnett** would be of great interest to readers of James Patterson, Melinda Leigh, and David Baldacci crime thrillers. Fans of Kendra Elliot and Robert Dugoni suspenseful mysteries would love the **Las Vegas Crime** series, featuring the tension-filled relationship between Baxter and Holt. Finally, her **Alex Hoffmann** series of political and espionage action adventure will enthrall readers of Tom Clancy, Brad Thor, and Lee Child.

Leslie has received much acclaim for her work, including inquiries from Hollywood, and her books offer something that is different and tangible, with readers becoming invested in not only the main characters and plot but also with the ruthless minds of the killers she creates.

A complete list of Leslie's titles is available at LeslieWolfe.com/books.

Leslie enjoys engaging with readers every day and would love to hear from you. Become an insider: gain early access to previews of Leslie's new novels.

- Email: LW@WolfeNovels.com
- Facebook: https://www.facebook.com/wolfenovels

- Follow Leslie on Amazon: http://bit.ly/WolfeAuthor
- Follow Leslie on BookBub: http://bit.ly/wolfebb
- Website: www.LeslieWolfe.com
- Visit Leslie's Amazon store: http://bit.ly/WolfeAll

Made in the USA
Las Vegas, NV
13 March 2022

45486839R10187